# THE DARK LIGHT

H DA

L IG

**SARA WALSH**

**SIMON PULSE**

NEW YORK  LONDON  TORONTO  SYDNEY  NEW DELHI

SIMON PULSE

An imprint of Simon & Schuster Children's Publishing Division

1230 Avenue of the Americas, New York, NY 10020

First Simon Pulse hardcover edition August 2012

Copyright © 2012 by Sara Walsh

All rights reserved, including the right of reproduction

in whole or in part in any form.

SIMON PULSE and colophon are registered trademarks

of Simon & Schuster, Inc.

For information about special discounts for bulk purchases,

please contact Simon & Schuster Special Sales

at 1-866-506-1949 or business@simonandschuster.com.

The Simon & Schuster Speakers Bureau can bring authors

to your live event. For more information or to book an event

contact the Simon & Schuster Speakers Bureau at 1-866-248-3049

or visit our website at www.simonspeakers.com.

Designed by Mike Rosamilia

The text of this book was set in Berling LT Std.

Manufactured in the United States of America

10 9 8 7 6 5 4 3 2 1

Walsh, Sara.

The dark light / Sara Walsh. — 1st Simon Pulse hardcover ed.

p. cm.

Summary: When seventeen-year-old Mia's ten-year-old brother becomes the latest child to disappear, she discovers that her town of Crownsville, Nebraska, adjoins another world, and with help from new friend Sol, she tries to rescue him from the Suzerain, who is trying to destroy her world.

ISBN 978-1-4424-3455-4

1. Missing children—Fiction. 2. Supernatural—Fiction. 3. Magic—Fiction. 4. Identity—Fiction. 5. Adventure and adventurers—Fiction.] I. Title.

PZ7.W168933Dar 2012

[Fic]—dc23

2011041701

ISBN 978-1-4424-3459-2 (eBook)

*For Mike. Always.*

# ONE

There have been strange lights in Crownsville for as long as I've lived here. Lights on the Ridge; lights on the river; lights that seep from the ground and then float to the sky in clouds of colored mist. No one really talked about them. No one really cared.

Until now.

The patrol cars parked on the corner of Birch and Main were the first thing I noticed when I left work that night. After what had happened in the neighboring town of Onaly that morning, I wasn't surprised. But seeing the cops in Crownsville still gave me the creeps.

The second thing I noticed was Rusty, my car, parked with his headlights glaring. I groaned.

"Mia . . . Why did you do that?"

I tried to remember even switching them on, but came up blank. That pretty much summed up my day. It was nine o'clock, which meant Rusty's crappy battery had been draining for three solid hours while I'd waited tables at Mickey's. Having only just liberated him from Reggie West's Motor Repair and Salvage—Rusty's second home—a dead battery was the last thing I needed. Now I would probably be stuck here while Jay waited for me at the Bakers'. Pete, as usual, was nowhere to be found.

I heard the door to Mickey's open and close behind me. As I rummaged through my bag for my keys, Greg, the night manager, stepped onto the sidewalk.

"You left Rusty's lights on," he said, stating the obvious.

"Yeah." I continued digging. Some of the stuff had been in my bag for months: spare socks; a million tissues (mostly used); a cigarette lighter, though I didn't even smoke. I swore to clear the purse out as soon as I got home. I mean, how much crap does a seventeen-year-old really need to carry around?

"And you forgot this," said Greg, passing me my jacket.

"Thanks, Greg." I took it from him with one hand as I pulled out my keys with the other.

"Something on your mind, Mia? You've been twitchy all evening."

I glanced at the cops, parked on the side of the road. "It's the Onaly thing," I said. "Have you heard of anything like this happening before?"

"In these parts? Can't say I have. But someone's taking those kids." He shook his head. "Five gone in six months and all within fifty miles of here."

I didn't need reminding.

The media called them the *Crownsville Kidnappings*, but only one of the boys who'd vanished, seven-year-old Simon Wilkins, had actually lived in town. Crownsville was a hub for the small towns and farms that surrounded it. This was the reason there were more than fifteen hundred students enrolled at school. Occasionally, kids went missing, but everyone knew where they were—Omaha, Kansas City, Sioux Falls. They bailed when they'd had their fill of rural Nebraska. But this wasn't the same thing. The boy who'd vanished from Onaly Crossing this morning was ten years old, the same age as my half brother, Jay, so don't tell me he'd gone looking for a new life in the city.

"I've got jumper cables in the truck if you need them," said Greg.

Which I invariably would. I had no one to blame but myself. He walked me to the car. I slipped into the driver's seat, patted Rusty's dash—a sacred ritual—and turned the key. The engine wheezed, then roared. It was the best news I'd had all day.

"These old homegrown beauties last a lifetime," said Greg. He slapped Rusty's hood. "See you tomorrow night, Mia."

Dark had fallen thick and fast. By the time I turned off Main Street, I'd switched on my high beams. It was a couple of miles to the Bakers' on rural roads that had seen better days. Having once mangled a rim in a pothole down here, I kept to the speed limit.

I'd gone about a mile when my phone burst into "The Star-Spangled Banner." That meant one thing—my best friend, Miss Willie Burkett. I pulled over to take the call.

"How was work?" she asked. Willie never wasted time with "hello."

"Usual crowd," I replied. "I swear the place is some kind of alternate dimension."

She laughed. "Have you spoken to Pete about this weekend at the lake?"

I cringed. "Haven't seen him yet," I said. In truth, I had no idea where he was. "Wills, I promise I'll talk to him. Just don't expect miracles."

"You *have* to be there, Mia. Andy is definitely coming. This is a chance for you guys to finally get together."

I wasn't so sure. Andy Monaghan was a drop-dead gorgeous

senior who drove a black Corvette that came straight from the showroom of his father's dealership. We'd come pretty close to dating a couple of times, but each time something had gotten in the way: Andy's broken leg, his ex-girlfriend moving back into town, me and Seamus McEvoy—a month-long fling I'd rather forget. But now Andy had broken up with his girlfriend, and Willie said he'd been asking about me around school. . . .

"I'll ask Pete as soon as I see him," I said. I picked imaginary lint off my jeans. "But I'm warning you, Wills; he hasn't been around much lately, and I can't leave Jay with this psycho loose on the streets."

"Pete needs to sort his sorry ass out," Willie muttered.

True, but I didn't see that happening any time soon.

I slumped in my seat and turned my head to the window. The lights on Rowe Boulevard were faint in the distance. Across the open fields, the trees that bordered the elementary school were silhouetted against the night sky. I watched their outlines swaying in the breeze, resigned to the fact that I was always the one who had to back out of our plans.

". . . and if he doesn't shape up, I'm gonna speak to Dad about it again."

I realized Willie was still talking.

"Don't you dare," I said, catching the tail end of her threat. A genuine threat. Willie's dad was Crownsville's sheriff.

"It's neglect."

"It's Pete being useless. Totally different."

"I guess." She sighed. "Come over and we can figure something out."

"I can't," I replied. "I've still got to pick up Jay."

Silence followed and I knew we'd strayed into difficult territory. Somewhere along the line, Willie had decided that I had the world's most horrendous life. You couldn't blame her; my dad had abandoned me at birth and my mom was in prison. I'd lived with my grandmother in Des Moines until I was eight. When she died, I was shipped here, to Crownsville, Nebraska, to live with Uncle Pete, my mother's brother. Pete wasn't the most attentive guardian, but things weren't that bad. I pretty much did what I wanted. But it also meant that Jay, who'd lived with us for the past six years, had no one to worry about him but me. I wasn't afraid to step up to the plate and take care of Jay. I was an honors student, had a 4.3 GPA, played volleyball and soccer, and still waitressed three shifts a week. I was doing fine.

Resigned to Willie's lecture, I stared out of the window.

And then the light caught my eye.

At first, I dismissed it, thought maybe it was the beam from a flashlight. I was parked on Route 6, and the light was far out, somewhere on the open land between me and Rowe. It was hazy in the faint glow of Rowe's streetlights, but definitely there.

I rolled down the window for a closer look, squinting through the darkness. The beam had widened, and I was sure I saw pastel shades in the light.

"You there, Mia?"

"Yeah," I said, though, of course, I wasn't. Whatever was out there had my full attention. It was like a reflection in one of those crazy mirrors at the State Fair—you expect to see reality, but what you get is indistinct and unreal. "Willie, I'll call you back."

"You're pissed at me."

"Course not." I watched, mesmerized. "I'll call you back."

Hanging up the phone, I stepped out of the car. The light danced in the breeze, the colors deepening. Red and blue and gold, the shades were vibrant against the surrounding silvery mist.

As I tried to rationalize what I was seeing, maybe fireworks or marsh gas, my peripheral vision caught a shadow low to the ground. A *moving* shadow, close to the light. It drifted to the left and, suddenly free of the light's glare, took form. It was a figure, hooded and cloaked, though I knew it must be a trick of the eye; there had been nothing but the light a second ago. Alone on a deserted road, with who knew what out there in the fields, I backed up to Rusty.

The moon broke free of the drifting clouds.

And then they were gone.

The light. The shape. They both vanished.

Mildly spooked, I climbed back into the car. Whatever had been out there wasn't there now. It was just the same old fields. The same old lights on Rowe. Still, I locked the door behind me.

By the time I reached the Bakers' to pick up Jay, I'd banished the incident into the "crazy story to tell Willie" category. Mrs. Baker answered the door with the widest smile I'd seen in days. She always made me feel welcome. Shrieks and screams came from somewhere inside the house.

"They're slaughtering orcs in the living room," she said. "Come on through."

I headed in to find Jay and his best friend, Stacey Ann, sprawled on the rug, Wii control pads clutched in their hands. Both turned when I entered, Stacey staring through those horrific glasses that magnified her eyes to twice their natural size, Jay brushing his wild mop of curly hair from his face. Picture any painting of a cherub. That's Jay Stone. Right down to the chubby baby cheeks and wide puppy-dog eyes. It's clear we only shared a father; my hair was chocolate brown, Jay's was more creamy caramel.

I got a chirpy "Hi, Mia," from Stacey Ann and a long groan from Jay.

"I love you, too," I said. "Time to lock and load."

As Jay packed up his Wii, Mrs. Baker saw me back to the door. "Thanks again for watching him," I said. "Pete . . ."

I paused. What could I say? That Pete was probably off drinking again, infecting the world with his soul-sapping outlook on life, when he'd known I'd had to work? Or that I'd arrived home from school to find Jay alone again at the house with the door unlocked? And Onaly Crossing less than a ten-minute drive on the highway . . .

"I just don't like leaving him alone with—"

Mrs. Baker put her hand to my arm. "He's welcome here, Mia. Anything you need. Any time. Just call."

I offered her a relieved smile. "Thanks."

Jay burst into the hallway with Stacey Ann glued to his side. "Ready," he said.

I grabbed him in a headlock, then marched him through the yard to the car. Rusty started on the first turn.

"That isn't why it starts, you know," said Jay, his feet up against the dashboard.

"I don't know what you mean," I replied, innocently.

"That stupid tapping thing you do. It's just a *car*."

I revved the engine, grinning ear to ear. "Hasn't failed me yet."

"Yet," said Jay. He waved to Stacey Ann as we pulled away.

By the time we arrived home, I was ready to call it quits. Only homework waited on my desk. Jay had other plans. We'd no sooner entered the kitchen than the Wii was out of his pack.

"Hold on one minute," I said. "Homework."

"Did it at Stacey Ann's."

I'd heard that one before.

He tossed a piece of paper onto the kitchen table. It was a detailed pencil sketch of our house. Memories flashed as soon as I saw it. It was the same assignment I'd had when I first moved to Crownsville. I remembered it clearly.

My art teacher, Mrs. Shankles—Cankle Shankles—had instructed us to draw our homes. I'd sat in the yard with my sketch pad. A few lines here, a few lines there. Porch. Windows. A couple of bushes, a couple trees. How easy was that?

But Cankles had been far from impressed. "You haven't tried, Mia," she'd said. "There's no detail. No *life*. I know you have more in you."

I don't think she ever realized how deeply I took those words.

I'd hid my grade from Pete, not that he'd been remotely interested. Then I'd taken my sketch pad back to the yard. I'd sat. I'd looked. I'd tried to *feel* the house and its land. Over the next two hours, I'd drawn it again. And Mrs. Shankles had been right; there was so much more to see. The wraparound porch sank to the right. The warped white siding had faded to gray. The green paint on the shutters was chipped. The walnut tree. The gravel driveway. I'd never noticed how much detail there was here. But from then on, I saw it. From then on, I stopped thinking about Grandma and Des Moines and started living in Crownsville.

I looked at Jay's drawing. He'd already noticed what had taken me so long to see.

"That's awesome, Jay," I said proudly, but tactfully. Jay wasn't big on fuss. "You should go to art camp this summer."

Jay was rifling through the snack drawer, completely unimpressed. "Art camp?" he blurted. "Too busy with baseball, Mia."

I laughed. Jay was a kid who knew exactly where he was going in life. I often wished I was more like him.

I waited at the kitchen table, the picture in my hand as Jay headed up to his room. There was a lot I didn't get about the world, but nothing shocked me more than what had happened to Jay. Jay's mom was my dad's second wife, and Jay had lived with them until Dad bailed again and the wife took revenge on him by dumping her four-year-old son with Pete! I mean, where do these people come from? At least Jay had our dad for a time, I guess. I wouldn't have known the guy if he'd hit me over the head with a mallet.

So, though Jay was my dad's kid and, therefore, not actually Pete's blood, Pete had taken him in too, and I'd gained the brother I'd always wanted. Don't get me wrong. Pete was pretty much useless. But he had saved Jay from a life without family, and he'd given me a family in the process.

I placed Jay's picture on the table, then headed for the shower to wash the scent of Mickey's fried chicken out of my hair. I'd barely settled in to study when the sound of Pete's truck brought me to my bedroom window.

Pete stood in the driveway, takeout bag in one hand, six-pack in the other. He looked out over the moonlit cornfields that bordered our land. His shoulders were back, his chin was up, and though I couldn't see his face, I knew his gaze swept those fields.

I frowned. It was so unlike Pete, who invariably stumbled when he arrived home this late. I quickly scanned the cornfield. There was nothing there. Yet Pete remained fixated on the horizon. I remembered the light and the shadow in front of Rowe.

"Maybe we're both cracking up," I said to myself. But I wondered if I wasn't the only one to have seen something strange that night.

# TWO

The next morning, I found Pete staring at the phone on the kitchen table. He looked like he hadn't slept.

"Where were you yesterday?" I asked.

"Omaha."

Better not to ask. I was pretty sure I didn't want to know the details.

I headed for the fridge. Two twenty-dollar bills were pinned beneath the magnet on the door. Right away, I knew they were mine. I always gave something toward the housekeeping fund and Pete always gave it back. Whatever Pete's problems, he had money. I didn't know where he got it, and I didn't ask. All I knew was that there was food in the fridge, and that Jay got everything he needed. He also got a lot of what he wanted.

Making no comment about the cash, I grabbed a yogurt and a spoon, then returned to the table. I sat across from Pete, hating that I was about to sound like a broken record. "Only, you didn't tell me you'd be out," I said. "Jay was here alone when I got back from school. He'd left the door unlocked. I had to call the Bakers. Again. You know how things are right now."

Pete didn't look up. "Shotgun's in the closet," he muttered.

Yeah. Like I'd blow some guy's brains out. Would Jay? Maybe. I didn't know which was a scarier thought.

I pushed the yogurt aside. "I need to talk to you about this weekend."

Pete looked up. He had the brightest blue eyes of any man I knew, but that morning they were definitely gray. His hair was dark, like mine, but it was so greasy that it appeared to be black. He'd probably once been a good-looking man. He still was, I guess, just disheveled, a little battered around the edges. He certainly looked older than thirty-eight. Right now, he looked about seventy.

"The guys are heading to the lake," I said, "but I can't go if you're not here for Jay."

"I'll be here."

Far too easy.

"I mean *really* here for him—not just present in some form or other."

"I'll be here," he said. "We'll do something. Bowling, maybe."

Pretty sure I'd heard right, I subtly sniffed for booze, but came away with coffee.

"Then I'll tell Willie," I said. It sounded more like a question than a statement.

I took my uneaten yogurt to the sink, all the time keeping one eye on Pete should he keel over from what, for him, was an overabundance of humanity. He'd gone back to staring at the phone. There were two crumpled lines in his forehead. They only appeared when Pete was deep in thought.

"Is everything okay?" I asked, wondering what had brought on this strange mood. Maybe he'd lost money, maybe he'd been in a fight.

"Another kid disappeared yesterday."

Wow. Pete caring about something other than his drinking buddies.

"I heard," I replied. "Onaly Crossing. Why do you think I'm so freaked about Jay? I mean, seriously, Pete. Onaly's ten minutes—"

"In Crownsville."

I spun back from the sink. *What?*

Pete again looked up. His eyes sparked with an emotion I couldn't pin down. When the muscles in his jaw tensed, I recognized it as anger.

"Last night," he said. "Alex Dash."

That couldn't be right. "Alex Dash from Jay's *class*?"

"Do you know any others?"

The Dashes ate at Mickey's every Thursday—today. I pictured them in their usual booth by the window. They always got the chicken special, family style. Four pieces of white meat, all you could eat of the dark. Mashed potatoes. Green beans. Cinnamon rolls. They always seemed so happy. . . .

My stomach turned, the news slowly sinking in. "Two in one day. The kidnapper must have come here from Onaly. What about the other kid, Pete? What did he do with him?"

Pete didn't offer a theory. He pointed to the phone. "Sheriff Burkett called late last night for volunteers. We've been scouring the town, the river, the Ridge. There'll be a real search now that the cops have rolled in."

I'd heard the phone ringing late last night but had just thought it was one of Pete's cronies trying to lure him back to the bar. Now I remembered the patrol cars on the corner of Birch and Main. Maybe they'd known that the kidnapper was cruising our streets. Thank God I'd sent Jay to the Bakers'. It was far too easy to imagine him here alone. The door unlocked. Jay, as always, oblivious to everything but his Wii. Over the sound of his game, he wouldn't hear some psycho inch into the house, checking the kitchen, grabbing a knife. . . .

My skin cold, I pictured Jay in Alex's place, locked in some guy's trunk. "I should stay home and help search."

Pete shook his head. "You get off to school, Mia. You need to keep up those grades. You're gonna have college to think about soon."

College? I couldn't think of anything but Jay, the Dashes, and the Thursday night chicken special.

"What do we tell Jay?"

Pete sighed. "Principal Shankles is calling an assembly this morning."

*Cankle Shankles*—the art teacher who'd taught me to open my eyes. I couldn't think of a better person to break the news to those kids.

I patted Pete's shoulder on my way out of the room. Now that the initial shock had worn off, I was touched that he'd been thinking about things like taking Jay bowling, my grades, college. . . . I turned back at the door. "About this weekend, Pete."

Pete made a small smile and that handsome face appeared, eradicating his usual weariness.

"You go to the lake, Mia," he said. "I won't let Jay out of my sight. I promise."

Only the arrival of the president himself could have knocked Alex's name off the lips of the students at Crownsville High.

"They're talking about a curfew," Willie announced. "For *everyone*. Us too!"

We were camped in the cafeteria with our boy buddies, Kieran and Seth. Seth's family lived next door to Willie's, so they often shared rides to school. He was also totally besotted with Willie. I couldn't picture them ever getting together; it'd be too twisted, a bit like dating your brother. Besides, they weren't what you'd call a great physical match. Seth was a little shorter than me, maybe five-five, five-six. On the other hand, Willie, our reigning queen of volleyball, at six-one, with long black hair, always made a statement.

Willie and I had been friends since my first day of school in Crownsville when we'd been teamed together during Music and Movement to depict winter. As the other teams had melted their way through summer and frolicked through spring, Willie and I had been struck with a hysterical fit of the giggles. Immediately banished to "time-out corner," it was a friendship formed from solidarity. Not much had changed since then.

After hearing her news, Seth all but collapsed in his seat. He covered his head with his hands, his eyes on Willie, as always. "Curfew? But this guy's after *kids*."

"If it is a guy," said Willie. "It could be a child slavery ring."

"Or one screwed-up psycho who's clearly not interested in us. They're not putting me under curfew. No way."

"The cops obviously know something they're not saying,"

added Kieran. He leaned back in his seat. "I wonder if anyone's mentioned it to the new kid."

Willie bolted upright, and a smug grin inched across Kieran's face. Willie's reaction was exactly what he wanted.

"Excuse me," she said, cupping her ear for news. "New kid?"

"Started this morning," Kieran replied.

As far as gossip was concerned, Kieran was the worst kind of fishwife. He was known around school as the Skunk, on account of a patch of gray on the side of his black hair. He touched the patch whenever he was about to spill a juicy secret, just as he was right now.

Intrigued, I leaned in to him. "Which grade?"

"Ours," said Kieran, "though Raquel Somers said he looked older. Apparently, he's related to the Crowleys. He's staying with Old Man Crowley down by the river."

"In that old shack?" asked Willie. "Crowley's completely insane. And here I was thinking no one could have a family worse than Mia's."

I blew her a kiss.

"You should take him cookies, Mia. Welcome him to the Dysfunctional Families of Crownsville Club."

"We've already reached our membership quota," I replied, then quickly changed the subject: "Is this curfew going to affect the lake this weekend?"

Willie threw up her hands. "I forgot to tell you about the lake!"

"That's what I love about you, Willie," said Kieran. He waved at the neighboring table of freshmen who were now staring at us. "Understatement."

"The lake's off," said Willie, and stuck out her tongue. "Andy can't get his dad's boat, which means none of his group wants to go. They're heading to the Ridge instead."

I didn't miss the look that passed between Kieran and Seth.

"So what's that got to do with us?" said Seth.

"I don't know what it's got to do with *you*," Willie replied. "But it means the rest of us are Ridge bound too."

"Because Andy Monaghan says so?"

"Because Mr. Monaghan and Ms. Mia have to hook up before he graduates. It's fated. The stars are aligning. This is the time when they finally get together."

I looked at Seth and shook my head. "She's delusional."

"Or right," Willie replied. She pulled from her bag a dog-eared paperback, one of the many soppy romances she devoured on a regular basis. "Meant to be," she said, and waved the book, *Destiny's Dilemma*, beneath my nose.

I groaned. According to Willie, all love was fated, and she was determined to prove this by matchmaking any single person who crossed her path. It had never made much sense to me. Fate is fate, right? It shouldn't need a helping hand.

Of course, this grand view of romance didn't apply to her own love life. Then she was more like, "That guy's hot. I'm going to ask him out." I'd never had that kind of confidence with guys. Nor did I believe in fate.

I hated to burst Willie's bubble, but Andy and I getting together was a long shot. I really liked him, but a lot had happened since the last time we'd almost gone out. Andy could have any girl he wanted. He was unlikely to still be interested in me.

Kieran snorted. "Will they, won't they? What does it matter if they put us under curfew? I mean, do you really think they can catch the guy in two days?"

"Dad has the whole town looking," said Willie. "Seems Alex disappeared a little after nine last night. That rat-dog of theirs got out, and he went after it."

"So he was close to home," said Seth.

"Last seen heading behind the elementary school on Rowe."

Andy forgotten, I straightened. "At nine last night?"

"Or thereabouts. Mrs. Dash isn't in a state to remember much of anything."

But I remembered. It had been at about nine when I'd seen the light in the same area. My heart kicked.

Maybe someone had really been there, someone with a flashlight, someone kidnapping Alex as I'd stood there and just watched! *No. It was coincidence. Had to be. I couldn't go to Sheriff Burkett with something like that. Had I even seen anything anyway?*

I recalled how the moonlight had appeared from behind the clouds and then, nothing. No truck; no van; no hooded, cloaked shadow. Certainly no Alex Dash. But if that was where he'd last been seen . . .

I almost screamed when the bell rang for homeroom. Kieran and Seth had already wandered away.

"Relax, Mia," said Willie. "There won't be any curfew. I'd make Dad's life too miserable being home every night."

We grabbed our bags and entered the tide of bodies that streamed into the hallway. My mind remained fixed on the fields by Rowe.

"Since you mentioned the lake," said Willie. "Does this mean you spoke to Pete?"

"Yeah," I replied, though suddenly it didn't seem so important. "He's gonna stay with Jay. He even talked about taking him bowling."

"Holy crap. Pete acting like a parent?"

I doubted Willie's disdain for Pete would ever die. Sure, he wasn't about to win any "Uncle of the Year" awards, but he'd stepped up when it'd mattered, and that meant more to me than him being there for bedtime stories and baking cupcakes.

"He's doing his best, Wills," I said.

Willie stopped, statuesque amid the jostling crowd. "Mia, why do you always defend him?"

I recalled Pete's face that morning, remembering his concern about my grades and college. "Because he's my uncle," I said. "And if he hadn't taken us in, I don't know where we'd be."

The Dashes didn't come to Mickey's, and the booth at the window stood empty all night. I caught Greg looking that way a couple of times during the shift. He shrugged and offered me a halfhearted smile.

"I can't believe it," he said. "Ten years old."

Mickey's was quiet all evening, but for the usual collection of waifs and strays who held court at the bar at the back of the restaurant. Thankfully, Pete wasn't with them. He and I had an unwritten rule: He never drank at Mickey's when I was on shift. Seeing him loaded with this crew would have been far too depressing.

By eight thirty, Rich Manning, who'd been Crownsville High's homecoming king in 1982 or something, had had far too much to drink. He grabbed my arm as I passed the bar.

"Fetch me a beer, Mia."

Getting stuck with Rich was the last thing I wanted. "You know I can't serve beer. Greg'll be back in a minute."

"You look old enough to me," he said. Leering, he patted the empty stool beside him. "Come on, I won't tell."

*Gross.* Sometimes I had to remind myself why I worked here.

I glanced at Gus Mason, who'd been patiently listening to Manning for most of the night. Gus shook his head. "You've had enough, Rich. Let Mia get on with her work."

"Used to be you didn't have to ask for a fresh beer in Mickey's," grumbled Manning.

"Used to be you knew when it was time to go home," Gus replied.

Gus had been in Crownsville since, I don't know—the Stone Age. He lived on the river near Old Man Crowley. Gus ran a ferry along the river in summer. It was popular with hikers who came to walk the woods along the Ridge. Willie and I would sometimes jump on for a couple of bucks, but I don't think Gus made much money at it. It was just something he'd always done.

"Whole place is going to the dogs," said Rich. "Whole town. Whole country!"

Glad to get out of his reach, I headed for the nearby wait station where I began to fold napkins for the weekend. Rich continued to gripe.

"Used to be everyone knew where everyone's kids were. Not now. It's the lights, Gus. Nothing good ever happens when the lights come to Crownsville."

As soon as Rich mentioned lights, I looked across to the bar. Don't get me wrong, Rich Manning wasn't what I'd call a reliable source of information. But still, I kept my ears open.

"And what lights would that be?" asked Gus.

"You know the ones. Up on the Ridge, out on the river. Saw 'em myself a couple of nights ago."

"Is that a fact?" said Gus. "From what I heard, you was in here a couple of nights ago. No wonder you saw stars." He glanced in my direction, just as I stifled a smile. He winked.

"It's the aliens, Gus. Feds know all about 'em. I bet the Feds know what happened to those kids."

"That must be it," said Gus. "Aliens."

"I've seen the lights on the Ridge."

Gus set down his beer. "Rich, you haven't seen anything more than a bit of Saint Elmo's fire or will-o'-the-wisp. Maybe you set fire to your own fart but were too drunk to realize it."

I covered my mouth, struggling not to laugh out loud.

"UFOs," Rich continued, undeterred. "Coming here from New Mexico. CIA's got files on it. Ask the CIA what happened to those kids."

"I'll be sure to," said Gus. He yawned. "When they're next in town."

As pathetic as Rich Manning was, I thought about what he'd said for the rest of my shift. Whatever it had been, I had seen something the night before. Maybe it was something important. With Alex still missing, it was time to come clean.

At the end of my shift, I called Willie.

"Is your dad home?"

"Just got back. Missed dinner and everything. What's up?"

"I need to talk to him."

"About what?"

"Willie, I'm not even sure, but I'll bring chicken."

"Then I guarantee you'll have his undivided attention. I'll tell him you're coming over."

Willie was looking out for me when I pulled up on her family's driveway. "What's the big news?" she asked, as soon as I left the car.

Not convinced I knew anything helpful, I shrugged. "It's just something I saw last night. It's probably nothing."

The Burketts lived close to the center of town in Crownsville's "Historic District," which was basically one long, tree-lined street. Dreaming of central air and her own en suite bathroom, Willie had been begging her parents to move to the new subdivision they were building to the west of town. I preferred this house with its overgrown trees, brick front, and lavender shutters. Over the years that Willie and I had been friends, it had become my second home.

She led me to the kitchen where Sheriff and Mrs. Burkett

were seated at the table. As soon as the sheriff saw my box of chicken and potatoes, he gestured me over.

"That's the kind of girl I love. Come sit down."

The sheriff was a man's man—tall and athletic like Willie but, unlike Willie, blessed with a healthy dose of good sense. He doted on Willie, and doted on *me* as if I were a long-lost daughter. No amount of wish fulfillment could ever make me imagine that my dad could be anything like Sheriff Burkett. When I thought of the sheriff, I thought of barbeque, touch football, and good-natured lectures about boys and speeding. When I thought about *my* dad, I pictured weasels.

Mrs. Burkett fetched plates, squeezing my shoulder as she passed. She was as unlike Willie as the sheriff was Willie's double. A little over five feet, she was fair-haired and soft featured. A real country mom.

"So what's this about, Mia?" asked the sheriff, putting some chicken on his plate. "Not Pete, I hope. He's been with us looking for Alex all day."

I glanced at Willie, sitting expectantly beside me. "It's not Pete," I said. "But it is about Alex. I think I saw something last night. I'm not really sure what it was, so I didn't know if I should say anything."

"Always speak out," said the sheriff. "And, believe me, we need all the help we can get. Kid just about vanished into air."

In my mind, I tried to rehearse what I wanted to say, but whichever way I looked at it, it still didn't make any sense. "I think I saw someone on the land behind Rowe," I finally blurted. "Someone with a flashlight. It was difficult to tell. I know Alex was last seen over in that direction. This was about the same time."

"What were you doing out there?" asked Sheriff Burkett.

"Heading to the Bakers' to pick up Jay." I glanced at Willie. "It was while I was talking to you. That's why I'd pulled over."

"I wondered why you went all weird on me," said Willie. "I thought you were mad about Pete."

"Something was out there."

The sheriff took a bite of drumstick. He wiped grease from his mouth. "The Bakers'. So you were on Route Six?"

"Yeah," I replied, relieved he appeared to be taking me seriously. "Almost parallel to the elementary school on Rowe."

"And you thought you saw Alex."

"No," I said. "Someone *else*."

The sheriff leaned forward. "Someone with a flashlight."

How to explain the light without sounding like Rich Manning? The holes in my story widened. *What exactly had I seen?*

*Pretty much zip.*

"It might have been a flashlight, or maybe a flare."

"What would some guy be doing out there with a flare?" asked Willie.

"It only looked like that."

"Well, it's something," said the sheriff. "We combed that land pretty good today. Didn't find a thing. I'll send another team at first light."

We polished off the chicken, talking of other things, including the infamous curfew, which the sheriff hinted might exclude the high school kids, at least for now. When I finally reached home, I was ready for bed.

I pulled up to find Pete on the porch swing, looking out over the Gartons' fields, which backed up to our land. It was quiet, too early for the first of the season's crickets. The house stood in darkness behind him.

"You're late getting home," he said.

"I swung over to Willie's," I replied.

"Then you must have heard the update on Alex."

"Yeah." I headed up the porch steps, unsure why Pete was sitting out in the dark. As with most things with Pete, it was better not to ask. "Rich Manning was in Mickey's. He says it was alien abduction."

"Rich Manning doesn't know his ass from his elbow."

*True.* I smiled. "Jay home?"

"He's in his room."

I folded my arms and looked out over the fields, remembering Pete on the driveway last night. Whatever he'd seen wasn't there now, no more than what I'd seen on the land behind Rowe. Just the moon, the stars, and the corn. Always the same in Crownsville.

"I'm gonna hit the sack," I said, and headed for the door.

Pete just stared into the distance. He was poised, as if at any moment he might vault over the porch railing and hurtle off into the fields. He leaned slightly forward as I passed, and as the swing tilted beneath him, I saw something that confused me more than his late-night vigil. A dull shape, previously hidden by the shadows, rested on his lap.

It was Pete's shotgun.

Frowning, I entered the house, flicked on the kitchen light, and sidled across to the window. All I could see was the back of Pete's head, the porch and the driveway, and a thick wall of blackness covering the fields.

# THREE

Friday. One day until the Ridge. Willie was plotting again.

"Andy loves red," she said. We sat on the lawn beside the gym during lunch, trying to avoid the chaos of the cafeteria. "So wear those skimpy denim shorts and a red tee. Gorgeous."

I figured it best not to say anything about my reservations and just go along with Willie's plans. Whatever happened would happen—probably nothing. I doubted a red T-shirt would make Andy collapse into my arms.

"Wills, you do realize it's just an afternoon on the Ridge?" I stretched out on the grass hoping to catch a few rays, especially since it looked like I'd be wearing shorts this weekend.

"Just the Ridge?" she replied, outraged. "Mia, let's wait and see."

"Wait and see what?" Kieran slung down his backpack and dropped to the grass. "Heard about the new guy?"

"Yeah," I said. "He lives on the river with Old Man Crowley. Didn't we cover this yesterday?"

Kieran gestured for silence. "Apparently, he has a *huge* tattoo."

*"What?"* cried Willie.

Real news. I scrambled up onto my elbows, eager to hear more.

"Yeah," said Kieran. "On his *back*. It's massive. Mike Woolley saw it."

Willie shook her head, clearly not buying it. I half suspected it was because she hadn't been the first to know. "And how *exactly* did Mike Woolley see the new kid's back?"

"In the locker room," said Kieran. "Everyone's talking about it."

"Everyone except us," I added. "Why are we always the last to know?"

"Beats me," said Willie. "So does this tattooed new kid have a name? You know, I still haven't even seen him."

"Yeah," said Kieran. "*Sol.* What kind of a name is that?"

I laughed. "The sunny kind?"

"And," Kieran continued, "he doesn't know how to play baseball."

"Again," said Willie. *"What?"*

"No lie. They're running pitching drills, and this kid's looking at Coach Wright like he's from another *planet*! Watch out for this guy. I'm telling you—he's a weird one."

Weird or not, I was grateful to the new guy for one reason: Without us even seeing him, he'd managed to distract Willie's attention from me and Andy.

That evening, I washed my jean shorts and ironed my red tee. Okay, so I was playing it cool in front of Willie, but I was going to be seeing Andy so there was no harm in a little prep. You know, like hair serum, a new lipstick, leg wax. That kind of thing.

On my way back from the bathroom, I tapped on Jay's door. Since Alex's disappearance, he had pretty much been keeping to his room, and I was worried how he was taking the news. I poked my head in to find him at his desk, in battle, as always, on his computer.

"Hey, Spud. Kicking butt?"

"Trying to finish this level," he replied, thumbs going crazy.

"Mind if I come in?"

He shook his head, but continued playing.

I'd never been into all those games with swords and stones and stuff. Life was crazy enough without axe-wielding maniacs bludgeoning each other to death. There were guys at school who played these games for hours. There was even a club, I think. To me, it was all just noise and comic book violence. And where were the women in these things? Lamenting the loss of their menfolk and gallivanting around in fur bikinis.

I sat on the end of Jay's bed just as a purple-horned behemoth condemned his avatar to eating dirt. I was about to ask him about Alex, when I noticed a photograph beside me on the comforter. It was an older shot, in color but grainy, of a young woman with mountains in the background. Her dress was kind of folky, like from the seventies or something, with billowing sleeves and a bodice front. Blond hair hung to her waist. Her eyes were wide like Jay's, but there was no innocence to them. They were sad eyes. Sad eyes in a gorgeous face.

I flipped over the picture, looking for a caption, but the back was blank. I turned it back over.

"What's this, Jay?"

Jay glanced away from his monitor. "Mom."

I didn't expect that.

So this was the woman who'd dumped Jay. I'd never imagined her as young and beautiful, more like a gnarly hag with a cigarette in one hand and a bottle of malt liquor in the other. But there she was, young and beautiful. She didn't look like a person who'd do something so cruel.

I remembered nothing about my parents—*nothing*. I'd been a baby when they'd left me with Grandma in Des Moines. But

Jay was different; he'd known our dad, though he rarely mentioned him. He'd known what it was like to have a mom, too.

"Where'd you get it?" I asked.

"Always had it." The colors from the game flickered on his flawless cheeks. "I keep it in my drawer."

"Do you remember her much?"

"Bits."

I looked again at the picture, staring deeply. I felt like she was watching me back. "What was she like?"

"Don't remember," he replied. "I only remember when they took her."

I looked up, chilled by Jay's statement. He believed that she'd been taken? Was that how he coped with what she'd done to him?

"She gave you up, Jay," I said, softly.

"Only because they took her." He paused his game, then turned to me. "Stacey Ann's brother said the cops were hanging around your school today. Why would they do that if the man's only taking kids?"

I saw the connections forging in his mind. He believed an unknown assailant had snatched his mom. Maybe someone else close to him could be next?

"Jay, it's just a precaution."

"Stacey said he's only after boys."

"Which is why you have to be careful," I said, desperate for the message to sink in. "Lock the door when you're home alone. No more, 'I forgot.' Make sure you're with someone when you're on the street."

"I guess."

"I'm serious, Jay," I said. "No one knows what happened to Alex."

"He's gone for good."

"Is that what Stacey Ann said?"

"Mrs. Shankles."

"Mrs. Shankles said he's gone for *good*?" I considered reevaluating my opinion of old Cankles.

"No," said Jay. "But I could tell that's what she meant."

Jay's alter ego was back in business on the screen. Golden stars glistened around its sword. The purple-horned behemoth ran for cover.

"They're gonna find him, Jay."

"And the other kids?"

I opened my mouth to reply and realized I didn't have an answer.

The avatar bounded over creeks and boulders before delivering the fatal blow. The behemoth, purple horn and all, vanished in a puff of silver smoke. Jay again turned back to me.

"Are you going out tonight?" he asked.

I placed the photograph back on the bed. "I'm staying home," I said. His look of relief just about broke my heart. I hid it behind a smile. "And Pete says he's taking you somewhere tomorrow. Maybe even *bowling*. Can you believe it?"

"It's not my birthday."

"So make the most of it." I headed for the door. "I'm gonna make popcorn. You want some?"

"Thanks, Mia."

Jay turned back to his game.

Though I usually avoided thinking about my parents, sometimes I couldn't help it, even though it was pointless, ridiculous, and a total waste of time and effort. Mothers were usually an off-limits topic of conversation at our house; *mine* in particular was guaranteed to send Pete straight to the bottle. She was a nasty little secret lurking in my past. I guessed Pete's silence had something to do with the reason why his sister had been thrown in jail. Whatever it was must have been bad; she'd been there for all of my life. I didn't know where. And I knew not to ask anymore.

But having seen the photo of Jay's mom, I couldn't help wonder about my own. Before bed that night, I went to my closet's top shelf, a spot Willie called the Black Hole of Crownsville. From beneath the mountains of shoeboxes and sweatshirts, I took down a blue velvet box. I placed it on my desk and opened the lid.

Inside was a necklace, the one thing I had of my mother's.

I don't know where my mother had gotten it, it was probably stolen. Pete had given it to me not long after I'd arrived in Crownsville. It was a weighty antique piece of twisted silver. Seven blocks of a translucent golden stone, like amber, hung from the ornate chain. The central gem was larger than the others, almost as big as my palm. Crimson veins ran through each stone like those old-fashioned marbles you could find at the five-and-dime. I held up the necklace, and the lamplight caught in the veins. They glistened like crimson rivers.

I sighed, annoyed with myself for even taking it out of the box. It was probably a piece of junk, just like all the other junk my parents had thrust into my life. I couldn't bear the thought of Jay nurturing hope that his own mother might return one day to claim him. Sometimes it was best to just walk away.

I placed the necklace back in the box, a weight lifting as soon as I closed the lid and it was out of sight. I wandered to the window. A little more than a mile away stood the Ridge, hidden in darkness. On a clear day I could sometimes see it from my room. My parents were ghosts to me, but out there, on the Ridge with Andy Monaghan and the promise of summer spreading before me? That was real.

I couldn't wait to get up there tomorrow.

* * *

There was only one thing to do after a sweaty game of touch football, and that was to hurl ourselves into the cool river. After swimming, Willie caught up to me as we climbed the steep boulders back to the Ridge. She was in a triumphant mood.

"Andy can't take his eyes off you," she whispered, after quickly checking that we wouldn't be overheard.

*Really?* I glanced to where Andy and his best friend, Jake, also climbed the rocks. I didn't know if there was such a thing as too perfect, but if there was, Andy was it. He was like an Abercrombie & Fitch model, all straight white teeth, perfect tan, and groomed dark hair. It didn't hurt that he'd stripped off his shirt to swim. Coach Wright clearly kept his seniors in shape.

I'd sworn I was just going to enjoy the day and not get sucked in to Willie's drama, which could only lead to a truck-load of disappointment. But I was surprised how nervous I'd felt since we'd pulled up at the base of the Ridge to find a shiny black Corvette already parked on the gravel lot.

Willie and I navigated the final boulders before emerging onto the wide, flat plateau at the top of the Ridge where the rest of the group was sprawled beneath the sun. The Ridge was one of Crownsville's best-kept secrets. It was all that remained of a humongous crater that had formed in about ten billion BC.

To the east, the plateau ended abruptly, plunging down to the river. Woodland bordered the gentle western slope, over which, on a day as clear as today, you could see across the plains. Our backs to the river, we sank to the grass with legs outstretched. The sun hovered above the Sleeper Hill Giant, the long mound outside Onaly with a flat peak that had eroded into the outline of a man snoozing beneath the sky.

"Just keep doing what you're doing," said Willie. "It'll work."

"What'll work?" I asked, determined not to check back on Andy.

"Pretending like this is all no big deal."

And here was I thinking I'd played it cool. "Am I that obvious?"

"It's a legitimate technique."

I laughed, giggled really, as if Willie and I were back in time-out corner. "You'd think he was the hottest guy on the planet."

Willie laughed back. "Definitely in Nebraska."

She jumped up before I could say anything more, leaving me for Kieran, who was trying to impress Sally Machin, one of the seniors, with a bizarre combination of kickboxing moves. Wondering why she'd suddenly bailed on me, I was about to call her back when Andy appeared at my side.

"You rocked that game, Mia," he said, beaming.

He sat beside me on the grass, river water dripping from his shoulders and hair. The temptation was to grin like an idiot, which I often did when Andy was around. He was just so laid back. I guessed his confidence came from living on a pedestal surrounded by his father's cash. And it wasn't only the students who'd put him up there; every mother in town hoped he'd date their daughter and spread some of those Monaghan dollars around. Andy also had *great* shoulders, the broad, muscular kind I loved. It was hard to focus when they were on full display.

"Maybe I should try out for the school team," I said, smiling back, and trying to ignore Raquel Somers, one of Andy's crew who'd been after him since kindergarten, watching us from her towel a few yards away. Andy showed no sign that he'd noticed. He shifted to face me full on.

"I feel like I haven't seen you in ages," he said, his swoony eyes the color of melted chocolate. "How's Jay?"

"He's good," I replied, my voice calm.

I was surprised how easy it was to slip back into Andy-mode. The last time we'd talked alone had been at Willie's birthday party about three weeks ago. But Andy had been there with Jessica, and he'd appeared very conscious of that fact. Now it was only us. Willie and the others didn't count. We were in our own little world.

He scraped back his hair, water droplets glistening on his shoulders. If I were to survive this conversation intact, I needed him to put on a T-shirt. Stat.

"Jay's a great kid," he said. "Are you going to the batting cages with him again this summer?"

I groaned. "Every summer. Jay rocks. I suck. Total humiliation."

His laughter echoed across the Ridge. "Then maybe I could take him. Jay cracks me up. It'd be a hoot."

I tried to figure out his intentions. He appeared to be playing the same casual game as me, but still. Jay and I had bumped into Andy and Jake at the cages a couple of times last summer. We'd all hung out, Jay showing off to the older guys and Andy and Jake egging him on. But Andy actually offering to take Jay to the cages? My heart picked up its beat.

"He'd love that," I said. "I mean, going with someone who can actually hit a ball."

Andy leaned back on his hands, muscles popping all over the place, as he looked out over the plains. "You heard about me and Jessica."

My heart raced a little faster. It was difficult to know how to respond. We were friends, and friends talked about dating and breakups and all that went with it. It didn't *mean* anything. Of course I knew they'd split—everyone knew. So why was he mentioning it now?

No. I was reading too much into things. Andy'd offered to take Jay to the cages because he was a really nice guy and he was into sports and he knew Jay didn't have a brother or anyone to look up to like that. He'd mentioned Jessica because it was big news, not because he'd wanted to push that he was single. I'd spent too long listening to Willie's fairy tales. I liked Andy a lot. I'd never denied it. That didn't mean Andy felt the same way about me. Did it? God, I was useless at this stuff.

"I only heard that you'd broken up," I said.

Andy turned to face me with those chocolate eyes and that chiseled jaw. He was about to speak when—

"OMG!" hollered Raquel.

Cursing her big mouth, I watched her dash to the edge of the Ridge. Completely uninterested in the drama, I looked back at Andy, silently urging him to continue.

"OMG!"

Andy smiled, dismissing whatever he'd been about to say with a shake of the head. "I think she wants us to follow her."

*Great. Why did something always get in the way?*

"I'm serious!" screamed Raquel. "Get over here! It's the new guy!"

# FOUR

oly six-pack," blurted Willie, her eyebrows almost in her hairline. "Or should I say, *twelve-pack*!"

Sol walked along the opposite side of the river in sneakers and jeans with a long-sleeved tee tied around his hips. I made no comment, as Andy had followed me to the edge of the Ridge, but the truth had to be told. We now had another item to add to the list of things we knew about the new guy:

1. He lived on the river with Old Man Crowley.

2. His name was Sol.

3. He had a smoking body.

Sol had muscles I hadn't known existed. And they weren't bulky gym-muscles, either. They were lean, real-life muscles, the kind that came from swinging an axe all day. Andy was tall, but even from across the wide river, I could tell that Sol was taller. Andy was broad. Sol was broader.

"Why can't we stay another year?" drooled Raquel. "I'd give up college. I'd give up *everything*." She looked at Willie. "You guys are so lucky; we don't have anyone like that in our grade."

I glanced at Andy, but thought it not the coolest move to disagree.

Jake was already wandering away. "You know, guys get all the flak for having one-track minds," he said. "Girls are fifty times worse."

I wondered if maybe he was right. I liked to think I was master of my hormones, but between what was standing at my side and what was stalking half-naked along the riverbank, I didn't know where to look.

Sol strolled on. He was now directly across from us, his dark hair turned golden brown by the sun, shoulders back, head tilted in our direction.

"Did you hear he lives with Old Man Crowley?" asked Sally.

"Once or twice," Willie replied. "You know, I haven't seen Crowley for ages."

As soon as she mentioned it, everyone agreed.

"Maybe he's sick," said Seth. He glared at Sol. "Maybe that's why the Incredible Hunk's come to stay."

"You mean Sol," said Willie, dreamily. "Like the sun. I've never wanted Monday to come so fast. We *have* to get his schedule."

"He's in my chemistry lab," said Kieran.

"And you tell us this *now*?" gasped Willie. "So unfair!" She grabbed my arm and pointed to the riverbank. "Mia, look— it's *true*."

Sol continued on, his back toward us. From shoulder to shoulder, from neck to hip, was a huge tattoo. It was a bird, a massive bird, with wings outstretched, talons down, its head proud and erect. Against Sol's tanned skin, it burst in vibrant reds, blues, greens, and golds. But most unusual was the way that Sol carried it. He must have known we'd see it as he passed, yet there was not a hint of self-consciousness in the way he walked. He simply ambled by, knowing we watched, not caring either way.

Us girls ogled him in silence until eventually Sol rounded the river bend and finally disappeared from view.

"Told ya," said Kieran.

Sally shuffled back from the drop, a stunned expression on her face. "Was that an eagle?"

"Not like any eagle I've ever seen," said Willie. "Mia?"

I didn't reply. I couldn't. Everything was out of focus, as if the world had narrowed and all I could see was Sol and his tattoo.

I *had* seen that bird before. And I planned to see it again the second I got home.

"So," said Willie on the drive back. "How did it go with Andy? You guys looked pretty tight there for a while."

Thoughts of Sol's tattoo had consumed me for the rest of the day and not even Andy's increasing attention had been enough to blow it from my mind. All I saw was the iridescence in its wings, its razor-sharp talons, its proud, steely eye. But now there was only me and Willie, and there was nothing on her mind but Andy.

"It went great." I thought of what Andy had said about Jessica and taking Jay to the cages, but pieces of the puzzle still hadn't fallen into place. "I'm just not sure I get it. Why would he be interested in me now? He'll be gone in a couple of months."

"So this is his last chance. Seriously, you two look amazing together."

"Maybe."

Willie shook her head. "*Maybe?* Mia, what's bitten you?"

Sol and his tattoo flashed in my mind. "It's nothing."

We pulled up at my gate. Willie turned to face me, her usually mischievous expression suddenly serious. "Mia, one day you're going to have to knock down that wall."

Willie wasn't serious very often, but when she wanted to

make a point, she sure knew how to hit the target. "I don't know what you mean," I said, genuinely shocked by the abrupt shift in her tone.

"You know exactly what I mean," said Willie. "I'm talking about the wall between you and any guy who might actually care about you."

Oh. *That* wall.

I glanced at the house, hoping Pete might magically appear and give me an excuse to escape.

"I date," I said, when it was clear Pete wasn't about to bail me out. It was the only defense I could come up with.

Willie wasn't impressed. "Little boys like Seamus McEvoy don't count." She held up her hand, her eyes twinkling with the first trace of a smile. "You don't have to explain to me, Mia. This is between you and Andy and that loser father of yours. There. Stated for the record."

"Statement noted?" I uttered.

"Good," said Willie. "Now go call Andy. Tell him you had a great time. Listen to Love Doctor Willie; she knows what she's talking about."

She leaned in for a hug. Relieved she'd finished her lecture, I hugged back.

"You know I think he's great," I said. "I just don't want to get my hopes up over nothing."

"You mean nothing like asking him to a movie or dinner or something?" she asked, squeezing back.

I pulled away and climbed out. "You're out of control."

"True," said Willie. "I blame the new guy. All that testosterone has melted my brain." She waved. "So long, Mrs. Monaghan."

I watched Willie's car disappear down the road, knowing full well that she was right about me and guys and walls and expecting things that were good to turn bad. But I didn't have time for that now, because there was something I really needed to do. I turned for the house on a mission.

Pete was making coffee in the kitchen.

"Where's Jay?" I asked, as soon as I got through the door.

Pete raised his hands in surrender. "I've been with him the whole time!"

"It's not that," I said. "I need to see him."

"He's just gone out back."

I found Jay at the side of the house trying to shoot baskets with an inflatable ball that was twice the size of the hoop.

"Hey," he yelled, when he saw me. "Look what I won at bowling. Pete pumped it up."

"That's pretty neat, Jay."

Arms folded, I watched the ball bounce up and down, all the time contemplating how I was going to handle this. It was probably nothing, just a stupid idea that had gotten into my head, but . . .

"Jay, I need a favor."

Jay didn't miss a beat. "No, you can't borrow my Wii."

"I don't want your Wii. I want your leg."

Jay turned to me just as the ball hit the rim. He let it fall to the ground. "Which one?"

"The left," I said. "Now hand it over."

If there was one thing that pissed me off about my dad and his parade of pathetic women, it's what they did to Jay. Not just abandoning him—like there could be anything worse. But this . . .

I crouched, and then rolled down Jay's sock to the top of his sneaker.

There it was. Just above the ankle. About the size of a Ping-Pong ball. A tattoo. Of a bird. *Sol*'s bird.

"Thinking of getting one?" asked Jay, with a cheeky grin.

I examined it closely. The same colors. The same lofty demeanor. The same razor-sharp talons.

"Not right now," I replied. I pulled his sock back up.

"Then what's the deal?'

"No deal."

I teasingly kicked the ball across the yard—"Don't pop that thing"—then headed back to the kitchen to find Pete pouring himself a cup of coffee. I immediately headed for the table.

"It's time we got rid of Jay's tattoo."

Pete stopped mid-stir. "What's brought this on?"

"He's ten years old. It's child abuse." I traced circles on the table with my finger, anything but look at Pete. I didn't want to explain to him about Sol. He'd only get the wrong idea and think this was me obsessing about some guy. It wasn't. It was about Jay. "That clinic in Omaha can do it. Doctor Peak said he'd arrange it, and then you never called. Sign the consent form and I'll organize it. I'll take him and everything."

He came to the table, watching me. Only then did I realize how closely. "Has something happened?"

"No," I said. "We should have done it ages ago. That's all. Heaven knows what Doctor Peak thinks of us leaving it there."

"I'll call him on Monday," said Pete. "See if we can get him in next week."

I don't know why I let something so stupid consume me, but for the rest of the weekend I kept picturing Sol on the riverbank. That a guy like him, so grown, so *mature*, could be walking around with the same tattoo as Jay just struck me as wrong.

I swore that if I ever saw my dad, I'd slap his stupid face. *Idiot.* How could he do that to a kid, to brand him when life was hard enough? It wasn't as if Jay and I had the advantages of Andy, or even Willie. If we were to make it in the world, Jay and I had to stand on our own two feet. We didn't need to be singled out as different. It may be fine for Sol Crowley, or whatever his name was, with his hunky muscles and devil-may-care attitude. But to do it to Jay—it was just infuriating.

I was grouchy at work on Sunday, grouchier still when I thought of Andy and realized I should have been on cloud nine, not stewing over Jay's tattoo. I wound myself up so badly that by the time I got into bed Sunday night, I couldn't sleep. Every time I conjured Andy's image, it spontaneously morphed into Sol. Everything came back to two questions: Why would Sol choose to get that particular design? And where did he get it?

It must have been somewhere seedy. Sol was a junior too, which meant he couldn't be much older than seventeen. The tattoo place in Crownsville wouldn't touch you unless you were twenty-one. And it didn't look like a standard tattoo, either—no love hearts and arrows, or tigers and snakes. Sol's bird had been *designed* and I was betting that whoever had designed it had also applied the ink. I hurtled toward an unnerving conclusion. They were the *exact same tattoo*. Whoever had done one, had done the other.

"That's ridiculous. It's coincidence."

Did I really believe that if I discovered who'd inked Sol's tattoo, I might find a link to my missing father?

\* \* \*

Monday. Lunch.

"It's a terrible idea," I said to Willie, for the fifth time. "I'm not searching the school for him."

"You don't have to," said Willie. She slid her tray onto the table, and then took a folded piece of paper from her bag. "I have Andy's schedule."

I appreciated that Willie was cheering me on from the sidelines. But with this latest move, I suspected her obsession for getting me and Andy together was racing out of control.

"Where'd you get that?" I asked, totally aghast.

"Sally. She's in all the same classes."

"Now Sally will tell him you asked for it."

Willie shrugged. "So? There is such a thing as playing *too* hard to get. You know, he was grilling Kieran about you this morning."

I laughed. I couldn't help it. "There's no way I'm hanging around his classes just to say hi."

"Whose classes?"

Kieran had arrived. I prayed he'd be on my side.

"Andy's," said Willie.

Kieran took the seat beside me. He threw his arm across my shoulders. "So where do you guys hang in the evening these days?" he asked, mimicking a deep, hunky voice. "Is Mia normally there? What nights does she work at Mickey's? What's her bra size, Kieran?"

So Kieran was getting in on the act, too.

"He didn't say that," I protested.

"'She doesn't wear one, Andy,' I said."

I shrugged off his arm. "As if you'd know."

Willie scoured Andy's schedule, completely deaf to the fact that I refused to stalk him. "He has Spanish last period," she said, her nose almost touching the paper. "You can easily get there from history."

"I'm not doing it!"

I glanced around the cafeteria for inspiration, or maybe a giant roll of duct tape for Willie's mouth. What I found instead was Sol. He was seated alone by the windows with an apple and a bottle of water before him. Even if I hadn't known about his tattoo, he still stuck out like a sore thumb. His T-shirt pulled tight across his shoulders, the muscles in his back visible as he leaned slightly forward. A couple of guys from our grade talked at the table behind him. Compared to Sol, they looked like kids.

"Then how about a compromise?" said Willie. "I'll ask Jake to a movie on Saturday, if you and Andy go with us."

She *still* hadn't given up? "But that'd break Seth's heart," I said.

"Kieran can amuse Seth. It's a simple solution. Jake's a fine man. We had a good time on Saturday."

"I thought he was your new love," said Kieran, gesturing left.

I could guess where he'd pointed.

"Scoped him the second we got in," said Willie, giving Sol a quick glance. "Yes, I would rather have a bundle of that, but, as he's yet to speak a single word to anybody in the school, I think we'll declare him a lost cause. Strictly eye candy."

I put my head in my hands, but it was just an excuse to take another peek at Sol. He'd turned his back to us, and sat with his feet on the chair beside him. I pictured his skin beneath his shirt, and the tattoo that had to have come from somewhere.

"Last chance," said Willie, waving the paper in my face.

I snatched it from her. "I'll think about it."

"You'll do it," she said. She checked her watch. "Yeuch. Physics."

I stuffed Andy's schedule into my bag and glanced at Sol. He'd gone, the apple and the water abandoned on the table.

"Willie, I'll trade you any day," said Kieran. "I've got chemistry lab *all afternoon.*"

I immediately looked to Kieran. *Chemistry lab.* If memory served me, that was exactly the class he shared with Sol.


I feigned a headache so I could leave history early. Andy would have to wait. I had other fish to fry.

I camped out at the lockers by Mr. Benbow's lab and rehearsed what I wanted to say. *Hey, Sol, show me your tat*, wasn't going to work. With half the girls already gaga over his very existence, I definitely didn't want him to think I was swooning over him too.

*Hey, Sol, can you take your shirt off?* The thought made me want to puke.

When the bell rang and the first galloping steps sounded on the floor above, I decided there was only one way to go. Wing it.

Doors opened along the hall and soon the flow of students meant that at least anything I said to Sol wouldn't be overheard. I pushed my way to Mr. Benbow's door, tried to ignore the butterflies fluttering in my gut, and hoped to hell I could avoid Kieran.

Sol was second out of the lab.

He entered the tide of bodies. Head and shoulders over most of the other students, he was an easy track. I hurried after him, several paces behind as he swung toward the gym and the parking lot at the rear of the school. A couple of shoves and a few wayward elbows and I'd almost caught up to him, just as he stepped outside.

"Sol?" I said. It didn't come out as decisively as I'd planned.

Though barely ahead of me, Sol didn't stop. He headed on toward the lot.

I shouted louder: "Sol!"

He turned around.

Andy aside, I'd never been one to fall at a guy's feet. They were just guys, right? But up close and personal, I suddenly understood the reason for all the fuss surrounding Sol. He was *hot*. Not just tall, hunky, handsome hot, which he was, but intense-looking, *gorgeous*. And not Monaghan gorgeous where everyone was after him and he knew it, but gorgeous like he knew it, and just didn't care.

All the things I'd noticed about Sol from the Ridge took on new clarity up close.

His hair was a shade lighter than his eyes; his jawline was straight and strong; his arms long, his feet huge. But again, he wasn't like the jocks—pumped-up boys parading as men. It was something more than that. It was the way he looked at me. I mean, *looked* at me. No embarrassment, no awkwardness like with other guys. He hadn't even glanced at my chest!

And then it struck me: There was no way this guy was seventeen.

Sol tilted his head and opened his hands as if to say, *"What?"*

Okay. So obviously not the friendliest guy. There was nothing to do but speak. I gripped my bag strap and took a few steps.

"I'm Mia," I said, cursing myself for thinking this a good idea. "Mia Stone. I know Kieran in your chemistry class."

*Great introduction, Mia.*

Sol didn't reply, but neither did he turn away. His expression was impossible to read. Bored, disgusted, mad? All I knew was that his gaze penetrated as deeply as the eyes of the bird he wore on his back. He waited patiently for me to continue.

But what to say? Under the pressure of his poised, self-assured air, all I came up with was this: "How do you like Crownsville? You live out by the river, right?"

He nodded. It was something. All I had to do now was forge a route from the river to the tattoo. Easy.

"Some of us were out that way over the weekend. You might have seen us? We were on the Ridge. You passed by."

The expression on his face never changed. I again tried to decode what it meant. *Who are you? What do you want? What the hell am I doing here?*

Rapidly getting nowhere, I sighed. This was ridiculous. "I was interested in your tattoo."

The voices of passing students punctuated the silence that followed. The gym door banged. Engines revved. Radios blared in the parking lot. And all the time, he stared at me. I started to wonder if I had ink daubed on my lips or huge boils on my face. Approaching Sol had been a huge mistake. He was clearly uninterested in everything and everyone around him. The chances of him opening up about the tattoo? Zero.

"What about it?" he finally asked.

So he *could* speak. His voice had a soft tone and a soothing depth, not ultra-deep, but in no way boyish. It was a bonus.

"I've seen something like it before," I said. Seizing the opening, I stepped toward him. "I wondered what it meant."

Though he was making this far from easy, I caught a glint of a smile on his lips. Up close, I saw shades of a whole different person. He was open and interested. What I'd judged to be arrogance appeared as curiosity. He was a mysterious bundle of contradictions. I wished him luck making friends at Crownsville High.

"It doesn't mean anything," he said.

"But it's *huge*. Where'd you get something like that?"

Again, that look, half guarded, half questioning. "No place around here."

"Then you got it in the town where you used to live?"

Sol's eyes narrowed. "I got it a long time ago," he said. And then he left, before I could say anything else.

Completely bemused, I watched him from the steps. He was one of hundreds heading through the lot, but he was the only one I saw. The new guy. So out of place. So *different* from everyone I knew.

He climbed into a blue truck and drove away.

Sol. Sol, with a man's knowing eyes and a tattoo like my brother's. Sol, who would think of me as that crazy girl with lots of questions. Not that I planned on seeing him anytime soon. One dose of humiliation was enough for me.

I headed for Rusty, determined to forget the encounter and move on with my day. But the image of that curious look in Sol's eyes lingered long after I'd left school behind.

# FIVE

ormally, I'd be desperate to confess to Willie that I'd spoken to Sol, but I kept silent for no other reason than I'd never told anyone about Jay's tattoo. I didn't plan on changing that now, especially with Pete promising he'd finally get rid of it. There were other issues I wanted to avoid too, like admitting that my fascination for Sol went beyond the tattoo. It was crazy, but I couldn't stop thinking about how he'd looked at me. And there was no argument on earth that would satisfactorily convince Willie of why Andy's schedule had taken me to Sol's chemistry lab. So when we sat down to lunch on Wednesday and Willie announced that the cops had been at Old Man Crowley's, I kept my ears open and my mouth shut.

"Got to be about Sol," said Kieran. "The 'never talks to anyone' act. The 'randomly shows up and no one knows where he came from' story. There was never any trouble at Crowley's until he came on the scene."

Willie, who as usual was tying knots in her french fries, tossed one of her creations at Kieran. "I hate it when you 'air punctuate,'" she said, mimicking Kieran's finger speech marks. "So the kid's new to town? Doesn't make him an axe murderer."

"Some 'kid,'" said Kieran. He flicked back the clump of mangled potato. "I'd like to know what kind of a 'school' he got kicked out of before coming here."

"Did he get kicked out?" asked Seth.

"Why else send him here? Did you see that tat? I bet it was a gang thing."

I was determined not to get involved in the conversation. But, a gang? The idea had merit; it would explain why Sol had been so cagey when I'd asked about the tattoo. Obviously, Jay wasn't in a gang, but maybe my dad had been?

"There are a million reasons for him to be here," said Willie, refusing to give it up. "Maybe his parents died and Crowley's his only living relative. Or maybe he's a storm chaser. Or he heard what a great town Crownsville was. If all the students looked like him, I'd say 'bring 'em on.'" She winked as she shot another air quotation.

"I bet your dad knows."

"My dad might know his favorite candy bar and his shoe size, and I wouldn't tell you."

"Meaning he does know something."

"Meaning, he wouldn't tell me if he did!"

Kieran pushed aside his tray. He looked at us one by one, intrigue clear in his eyes. "Think about it. All these kids disappear, Sol turns up, and then Alex Dash goes missing too."

Willie shook her head, then gestured like Kieran was crazy. "So that means Sol's snatching kids? Get real, Kieran. Boys were disappearing long before he showed up."

"But if we knew where he came from, then maybe we could find out if the same thing had happened there."

I couldn't help thinking that maybe Kieran had a point. Not his ridiculous theory that Sol was the Crownsville Kidnapper (that was just typical Kieran hysteria), but that Sol was far too mysterious. I'd asked about the tattoo and he'd given me nothing. Why be so secretive? Maybe it was a gang symbol, maybe it wasn't. Whatever the truth, it all pointed in one direction: Sol was hiding something.

The bell saved us from more of Kieran's conspiracies.

"Unbelievable," muttered Willie, as soon as he and Seth had gone.

We grabbed our bags, then dumped our trays at the mess station.

"Time for study hall," I said. "Any plans?"

Willie grinned. "Yeah. I'm gonna run circuits in the gym. Want to come?"

I really did. "I can't. I haven't finished Rifkin's debate prep. He's getting harsh with his grading."

"You mean the 'It's about time you all grew up and faced the disappointments of adulthood' speech that he gave last week?"

"Yeah. That. I'll catch you later, Wills."

Glad for a distraction from Sol, tattoos, and psychopathic kidnappers, I hurried to the library and bagged the largest table I could find to accommodate the mountains of books I'd need for Rifkin's assignment. It was a monster—"Resolved: The clash of civilizations has no basis in reality." Yikes. I grabbed the reading list, hit the shelves, and began taking notes.

Twenty minutes later I realized I'd only written three lines. Opulent blooms filled the margins of my page. A theme appeared between the doodles: Scrolling, curling *S*s.

*Give me a break.*

I blamed Kieran that I was so distracted. All that garbage about Sol and the cops at Old Man Crowley's—as if Sol had anything to do with those kids. The real mystery was his tattoo. Find out where he got the tattoo, find a link to my dad. Find a link to my dad and . . . Then what? Track him down? Was that what I really wanted?

My brain was beginning to melt. Trying to refocus, I reached for a different book. I didn't expect what I found. An open book lay on top of the stack. And there, on the page, was a drawing of Sol's and Jay's tattoo.

Stunned, I glanced around. Sol was nowhere in sight. Heart racing, I looked again at the book. The colors burst from the page. It was definitely the same bird, a strange, otherworldly eagle. Its steely eye watched me.

The caption read: "The Lunestral, or dream bird, which descends to earth in a column of light, signifies resilience, protection, and hope. The Lunestral is said to appear in dreams and offers protection from demons in the night."

The book, *Symbols in Legend and Mythology*, didn't look like it'd spent much time off the shelf. I turned it over and examined the spine. No Dewey number. No Crownsville High stamp. I skimmed through the pages before turning back to the bird.

Resilience. Protection. Hope.

That didn't sound very gang-like to me.

But I felt like I was now privy to some great secret. After all these years, Jay's tattoo had meaning.

Again, I scanned the library. And there he was, watching me from the door. Sol.

He couldn't have been there for more than a couple of minutes, but the thought that he'd been watching me sent a shivery thrill through my spine. He leaned against the wall, his long arms folded, his expression totally unreadable.

I looked down at the book and wondered whether I should chance a smile. But when I looked up again, Sol had gone.

The wasted study session saw me back in the library at the end of the day. I set to work, but time and again my gaze wandered to the door. There was no question Sol had sneaked the book onto my pile. But why didn't he think he could hand it to me in person? I took the book from my bag and opened it to the dream bird.

"You know this place causes dandruff."

I just about sprang out of my seat at the voice. I was doubly surprised to see Andy, a species usually found in locker rooms, not libraries. The thrill from when I'd caught Sol watching me during study hall returned. Only this time, it was different. With Sol, I felt drawn, like he was luring me toward him. With Andy, everything felt fresh and real and now. My stomach tightened with nervous anticipation.

"You scared me to death," I said.

"Sorry." He slid into the seat beside me, his hair wet like he'd recently showered. It was a regular look among the senior jocks. "Overtime?"

"Debate for Rifkin." I quickly covered the dream bird with

my notebook. "He's ranking our grades on this, and only giving five As."

"And you want one?"

I shrugged. "Wouldn't hurt."

Andy's eyes sparkled in the library's fluorescent lights. It was clear he wanted to be here, unlike Sol whose gaze seemed to question everything about me. I had no idea why I was comparing the two of them; it was a bit like comparing gingerbread to prime rib. Both were delicious, but one was all warm and comforting, the other all flesh and blood. It didn't take much to guess who was who.

"I had a great time last weekend," I said, trying to rein in my excitement. "I haven't been on the Ridge in ages."

"Me neither," said Andy. "We used to hang out there a lot."

He shuffled, nodding as if the conversation continued in his head. I watched and waited, wondering why he seemed so restless.

"I never finished telling you about Jessica," he finally said.

Jessica? My heart sank. This was the part when he'd tell me they'd gotten back together.

"Oh?" I asked.

"Yeah." He fidgeted again. It was so un-Andy. He was usually so calm. But it was kind of adorable, too, with his damp hair flopping onto his forehead. Shame I was probably about to get bad news.

"Me and Jessica should never have gotten back together last time," he said. "It's definitely over now. I just wanted you to know that."

Hope rekindled. *He just wanted me to know? Me?*

Andy looked me straight in the eye. He took a deep breath. "Mia, come to the prom with me," he blurted. "I mean, would you like to come to the prom with me?"

I couldn't speak.

Obviously, he misunderstood my silence. His face fell. "I only mentioned Jessica because I didn't want you to think this is a rebound thing. It isn't. I swear." He slumped. "Look, Mia, you know I've always liked you. We get along really well. If it hadn't been for Jessica and . . ." He shook his head. "You don't have to answer right away. You probably already have a date, right?"

Was he kidding me?

"I'd love to go."

He faltered. "You looked kind of stunned."

"I'd love to go," I said, again.

He smiled and the scent of freshly grilled prime rib faded. "Then I'll get us tickets." He touched my arm, and for a second I thought he might do something really crazy, like kiss me right there in the middle of the library. He didn't.

"I should let you get back to debate," he said, and stood up.

If I wasn't mistaken, he looked hugely relieved. "Don't work too late. The fog's coming down out there."

Half shell-shocked, half boogying on my happy cloud, I grabbed my cell as soon as Andy left and shot Willie a text: "jst saw AM in libr. Gt bg nws! TTYL!"

There was no way I could tackle Rifkin's debate now. Those clashing civilizations would just have to try to get along until my high wore off. Andy had just asked me to the senior prom!

I dumped my books on the cart, and then snatched up my notebook. Beneath it, the dream bird stared at me. I paused.

*The dream bird, which descends to earth in a column of light.*

But there was no light when I thought of Sol and his tattoo, only mystery and shadow, the kind of dark things I wanted to obliterate from my life. I saw light when I thought of Andy— Andy who'd been so sweet and nervous when he'd asked me to prom, choosing me over every other girl in school. So what if Sol and Jay had the same tattoo? It probably meant nothing. And even if it did, was that something I wanted to bring into my life?

I dropped Sol's book into my bag and made a decision. It was time to turn my back on shadows for good.

Andy was right. By the time I hit the parking lot, the mist was pretty thick. Morning and evening were often foggy in Crownsville, because of the river. It probably wasn't smart to head out of town, the mists would thicken as I neared the water, but there was no turning back when I was in such a decisive mood.

It was a simple plan: I'd drive to Old Man Crowley's, thank Sol for the book, hand it back, and then put him and the tattoo out of my mind for good.

As predicted, the mist became a dense fog as I neared the bridge and the landing for Gus Mason's ferry. Visibility sucked. I turned on Rusty's low beams and kept below thirty.

About ten minutes later, two red orbs glowed in front of me. The traffic signal at the river bridge.

I hadn't realized how far I'd come without anything to guide me but the winding road. The river bridge was narrow—only one car could cross at a time. Though I was little more than twenty feet away, the wooden railings on either side, which prevented a plunge into the river below, were barely visible.

Doubts surfaced. Could I even find the turn onto Old Man Crowley's land? What if Sol wasn't there? I had to put the book into *his* hands if I was to gain closure on this festering obsession.

The red light turned to green, and I came up on the clutch. Rusty shuddered, then died. Thinking I'd stalled him, I set back to neutral, tapped the dash, and then turned the engine. Nothing.

"Oh no," I groaned. "Come on, Rusty. Please, don't."

I ran through the entire ritual again, conscious of draining

Rusty's less than reliable battery with every try. Still the engine refused to turn.

"This is bad."

I grabbed my phone, called Pete, and begged for once that he'd answer. He didn't. After garbling a voicemail, I turned on my hazards, climbed from the car, and took stock.

I was at least a couple of miles from home, farther if I had to backtrack to town and walk on from there. I also had to get Rusty off the road before someone tore up behind me. Whatever happened, I was going to have to explain why I was out here. There was nothing else to do: Willie would have to come to my rescue.

I was about the make the call when a voice came from the right, close to the bridge. "Hello, there." A rustle in the undergrowth followed.

Suddenly conscious of being alone in the middle of nowhere, I spun around.

"Who's there?" My heart pounded.

"That you, Mia?"

A short figure appeared on the towpath. I squinted through the fog. "Mr. Mason?"

Gus Mason emerged from the mist. Never had I been so happy to see him.

"What you doing out this way?" he asked.

Now wasn't the time to explain. I skipped ahead. "My car died."

"We should get it off the road, then," he said. "Can you push?"

I knew I could. I was more worried about Gus, who had to be at least seventy years old.

"Just to the side here, Mia. I'll take off the brake."

I handed Gus the keys, cringing at the empty soda cans on the floor and the sports bra dumped on the backseat. Gus didn't seem to notice.

Together we pushed Rusty onto the grassy shoulder. Problem one: solved.

"I can't thank you enough," I said, as I grabbed my bag from the backseat and stuffed the bra into one of my old sneakers.

Gus hoisted his baggy jeans onto his waist. He scanned the fog. "Pete coming for ya?"

"He's not answering his phone," I replied, hating that I had to give testimony to Pete's unreliability. "I'll probably walk back to town."

Gus waved the idea away. "No need for that. I've got the ferry at the landing. I was about to take her back to the boathouse when I heard you cut out. Jump on. I'll take you to Miller's Crossing. It can't be more than fifteen minutes for you from there."

I couldn't have been more grateful. I resisted the urge to throw my arms around Gus's neck and plant a huge kiss on his shiny forehead.

"Have you been on the water in all this fog?" I asked, as we navigated the undergrowth to the river's edge.

"Fishing for perch," he replied. "Didn't catch so much as a cattail. Lucky for you, hey?"

The path veered and the first boards on the dock appeared beneath us. Another twenty feet and the ferry emerged from the mist.

Gus's ferry was a thing of magic to any kid younger than ten in Crownsville. More pontoon than boat, it was painted scarlet and decorated with scrolls and flowers reminiscent of gypsy wagons. A yellow awning, strung with fairy lights, sheltered six wooden benches. The captain's station stood at the stern. Beside the wheel lived Admiral Sunday, a stuffed parrot complete with an eye patch and spotted kerchief. He perched over the rusted tin where, as a kid, you dropped your quarters when you boarded, and Gus, an awful ventriloquist would squawk, "Welcome aboard, shipmates."

I pulled my jacket around me as I huddled on one of the benches and tried to avoid Admiral Sunday's eye. In truth, the scrawny thing had always given me the creeps. Gus started the engine and the lights on the awning twinkled on. We drifted from the dock and onto the river. The vague outline of rocks and trees loomed on either side.

"How's school these days?" asked Gus, who looked ahead, at what, I didn't know.

"It's good."

"And how's that little brother of yours?"

"He's fine."

"Not straying from home on his own, I hope."

"No, we keep close tabs on him with the way things are."

Vibrations from the engine rumbled through the hull. My hair and clothes grew cold and damp. I watched Gus steer and thought of that night at Mickey's with Rich Manning. And then I thought about Alex and the light I'd seen on Rowe.

"Mr. Mason?"

"Call me Gus. Mr. Mason makes me sound like an old fart, which of course I am, but no harm pretending otherwise."

I smiled. "Do you remember what Rich Manning said about Alex Dash?"

"Rich? Who can remember anything that comes out of his crazy mouth?"

"He said there were lights in Crownsville—that nothing good happened when they came here."

Gus continued to stare off the bow, and the glow from the fairy lights caught in his pale blue eyes. For a second I could imagine I was at sea or some faraway place, visiting worlds only Gus knew how to find. His thick eyebrows dropped with his frown. I checked ahead into the fog, certain something must have caught his eye. A white blanket remained.

"It's a strange place, Crownsville," he remarked.

I turned back, surprised by the change in his voice. He looked like the same old Gus with the same old Admiral Sunday guarding his shoulder, only he *wasn't* the same in that moment. It was as if he saw that faraway world—*something* just out of reach.

"Did *you* ever see lights?" I asked.

"No, Mia," Gus said. "No lights."

Silence descended as we turned sharply west. The fog started to lift in front of us and trees appeared on the banks. I recognized the landmarks and knew we were close to Old Man Crowley's.

We rounded another bend and Crowley's tiny shack appeared. Everyone knew it was a ramshackle place, a clapboard cottage built on top of a gentle rise. Tall trees surrounded it, like a woodland hut from a long forgotten tale. Lights shone at the windows. But it wasn't Crowley's home that made my heart kick, then race.

Sol stood on the overgrown lawn, watching the ferry as we drifted by. Instinct told me to look away. I couldn't. He watched, like a sentry, a lone statue in a sea of mist. The fog remained thick on the edges of Crowley's land, but on the yard, it retreated, like a curtain opening at the beginning of a play.

Why Sol was outside in weather like this didn't enter my mind. He *belonged* there, as much as Gus and Admiral Sunday belonged on the river. But the ferry puttered along, and soon we'd passed. I turned to take one last look before Sol and the house disappeared from view.

Gus also looked at Sol. I caught the two of them—the old man on the river and the young guy on the shore—staring intently at each other.

I pulled my jacket tighter around me, unnerved.

The magic had passed. Gus was Gus again, his eyes trained on the river. But I couldn't shake the shiver that traveled my spine.

In that final moment, before Sol had disappeared from view, I was certain I'd seen Gus *bow*.

# SIX

O f everything in the world," said Willie. "Shopping, chocolate, volleyball—it's being right that I like best."

"Then you should be really happy," I said. "Because you were right."

She was inspecting my closet's pitiful selection of formal wear while I sprawled on my bed, glowing from Andy's invitation.

"Willie, I'm buying something new. That cream one's putrid, the blue's too slutty, and I barely fit in the green anymore."

With one eyebrow raised, she turned from my closet. "Then why are they hanging here?"

"I might need them," I said.

"For?"

"I'll think of something."

"Why do I believe you?" She took putrid and slutty from the closet. "Hanging on to garbage is a defense mechanism against all the misery in your life."

"But I don't *have* misery in my life," I said.

"Yes, you do. Take Rusty, for example."

You think she'd give me a break after Andy asked me to prom. I groaned. "Do we have to?"

Hours had passed since my adventure on the river and I didn't want to revisit it now. The more I'd dwelled on what I'd seen, the more convinced I'd become that Gus had bowed to Sol. The more convinced I was, the more confused I became about what it meant. It was the kind of circular thinking that only Sol Crowley could inspire. I'd had enough of it to last a lifetime.

"What are you going to do about him?" asked Willie.

"Rusty?" I sighed. "Pete towed him to the shop. This time, I think it's terminal."

"Good. You've been a slave to that machine for long enough." She pulled out my little black dress. "What about *this*?"

"For *prom*?"

"I'm just looking for ideas. Of course, we have to shop." She tossed the dress back into the closet, then flopped into my chair. "I was serious about Jake, you know."

"About a date?"

"We get along."

"Then do it. Ask him out." I imagined us together at prom. "He's cute."

"And tall," said Willie. "You know I can't date anyone shorter than me. That severely limits my options." She reached for the box with Mom's necklace, which I'd left out from the other night, and opened it before I could stop her. "*Nice.* You should wear this." She held it up. The amber stones with their crimson veins twinkled in the light. "Where'd you get it?"

With Willie already trying to unearth the misery in my life, I wasn't sure I wanted to confess. "It was my mom's," I replied, tentatively.

"No!" She draped it across her front before placing it back in the box. "You *have* to wear it for prom. No one will have anything like it."

I really couldn't see myself wearing the necklace; it was far too ostentatious. In fact, I couldn't imagine anyone wearing it but a powdered old lady with diamond earrings and a mink stole.

Willie strolled to the window, a satisfied smile on her face. "I still can't believe he was nervous. Andy Monaghan. *Nervous!* Jessica is going to freak when she hears about this. Seriously, Mia . . ." She paused, her forehead pressed against the window pane, "Is that Jay out there?"

I glanced at the clock. It was almost ten, far too late for Jay to be wandering around outside. I scrambled off the bed and joined Willie at the window.

Jay stood on the edge of the cornfield, his outline faint in the light from the kitchen window. He ducked, peering through the new growth as if searching for something in the foliage.

"Mia, what is he doing?"

"Maybe he lost something," I said. "I'd better go see. You get rats the size of coyotes out there."

I bounded downstairs, through the kitchen, then out into the yard. The worst of the fog had cleared, but the air was still cool and damp. Moisture glistened on the driveway.

"What you doing, Spud?"

He turned as I reached his side.

"I thought I saw something," he said.

I scanned the edge of the field. All that moved were fine vapors of mist coiling around the stalks. "I don't see anything. Was it a fox?"

Jay shook his head. He looked back into the corn, his eyes narrowing, searching.

There was nothing there.

I glanced up to the bedroom window where Willie still watched. I shrugged at her, confused. "What did you see, Jay?"

The corn whispered quietly around us.

"Jay?"

"I'm not sure," he said. He took my hand. "I thought I saw my mom."

I spoke to Pete in the kitchen first thing the next morning.

"I think we have a problem with Jay," I said. "And I think it might be my fault."

Pete looked up from cleaning his shotgun. "What kind of problem?"

I slid into a chair and braced myself for what I knew would be a difficult conversation. No matter how much Pete avoided talking about family, I had to tell him about what Jay had said he'd seen. I was worried.

"I think I might have stirred something up about him and his mom," I said.

A long, awkward silence passed. Finally, Pete dropped his rag. "What about her?"

"It was the other night," I replied, determined to be as delicate as I could. "He had this picture of her, so I asked him about it. Nothing heavy, just if he remembered her, that kind of thing. Only, he made up this tale about her being taken from him. He seemed worried that I was going to get snatched too. With Alex gone, I just thought he was mixing everything up. At least, that's what I thought. Then last night I found him out by the cornfield. He said he'd *seen* her out there."

"His mother," said Pete. He didn't once blink.

"Yeah," I replied. "In the *cornfield*."

I expected Pete to dismiss it as crazy kid talk. But he stared at me as if he were really listening. A first for Pete.

"What else did he say?" he asked.

"Nothing yet. I wish I hadn't asked him about her. Stacey Ann's probably been filling his head with crap about Alex. Now he thinks he sees his mom. I just wondered whether we should mention it to Doctor Peak. Did you call him yet?"

As soon as I mentioned Doctor Peak, Pete went back to his gun. "Haven't had a chance."

"But you're gonna call him, right? About the tattoo?"

I regretted saying anything as Pete slid into one of his moods.

A horn tooted from the driveway.

"That'll be Willie," I said, and grabbed my bag.

Pete didn't look up, no good-bye, no have a nice day. I knew what it meant. He'd take off somewhere and wouldn't be back until late. I had work after school, which meant Jay would be alone for most of the evening unless I called Mrs. Baker and asked her to watch him.

Mothers. The Stone family taboo.

When would I ever learn to keep my big mouth shut?

* * *

In my experience, days that start badly rarely get better.

First period: Rifkin, Lord of Grumpton, piled on yet more homework. Seth was sulking at lunch having heard that Willie planned to ask Jake out. And then Sally Machin must have heard about me and Andy going to prom because she bashed into me in the hallway, and then flounced off after sending a fatal look in my direction.

By the end of the school day, I was ready to climb into bed. Except I had a shift at Mickey's. Worse still, because of Rusty's demise and Willie's club volleyball practice, I had to go there straight from school . . . on the bus.

There was something about the school bus that made me want to give up the will to live. First, it smelled like an old folk's home, a mixture of baby powder and urine. Secondly, it picked up from the elementary school before it came to Crownsville High, and the little twerps on my route thought it was hilarious to yell "boobs" and pinch the asses of anyone over the age of fifteen who got on. I stood close to the school steps, staring at the beast as if it were my nemesis, here to vanquish me.

"Mia?"

"I know," I snapped. "I'm getting on the wretched thing."

As soon as I spoke, I realized it wasn't the usual scolding voice in my head. I spun around. Then I cringed.

Sol stood behind me. He glanced at the bus.

"You crept up on me," I said, wanting to add "Again!" I was curious, though, about what he wanted.

"Sorry about that."

I couldn't help but accept his apology. The piercing intensity had gone from his eyes and—did I dare say it?—he appeared *approachable*. Of course, approachable is easy when you have the upper hand. I mean, he had just caught me talking to myself.

"In my defense," I said. "I don't always talk to myself. I was getting psyched up for the bus."

For the first time ever, Sol Crowley smiled. And what a smile it was. It reached every part of his face, especially his eyes. At the same time, with a subtle shrug, he shifted his weight, left to right. His wide shoulders relaxed. His long, tanned arms hung loose at his side, and suddenly he didn't seem as intimidating as the Sol I'd first spoken to only days before.

"You should sit next to that kid who's licking the windows," he said.

It was intriguing to hear him speak again. He had that sexy voice that came from somewhere deep inside his chest, one I could listen to all day. I was going to prom with Andy, but I was still human. Sol *was* hot. There was no way around it. I smiled too.

"Who, Ike?" I said. I pointed to the bus where Ike Greenwald was, indeed, licking the windows. "He's my best bud."

The bus door closed.

"I should go," I said, though for some reason, I really didn't want to. Yes, I'd made my decision yesterday: No more dark, moody mysteries. Life from here on in was going to be light, bright, and fluffy. But Sol was smiling, making jokes. And I was curious—*everyone* was curious—about him. Besides, I still had to return his book.

Two girls approached from the right, walking straight at Sol, obviously hoping to brush past him by the giggly expressions on their faces. Without so much as a sideways glance, he leaned away, foiling their plan. He had to have known he was their target, but he didn't acknowledge it. I guess when you looked as good as Sol, you got used to being stared at all day.

Torn, I glanced at the bus. Ike's face was still pressed against the glass. Time for a decision. Get on the bus now or risk being late for my shift.

"I'll give you a ride," said Sol, as if reading the torment on my face. "I can't let you put yourself through that."

His motivation for the offer was a mystery. Maybe he wanted to talk about the dream bird or last night on the river. Maybe he'd finally decided to try to make friends at Crownsville High. But a ride? I didn't know anything about him. Would I get into a car with a potential psychopath? Even if he was a cute one? Apparently, yes.

"I'm actually heading to work," I said. "At Mickey's. On Main."

"I've seen you there."

The bus pulled away. Decision made. Sol Crowley was about to drive me to work.

Everyone takes a turn feeling watched when they are in high school, but strolling across the parking lot with Sol, I *knew* every eye was on us. Word was bound to reach Andy that Mia Stone had climbed into the new kid's truck. Half the school already knew Andy had asked me to prom. I felt my reputation begin to tatter. But it was too late to turn back. Sol actually *held open* the passenger door of his truck. He gestured for me to climb in.

"Unless you think I'm the kiddie snatcher too," he said.

My cheeks burned as soon as he said it. "Of course not," I replied, and to prove the point, I got in.

But I wondered if I'd made the right choice when Sol got in and closed the door behind him. The cabin suddenly felt very small. His long limbs and broad shoulders filled the space. He pulled out of the parking lot.

"So how do you like Crownsville?" I asked, unable to think of anything else to say, and wondering if this time I might get an answer.

"It's different," he said.

We stopped at a red light, and I caught him watching me out of the corner of his eye. I got the feeling he was studying me as much as I'd studied him.

"No one *really* thinks you took those kids," I said.

He smiled. "I didn't think they did until about a second ago."

*Shut up, Mia.*

The light turned. Sol went back to watching the road. It was a relief. There was something about him I couldn't pinpoint. It was as if he already knew me, or expected me to say something, but I wasn't sure what. It was a little like when Rifkin called on you in class, and you realized that you'd been daydreaming and had no idea what the question was. I hated those moments because usually I filled them with pointless chatter like, "Is Crownsville High much different from your old school?"

"Very," he said.

"And where was that?"

Sol stared at the road. It was difficult to know where to look. His face in profile, with his straight nose and strong jaw, was as gorgeous as he was head on. His smile faded. I wasn't sure why, but I was suddenly cast back to the ferry and Gus's intensity as he gazed into the fog. Sol's huge hands gripped the wheel, the tendons in his arms straining as he twisted the vinyl. "It was some place far away."

Another red light. I hadn't noticed how many lights there were down here. As soon as we stopped, Sol again faced me.

"Why were you on the river last night?" he asked.

The cabin seemed to shrink even further. All I could see were Sol's wide shoulders, his long arms, and the questioning look in his eyes. I glanced at his hands, which moments before had squeezed the wheel, and thought of Kieran and his crazy conspiracies. They *were* pretty big hands. Strong hands. The kind that could easily grab a kid off the street. I swallowed.

"My car died," I said, cursing Kieran for making me feel so uneasy. "Mr. Mason was giving me a ride to Miller's Crossing."

"But why were you up there?"

"Well . . ." I took a breath. There was no reason to feel this nervous, no matter how hard he'd twisted that wheel. Whatever the rumors were about Sol, he'd done nothing to deserve them. He wasn't the most open guy, but he had just started at a new school. I couldn't blame him for keeping his distance. It didn't mean he was about to leave me dead in a ditch.

"I was coming to return your book."

"So you know where I live."

"Everyone does."

"Are you often up at the Ridge?"

A horn honked and our eyes snapped forward to find that the light had changed. Sol drove on.

"Sometimes," I said. "Mainly in summer. Sometimes we go to Jacob's Lake. It's about fifty miles from here. A couple of guys from school have homes up there."

"And the rest of the time?"

"I don't know. Just what anyone does in a town this size."

We pulled up in front of Mickey's, ending what had almost been the longest ten minutes of my life. I reached for my bag. "Thanks," I said, and handed him his book.

Sol took it. He continued to watch me as if my face were covered in a thousand captions and clues. "You never did tell me where you'd seen the Lunestral," he said.

"You never asked."

"I'm asking now."

This was unknown territory. Having a mother in prison, a loser father, a depressive uncle. No problem. I'd admit it to anyone who asked. But admit that Jay had a tattoo?

"My half brother has the same tattoo," I said, shocked to hear the words coming from my mouth. "Only, he's much younger— he's only ten. My dad and his wife gave it to him before he came to live with us; we planned to remove it. It's an unusual design, so I just wondered—"

"If you knew where mine came from, you might discover where your brother got his."

He was smart, at least.

"Yeah," I said. "I guess I did."

Sol leaned back in his seat, his face tilted in my direction. "Then I wouldn't look too hard, Mia," he said. "I doubt you'd find the answer you're searching for. But remember, even if you remove it, once the dream bird's touched you, you'll always have its protection."

Sol's gaze held me. Tiny veins of golden flecks ran through the brown in his eyes. Almost hypnotized, I watched him, as if he'd stepped from the book of myths and legends that now lay between us on the seat. How was I ever going to explain this to Willie?

"You should get to work," said Sol, and the moment vanished.

He was right. After all, it was Thursday night. Chicken special. Always a winner at Mickey's.

"Thanks," I said, though I wasn't certain what I was thanking him for. The ride? The book?

Clutching my bag to my chest, I opened the door, part of me reluctant to leave. Whoever Sol was, wherever he'd come from, he'd brought the dream bird to Crownsville and had given meaning to Jay's tattoo. For that, I was grateful.

I shot him a half smile. "I'll see you around."


I returned from work that night to find the house empty and a note from Pete that Jay was at Stacey Ann's. I stopped when I entered the living room. An empty whisky bottle stood on the end table beside the couch. The scent was thick in the air. Just when I'd thought Pete was doing better. But then it was always the same with Pete. One trigger and he'd be off again.

I showered, then threw on my sweats. Rifkin's assignment waited on my desk. It felt like years since I'd sat in the library with the dream-bird book as Andy invited me to the prom. But the world continued on and with it, Rifkin's assignment. I flicked through my notebook until I came to the page of doodled Ss.

Sol.

It was no good. Rifkin's clash of civilizations couldn't compete with the images of Sol that swirled in my mind. Sol, who came from some place far away. I wished myself there now.

Distracted, I reached for my mom's velvet box and flipped open the lid. Twenty-four hours ago, the necklace had been part of Willie's plans for prom. It had been all about Andy, about finding the perfect dress. Now the color of the golden stones reminded me of the flecks in Sol's eyes.

I took the necklace to the mirror and fastened it around my neck. It actually looked better on than it did in the box. I'd never really thought I'd wear it to prom, but now it struck me as kind of vintage, a sort of shabby chic.

Headlights appeared outside, followed by the soft rumble of an engine. I wandered to the window as the Bakers' car pulled up. Jay climbed out.

Satisfied that he was home, I returned to the mirror, again checking the necklace. *Vintage.* I liked the sound of that.

Voices carried from outside. Tires crunched on gravel.

Golden stones. Crimson veins. Maybe a red dress? After my excursion with Sol, I might soon be known as the scarlet woman of Crownsville High.

I was lost in the thought, when light began bouncing off the side of my face. Pink. Green. Blue. It looked so pretty against my cheek's tanned skin.

Pink . . . green . . . blue . . .

My gaze drifted to the desk lamp.

Pink . . . green . . . blue . . .

The lamplight was yellow.

I turned to the window.

Two columns of celestial light—pastel ribbons—danced in the breeze from somewhere deep within the corn. Just like that night behind Rowe. But brighter, closer, stronger.

*Voices outside. Tires crunching on gravel . . .*

But what about the slam of the porch's screen door? Where were the cabinets banging in the kitchen, the rustle of snack wrappers, the laughter on the TV? Where were the footsteps on the stairs?

Outside, the lights danced.

I dashed into the hallway.

"Jay?"

Silence.

"Jay?"

Into Jay's room. Bed empty. Computer switched off.

"Jay?" Louder this time.

Colored mists floated in my mind as I descended the stairs in three giant leaps. The lights were visible through the kitchen window. They'd moved deeper into the field.

The screen door slammed behind me as I emerged from the house. Rustles in the cornfield echoed through the darkness. Jay's schoolbag lay on the edge of the field, dumped on the dusty yard. Trampled corn stalks lay beyond it.

Drunk on a cocktail of panic, denial, and disbelief, I sprinted.

Then I screamed Jay's name.

# SEVEN

Terror propelled me. I had to reach Jay before Jay reached that light, and I had nothing to guide me but the indistinct path he'd forged through the corn.

The lights. Alex Dash. Jay.

Those three thoughts converged, like a connect-the-dots puzzle when the hidden picture becomes clear. This wasn't marsh gas or will-o'-the-wisp. It wasn't fireworks or aliens from outer space. This was the same light I'd seen on Rowe, the same light I'd seen the night that Alex disappeared.

Though not yet grown to full height, the corn formed a barrier around me. It scratched my outstretched hands. It clawed my hair. Twice it tripped me.

"JAY!" My own gasping breath was the only reply.

With every step, the light moved farther away, the two columns merging into a wall of mist. There was no one to help. No one to hear my cries.

"Jay! You stop right now!"

I battled blindly on, trampling anything in my path, until *finally* I stumbled out of the cornfield and onto open land. The colored mist had vanished.

The Gartons' farm was to the left. The faint lights of Crownsville lay beyond. Stars shone overhead. Far to the right stood the Ridge, its black mass silhouetted against the velvet sky. A tiny figure sprinted across the fields toward it.

I cupped my hands to my mouth. "Jay!"

Nothing.

"Jay, stop!"

It was no good; either he couldn't hear me, or he didn't want to stop. I lowered my head and ran on. Soon I reached the first trees at the base of the Ridge. Jay was no longer in sight. Worse still, the light had returned. As I scrambled through the undergrowth and into the woods, the light shone from somewhere above. Peachy tints hit the trees and caught in the leaves. A static-like charge filled the air. My skin tingled.

"JAY!"

Vaulting rocks, I hurtled up toward the Ridge. Birds

squawked, disturbed as I passed, and took to the sky in a mass of frantic wings. My muscles screamed. But I couldn't stop. Not when Jay was alone with whatever it was that I was certain had taken Alex.

I reached the last of the trees before the plateau. A wall of tinted mist covered the top of the Ridge. As if two great hands pushed from the edges, compressing the light into a narrower and narrower strip, it receded. Faster and faster. Little more than ten feet of light remained.

Nine.

Eight.

A faint figure stood inside the ever narrowing gap. With a final burst, I tore onto the Ridge.

"Jay!"

In the second I broke from the trees, the light reversed its course. It expanded rapidly, up and out. Like a gateway to Heaven, it was brighter than anything I'd ever seen. Soon color covered the entire Ridge. Dazzled, I shielded my eyes, peering between my fingers at Jay. His back was to me and he moved forward as if to reach for something unseen. A few feet more and he'd walk right off the edge of the Ridge and plunge into the river below.

"Jay, don't! Stop! That's the—"

A second figure appeared in the light. It was tall, shrouded in a long black hooded cloak. Images flashed of the shadow behind Rowe, of Alex Dash and the empty booth at Mickey's. I didn't know where that figure had come from. From within the light? I didn't know. All I knew was that I had to get to Jay.

The figure reached for Jay. I screamed, dove forward, lunging for the light. The hooded figure glanced back, and a great weight bowled into me from behind, knocking me off my feet. The wall of light flashed once, and then vanished. The hooded figure was gone.

So was Jay.

Frantic, I lifted my chin off the ground, spitting dirt from my mouth as I pushed to get up. I couldn't. Whatever had knocked me down, still pinned me.

The weight lifted.

My fingers clawed the dust as I scrambled forward. "Jay!"

"Mia, no! Wait!"

I spun around. A second figure rose in the gloom.

This wasn't happening. The kidnapper had returned to cover his tracks!

"Mia."

The figure knelt. Pale moonlight struck the side of a familiar face.

"Sol?"

"It's me," he said.

I didn't question why he was here. He simply was. That was all that mattered. I grabbed his arm. "Sol, did you see it? Jay! He was there." Gripping Sol tightly, I scrambled to my feet, dragging him toward the drop. "He must have gone over."

I peered into blackness. The sound of rushing water clashed with my ragged breathing.

"Jay, hold on!" I yelled. Hands trembling, adrenaline gushing through my limbs, I yanked my phone from my pocket. "I have to call the sheriff. Sol, do you see him? He has to be down there!"

Sol did not reply. His gaze remained on the river below.

I seized him again, desperate for him to understand. "It was the light, Sol," I said. "Tell me you saw the light."

Sol stood as still as when I'd seen him from Gus's ferry. A deep frown covered his brow. Not a word passed his lips. It had to be shock that had silenced him. I couldn't blame him; I could barely believe what I'd seen myself. But with Sol beside me, I felt hope rise. I wasn't the only witness to what had happened.

With hands shaking, I called the sheriff's number.

The rest of the night passed in such a blur that I could barely distinguish one part from the next. One moment I stood with Sol on the Ridge. The next, distant engines, flashlights, voices. Pete was there. I hadn't seen him arrive. There were ambulances on the Ridge road, patrol cars, and Sheriff Burkett asking me over and over about what I'd seen. Each time I told him, he glanced at Deputy Monwright, and then asked me to explain it again.

"It was like that night," I said, urging them to believe me. "There was a man and these colors and this light." I glanced at Pete, who stood back with arms folded, watching me closely. "It must have been lightning, a tornado."

"There was no tornado tonight," said the sheriff.

"Then a microburst! *Something!* Jay has to be somewhere. You're checking the river, right?"

"We're checking, Mia."

The sheriff drifted away. I was alone with Pete.

"This can't have happened," I said, wanting it to be true. "Pete, there were lights at the *house*. They *came* for him."

Pete didn't reply. He stood, motionless, cast in shadows as black as the hooded figure I'd seen with Jay. "Pete! This is Jay! Say something!"

As soon as I got close to him, I smelled booze. Rage gripped me. "I'm going to help look," I snapped. "Seeing as no one else in his family gives a damn!"

I stormed back onto the Ridge, pushing past the officers who scoured the ground for clues. I'd almost reached the edge when I noticed Sheriff Burkett standing to the side with Sol. Relief hit. Sol was talking. Now they'd have to believe me.

"And you didn't see this light," repeated the sheriff.

I froze.

"I saw Mia on the Ridge," Sol replied. "I thought she was going to jump, so I grabbed her."

*Thought I was going to jump? That wasn't how it had happened. Why the hell would I jump? He'd seen the lights. Sol knew what had happened.*

"Why were you out here?" asked the sheriff.

"Just walking."

"And you're staying with Stan Crowley?"

"Yes. I know Mia from school."

"What about this hooded man?"

Sol shook his head.

The sheriff rejoined the others, but I stood, rooted in place, staring at Sol. It was only then that he noticed me watching.

"You think I'm crazy," I said.

The look in Sol's eyes hadn't changed from when we'd stood on the edge of the Ridge. Distant. Remote. "No," he said.

The cops moved around us, radios crackled, lights swept the ground.

This was a dream. It had to be. "You saw the light, Sol."

He swallowed deeply. "I saw nothing."

I shook my head. I'd been so relieved when he first appeared, but now it was as if I were facing a stranger. This wasn't the Sol who'd shown me the dream bird. It wasn't the Sol who'd driven me to Mickey's. This was a guy who'd come to Crownsville from some place far away. He showed no sign that he was lying about the lights. He simply watched me, expressionless.

"You've had a shock, Mia," he said, calmly. He turned away. "I think you should go home."

My gaze followed Sol's path as he wandered past the officers and was eventually consumed by the dark. I waited, stunned, expecting him to come back at any moment and say that he'd lied. Sol did not return.

Frantic activity continued around me. But not once did I move until Sheriff Burkett reappeared and I finally let him lead me away.

Ten o'clock. Eleven. Midnight. We remained in the kitchen—me, Pete, the sheriff. From time to time, Sheriff Burkett's radio buzzed and my heart would leap as he took the call. But there were no reports of Jay. It was too dark. It was time to wait for dawn.

"I'll call Principal Cook," said the sheriff, when he got up to leave. "I'll tell him you'll be staying home tomorrow, Mia. You got that, Pete?"

"She'll stay home," said Pete, simply. His fingers gripped the edge of the table. He stared into his lap.

Still disgusted that he'd been out drinking when this had

all gone down, I turned my back on Pete as soon as the sheriff left. I headed for my room. Jay's door remained closed, taunting me.

How many times had I passed it on my way to bed and never poked my head inside to wish him good night, to ask about his day, to tell him I loved him, like an older sister should? It was like a great secret, a great *conspiracy*, rested on my shoulders. No one believed what I'd seen, and the only person who shared in the secret had lied.

I pressed my cheek against Jay's door, eyes closed as I prayed for the sound of his squeaking bed or for an explosion from one of his games.

Silence.

I didn't sleep. *Couldn't* sleep. Every time I closed my eyes, I saw Jay in the darkness. Colors swirled around him. Then the dark figure would turn, his face shrouded by the hood. I'd reach out, stretch for Jay's hand, then—gone.

But where? Jay had vanished into thin air. But that couldn't be. He must have fallen into the river. He would be out there, floating, cold and alone.

"But it wasn't like that," I muttered.

Jay *hadn't* fallen. It had started way before. Something had *drawn* Jay into the cornfield. I remembered him taking my hand, telling me he'd seen his mom. What if someone had really been out there? What if whoever had taken him had been targeting Jay for days? Watching. Waiting for the moment to strike.

But Sol hadn't seen anyone on the Ridge.

But Sol was lying. Had to be.

But why?

The door downstairs banged followed by the sound of Pete's truck as he pulled away. I rolled onto my back and stared at the ceiling, as the jumbled mess of events ran through my mind again.

Pete returned at seven the next morning. Still unable to sleep, I headed for the kitchen.

"Anything?"

He shook his head. "They're bringing in divers."

My heart sunk. Jay was a strong swimmer. He might have dragged himself from the river and gotten lost in the woods. Lost was good. What was lost could be found. But divers? Divers meant he was never coming back.

"I should have been here last night, Mia. I'm sorry."

I remembered with shame my outburst on the Ridge. So Pete had been out drinking—what was different? I'd known about the lights, but I hadn't run fast enough. I could've saved Jay if I'd tried harder. Blame lay thick in the air.

"You couldn't have known, Pete," I said. "All that matters is that we get Jay back."

"We'll get him."

"I wasn't lying. I saw everything I said I did. It was the same thing I saw when Alex Dash disappeared. Jay's somewhere on that Ridge. I know it."

Pete offered a nod so slight I barely caught it. "You're not to go back up there," he said.

I made no reply.

"I'm serious, Mia. It won't do any good wandering around up there. Get some sleep. We'll find him."

"Are you going back out?"

He opened his hands and gestured to the mud that covered his jeans and boots. His hair lay damp across his forehead. Stubble covered his chin. "Just came for a change of clothes."

I lingered at the table as he headed out of the room.

"Promise you won't go to the Ridge," he said, glancing back.

"I promise."

It was an easy promise to make. I had no intention of returning. There was still a piece of the puzzle to solve, the huge question that had kept me awake all through the night. And as soon as Pete left, I headed out to get some answers.

I dumped my bike on the track outside Crowley's. I had only ever seen the house from the river, but from where I stood it appeared to be in an even worse state than I'd imagined. Only an undiscovered law of physics could explain how the structure survived. The dilapidated roof sank to the right. The tiny windows were crooked. If the storm season didn't finish it off, then the overgrown yard would soon envelop it.

I walked the dirt path to the door, passing a garage and outbuilding, both as ruined as the house.

I knocked.

Crows squawked in the trees. Squirrels bounded through last year's fallen leaves.

I knocked again.

I'd been so focused on confronting Sol that it hadn't occurred to me that he might have left for school. The house looked as empty as always. There was no sign of the blue truck.

Willie's words echoed: *I haven't seen Old Man Crowley for ages.*

Neither had I.

I knocked twice more.

I sidled to the window. Cobwebs and grime covered the glass, inside and out. I rubbed away what I could before peering inside. Beyond was the living room with a fireplace and hearth. Paper had peeled off the walls, exposing rotten boards blackened by mold. Two folding lawn chairs faced the fire with an upturned crate forming a makeshift table between them.

There was no TV. No pictures. No rug.

I stepped back and glanced up at the second-floor window. The drapes were drawn.

Something was wrong here. Did Old Man Crowley really live in a house with foldaway chairs and a crate for a table? And where exactly was he? He could always be seen on Main Street, grumbling to himself as he bought junk at the hardware store or buckets of rusty nails from the flea market on the edge of town. Whatever the weather, he was always scurrying somewhere in that long black coat he wore. But not recently. Not since Sol had arrived.

The smart thing would have been to turn tail and get the hell out of there, but since the moment I'd seen the lights from my bedroom window, smart had been low on my list of priorities. Jay couldn't wait for the smart, sensible, and rational thing to do. He needed help *now*.

I checked behind me. All clear. Then I crept to the rear of the house.

That's when I saw Sol.

He sat facing the river about halfway down the sloping yard, his knees up and his arms draped across them. Chances were he hadn't heard me knock, but I wasn't convinced. I fought through the brambles, stopping about ten feet away.

"I had a feeling you'd come," he said. He didn't turn around. His feet were bare, the bottom of his jeans wet from the dew-covered lawn.

I'd been adamant that whatever Sol was hiding couldn't be as dramatic as Kieran had surmised. Now I wasn't so sure. There was no good reason for Sol to have lied about what he'd seen on the Ridge. Unless he was involved. Unless he knew the identity of the man beneath that cloak.

"Then you know why I came," I said. My stomach churned, but my voice remained steady and strong. No matter how I felt inside, I couldn't allow any hint of weakness to surface. Not if I was to stand up to Sol.

Sol rose slowly, his long limbs unfurling until he stood at full height. Physically, we were no match; if he wanted to, he could overpower me in a second. But that wasn't my concern. Sol's real power lay in his eyes. Commanding. Controlled. A barrier to rival the wall Willie was convinced I'd built around myself. With Jay's life on the line, I was determined to break through it.

"Why did you lie?" I asked. "You were right there. You saw the light."

The muscles in his jaw tensed. "I told the sheriff," he said, "and I'll tell you now: I was walking, I heard shouts. I came over, I found you. That's it."

"You're lying."

As soon as I said it, he flinched and looked away. A weakness. Brief, but visible. I seized the advantage.

"Sol, my brother is missing," I said. "If you know anything . . ." I trailed off.

Sol's lips were clamped together, his frown deep. He *knew*. I could see it all over him. "Mia . . ."

Everything fell silent and still.

Sol closed his eyes, chest expanding as he drew a deep breath. His tormented expression vanished. He looked up, chin raised, again in control. He'd never seemed so gorgeous.

"I don't know what happened to your brother, Mia," he said. "I'm sorry."

But not half as sorry as me. In the second it took him to say those words, I'd already formulated the next part of my plan. This wasn't over. Not by a long way. Not until I'd uncovered the reason why Sol was lying.

# EIGHT

'd never before done anything this risky, so when I returned to Crowley's that evening, I was so nervous I almost puked. But I was determined. Sol had been close to telling me something, of that I was certain. With no trace of Jay, I had to find out what that something was.

I dumped my bike far from the house and hiked the remaining half mile. Sol's truck was parked outside. The occasional shadow moved through the living room. Crouched, I waited.

Sol left at eight. I lingered for ten minutes, zippered up my jacket, and then got to my feet. I was going in.

The house loomed in the dusk, like a wicked witch's lair in

a kid's fairy tale. With no notion of what I might find, I pictured children's bodies, cages, ropes.

And Old Man Crowley? The only thing I knew for certain was that OMC was no longer here. Where he'd gone was a mystery.

I battled the undergrowth to the rear of the house and tried not to think about Sheriff Burkett and all of his "talks" that Willie and I had endured over the years. Somehow, we'd never covered breaking and entering. I tried not to imagine his look of disappointment if I were found here. It was reason enough not to get caught.

The back door was locked, so I trampled rampant ivy to the window. I placed my hands to the glass and immediately noticed a creak as the window shifted. The frame had warped and was only wedged closed.

I pulled. Damp, musty air hung inside the house. Scrambling up, I heaved my body through the gap and into the kitchen. A board rested between two cabinets beneath me. It swayed as I lowered myself down. I caught my breath. I said a prayer. The counter held.

I took stock as soon as my feet hit the linoleum floor.

Okay, I'd hardly been raised in a palace, but the place was a dive. There were four rickety cabinets with paint peeling from their doors. A sink with a single faucet. Two electric rings for cooking. No oven. No fridge.

I opened one of the cabinets. The shelves were lined with damp, peeling paper. There was a bowl inside, two cups, and a stack of paper plates. A can of soup. A wholesale box of Snickers. A bag of trail mix.

Palms clammy, I closed the cabinet and headed deeper into the house where stairs led off a narrow hall. The living room was to my right. To my left stood a closed door. I gently pushed it open and peered into the room beyond. Hampers, boxes, and crates filled the space, haphazardly piled like a life-size game of Jenga. If I'd pushed my luck with that make-shift counter, then rifling through these cardboard towers was tantamount to suicide. But somewhere in the house there *had* to be a clue.

I had just pulled back from the doorway when my phone beeped. A brief heart attack followed. I searched through my pockets. It was a text from Willie.

I'd dodged her calls all day, but sent a message that I was fine and that we could talk tomorrow. She'd left a voice mail earlier with an update: Still nothing of Jay, no trace of the man, no trace of anything but the trampled path we'd made through the Gartons' fields. *Hang in there, Mia. Dad's gonna find him.*

I checked her text. It was two words: "Luv ya."

I sank onto the bottom of the staircase and stared at the screen. A second ago, I'd felt like the world's only living person, creeping like a criminal through Old Man Crowley's home. Now I felt Willie beside me. I knew exactly what she'd say: *We should check upstairs. Find out what he's up to. You go first.*

"Luv you too, Wills," I whispered.

I switched off my phone and began a slow climb to the upper floor.

I headed for the bedroom at the front of the house. The curtains I'd spotted earlier had been opened. I peered through the window. There was no sign of Sol's truck.

"Don't do this, Mia. It's crazy."

Maybe so. But Sol had given me no choice.

Crumpled sheets covered a cot beneath the window and there was a long, low chest beside it. On top of the chest sat a glass, a flashlight, and a loosely rolled scroll of paper, about a foot in length. It was caught beneath a pile of clothes—jeans, T-shirts, hoodies. Sol's clothes.

Taking care not to disturb the pile, I inched out the scroll, marking its position so I could put everything back just right.

The scroll was thick, crumpled, and worn. I unrolled a couple of inches, just for a quick look. It was constructed from two sheets; some kind of vellum had been taped across the top edge of the lower sheet, forming a transparent overlay. On the lower sheet was a map.

I took the flashlight from the chest, placed the scroll on the bed, and fully unrolled the papers.

The bottom map showed Crownsville, with Onaly to the north and west. Not quite a street map, but detailed enough. The vellum overlay showed something quite different: Patches of dark shading that, when placed over the map, covered most of the two towns. And there were randomly dotted stars, too, at least fifteen or twenty in number. A dense cluster of tinier stars formed a line close to the center of the map, where there was no shading. I smoothed the vellum and the map of Crownsville popped into focus. What lay under the vellum's starry line became clear: It was the Ridge.

I lifted the overlay to ensure I'd read it right. There was the river. The woods. If I followed it just an inch, I could put my finger in the exact spot where I stood.

I replaced the overlay and tracked the path of the other, larger, stars. There were a couple in Onaly, right in the middle of a shaded patch. There were four or five in the middle of nowhere, most close to the river. But then one, over the dark area on Crownsville, caught my eye.

My fingers skimmed the vellum. Along Rowe to the elementary school. Along Route 6 from town. Between them empty land. And on the empty land . . . a star.

My throat dried. My scalp tightened. There was only one

other location to check, but I was beginning to guess what those stars meant. And there were two of them, right on the land by our house.

Barely breathing, I glanced around the room. A pair of mud-stained boots lay beneath a wicker chair that was nestled between the eaves of the sloped ceiling. A second pile of clothes lay on its seat. A swath of dark fabric was draped across the back.

I abandoned the map and grabbed the flashlight, shining it into the corner of the room. Whatever hung on the chair was long and black, just like the cloak I'd seen in the light.

The walls closed in. I'd come this far. I *had* to know.

I tucked the flashlight beneath my arm, darted for the chair, and then reached for the fabric.

The first thing I noticed was the weight. It had to be twenty pounds. The same mud I'd seen on the boots was daubed across the hem. Sleeves slipped from the folds as I held it up.

A collar. Cuffs. But no hood. It wasn't the cloak I'd seen on that figure.

Had I really thought it might have been Sol beneath that hood? That he'd conjured some elaborate light show by which to snatch Jay? Anyway, it could never have been Sol. He'd been with me when I'd seen that hooded man.

But how to explain the map? Alex on Rowe. The lights in the cornfield. Jay on the Ridge. All covered with X marks the spot. Still I needed something more. Proof. Solid, undeniable proof. I put the coat back, and then shone the flashlight once more around the room.

There was a trunk close to the door. Long and deep, it was carved from a dark wood. Thick metal bands crisscrossed the lid. There was no keyhole. No padlock.

I looked through the window again. No sign of Sol. There was time.

I crouched in front of the trunk and threw back the lid. Clothes and blankets covered the contents. On top of them lay a sword.

I'd seen swords before. Sheriff Burkett had a few on the wall in his den. But they were fancier, elegant, I guess. Not this one.

First, it was huge. It ran the full length of the trunk. Secondly, it was plain. No etchings or scrolls decorated the blade like the ones at the Burketts'. The only ornamentation was a thick band of worn brown leather on the grip. It was brutal-looking, a weapon designed for one purpose: running something through.

I reached for the sword, my fingers curling around the hilt. It was heavy, like, *really* heavy, heavier than the weights Willie and I lifted during circuit training in the gym. This was a real, solid, blood-and-guts weapon.

I plunged my hand down the side of the trunk and rifled

to see what was hidden beneath. There was a handgun. A box of bullets. More clothes. There was a deep green shirt of linen or hemp, embroidered with tiny silver stitches. Another, heavily woven in the deepest of red. And then other things, things I'd never seen before. A marble-sized glass sphere inside a tiny box. A pouch that jingled as if filled with coins.

I eyed the T-shirts and jeans beside the bed. It was the uniform of every guy at Crownsville High. Not like the clothes in the chest.

I lifted the embroidered green shirt. Sol's scent rose from it, like the woodlands alongside a river. It was the outdoorsy scent of Sol's truck that I recognized from when he'd driven me to Mickey's.

As I carefully replaced the shirt, I tugged at the spine of a book, wedged down the side of the trunk.

*Symbols in Legend and Mythology.*

The dream bird book. As I pulled on the spine, the book caught on something beneath.

"It can't be . . ."

I reached in, and then slowly withdrew my mom's necklace.

With all that had happened, I hadn't given it a thought. Now I remembered. Almost twenty-four hours ago the necklace had been around my neck. I'd worn it when I'd taken off after Jay. I saw myself in the kitchen with Pete and the sheriff, standing outside Jay's room, lying in my bed. I hadn't been wearing it then. I was *certain*.

It was definitely the same necklace; only the clasp was broken. A long strand of chocolate-colored hair was tangled in the links.

Images flashed. Sol bowled into me from behind. *Was that when he'd taken it?* But why? I didn't feel it fall. Because it hadn't fallen; the broken clasp was evidence of that. It had been torn from my neck.

The light brightened in the room. Necklace tight in my fist, I sprang to the window. Sol's truck pulled up outside.

My feet barely hit the stairs as I bolted for the kitchen, every nerve in my body on high alert. How long did I have? Minutes? Seconds?

I hurtled into the back door. The necklace snagged in the latch as I battled to slide it free. The harder I pulled, the more the latch refused to budge. Footsteps approached outside.

"Come on. *Think!*"

My gaze swept down and relief followed. The bolt was pushed down in its cradle. It slid effortlessly when I lifted it. Cool air rushed inside.

I'd barely cleared the lawn when Sol shouted. The darkness between the trees beckoned. It was like last night all over again, only this time *I* was the one pursued.

I heeded no obstacle, barreling through branches and brush, darting between the never-ending trunks that threatened to block my path, fleeing from that sword and the map and a truth I was no longer certain I wanted to know.

All the time, Sol drew closer, the sounds of his pursuit echoing through the wood.

On and on. Like an out-of-body experience, I saw myself as if from above. Only the biting pain from the necklace, tightly crushed in my fist, anchored me to my body.

My pace slowed as the land rose. I didn't look back. The river on my right kept my path straight. Rocks appeared beneath my feet. I approached the Ridge.

Head down, I powered up the final rise. Any second I'd burst free of the trees and could turn for the road and pray that someone passed. Maybe the officers and deputies were still out searching for Jay. The thought spurred me on. A hundred feet. Fifty. I neared an opening in the trees.

Only seconds passed before I lunged out of the shadowy darkness and out onto the Ridge. The final tips of sunset faded out to the west. The moon hung low in the east. But there were no officers, no sheriff, nothing to mark this as the place where Jay had vanished.

I'd barely cleared thirty feet from the trees when Sol bolted onto the Ridge.

"Mia! Stop."

"The sheriff's on his way," I yelled. I continued to run, panicked, picturing him seizing me and hurling me into the river.

No reply came.

Hoping the threat would make him flee, I veered toward the
track that led back to the road. Leaves rustled to my left.

Sol emerged, lower on the slope—he must have ducked
back into the woods and swerved around. He stood within paces
of the path, my only route to the road. Flight or fight governed
my response. I turned and fled back toward the Ridge.

His heavy steps followed as soon as I moved. "Don't! Mia."

I spun around. Sol had stopped, a safe distance away. He
watched me intently. His shoulders and chest rose and fell with his
rapid breaths. He reached out his hand. "Come down, Mia," he said.

I shook my head. "Where's my brother?"

"Mia." Sol took several steps.

I stepped back, inching closer to the edge of the Ridge and
the forty-foot drop to the river.

"Mia, don't."

I glanced behind me. The drop was less than twenty feet
away. "Don't come any closer," I warned. "I'll jump."

With hands raised, Sol approached slowly.

"I'm serious." I cried. "I'll jump!"

My eyes darted left and right, frantically searching for

escape. With Sol's hands still raised, I imagined them around my neck, him squeezing just like when he'd twisted the wheel in his truck.

To my surprise, Sol stopped. He lowered his hands. "Come down from there, Mia," he said. "I'll explain. I promise."

"How will you explain this?" I yelled. Almost defeated, fighting back tears, I brandished the necklace tight in my fist. "You lied, Sol. You saw the light. You saw the man. I saw the map! Tell me who took Jay!"

Sol's eyes widened. "I promise I'll tell you everything," he said, rapidly. "*Please*. You have to come down from there."

I took another step away.

"MIA, DON'T!"

Something in Sol's voice stopped me. He dashed up the Ridge. Every movement registered in my mind in slow motion. Shock covered his face, yet never once did he look at me. His gaze was fixed behind and beyond.

Cautiously, I turned around.

Light covered the Ridge. In the center, ribbons of color tumbled through a bright opening. The light widened and stretched. Still it grew—stronger and more vibrant than the night before. It spread to the trees and reached for the sky, a massive gemstone wall eclipsing the night.

Mesmerized, my gaze fixed on the bright epicenter.

"He's in there," I whispered.

The threat of Sol forgotten, I saw Jay's empty room, his computer idle on the desk, his clothes unworn in his closet. There were no more sounds of Jay and Stacey Ann clowning around in the yard. No more *thump, thump* of the basketball against the side of the house.

The light covered everything. Was it Heaven? Was that where I'd find Jay?

As if from a million miles away, I heard Sol yell my name. I didn't care. All I wanted was Jay.

Closing my eyes, I walked into the light.

# NINE

The light vanished. The breeze lifted. Once again, I found myself facedown in the dirt. I must have blacked out. But then I remembered Sol on the Ridge and the fear in his eyes. He'd seen the lights too.

Disoriented, I pushed myself onto my knees, but got no higher before a hand grabbed my arm. A sense of danger crashed over me and I prepared to scream. The hand on my arm covered my mouth, silencing me before I could shout.

"Quiet! They'll hear," hissed Sol.

With one hand still covering my mouth, his other gripped my arm so tightly it felt as if his fingers were pressing into the bone.

Struck with terror, I couldn't take my eyes off his face. He scanned the horizon. The scent of wood smoke drifted on the air.

"Don't make a sound," he whispered.

So this was it. Death. Sol didn't have the sword, but he could easily have a gun or maybe a knife. I knew his secret: He *was* connected to Jay and those boys. There was nothing left for him to do but finish me off.

I screwed my eyes shut and tried not to imagine what the end would feel like. A quick stab, a short burst of pain, and then over? Or maybe he'd do something worse—leave me here far from aid, slashed and torn, powerless to stop my life from seeping into the dirt. Somewhere in the blackness, a bell tolled like the death knells I'd read of in Gothic novels. I knew it rang for me.

But the stab, the pain, the shot never came.

"We have to move."

Stunned, I peeked open an eye. Sol's hand remained over my mouth. He pulled my body against his chest. "Can you get up?" he asked, his face inches from mine. "Are you hurt?"

Confusion replaced fear. Sol wasn't trying to kill me. His eyes were wide, his body tense. He looked as scared as I was. And the way he was holding me . . . it was almost *protective*. He scanned the darkness, poised, alert. And then it struck me: *What the hell was that bell? And if it didn't ring for me, then why?*

My eyes tracked the path of his gaze. My mouth dropped open behind his hand.

We were on the Ridge, or at least it looked like the Ridge. There were the same trees and the same grass. Water flowed behind us. But ahead, where the road once ran, the trees were more widely spaced than those that surrounded the Ridge. Distant lights hung between the trees. Unlike the lights that had taken Jay, these were orange beacons like lamplights suspended in darkness. Around them stood the silhouettes of squat buildings. The scent of smoke strengthened. The bell continued to toll.

Panic surged as I struggled to make sense of my surroundings. There should be farmland and prairie all the way to Onaly! No buildings. No lights. Nothing.

Mind in meltdown, I pushed away from Sol's arms and tried to rise. Strength fled from my legs and I toppled back onto my butt.

Sol grabbed me. He clamped his hand over my mouth again.

"Mia, don't!" he said. Slowly, gently, he turned my face to his. "I will let you go, but you can't make a sound."

I stared into his eyes, clinging to his voice as if to a raft at sea. It was the only thing here that made sense.

"Don't speak," he continued. "Don't even think. We're going to get up, and then we're going to run."

Leaves rustled to our right. Sol's gaze swept toward the

sound. He squeezed my hand and sniffed the air like a dog on the scent of impending danger.

"Now!"

Though he almost tugged my arm from its socket, I didn't let go of Sol's hand. He wasn't going to kill me—that much was obvious. Not yet, at least. Whatever was happening, I had only one mission: to stay on my feet.

Vaulting rocks, we tore into the woods. A growl rose from behind. The sound came from deep within the chest of something best left unseen. Terrified, I ran hard. Another growl. This time from the left. A shriek carried through the night as if in answer to the guttural growl.

Sol stopped. This time he pulled me down. *"Wait."*

Crouched in the undergrowth, I looked from tree to tree, every muscle in my body on alert. A town was now visible at the bottom of the hill. Empty, burned shells of houses and shanties made of wood and stone edged the settlement. It wasn't Crownsville.

"What is this place?" I whispered. "Sol?"

I turned to face him, expecting no answer, simply needing to remind myself that I wasn't alone. Something in Sol had changed. His shoulders were back and straight, his chin raised. The fear had fled from his eyes.

"This is the other world," he said. "The one you're not meant to see."

* * *

After clearing the woods, we sprinted a short distance to a metal shack on the edge of town, ducking into the shadows beneath its overhanging roof. Safely out of sight—of what, I still didn't know—Sol surveyed our path.

"It seems clear," he said. "But we're not there yet."

A long scream resonated across the town. Two more followed. Whatever shriek we'd heard in the woods, this was not it. This was human. I backed up against the shack. Sol must have seen the look in my eyes. He shook his head.

"Mia . . ."

Throat constricting, mouth dry, I whispered, "I won't yell," though the scream rang in my ears. "Who was that?"

Sol sighed deeply, the sound laced with regret and despair. "Someone who got careless," he said.

The hut was cold against my back, but I couldn't tell if that or the scream chilled me more. Or maybe it was the expression on Sol's face. But as always with Sol, it didn't last. No sooner were his feelings visible than he reined them back.

"You take your chances in Bordertown at night," he said.

Bordertown? The border of what?

I watched as he crept from the shadows and checked the road ahead. Finally, I understood.

"You know this place," I whispered.

The bell rang, followed by another scream. But I saw and heard only Sol. He turned his head to his shoulder, his strong profile lit by the faint orange lights of the town.

"It's where I come from."

His words lingered, echoing through my mind as if I heard them from the bottom of a deep, deep well. This was a dream. It had to be. Sol was the new guy at Crownsville High. He'd moved to Crownsville for a fresh start or to get away from trouble like Kieran had said. He couldn't have come from here; there wasn't any place on the Ridge for him to have come from. But the map. The *sword* . . .

I went to his side. It was as if we were meeting for the very first time. Everything I thought I knew about Sol collapsed, but now his silence and secrets made sense.

"We'll cut between those houses," he said, pointing to the right. "Don't stop for anything. Just believe me. We're in danger."

We kept to the muddy alleys, passing building after building each different from its neighbor. The farther we ran into town, the more houses appeared. But not homes like in Crownsville or Omaha. These were tightly packed, smaller, some of stone, some of wood, most patched with sheets of metal or nail-ridden planks where chunks of plaster had fallen.

Streets twisted and turned until I was hopelessly lost. Cobble-stones paved one street, then the next was dirt, straw, then stone again. There was no pattern, no consistency, but the tolling bell, and the occasional light from a shuttered window.

We ducked down another alley, far from the Ridge. It smelled of bread, earth, and something sweet, like long-ripened fruit. A low-lying mist hung over the ground. It thickened at the head of the alley.

Sol raised his hand. *Wait!*

Through the mist, I caught movement near the ground, by where the alley opened onto the street. Limbs appeared and something scurried away. I grabbed Sol's arm as he crept closer still. "Are you crazy?"

There were more tap-taps of claws against stone. Whatever had been growling before in the woods was there lurking in the mist, I knew it. For the first time in my life, I wished I had Pete's shotgun. A chirrup, like a chipmunk or water rat, echoed and the creature appeared.

It was a child, or seemed that way, maybe five or six years old, but much, much smaller, and scurrying on all fours, its butt up in the air. Huge round eyes skittishly peered our way. Its neck was long and swayed side to side. At the end of each finger grew a thick claw, which it tapped against the stone. It chirruped again, spun one-eighty, then scampered off into the streets, flicking a long, hairless tail before disappearing into the mist.

Sol let out a deep breath. "It's just a gutterscamp," he said.

"They feed on the trash after nightfall. Come on, we need to move."

I stared into the space where the creature had been, as stunned as if I'd watched a plane fall from the sky. Everything I'd seen and heard collided in a jumble of images and sounds. I sank to my knees.

Sol dashed to my side. "Mia," he said, his expression earnest. "You have to get up. *Now*. You're coming with me, whether on your own feet or over my shoulder. Your choice."

It didn't seem like much of a choice, but what other did I have?

The labyrinth seemed endless. I was about to ask how much farther, when we stopped in front of a door on a narrow, cobbled street. Sol knocked. Long moments passed as we waited. Freaked to the point of hysteria, and convinced that whatever followed us was only steps away, I was about to bang on the door myself when footsteps shuffled inside.

"It's late," barked a man's voice. "What do you want?"

Sol leaned against the wood. He whispered words I couldn't make out, or maybe words I simply didn't know. Finally the door opened. Without word, Sol ushered me into a long, narrow room with a table and benches in the center. To the left, two straight-backed armchairs faced a stone fireplace.

The man hurried away, disappearing through a doorway at the

rear of the room that stood beside a wooden staircase. Footsteps sounded overhead. I looked to the stairs. No one came down.

Though we were safely inside, Sol remained at the door. He pressed his ear to the wood and gestured for me to remain silent.

"Were we followed?" I whispered.

"I'm not sure."

I backed away, determined to hold myself together and not imagine what might be prowling the streets. It wasn't easy. Here in this room, this world suddenly felt far too real.

The man who'd let us in returned, brushing past me as he made his way to Sol. He was older, maybe Sheriff Burkett's age, but shorter, and wore baggy brown pants and a long linen shirt. His hand clasped a sword, which he offered to Sol.

Sol took the weapon without question. I followed the sweep of the blade down to the tip, which despite Sol's height, almost grazed the stone floor. "I think we're safe," he said. "We got lucky."

Lucky? I didn't feel lucky at all. Lucky was when you got called first for debate and didn't have to wait the entire class for your turn. Lucky was when Rich Manning's mom was in town and he missed a night of drinking at Mickey's. But this? *Lucky?*

"Why are you here?" the older man asked, his face sweaty and red. I noticed his teeth were widely spaced and filed into tiny, sharp points. "We saw the Barrier open."

Before Sol could reply, footsteps sounded overhead, and a

guy bounded down the stairs. He appeared about Sol's age, was of a similar build, and had dark hair, much darker than Sol's, almost black. His clothes, a thick blue shirt and loose black pants, cast me back to Sol's bedroom and the woven shirts I'd found in his trunk. He headed straight for Sol. Unnoticed, unwatched, I remained in my spot.

"They passed by," the guy said, without greeting. "Headed toward the square."

"How many?" asked Sol.

"One sentinel. Two visage demons. But the alarm's ringing; there'll be more."

It was clear Sol knew this guy well. It was like Willie and me: no fuss or nonsense, just straight down to business.

Sol placed the sword on the table. He slumped onto the bench closest to the door. "They must have seen the Barrier open," he said.

"It was hard to miss," replied the guy. He shot me a questioning look. "Just about lit up the whole town."

"Then they already know."

If I'd dared, I would have asked whom he was talking about and what it was they now knew. But I pretty much knew the answer. Someone—*they*—knew I'd tumbled into a world I wasn't meant to see. I was also pretty sure *they* wouldn't care that it wasn't my fault.

"She opened the Barrier," said Sol. All eyes turned on me. "They'll want to find who did it. We have to get her back before they do."

The man with the pointed teeth watched me as if I were one of Rich Manning's aliens. "That was no little opening," he said. "That was an Equinox, or as close as you can get. How'd she do it?"

Sol watched me in the same way that other two watched me. As if I were the strange one. "With solens," he replied.

"From *where*?" asked Pointy Teeth.

Sol ran a hand across his mouth, all the time watching me closely. I couldn't tell if he'd paused for impact or if he simply couldn't decide how to answer.

"It was the Solenetta," he said.

Pointy Teeth collapsed onto the bench. He continued to gape. Though I barely understood a word of what they'd discussed, I suddenly felt bare, dissected. I didn't like it at all. My temper flared.

"Tell me what's going on," I demanded.

Silence.

"Well?"

Glances were exchanged. It was Sol who finally replied. "Your necklace," he said.

My *necklace*? I immediately glanced at my hand or, more

specifically, at the hand that had held my necklace. I'd not given it a thought since the Ridge.

"It's gone," I said.

The previous silence had been ponderous. This was one was downright oppressive.

Sol shifted in his seat. He leaned over the table, frowning deeply. "What do you mean 'gone'?"

I shrugged. "I had it in my hand. I must have dropped it."

Sol sprung to his feet, moving toward me with such speed that I instinctively backed away. "Check your pockets," he said.

"It's not in my pockets." I patted the front of my jeans and jacket to prove the point. "It was definitely in my hand. Why does it matter? It's just a necklace."

Sol's face looked like he'd just found his home burned to the ground. Shock. Disbelief. Fear. He turned for the door. "I have to go back."

The younger guy offered Sol the sword, "It'll be crawling out there. You'll never make it."

Sol paused at the door. "What choice do we have?" he asked. He placed a hand on the other guy's shoulder. "If they find it, we're finished."

I don't know how long I waited on that bench for Sol to return. Pointy Teeth disappeared upstairs not long after he left. It was just me and the other guy, like a pair of shy freshman thrust together in the cafeteria. It didn't matter. I'd decided that none of this was real. Any minute I'd wake up on the Ridge. Unless I really was dead and this was Hell. I surveyed every inch of the walls and waited for the joke to wear off.

On one of my many sweeps of the room, I caught the other guy's glance. He offered his hand. "Delane," he said.

I guessed it was his name and shook back.

"Mia Stone." Then added, "From Crownsville." If that even existed anymore.

Delane nodded. With his black hair and blue eyes, he reminded me of someone. He was a really good-looking guy, tall and strong like Sol, definitely Willie's type. I studied him closely, trying to put my finger on why he felt so familiar.

"I've never seen Crownsville," he said. "I've been stuck here since Solandun volunteered to go over."

*Solandun?* Confused, I shook my head. "You mean Sol?"

"Yeah," said Delane. "Welcome to the Other Side."

Whoever Delane was, he didn't seem afflicted with the same reticence as Sol. He was open and friendly, his manner warm. If there was a chance for answers, it was now.

"So what is this place?"

"This place?" he asked. "It's Rip's house; he keeps it so we've got somewhere to—"

"No," I said, gesturing all around. "*This* place. This *whole* thing."

"Well . . ." He paused. His icy blue eyes narrowed and two deep lines appeared on his forehead. It was an expression I'd seen before, and I realized who he looked like. Those lines on his forehead were the same as when Pete was deep in thought. He was a young, friendly version of *Pete*.

"How much do you know?" he asked.

I shrugged. "How about 'nothing.'"

"Then this could take all night."

Only, we didn't have all night. I had to get back to the Ridge. To do that, I needed to know what I was up against. "There were lights," I said. "On the Ridge."

"That's the Barrier," Delane replied. "It's what you passed through. It protects us from you, and you from us."

Every question I wanted to ask led back to yet another question and then another and another. I tried backing up: "This place is *real*?"

"I hope so," said Delane, laughing. "Or I definitely ate something I shouldn't have."

I knew the feeling.

"The Barrier's been here forever," he continued. "More or less. It's an energy created from magic."

So this was a dream. I *was* unconscious on the Ridge. "*Magic?*"

"Old magic."

"But there is no magic."

"Not on your side. Some wanted it the same here, too. Course, it didn't quite work out like that. Why do you think we're in this mess?"

I didn't get a chance to hazard a guess. Another knock came at the door. Footsteps thundered overhead. Delane was already at the door when Pointy Teeth hurried back into the room.

"It's Solandun," said Pointy. "I saw him from upstairs."

Delane opened the door, and as soon as Sol entered, I knew my opportunity to ask questions had gone. He didn't look happy.

"I couldn't find it," he said. "It's crawling with masks."

"What do we do?" asked Delane.

"We get Mia back," Sol replied. He offered me a cursory glance. "Do we have grains?"

Delane shook his head. He looked to Pointy. "Rip?"

"Maybe I can get a couple," Rip replied. "*Maybe*. But you can't take her up there until they've cleared out. It's too great a risk."

"If she's found here, it'll be worse."

The argument raged back and forth, but I no longer heard their words. If I'd disappeared through the lights and come here, so had Jay!

I leapt up and pushed past Delane, positioning myself right in front of Sol.

"Sol, *Jay*!"

Sol nodded slowly. It was all I needed.

"You knew," I gasped. "About *all* of this. And the man I saw—the hooded man."

Again, he nodded.

"We have to find him."

"You can't go out there."

"I have to. Jay's here, Sol!"

Sol didn't blink. "Yes."

*"Yes?"* I blurted. "That's all you can say? What about the other kids?" I looked from Sol to Rip to Delane. "They've taken six other boys."

"They've been bringing them over," said Rip. Then to Sol: "That's what I was trying to tell you about the Barrier. The same thing happened last night. It was like an Equinox began and then just stopped. We think they have solens."

"It was us," said Sol, wearily. "They took Mia's brother, Jay, last night. Mia was there. She was wearing the Solenetta."

"My necklace?" I asked, increasingly uneasy. "It's just a piece of junk."

No one replied.

"And what's it got to do with Jay? Why did they take him?"

Silence.

"Sol, *why*?" I couldn't stand it any longer. He was wasting time when Jay was somewhere in this nightmare. "We have to do something. He's my brother, Sol. He's ten years old." I took a step for the door.

Sol blocked my path. "He'll be found, Mia."

Yeah, *right*. Sol had known that Jay was here all along and he'd said nothing. Now he expected me to believe that Jay'd suddenly just appear? "Who's going to find him?"

"We have people looking."

"Really? And why would anyone here be looking for Jay?"

I tried to push past him, but getting by Sol was like trying to walk through a wall.

"If they find you out there, they'll kill you," he said. He raised his hands like he was trying to calm me. "Mia, I'm not going to let that happen."

"We'll see about that." Pumped, ready, I remembered the phone in my pocket. "I'm calling the sheriff. See what he has to say about this."

I switched on my phone. The display was blank. It must have gotten crushed on the Ridge. The thing *was* ancient. Again I pushed the power button. Held it down. Nothing.

"Fine," I said, refusing to look at Sol. "I'll just go back and open that Barrier-thing. I did it once."

"With solens," said Sol.

"Then I'll get more. Someone in this town must have some."

Sol glanced at Rip and Delane, then looked to the ground. "Mia, there aren't any others," he said, softly.

I faltered. "Then how do we get back?"

Rip thrust his hands into his pockets. Delane studied the wall. Only Sol would hold my gaze.

I watched him back. Stuck? This nightmare was plunging into new depths of terror. I pictured Pete wondering where I was, if he'd even noticed I was gone. And Willie. She'd go nuts if I disappeared. I'd told her that I'd call her. I glanced at my phone in my hand. The useless phone. My only link to Crownsville.

"It can't be," I whispered.

Trapped here. Only, here was exactly where I needed to be. I thought of Jay in the hands of a psycho somewhere in this hellish world. His time was ticking away.

"Look, Mia," said Sol. He sighed, his hand grazing mine with the slightest touch. "Whatever you think, I'm not trying to be difficult. I know you're upset about your brother. But I have to get you home. You shouldn't be here. Believe me. There is another way to get you back, but it means returning to the Ridge and we can't do that until they give up looking. You'll have to stay. For now."

I'd barely processed his words before he walked away from the door. Rip and Delane did the same.

"She can sleep upstairs," said Rip, sounding relieved that the discussion was over. "As soon as dawn hits, I'll go out for grains. We might get lucky. But we should all get some rest. Tomorrow could be a long day."

I had no choice but to go along with their plan tonight, but there wasn't a chance in this world, or any other, that I was leaving this place without Jay.

Reluctantly, I followed Rip upstairs to a bedroom at the front of the house. The wooden floor, like the beams in the ceiling, was buckled and bowed. I perched on the bed until Rip had left, then crept back to the door and opened it a crack. Rip's steps sounded on the staircase. Then the three resumed their conversation, their voices muffled.

"So how much do we tell her?" asked Delane.

A pause followed before Sol replied. "I don't know," he said, his voice deep, weary. "What's the point, when she has to go back?"

# TEN

waited until the house fell silent, then tiptoed downstairs into the darkened room below. I had a two-point plan: Find Jay, then get the hell back to Crownsville. I'd almost made it past the table, when—

"I wouldn't do that."

Heart pounding, I spun around. A candle lit near the hearth. Sol became visible in one of the fireside chairs. Busted.

"I knew you'd try to leave," he said. There was nothing cocky in the way he spoke. He was calm, resigned, as if he'd seen me coming from a mile away. He leaned forward, elbows resting on his thighs, his hands dangling between them as he watched me.

I folded my arms. So he'd guessed what I was up to. It didn't matter. I'd made my decision and nothing he could say would change my mind. Nobody was searching for those boys. Alex Dash had been gone for a week, others for months. Surely they would have been found already if someone had been looking. But Jay had only been gone for twenty-four hours. He couldn't have gotten that far. Every second I waited here was a wasted moment.

"I have to find him, Sol."

Determined to remain composed, I turned for the door. I could cope with the insanity of stumbling into another world, but only if I focused on Jay. Sol would get no tears or tantrums from me; I wasn't going to beg for his help. He'd known the boys were being brought here from the moment we'd first talked at school. He'd had plenty of chances to help. He'd done nothing.

"I'm going to start with the streets," I said, determined he accept that I was going to find Jay. "Then I'll check the Ridge. Someone must have seen him."

The door was both latched and locked, but a small black key hung from a hook to the right. I took the key and placed it in the lock. Sol's hand slammed against the door. My heart leapt into my mouth. Refusing to turn around, I felt him close behind my shoulder. I hadn't heard him cross the room.

"You don't trust me," Sol said, his voice low, and close to my ear.

"Can't imagine why you'd think that." I tugged at the door handle, ready to strike him with an elbow if he didn't back down.

I tugged again. Sol's hand darted to the lock. In one swift motion, he palmed the key, and then forced his fist back against the door. On the other side of my body, his other hand smacked against the wood. I was caged.

"Believe of me what you will," he said, his breath warm on the side of my neck. "But I can't let you go out there. I won't."

I studied the prison he'd formed around me, the muscles in his arms straining as he pushed against the door. There was no way he was going to give up.

Cautiously I turned to face him. I no longer believed Sol wanted to kill me, and that was something. But with him standing this close, I felt like I had on the day he'd given me a ride in his truck. His presence consumed the space between us. The way he loomed over me—there was just something so physical about Sol.

"I don't understand why you won't listen to me," I said. He wasn't going to scare me. "What do you expect me to do?"

The only light in the room came from the hearth. It caught just one side of Sol's face. The golden flecks in his eye glimmered. His jaw cast deep shadows across his chest. Darkness and light.

"I want you to trust me," he said, towering over me.

But how could I, when all he'd ever done was lie?

Defeated, I lowered my head. This wasn't real. It wasn't my life. Life was school. It was Mickey's. It was going with Andy to prom! For once, everything was how I'd wanted it to be. And then Sol had entered my life. Now I didn't even know where I *was*.

"I don't know what to think," I whispered. "Is any of this even real?"

Though I remained between Sol's outstretched arms, he didn't once touch me. I could smell him all around me. It was the scent from the shirt in his bedroom and from the cabin of his truck. It reminded me of Crownsville.

"It's real, Mia," he said.

Finally, he lowered his arm and backed away. He wandered across the narrow room to the fire. After placing the key on the arm of the chair, he reached for a brown bottle on the hearth.

It was only then that I realized how fast my heart was pounding. And it wasn't from fear of all that had happened since the Ridge. It was *him*. *He* did this to me. It wasn't the same nervousness I felt when I was with Andy—those feelings were explainable, understandable. They were right. With Sol, the feelings were deeper, more mysterious. It had been easier to avoid those feelings in Crownsville. I could just stay away from him. Now I couldn't escape them—couldn't escape *him*. Sol was my only link to Jay.

I glanced at the bottle on his lap. "Poison?" I asked.

"Almost," he replied. "Rip makes it. It's not good." He offered me the bottle.

Resigned to the fact that I wasn't going anywhere, I sighed. I mean, what could I really do? I didn't know where to find Jay. And even if I could find him, I'd then have to return to the Ridge and get us both to Crownsville in one piece. I didn't even have my necklace, which clearly was part of the reason I was here.

I headed for the fire, dropped into the opposite chair, and took the bottle from Sol. I drank a long swig. A spicy, burning liquid set my tongue aflame and brought tears to my eyes. Almost choking, I handed it back. "You know I'm not twenty-one."

Sol smiled. It was the first smile I'd seen from him since we'd stepped through the lights on the Ridge. "Me neither," he said. "I won't tell."

"How old are you?"

"I'm nineteen."

So I'd been right. He wasn't seventeen.

"Then what the hell were you doing at Crownsville High?"

He looked away. It was a classic Sol move. But as trapped as I was, Sol was trapped here too. This time he couldn't escape my questions. "You promised you'd explain," I said, dipping my head to reclaim his gaze. "When we were out there before. You said you'd tell me everything."

"All right." He pulled back his shoulders. "Mia, I was in Crownsville because of those missing boys. We believed they might snatch someone older next. We needed to be on the inside."

Okay. It was something, including a confession that he knew exactly what was going on.

"Then you know who's taken them. You know who has Jay. Sol, you have to—"

"He calls himself the Suzerain," Sol said, before I could finish. "And he's taken over Brakaland from here to the mountains."

I paused. It wasn't just because he'd answered so openly. It was the tone of his voice, heavy and filled with distaste for this person who'd taken Jay. I shivered. It was like finding Sol's sword in the trunk. I *had* to know. But did I really *want* to? "Brakaland?" I whispered.

He nodded. "That's the name of this country."

This country? The country I'd tumbled into. Suddenly I felt very small.

"The guy who has Jay," I asked, needing to understand. "When you spoke of him, it didn't sound like you were much of a fan. Why?"

Candlelight flickered on Sol's face as he drank deeply from the bottle. He stared distantly at the candle's flame, frowning as if he saw something I couldn't see. "Because he wants to destroy your world," he said.

\* \* \*

"We live in the spaces you don't use," said Sol, "in a parallel world hidden by the Barrier. But our world is shrinking. As your populations and cities grow, we lose more of our land. There were some who wanted to send emissaries, to bargain and keep the peace. Another force wanted to fight back."

Just a moment ago, I'd thought no further than Jay and the Ridge and the twisted cobbled streets of this godforsaken town. Now a whole world opened up around me. One I didn't know. One I didn't understand. One that had taken Jay.

But, in debate class, Rifkin always said that the crux of any argument was knowledge. He taught us that the speaker who truly knows a subject, who can interpret it, bend it, examine it from every angle, was the speaker who won. If I was going to find Jay, I needed to know everything.

"The Suzerain is a man called Finneus Elias," said Sol, as if sensing that I wanted him to continue. "He's a man of magic and persuasion. He knows your world. He has been there many times. He convinced some that if he were in control we could fight to hold back the boundaries of your world and protect our own. Many disagreed and the two sides split. It turned into a great war. Eventually, he was defeated, but Elias didn't give up his cause; he just went underground. He abducted those who were skilled in magic to build a new force.

"Years passed. No one thought Elias would ever return. And then he came back, only this time the force of his magic was much stronger than anything Brakaland had ever seen. He opened gateways, other Barriers to worlds within worlds, gateways that were not meant to be opened. He liberated the Warnon Mines in the southern deserts, which was once a Barrier to a demon world."

"Demons?" I spluttered.

This was insane. It was a story from one of Jay's games. It had to be. I reached for Sol's bottle. Maybe that drink wasn't so rotten after all. The initial sting from my first gulp had worn off. Now I just felt numb inside.

Sol leaned back in his chair, his gaze once again distant. "They've infested this place," he said. "The Suzerain claims he's the only one with the magical power to protect Brakaland from the demons. But the war between the Suzerain and the demons is a false one. He purposefully released the demons to start this war. To make himself irreplaceable. He is their master."

And this was the man who had Jay. My panic rising, I could barely speak. "Was it him? The man on the Ridge?"

I only realized I was clutching the bottle when Sol gently took it from my hand. He watched me closely, like he was ready to catch me if I fell. I could only imagine the look on my face.

"I need to show you something," he said. "It will make it easier for you to understand."

He placed the bottle back on the hearth, then headed to the door beside the staircase at the rear of the room. With legs like Jell-O, I followed, my mind racing with visions of Jay on the Ridge. I thought of the night that Alex had disappeared. I should have done something more. I should have gone into the fields and stopped it, and then maybe Jay would never have been snatched. But why had he been snatched? For what possible reason could this Suzerain want a ten-year-old boy?

A small, shadowy room lay behind the door. Shelves lined the walls and the glint of bottles and jars was visible in the dim light. Sol must have known what he was looking for; a second later he returned with a large leather-bound book in his hands. He took the book to the table in the center of the main room.

"This is why the Ridge is so important," he said, as I joined him.

He opened the book to a map, the same map I'd seen at Old Man Crowley's with that line of tiny golden stars. I viewed it with increasing trepidation. Now I knew what it meant.

"It's the way through, isn't it?" I asked. It was a struggle, but I had to remain calm. Analyze. Understand. *Think*. Jay needed me to be strong.

"The Ridge is the weakest spot in the Barrier between Brakaland and your world," said Sol. Every time he spoke, he looked at me, whether to check that I understood or to ensure I wasn't about to collapse, I didn't know. But his presence beside me, his controlled expression—it was reassuring.

"There are many weak spots in the Barrier," he continued, "but none more vulnerable than the Ridge. The weakness there has formed a true gateway and the power in the solens reacts to it."

He turned the page to a drawing of an amber-colored stone with sunbeams radiating from its surface. "Solens are crystals," he added, as I peered closely at the drawing. "A rare stone. They take thousands of years to form and can be mined in just one corner of our world. A complete solen is incredibly powerful, so most are ground into a powder. Each grain holds a weakened spell." He closed the book.

"One grain will open the Barrier long enough for a man to pass through. It can be done here or at a couple of other places. Most Barrier weaknesses are no longer used; a grain isn't strong enough to open them. But if Elias is to attack your world, he needs to bring down the Barrier. He can't do that with grains, Mia. He needs solens—complete solens. And he'll do anything to get them."

Sol's words were sinking in. This man planned to attack Crownsville! You couldn't find a more harmless town, but trouble had found us. No one had any clue that a war was brewing on our doorstep. But then Bordertown was right next to Crownsville, and Sol said that Brakaland shrank as we grew. Crownsville had grown a lot during the last few years. There was even talk of a mega-mall on some farmland off Route 6.

Thinking of home, my mind drifted to the image of me standing at the mirror in my bedroom, thinking about prom with seven golden stones draped around my neck. "My necklace," I whispered.

"Mia, your necklace contains seven of the largest solens ever found," said Sol. "It is the Solenetta. It alone has the power to fully open the Barrier and to keep it open—the Equinox."

The velvet box on my desk. Pete had given it to me when I'd first arrived in Crownsville. For years, it had sat on my closet shelf, forgotten, buried beneath sweaters and empty shoeboxes. Increasingly uneasy, my voice trembled. "Sol, my mother left me that necklace."

He was about to reply when a red orb glowed on the hearth. Breathless, my mind again spinning, I watched as he headed to the door and pressed his ear to the wood. A distant knock sounded from somewhere on the street.

"Upstairs," he said. "Quickly."

We scurried to my room. Sol headed for the window. He carefully pulled back the threadbare drapes, and then peered onto the street below, beckoning for me to join him.

Two tall cloaked figures walked the cobbled street. They

lingered at every window, pressing their shrouded faces against the glass, knocking on every door. I held my breath as they approached Rip's house, fighting the urge to duck or to dive onto the bed and hide beneath the blankets like a child. One of the figures turned when it reached our house. Its head tilted, slowly sweeping its gaze to our window. I could see nothing beneath the shadow of its hood.

"Don't move," whispered Sol. "It senses our vibrations."

Believe me, I had no intention of moving. But it appeared that mattered little. It *knew* we were here, though we were as hidden by darkness as it was shrouded in shadow. It raised its arms toward us. Something told me to close my eyes, but frozen, I could only watch.

Gnarled hands appeared out of the sleeves of its cloak. Long, bony fingers lowered its hood, revealing a chalk white face with skin stretched tight over a bald, elongated skull. There were no eyes, no nose, no mouth—*nothing*. Only pale ghastly skin and a mannequin's blank face waiting for an artist to give it life.

Then that life appeared. Gradually, features emerged. Wide eyes, cherub cheeks . . . I covered my mouth to stifle my scream. The creature had turned into *Jay*.

"What do you see?" whispered Sol.

I couldn't reply. Every curve, every line of the creature's face was a perfect replica of Jay's. It had the same look in its eyes, the same turn of its mouth. And if it hadn't been standing almost seven feet tall, I would have sworn that it *was* Jay.

Sol pulled me back from the window, his hand gentle on my arm. "I wanted you to see it," he said. "So you know."

Barely daring to move, I shuffled away from the window and dropped onto the bed. Nothing in Sol's tale had prepared me for what I'd just seen. Before his story had been only words. In the face of that sinister creature, it was real.

"It's a visage demon," said Sol. "We call them masks."

Shocked, sickened, I could hardly speak. "It was Jay."

"It's whatever image they pluck from your mind and cast onto that canvas."

"You saw different?"

Sol shook his head. "It wasn't focused on me. They're tainted by dark magic, created by the Suzerain from one of the breeds he released from the Warnon Mines. Their bodies can change too. They know your thoughts, Mia. Show you exactly what you want to see, holding your attention until you've stared so long, it's too late to get away."

The tall, hooded figure on the Ridge. I tucked my trembling hands beneath my thighs. "That's what took Jay."

"They control the Barrier for the Suzerain."

"But why would Jay go with something like . . ." I closed my eyes, no longer needing Sol to answer that question. I knew what had happened to Jay. Though I was the master at restraining my emotions, this time I couldn't hold back the tears. All I could see was myself and Jay standing in the yard with misty vapors snaking through the cornfield. *They show you exactly what you want to see.*

"He told me he saw his mom," I choked. "He thought it was safe."

We stayed in silence for the longest time. Not once did Sol try to comfort me or tell me that everything was okay. He'd shown me the visage demon for a reason. Everything was not okay.

"Mia, you can't go out there alone," said Sol. "There are other demons out there, creatures worse than the masks. They know something powerful opened the Barrier. They'll be looking for you."

Though Sol was here, I'd never in my life felt so alone, not even after Grandma had died and I'd stood on Pete's driveway with a suitcase at my feet, gazing up at a house and a man I didn't know. This was worse. At least then I'd understood something of my surroundings. It had made some kind of sense.

"We have to find my necklace," I said.

"There's a good chance we will," said Sol. He crouched in front of me, taking my hand in his strong grip, forcing me to keep my gaze on him. "There are some who make a living smuggling goods across the Barrier. Runners. They bring in contraband and then use the profits to fund solen grains for their next trip. One grain to get across, one to get back. Gangs of Runners operate in any town where there's a weakness, *especially* here in Bordertown. Nothing happens on the Ridge that they don't know about. That's our hope for finding the Solenetta."

I didn't let go of his hand. "And Jay?"

Sol narrowed his eyes as if searching for the right words. "Finding Jay will be complicated," he said.

As complicated as it felt to have my hand in Sol's as he finally opened up to me. My feelings were never complicated around Andy. Andy was straightforward, even with the drama of his on-off relationship with Jessica and Willie's dreams of romance and fated love. But Sol . . .

"Why did they take him?" I asked. "The other kids too?"

"It's complicated," he said, again.

"*Where* are they taking them?"

"They're taking them to Orion. It's a city here on the plains and the seat of the Suzerain."

Every time I heard that name—*Suzerain*—a shiver traveled my spine. "How far is it?"

"Depends on the route," said Sol. "Less than two days on the road."

I squeezed his hand, desperate for him to understand. "Then we have to go there, Sol."

He watched me for a long moment, then slowly got to his

feet. As his hand slipped from mine, all trace of emotion fled from his face. "We have people there," he said, straightening. "We're looking for those kids, Mia. All that matters now is that we wait for the Ridge to clear and get you back to the Other Side." He turned for the door. "You should sleep. I'll fetch you in the morning when we know more."

I let him leave, but only because I knew he wouldn't tell me what I wanted to know. Whenever I'd mention Jay, he'd pull back. He was hiding something and I was getting better at spotting when he did. There were holes in his story, great, gaping holes you could almost step through. He knew it too. It was obvious in his face. He knew where this story led.

My parents. Somehow they'd been involved in this. How else would I have had the Solenetta? My mother had clearly taken the necklace from somewhere and it had landed her in a heap of trouble. But in trouble where? Here? Or on the other side of the Barrier? I didn't doubt that my father was mixed up in there somewhere, too. There was only one conclusion that made sense: My parents must have been Runners.

I listened for Sol's steps on the stairs, seizing this moment of quiet to process what he'd told me. There was still Pete to consider. Where did he fit in all this? He must have known his sister was involved in something huge. Was that the reason for his brooding silences?

Exhausted, but too wired to sleep, I knelt on the bed and peered out the window. The visage demon stared up at the house, Jay's image still cast on its face. It hadn't moved from its spot—not an inch—since we'd seen it. Would it stay there all night? Would it still be waiting in the morning? Whatever image it had found in my mind, I'd seen the creature change. I knew what it really was. It couldn't trick me as it had tricked Jay.

Chilled, I sank down and stared blankly at the wall, the only thing separating me and a demon tempting me with my brother's face.

# ELEVEN

I lay awake for most of the night, torturing myself with images of the visage demon and Jay on the Ridge. As the first light of dawn came through the window, I took another peek outside. The visage demon had gone.

Though he'd promised to wake me, Sol didn't appear at my door. So when it was clear from the voices below that the others were up, I went downstairs to find out the plan.

Sol and Delane were nowhere to be seen. An older man sat at the table with Rip. A man with bushy white hair and laugh lines around his eyes and mouth.

"Old Man Crowley!" I blurted. "I mean, Mr. Crowley. I mean—*what?*"

Crowley's aged face beamed as if this were the most natural meeting in the world. I wasn't sure if he would have recognized me in Crownsville if I'd run him over with Rusty, but it appeared he was more than comfortable seeing me here.

"Mia," he said, his voice wheezy and light. "Rip's been telling me about your adventure. Quite the turn of events, don't you think?"

The black coat he always wore around town lay on the bench beside him, a reminder of how close I was to home. Close, but out of reach.

"I don't understand," I said.

Grinning, he gestured for me to join them. The broken capillaries on his cheeks glowed with his smile. "Tiamet Crow's the name," he said, as I sat. "At least, it is on this side of the Barrier." He flashed a conspiratorial wink.

"But what are you doing here?"

"I live here," said Crowley, Crow, Tiamet—*I couldn't keep up*. "You didn't really think I lived in that old shed?"

"Actually, I did," I said, apologetically. "So you know all about this?"

Rip offered me a cup of something hot and dark. I thought of the drink I'd shared with Sol last night and wondered whether this latest concoction was safe to taste.

"Tiamet's a Runner," said Rip. "Best Bordertown Runner for fifty years."

"And getting too old for it," said Crowley. "We've been watching Crownsville ever since Elias crept back out of the dirt. It's not an easy job. When I heard Solandun was coming over, I seized the chance to slip away."

Sitting beside Crowley, my confidence grew. Crowley meant Crownsville—home. Home, I understood.

"You said, '*We've* been watching Crownsville,'" I stated. "There are others?"

"A few," Crowley replied.

A few being two, three, four, or fifty? Did everyone know about Bordertown and Brakaland, except for me? I was always the last to know. "My uncle," I said. "Pete."

Crowley nodded, seemingly happy to chatter away about anything and everything. It was a welcome change after having to pry information out of Sol. "He knows this world," he said.

Then Pete must have known what had happened to Jay, the others kids, too. His moods made sense at last. No wonder he often acted like it was the end of the world. If he knew there was a war on Crownsville's doorstep, it almost was. But how deeply involved was he? Did he talk with these "others" who knew about Brakaland? Did he meet with Crowley, or even *Sol*? Would he tell the sheriff that I'd disappeared too?

As soon as I thought of the sheriff, I pictured Willie and a new day in Crownsville starting without me. It was Saturday, she'd be at volleyball, and probably wouldn't even know I'd vanished if Pete hadn't said anything. Maybe she wouldn't find out if Pete came over to fetch me first. Jay too! If Pete rescued us, we could slip back and no one would notice I'd been gone.

Pete would no longer be able to keep his silence. I knew about this place—*Brakaland, Bordertown*. I knew about a world on the Ridge, hidden by the Barrier. I knew there was more to my mother's story than Pete had let on. Sol hadn't been willing to tell me about her either, but I had an idea.

"Pete'll be freaking out," I said to Crowley, as casually as I could. "It must be like Mom and Dad all over again."

Crowley's grin faltered. He glanced at Rip. Rip immediately looked away. Jackpot.

"Pete doesn't like to talk about it," I continued, as if I knew everything there was to know. "It's hard for him, what happened to them."

Crowley watched me out of the corner of his eye. "Sometimes life's like that," he said. "But Pete's a big boy. He knows what's what."

"If only Mom hadn't taken that necklace, right?"

I knew it was lame. I knew *I* was lame for trying it, but what did I have to lose? I had to seize my chances when they came.

"Well," said Crowley. "I—"

The door opened and a cool breeze wafted into the room.

Sol and Delane had returned. I held in my groan. Old Man Crowley had been close to letting something slip!

"Duddon Malone's men were seen at the Barrier last night," announced Delane, closing the door behind them. "They were talking to sentinels. Malone was up there again this morning. His gang left town at dawn. Heading west."

"Then they must have something to sell in the city," said Rip.

Sol sat beside me without greeting. His Crownsville clothes were gone. He was dressed like Delane—dark, loose pants, gray linen shirt, black leather boots. He looked good. Strangely *right*, as if the jeans he'd worn in Crownsville had been part of a costume. I guess they were.

"We think it might be the Solenetta," he said. Then, to Crowley: "We need grains, Tiamet. Rip's been all over. The town's dry. Can you get them?"

"Why do you think I'm here?" Crowley replied. He shot me a quizzical look from beneath his eyebrows before refocusing on Sol. "Last I heard, the Dobbs twins had grains, but they're not likely to sell. They need them for business. I hear there's a Runner gang selling in Fortknee. Supposedly they're heading this way, but if they're selling, they might not have any left by the time they reach us."

"We could ride for it," said Delane to Sol. "Fortknee's less than eight hours."

Sol appeared to give the suggestion serious thought. He watched Delane, and from the look on Delane's face, it was clear the conversation continued between them unspoken. It was just like me and Willie.

"Fortknee is too far," Sol finally said. "By the time we got there, Malone's gang would almost have reached Orion with the Solenetta. We'd never catch them."

"*If* they have the Solenetta," said Delane. "They could be selling anything."

"We can't take that chance. Tiamet, any way you could get to Fortknee?"

"With my back?" said Crowley. "It'd take me three weeks."

"Then we have to make a choice," said Sol. He looked from one to the other. "The Solenetta can't reach the Suzerain."

"If Malone has it, he'd be with his gang right now," continued Delane, enforcing his point with a tap on the table, "riding full pelt to Orion."

"I doubt it," said Sol. "That would announce that he has something special. He'd stay well away, travel alone. He wouldn't want to draw that kind of attention from the other gangs."

"Or he'd give it straight to the sentinels."

"And miss an opportunity to bargain for the best price? Not Malone."

Delane shrugged. "Then we're back at the beginning."

"Not quite," said Sol.

I was happy to listen and soak up whatever information I could. It might help me find Jay. But I found myself drawn in to Sol's words, his presence. I was not alone. Rip hung on every word, and Crowley, at least fifty years his elder, nodded at everything Sol said. At this table, Sol was respected.

"Rip can send a couple of men to Fortknee," said Sol, seemingly oblivious to the way they watched him. Or maybe he was just used to it. "That way we at least know there's a chance for grains. Mia can hide here until they return."

*Wait here?* I hadn't agreed to that. After everything Sol had told me last night, he expected me to sit here and do nothing?

"Then we head off after Malone's gang," said Delane. "At last. Some action."

"Not yet," said Sol. "I'd rather not leave Mia alone unless we absolutely have to. Let's find out what Malone's got." He looked at Crowley. "It's time to make a house call."

It was time to speak up. "I'll come too," I said.

"The only place you're going is Crownsville," Sol replied.

"Not without Jay. You brought me here, Sol, don't—"

He stiffened at my side, the gold in his eyes flaring as he turned to face me. "I told you to stop on the Ridge," he said. "I told you not to do it."

"You told me nothing!" I replied. "But now I'm here and

until we find Jay, everywhere you go, I go. I'm coming, Sol, and there's nothing you can do about it."

A wheezy chuckle split the tension. Old Man Crowley struggled to his feet. "She's a Crownsville girl, all right. Bring her along. Malone won't know what's hit him!"

My new number one favorite person in the world—*any* world—Old Man Crowley, headed for the door, but turned back when we began to follow. He looked me up and down. "Second thoughts," he said, offering me another top to tail. "You can't go out looking like that. Not unless you plan on setting yourself up as a new Runner in town."

Suddenly, all eyes were on me. I checked to make sure I hadn't sprouted a gutterscamp's tail overnight, then noticed my jeans. "Oh no," I said. "If you think I'm wearing a dress, you can forget it!"

Rip happened to have one dress, a red, floor-length sack that weighed about ten pounds and reeked as if it had spent the last two years rotting in the bottom of an old chest. Of course, it just had to be my size. Surely, wearing a sandwich board with "I'm not from around here" in huge letters would have been less conspicuous. The feeling disappeared as soon as we stepped outside.

Daylight had filled the streets of Bordertown with people, the likes of which I never could have imagined. The first man

I saw outside the house looked as I would have expected, but for his thick, long black hair, which had been braided like rope, coiled around his torso, and tied in a knot at his waist. A portly, elderly woman had tattoos of plants and flowers, the species of which I didn't know, across her arms and neck. I also saw tails. I saw *scales*. Eyes of every color. Skin of every shade. My plain red dress looked as everyday as jeans and a T-shirt in Crownsville.

I tried not to stare as everyone went about their business. But when a woman Willie's height, half her weight, and with a ridge of iridescent green spines along the back of her arms passed us, I couldn't help but ask.

"What's wrong with them?" I whispered to Crowley.

*"Wrong?"* asked Crowley. "Many are pure, maybe the only pure things left in this world of a thousand races."

I'd assumed this world was filled with people like Sol and Delane, regular-looking people. But a thousand races?

"So many?" I asked. "Aren't they human?"

"They're all kinds," said Crowley. "Plenty look like you, too."

I guessed he was right. There *were* regular-looking folk. It was just easy to miss them among the spectacles.

"What kinds of races are they?"

"Who can name them all these days?" he said, as if it was no big deal. "There were originally five great families. The Bala and the Samu. The Beseye and the Simbia. And then the Norgoncar, a family of spirits. Over time, Samu bred with Simbia, and Beseye with Norgoncar. And look what you get! Better than everyone looking the same, don't you think?"

Honestly? I didn't know.

"So what are you?" I asked. I tried not to stare as a bearded woman passed on my right. "You look human."

"As do you."

"I *am* human."

"Then that's what you must be. As am I."

Totally befuddled, I looked at Sol and Delane, who walked ahead. I thought about Sol's tattoo and the golden flecks in his eyes, but thought it was probably impolite to ask Crowley outright about Sol's family.

We turned off the road and onto a side street encased in shadow. Sol and Delane stopped at a low wooden door.

"Mia, stay quiet in here," said Sol, as Crowley and I joined them.

I was still kind of annoyed that he blamed me for being here. After last night, I thought we'd moved beyond all that. I put a finger to my lips.

"I'm serious," he said. "If someone wanted to buy Malone's mother's blood, he would slit her throat and bleed her dry."

"I can't wait to meet him."

"Just don't forget what he is."

"And what's that?" I asked, feigning boredom.

"He's the leader of the largest Runner gang both here and in any of the towns with Barrier weaknesses," said Sol. "He buys, steals, and sells to the highest bidder. And not just things, Mia—people, information. Nothing happens in this part of Brakaland that he doesn't know about. He'll know someone came through the Barrier. He's been talking with sentinels and they work for the Suzerain."

"Then I'll keep my mouth shut," I said, knowing I sounded peevish. "Glad to help."

"I'll go first," said Crowley. He pushed to the front. "Malone owes me a favor after the last load I brought across for him. Let's see if we can't keep this friendly."

Crowley put his hand on Sol's arm as he knocked, and I couldn't help but think that his final comment had been directed at Sol. Crowley knocked again. Then, without waiting for an answer, he opened the door and the two stepped inside. I followed with Delane, curious to meet a man who'd sell his own mother's blood but annoyed that Sol was right. Sometimes it was best to keep your mouth shut. This was probably one of those times.

"Stay behind me," whispered Delane, as he closed the door. "This one's a clawcurler."

Careful not to trip over my dress, I shuffled into a vast, but low, room. Crates and boxes, stacked floor to ceiling, formed long, gloomy aisles, like a Target from Hell. Lining the aisles were piles of chairs, rugs, suitcases. Posters of sailboats, kittens, and cityscapes hung on the walls. There was a bicycle, a child's drum kit, hat stands, cabinets, all stacked randomly, like the car tire on the ottoman to my right, and the lawnmower draped with ladies' scarves. A grandfather clock ticked in the corner. Everything here came from my world. Most of it looked like junk. I wondered how much had originated in Crownsville and whether, if I looked long enough, I might happen upon the ice skates I'd "lost" in seventh grade.

"Look who it is."

The voice came from the rear of the room, but with Sol and Delane blocking my view, I couldn't yet see the infamous Malone. I peered over Delane's shoulder, but couldn't spy anyone amid the boxes.

Shuffling footsteps followed and then Duddon Malone appeared. I don't know what I'd expected. A dark, swarthy villain with scars and an eye patch maybe? What I saw instead was a small, fat man with curly gray hair, red cheeks, and eyes to match. He bobbed as he walked, like a little red robin snuffling for worms.

"This is a rare honor," he said, his voice deeper than I expected from a man of his height. "Come for something in particular?"

"We've come for information," said Crowley. He stepped in

front of Sol. "About what happened last night. The whole town saw it."

"And the whole town's talking about it," said Malone. He waddled closer and caught sight of me peering out from behind Delane. He looked at Sol. "Sure I can't tempt you with something expensive instead? For the young lady, perhaps?" His smile revealed teeth more sharply pointed than Rip's. "I'm certain to have something she'd like."

Though Sol was almost twice Malone's height and probably could have sneezed him to the ground, the guy still creeped me out. Given a choice between a staring contest with Malone's pink eyes and the visage demon beneath my window, I'd take the demon on every time.

"Let me show you this," he said, and, without looking, forced his arm into the clutter on a nearby desk. "I know I left it somewhere. Ahh, here it is."

He withdrew a plastic tiara, like from a child's costume box, but it was the tattooed eye on the back of Malone's hand that caught my attention. The eye was large and lined thickly in black, the iris green. I felt it watching me. In fact, I was certain Malone had used the eye to find the tiara. It wasn't a comforting thought.

I glanced at Delane for a reaction, but he looked bored. Crowley's expression showed something different: He still expected trouble.

"Just information for today, Duddon," said Crowley. "You can at least spare that."

"Tiamet," said Malone. He placed the tiara back on the desk like it was the Queen of England's jewels. "What can I say that you won't already know?" His gaze shot again to Sol, but the eye on his hand stared at me. I shuffled closer to Delane and conceded Sol's point. I probably shouldn't have come.

"How about a charm?" continued Malone. "Or maybe a bracelet. Or perhaps a necklace."

A loud crash followed. I jumped about a foot in the air. Sol had knocked a crate of dishes off the shelf beside him. China shattered at our feet.

Without word, Sol headed for Malone, Delane close on his heels. Crowley immediately intervened.

"Duddon, just tell us what you know and we'll be gone."

From the purpose in Sol's strides, it didn't appear that he was ready to play Malone's games any longer.

"How about a necklace?" Sol hissed. He towered over Malone's quivering mass. "Now that you mention it. Something in yellow. Got anything like that?"

Malone's ratty eyes darted left and right. "Afraid I don't," he gasped. "Sounds expensive, though. Wouldn't have any trouble finding a buyer for something like—"

Sol grabbed Malone's throat. I felt like I should look away, but another part of me wanted to see Malone get what he deserved. More than that, Sol and this sudden show of force gripped me. I'd seen him with a sword in his hand, but it hadn't registered that Sol would use it as a weapon. With his fingers around Malone's throat, Sol had unleashed a power that always simmered inside him.

"What happened at the Barrier last night?" he spat.

"Two people came through," spluttered Malone.

"Who?"

"No one knows! They were gone by the time the sentinels arrived."

"What else?"

"Nothing else." Malone's skin was turning purple.

"Then why were you on the Ridge this morning?"

Malone's chubby fingers grappled Sol's grip. Sol did not let go.

"You know the rules," he wheezed. "Everything that enters Bordertown comes through me."

"Rules can be changed," Sol growled.

"I was just fishing for gossip," replied Malone, trying to shake his head. "The Barrier's my business. Pick on Tiamet. He's up there often enough."

Sol shoved him back, almost knocking Malone off his feet. "You getting cozy with sentinels is *my* business," he spat. "If you want to keep this operation going, you'd better learn to *cooperate*. Do you understand?"

Malone stayed back, his hands at his throat, his gut heaving as he breathed. "I know how things work around here."

"Then don't forget it," said Sol, turning toward the door.

We all followed. Happy to be leaving, I lifted my skirt to navigate the broken china. I glanced back, uncomfortable letting Malone out of my sight. Malone leaned against a cabinet, arms folded, with a sly smile plastered across his face. His gaze dropped to my feet and lingered there. With a very bad feeling, I hurried after the others and back onto the street.

"He knows," said Sol. "Tiamet?"

"He's got it, all right," Crowley replied, puffing to keep up with Sol's long strides. "So what do we do about it?"

"We go after them. Mia can stay with Rip until we can get grains."

I was almost jogging to keep up, the sights and spectacles around me all but forgotten.

"Guys," I said. "I think—"

"We can make it if we head straight out," said Delane. "Cut them off before Malone sends a warning."

"Cheating little rat," said Sol.

I jogged a few more steps. *"Guys!"*

Finally, they stopped and turned. I looked from one to the

other, hating to break bad news, but, "I think we have a problem."

"A big problem," agreed Delane. "The Solenetta is definitely en route to the Suzerain."

"A different problem." I checked the street, then raised the hem of my skirt.

*"Sneakers?"* exclaimed Sol.

I sagged. "I think he saw them."

"Rip gave you shoes."

"They barely fit! Besides, I've seen other people wearing sneakers. Look!" I pointed to a scaly guy across the street. "They're Nikes."

"It's not the same," said Sol. "Did Malone see them or not?"

I nodded.

"Then it won't take much for him to put the pieces together," said Delane. He placed his hands on his head. "People in sneakers? Mia, he knows where they got them. He sold them! He's going to be suspicious of anything from your world that didn't come through him."

I stood in that street in that stupid dress with Sol, Delane, and Crowley looking at me like I *was* stupid. One little excursion and I'd already caused trouble. And here I was thinking I could rescue Jay. If only Willie were here, she'd back me up on this—she'd tell them that you can't walk around in shoes that barely fit! But Willie wasn't here. I had no one.

The bell we'd heard last night began to ring. People stopped. Murmurs rose from the crowds. Sol paced the width of the street, muttering beneath his breath in a language I was certain I didn't know. *"Banda nutidi . . ."* or something like that. I didn't need a translator to work out what he said: We were in trouble.

"He's summoned the sentinels," said Crowley, the only one of us who still seemed to have kept his wits. "They'll tear this town apart looking for her."

I checked left and right, convinced that *everyone* was looking at me. They weren't. Some looked to the air, some at the ground. Most simply made an about-face and hurried away.

Sol pulled himself back together. He took my arm. "Can you ride?" he asked, as we ran for Rip's.

"Like a bike?"

"Like a horse."

"I can drive," I offered.

"That's a little more conspicuous than we want."

Delane sprinted to our side. "It's not boring with you around, Mia," he said, grinning like he was having the time of his life. "Guess the decision's made. You'll have to come with us to Orion."

# TWELVE

tossed what clothes I had into the bag Rip gave me. I was grateful for the task; it gave me something to do with my hands. I could hear the others moving around downstairs. We didn't have long until we left.

I rummaged through the bag for my jeans, and pulled my phone from the pocket. If I could get power, just the faintest signal, I could text Pete: "Iv crssd barrier + J's hr. Help!"

My phone was still dead. "Crap."

But at least one thing had turned in my favor. We were headed for Jay.

A door downstairs banged. I shoved my phone back into the pack and went to the stairs. Rip had returned. The second we'd told him what had happened, he'd darted into town for the latest news.

"The town's swarming with sentinels," he said, "and they're heading this way. I got horses from the Dobbs twins. You'll find them at their mother's place."

I scurried to Sol's side, hoisting my pack onto my shoulders, praying for the strength to see this through. It was what I wanted—to be searching for Jay. Yet still I felt like I was about to plunge off the edge of a cliff.

Rip continued to pace. "One of Malone's cronies has already left, riding full pelt on the Orion road. He must have gone to warn the gang that you're onto them. You'll never catch them now."

"Then we'll have to cross Welkin's Valley," said Sol. "Cut them off before Orion's gates."

Rip stopped dead. "The valley? You're not serious."

"I'm serious," said Sol.

Dentally challenged as Rip was, the guy had clearly been around the block. That he wasn't happy with Sol's plan did not inspire my confidence. He repeatedly shook his head.

"Solandun, there's naught in the valley but demons. The place is cursed."

"It's the fastest way," said Sol.

"Nobody willingly enters the valley unless—"

Sol placed his hands on Rip's shoulders, squeezing them gently. He looked Rip square in the eyes. "We can do it," he said, quietly and confidently. "We *will* do it."

I'd never seen anything like it—a younger guy holding an older man's gaze with a self-assurance beyond his nineteen years.

Crowley, red in the face from sprinting back from Malone's, came to Sol's side. "Then you'll need more weapons," he said to Sol, almost proudly. He turned to Rip. "That means repeller orbs and decimators, Rip. As many as you've got."

The tension between Sol and Rip broke as everyone set into a second flurry of activity. This was it. The start of our journey.

I looked at Old Man Crowley. "You're coming, right?"

Warmth filled Crowley's eyes. "Not me, Mia," he said. "I'd just slow you down. Besides, someone's got to stay with Rip and cover your tracks."

Of course. I'd never considered the mess we were leaving behind in Bordertown. Malone knew two people had crossed the Barrier last night. He knew Sol wanted the Solenetta. He'd seen me, a stranger in sneakers from the Other Side. He would have to be an idiot not to put it together. Clearly, he wasn't.

"Can't you slip back to Crownsville and tell Pete what's happened?" I asked, unable to believe why I hadn't thought to ask earlier.

"Got no grains," Crowley replied.

"Of course," I said. "I keep forgetting."

I pictured the cafeteria at Crownsville High and all the times I'd sat there talking with Willie and Kieran and Seth. We were a team, we shared everything. A new team was forming around me, one I knew nothing about.

"I don't get it," I said to Crowley. "Malone's already got the Solenetta. Why does he care about me?"

Crowley, *Tiamet*, reached for my hand. "Don't worry about the details, Mia, or you'll drive yourself insane. Just keep yourself safe. Trust Solandun. Trust Delane. They know what they're doing."

And so it seemed. Sol thrust a sword into my hand.

"I have to fight?"

"Just try to stay alive," said Sol.

I lifted the sword. It was lighter than the one in Sol's trunk and shorter than the one Sol had taken when he'd gone back to look for Solenetta last night. Nevertheless, it was heavy and wobbled in my grip. "I can't use this."

"Mia, you may have to," said Sol.

I tried to imagine what it would be like to actually use it. I was always the peacekeeper at school, getting between Kieran and Willie when they were at each other's throats. There was no way I could go after someone with a sword. But I thought of

Jay hacking and slashing his way through his video games. He wouldn't show fear. But Jay didn't have a sword to protect himself, and I did. I owed it to him to use it.

As the others finished packing, Delane hurried over with a belted scabbard. "Left or right?" he asked, and then when it was obvious that I had no clue what he was talking about: "Do you use your left hand or your right hand?"

"Oh," I said. "Right."

He laughed as he strapped the belt across my hips. "Don't panic. You probably won't have to use it."

He tightened the belt almost down to the last loop, then stepped back to take a look at his work. "Perfect fit." He winked. "Well, almost. It's lucky you're quite tall. Try it."

I'd never predicted that one day I'd be sliding a sword into a scabbard. But my reach was long and the sword fit, almost as if it was meant to be.

"Now draw," said Delane. He mimed drawing the sword.

I mimicked him, my sword slipping swiftly from its sheath.

"Great technique," said Delane, as I slid it back inside. "We'll make a warrior of you yet."

That I highly doubted.

The packing complete, Sol joined us at the door. He peered outside.

"Keep to the back streets," said Crowley, as he handed Delane his pack. "They're bound to come here. We'll stall them for as long as we can."

As we left the house, I took a final look at Crowley and Rip, standing there like friends I'd known my whole life.

"Remember, Mia," said Crowley. "Trust them."

With that, the door closed and I was alone with Sol and Delane.

Chased by the bell, we sprinted through Bordertown's deserted alleys. My pack bashed against my back. The skirt wrapped around the scabbard with every step. Several minutes later, the gap between the houses widened, diminishing the number of places to hide. Soon we crossed open land, peppered with the kind of shacks I'd first seen on entering town. Gnarled trees sprouted between the huts then thickened into a grove. Vines with scarlet leaves smothered the trunks like blood-filled ivy sucking the life from the boughs. Overgrown, they trailed from branch to branch, a vast red web that shimmied in the breeze and cast deep shadows onto the ground.

At a run, we ducked beneath the trailing leaves and headed into the grove.

"Still no sign," said Delane. "They'll be cutting off the roads leading out of town. There's no way they'll think us crazy enough to take on the valley."

"What is this valley?" I asked beneath my breath.

"It's been deserted for years," replied Delane, with his usual cheery tone. "Best to just leave it at that."

Sol slowed, peering between the low-hanging vines. "I see the horses."

"Sentinels?" asked Delane.

"None," he said. "It doesn't feel right."

I peeked through the scarlet foliage into the clearing ahead. On it stood a circular house, about ten feet in height and constructed from pale blue stone. Two horses in full tack were tethered to a post in the yard, nibbling at the sun-scorched grass. No one else was in sight.

"Only two?" I whispered.

"You can ride with me," said Delane. He leaned in to my ear. "Don't willingly get on a horse with Solandun. He rides like a maniac."

I laughed. Just a little. No matter how bad things became, nothing seemed to get to Delane. I wondered what other information I could get from him about Sol.

Simply grateful our escape didn't depend on me riding alone, I stepped into the clearing, following Sol to the horses while Delane kept watch at the rear.

"Untie him," said Sol, gesturing to one of the two.

It was a huge animal, brown to the point of black. A single strip of white ran down its face. It stamped when I approached.

"He knows you're scared," said Sol, with a smile.

"That's good, isn't it?"

"Not if you want him to listen you."

I inched closer and tried to woo the beast with charm. "Hey there, boy." I patted his side. It didn't work any better than it did to coax Rusty. The horse sniffed my forehead as I went for its reins. Something cold and wet came away on my skin.

Sol had already mounted. He held my reins as Delane joined us, mounting our ride as easily as Sol had his. Delane offered me his hand.

"Just hold tight."

"That's the plan."

I hoisted my ridiculous skirt above my knees, and then scrambled up with Delane's help. Almost six feet off the ground, I grabbed his waist. "Okay," I said, feeling secure. Well, kind of.

I peeked out from behind Delane's back and caught the glimmer of Sol's sword as he raised the blade. Just like the night before on the Ridge, he leaned forward and sniffed the air. "They're here," he murmured. "Back up."

The horse moved beneath us, but my gaze remained on the trees. I held Delane tighter, anticipating visage demons creeping into the clearing and again confronting me with Jay's face. I instinctively lowered my hand to my sword, though I knew I couldn't use it. I couldn't strike at anything that bore Jay's face.

"What's out there?" I whispered.

"Sentinels," said Sol. Still leaning forward, he turned an ear toward the grove. The sun shone in the clearing, casting golden brown light through his hair. His eyes narrowed. "They're trying to surround us."

"I don't see anything."

A ripple carried through the vines like a whisper traveling leaf to leaf. The first sentinel appeared. It was tall, at least seven feet, and as bald as a visage demon except for a tail of coarse black hair that sprouted from the top of its head. Its empty, glassy eyes were round and widely spaced like a shark's. A black, sleeveless tunic covered its gargantuan chest. Muscles bulged in its arms, and thick blue veins, as wide as my finger, pulsated beneath its skin. Below the tunic, bare legs displayed massively oversized quads and gigantic feet, both hugely out of proportion to the rest of its already impressive frame.

They appeared one after the other, each identical to the first, encircling us, moving as a unit to cut off our escape. Twenty. Thirty. I lost count. They watched us. Waiting for what, I didn't know. Anticipation rose. Were more on the way? We were already hideously outnumbered, but we had horses.

"Time to go," said Delane. "Solandun?"

I caught Sol's nod, clutched Delane tighter, and prayed the poor guy could still breathe through my grip. Him turning blue was the only thing that would make me let go.

The front sentinel raised a gnarled arm. Its mouth opened: "Ni'ah."

That one word, whatever it was, shattered the moment.

Sol, then Delane, rounded the horses, and charged for the woods behind us. I ducked to snatch a breath against the rushing wind.

I knew within seconds why the sentinels hadn't come with horses. They didn't need them. They sprinted after us, their humongous steps powered by their massive thighs. Thunder sounded at their charge. Screams, like warrior's cries, echoed. I'd never seen anything on two legs run so fast. Within seconds, they'd flanked us. They bounded over shrubs, bowled through saplings like a giant herd escaping a predator.

Only, they were the predators and we were the prey.

I clung to Delane, certain I felt a sentinel's breath on the back of my neck, but too terrified to look. Delane sat low across the horse's neck, riding in stride with Sol at our side. Neither checked back.

We weren't going to make it. Several of the sentinels on our flank drew closer. Those in the lead veered toward our path. Sol pressed on, ahead by several strides. He caught the turn in the sentinels' direction as six or seven bounded ahead to our left. Seconds more and they'd cut off our escape.

Sol steered his horse to the right. Delane followed.

The woodland thickened. Low-hanging branches threatened to topple us. But there must have been a route through the undergrowth; never did Sol's speed waver. A dark tunnel of trees appeared ahead and Delane's cry, carried by the wind, rushed by my ears.

"Hold tight!"

The sentinels' thundering strides drew closer on both sides. A strong current of beastly odors thickened. Six feet was all that separated us from the beasts sprinting at our side.

"They're too close," I yelled.

"Just hang on!"

Five feet. Four feet. I was within reach of the sentinel at my side. Blackened fingernails—*claws*—grazed my arm.

"Delane!"

The horse, as if sensing my terror, lowered its head and charged again. The sentinel fell back.

I risked a glance over my shoulder. The pack had formed a wide arc behind us. Maintaining their pace, they pressed forward, forcing us from the path Sol had found through the woods. Though they moved as one, never did they shout an order or command. It was as if instinct guided them.

"They're cutting us off from the valley," yelled Delane. "Solandun, they're pushing us north!"

Obviously, Sol had noticed it too. "They're herding us," he shouted back. "Just keep moving."

Herding us *away* from the valley? "Why are they doing that?" I cried.

"They're trying to corner us," said Delane.

But I didn't see any place where they could trap us, only the sentinels and the trees. On we went. A mile. Two. The sentinels drew no closer.

The trees began to thin. Rocks appeared underfoot. Daylight beckoned. I focused on what lay ahead, conscious that with one mistake, one stumble, they'd be on us. They were pushing us somewhere, and we had no choice but to oblige.

The trees were now sparse. No leaves covered their branches. Their bark was gray, as if it had withstood a wildfire, though the ground was not charred and the lengthening grass showed no sign of damage. A fine layer of silvery ash blew from the trees and was carried away by the wind.

Ahead, Sol's horse whinnied, then stopped. Confused, I realized that Delane had slowed too. We pulled up at Sol's side. Both horses turned to face the sentinels.

The creatures stood behind us in a line, blocking the route to Bordertown with an impenetrable wall of bodies. Beyond them lay the woods, the canopy a thick, deep green. Before us lay the desiccated trees with their jagged, leafless branches. It was as if someone had drawn a line across the ground. On one side, where the sentinels waited, was life. On the other side, our side, was death.

"We could fight," whispered Delane.

I caught Sol watching me, and as if that had sealed the deal, he shook his head. "There's too many," he replied. "We've barely enough decimators to get through the valley."

"Then it's your decision," said Delane. "They've got us where they want us. They don't think we'll go on."

I glanced over my shoulder to where gently rising grasslands spread away from the forest. It was the perfect place to gain some speed and put the sentinels behind us, or for the sentinels to charge us down. But no sentinel moved.

I looked at Sol. His head was high, his back tall and straight. There was no fear in his eyes. Old Man Crowley's words returned to me: *Trust Solandun. Trust Delane. They know what they're doing.*

I couldn't take my eyes off Sol. Never once looking away from the sentinels, he leaned in to his horse's ear. I didn't catch what he said, but it must have done the job for the horse took several faltering steps back.

"Delane," he said, his voice low.

We too retreated.

Feet stomped in the sentinels' line. Teeth bared. Black eyes stared. Toward the center of the pack, one of the sentinels took a forward step. The one beside it shot out an arm to block its path. Then came a bark, a sound I recognized from when we'd tumbled through the Barrier on the Ridge.

"The Wastes," it snarled. "Leave them. They're as good as dead."

# THIRTEEN

've changed my mind," said Delane. "This was a bad idea."

About ten minutes had passed since the sentinels had abandoned their pursuit. The last time I'd looked, the woods had been visible behind us, the sentinels a shrinking line of pale flesh. Clearly, they weren't about to give up their post, leaving us no choice but to press on. Not that we were making much progress. For every step the horses took, we had to coax them into taking one more.

The landscape changed little. Knee-high prairie grass, endless clear sky, and the occasional barren tree was all I could see of the gently sloping hill that we climbed.

Sol's horse bucked. "It's no good," he said, and dismounted.

"We'll have to lead them. They might be better if they have something to follow."

"What's wrong with them?" I asked.

Delane twisted in the saddle to face me, and for the first time since I'd met him, his expression turned completely serious. "No animal willingly sets foot in the Wastes."

Yet here we were. Wherever here was.

I swung my leg over the horse's rear end, preparing for an elegant dismount. It didn't quite work out. My foot caught in the folds of my skirt, and I slid sideways, almost taking Delane with me.

Sol must have noticed me falling. "Careful," he cried.

He dashed over and grabbed me tightly around the waist. My back against his chest, he lifted me down.

Though I was safely on solid ground, Sol did not let go. I turned in his arms, hugely aware that he was still holding me. "I slipped," I muttered sheepishly.

A flicker of amusement entered Sol's eyes. Undoubtedly, he'd pictured me landing on my butt with my skirt around my shoulders. But there was softness in his expression too, like when he'd joked about the bus outside school. It was a welcome change from his usual serious silences.

"You have to take care of yourself," he said. "Land badly on your ankle and this will be a really long trip."

Delane jumped down beside us and Sol let go of me, as if

he'd just realized that he was still holding my waist. He headed for his horse and gathered the reins. "It's time to move," he said, back to business.

I was about to follow when a squeak came from somewhere close by. Surprised by the sound, I peered behind me to the spot where I thought it had originated. I almost hurled.

It might have been a rabbit—once. That is, a rabbit that had spent a fair bit of time in a pit bull's mouth. A little fur remained on one of its hind legs, but other than that it was just a mess of flesh and bone. But it was alive. Somehow. It lay, twitching on its side, its bloodied front paws occasionally tapping the ground. I stumbled back.

"What the hell is that?" I gasped, and shot out a hand to grab Delane.

Delane peered into the grass. "It must have wandered in and gotten lost," he said. He wrinkled his nose. "Looks like it's been here a while."

"Something's been at it," I said. Its paws twitched. "We need to put it out of its misery."

My cries brought Sol back with his horse. He took one look at the rabbit and then turned his head in disgust. "It can't be killed," he said. "Not here."

I frowned. Uneasy, I scanned the prairie, noticing the stillness, the silence.

"The Wastes," I whispered.

"The Wastes are the places in our world that the Barrier has abandoned," said Sol. "It is reality shattered. No life. No death." He glanced at the rabbit, his expression of disgust gone. He looked sad. "It's being absorbed by the Barrier."

My stomach lurched again, my mouth dry. "They did this on purpose," I said, panic rising inside of me. "The sentinels. They knew they'd trap us. That we'd give ourselves up rather than come here."

"It is the Wastes," said Delane. "Get stuck in here for too long and the Barrier will begin to absorb you too."

I straightened, imagining the three of us collapsed on the grass, our flesh melting, too far gone to ever escape the Wastes. Already, we'd stood here too long!

"Then we have to move," I gasped. I immediately headed up the hill, picking up the pace with each step, chased by something intangible, yet far more dangerous than Duddon Malone or the sentinels at the forest's edge.

Sol called me back. "Mia, wait! There's something else you should know."

Freaked, I glanced back over my shoulder. "Sol, I think we know enough!" I cried. "Or do you want to end up like that?"

The land flattened as I approached the final rise. I stopped. A quarter mile in front of me was a second hill, taller than the one on which I stood, and wider, too, its plateau shaped like the outline of a man dozing beneath the sky. I would have recognized it anywhere. I'd seen it from the Ridge a hundred times. There was no mistaking the Sleeper Hill Giant.

To the side of the giant lay a dense, jumbled mess of buildings. Some were in sharp focus, like the unmistakable white wooden cupola above the Onaly Free Church. A hazy nothingness covered other parts of the town as if I saw it through condensation on the inside of a window.

Though I saw no cars, muffled sounds of traffic came from a distance. Every so often, the sounds would stop abruptly and silence would fall.

Sol, Delane, and the restless horses came to my side. "It's Onaly Crossing," I said, breathless. "Sol, it's *Onaly*."

A flash of light sped past the front of the church. A blue car burst into focus and then vanished as quickly as it had appeared.

"I tried to warn you," said Sol, regret clear in his tone.

Sol had tried to prepare me for what I was about to see, and once again, I'd ignored him, charging off on my own as if I knew better, when clearly I knew nothing at all.

"This is what happens when the Barrier encounters one of your towns," he said. "The Barrier embraces nature. Life. Where it finds those things, both our worlds exist undisturbed, one within the other. But the Barrier was created thousands of years before all of this." He gestured to Onaly. "It didn't know what was coming."

It was overwhelming. Sol's shrinking world lay bare before me. The shading over Onaly and Crownsville on the map at Old Man Crowley's finally made sense.

"The Barrier can absorb *some* things on your side," said Delane, with a shrug. "The occasional road, a farm. But your towns and cities are too dense. They're too packed with materials it doesn't understand. It loses itself, unable to understand what exists on the Other Side. Lands we have once shared have become yours."

It was monstrous, grotesque, unfair. Below, another car appeared and then vanished. Two houses stood fused together, one a Brakaland house, judging by its stone walls. Two worlds colliding.

"We won't make it out, will we?" I asked. "That's why the sentinels let us go."

"We'll make it," said Sol. "We have no choice but to pass through the town. North takes us too far from our trail. South, and the land turns craggy and steep as it approaches the valley. We'd never get the horses through. The quickest way is to forge straight on. In less than an hour, we'll put the Wastes behind us and reach the Shorlan Pass. From there we can enter the valley."

Bookended by the two guys, I looked from one to the other.

Sol, strong and restrained on one side, Delane, energetic and optimistic on the other. It was time to trust them.

"Then let's do it," I said.

Maybe my resolve had surprised him, but when I looked at Sol to confirm that we should move, I caught him watching me with admiration. He pulled back the look as if realizing that I'd noticed. His gaze turned to Onaly. "We stop for nothing," he said. "Every minute we spend here, the Barrier is trying to absorb us."

I glanced back down the hill toward the rabbit. "And what about him?"

"It's not truly alive, Mia," said Sol, softly. "It's probably been here for months, even years. I'm sure it reached the point of oblivion a long time ago."

The walk into Onaly was the strangest of my life. The closer we came to the town, the more I caught reality turned on its head. Remains of the Brakaland homes that had once stood there appeared more frequently. Few were intact. A wooden wall with a window at its center bisected a picket fence in the garden of one of the Onaly homes. A sidewalk had half swallowed a wooden door, like a tooth sticking out of concrete gums.

Voices and traffic noise burst from the air. An invisible car door banged. Footsteps followed, then faded away, a snippet of a ghostly half-life that existed unseen. On the other side of the Barrier, it was just a normal day in Onaly.

"How do you feel?" asked Delane.

My skin tingled. My ears buzzed. "Weird," I replied. "I know these places."

As we passed through downtown, I touched the wall of Harper's Ice Cream Parlor. I always got my favorite combo there—black raspberry, chocolate chip, French vanilla. Two doors down, a pale pink fog covered Rainy Days, the junk shop where Willie and I had bought gag gifts for the volleyball team last year.

About fifteen minutes later, we were at the junction of Main Street and Third. A couple of blocks and we'd pass the church and Onaly would be almost behind us.

"It's not far now," I said.

Finally, the buildings receded and the road disappeared beneath a blanket of grass.

Once clear of town, I took a final look back. Onaly lay under a hazy mist.

"There's nothing that can be done," said Sol, with a rueful shake of the head. "You should put it from your mind."

But how could I when all over this world a short-circuited Barrier was struggling to maintain its hold?

Back on the horses, we pressed on across the prairie. Soon a cool breeze touched my face. Reality returning. Forested peaks waited ahead, the landscape turning from grassland to rock. Patches of red mist appeared in pools.

"It comes from the valley," said Delane, gesturing to the fog. "We're close to the Shorlan Pass."

Riding behind Delane's broad back, it was difficult for me to make out the pass until we were almost on it. Pine and spruce grew beside a rocky path. Little more than a few feet wide, it descended steeply into dark forest below. Two life-size male figures, carved from wood, guarded either side of the trail. One faced in toward the valley, the other out toward the prairie. The red mist covered their feet.

"Freemen," said Delane. "Here to welcome us to the valley."

It wasn't much of a welcome. There really wasn't anything here. The mist thickened as soon as we entered the forest. Little sunlight penetrated the canopy above.

I ached all over, but at least another hour passed before Sol slowed. We'd still not cleared the woods.

Delane drew up alongside. "Do you smell something?" he asked.

Sol held a red crystal in his palm, the one from Rip's hearth that had glowed when the visage demon had appeared the night before. Light radiated from it. "Something's tracking us," he said. "That didn't take long."

My heart sank. I didn't know how much more of this I could take. I felt ignorant and useless, cast off from the things I knew. It was Saturday. I was supposed to have an extra shift at Mickey's.

Rifkin's debate waited unfinished on my desk. Only, that life no longer felt real. There was no Willie, no Kieran or Seth here. That was all just a game I'd once played.

Movement came from trees to my right. It was so rapid that I was barely even sure that I saw it. I held on tight to Delane.

Again. To the left. Something was out there, and not the sentinels with their thundering steps. Whatever it was moved even faster. One moment there, the next, gone.

The horses stirred. Ours took a backward step.

"This is bad," I whispered.

A gray face suddenly stared up at me from the side of the horse. Its head was narrow, its features stretched, the skin mottled with blue. Black eyes, with a thousand faces, watched me. A skeletal hand reached for the horse. Then it vanished.

Our horse reared before I could even scream. Down I went. I landed with a breathtaking thud, the hilt of my sword hard beneath my hip. Sol and Delane leapt to the ground. Both raised their swords, standing between me and the woods.

"It was a shadow imp," said Delane, gasping. "It appeared right by us."

Sol scanned our surroundings, every muscle in his body braced. "Did you see where it went?"

Delane shook his head. "We'll have to wait until it reappears."

I scrambled to my feet, drew my sword, and then wedged

myself firmly between Sol and Delane. "It was gross," I said, barely able to catch breath from the fall. "All gray and funny-looking."

"They're blood hunters," said Sol. "A type of demon. It's after the horses."

I patted our horse, who was freaked. I knew just how the poor thing felt.

"There," said Delane, pointing to our left.

In a flash, the shadow imp appeared less than ten feet away. Another flash. Then another. Now there were three. Both horses reared and then bolted into the trees. Just as fast, the imps disappeared. Without word or warning, Sol sprinted after them.

"Don't!" I yelled. "Sol!"

Too late. The gloom consumed him in seconds. I made to follow, but got only a couple of steps before Delane yanked me back. "Mia, you can't."

"They'll kill him!"

I tugged my arm free, horror-struck that Sol would do something so reckless. "Sol!"

I again made to follow. This time Delane grabbed my hand. He didn't let go.

"It's okay," he said, wrestling me back. "Mia! They can't touch him!"

"But—"

I didn't finish. A gray face peered out from behind a tree. Deep scars covered its chin where the clutch of black fangs that hung from its mouth had torn the skin. Clawed fingers scratched the bark.

Delane spun me around. "Back! Mia, get back!"

I froze.

The shadow imp lunged. Instinct kicked in. I blindly thrust my sword and prayed for a hit.

The shadow imp leaped clear of the stroke. Its arms whipped the air, striking Delane across the side of his head, lifting him clear off his feet. Delane crashed to the ground. He didn't move.

Blade out, I forced myself to hold the demon's gaze. But the creature wasn't intimidated. It wanted one thing: Delane's blood.

"Don't even think about it," I yelled, recalling something I'd seen on *Animal Planet* about grizzly attacks and making yourself big and mean. Or was that lie down and play dead? I could never remember. But my yell was enough to regain the demon's attention.

*Pop.* It was gone. A heartbeat passed. The imp reappeared, inches from my face. Breath, like vomit, poured from its mouth as its fangs aimed for my neck.

I started to shove the creature back, then remembered I still gripped my sword. With a scream, I pulled back the blade, the fangs almost at my throat, and thrust with all my strength. My stroke grazed its side.

The imp hissed. It staggered forward, its weight crashing into me. Off balance, I stumbled. The hem of my skirt caught beneath my heels and I toppled back. Together we fell, its arms around me as if I were dancing with death.

I landed with a thud. Time slowed. The imp writhed against me. Then a yell, a scream. A flash of color like a matador's cape swept over us. Delane's blue shirt. *He was alive!*

The imp pummeled my chest as it tried to escape. My lungs emptied beneath the blows.

Then blackness seized me and I was out for the count.

# FOURTEEN

The first thing I saw when I came to was a blurry face staring down into mine. I blinked a couple of times and Delane's smile slipped into focus. "Mia?"

Sweat glistened on his forehead. Leaves clung to his hair.

"You're okay," I said, in a daze.

"Just a bump," Delane replied. "Can you get up?"

My chest felt bruised where the imp had struck me and my hip sore from when I'd fallen from our horse, but everything seemed to work fine. "I think I'm okay. The imp?"

"It got away," said Delane. "Shadow imps won't fight when they're cornered. It disappeared into the forest not long after you collapsed. There wasn't much I could do to stop it. You saw how fast they are."

I made to rise. "Delane!" I gasped. "Sol!"

"Not back yet." He helped me to my feet. "But he'll be fine, Mia. Trust me on this."

Seemingly satisfied that I wasn't about to collapse, he released his hold. I brushed the dirt from my dress, took a couple of breaths, and felt some of the tightness lessen in my chest.

"It's the dream bird, isn't it?" I said.

Delane pulled back as if he wasn't sure what I meant.

"The Lunestral. On Sol's back. He told me it protects him from demons."

"I didn't realize you knew."

"Sol told me about it in Crownsville," I replied. "Jay has the same tattoo. Didn't work so good for him."

Delane made an apologetic shrug. The gesture said more than words, its meaning clear: *Don't worry. Jay will be fine.* He squeezed my hand and in that moment I thought he might actually be one of the nicest guys I'd ever met.

I grabbed my sword from the ground. There was no blood on the blade. "I thought I hit it," I said, disappointed.

Delane shook his head. "But from the part I saw, you made a good go at it."

I sheathed my sword. "I pretty much fell on my ass, didn't I?"

I laughed, couldn't help it. Soon, Delane laughed too.

"Pretty much," said Delane. "But it was a valiant effort."

He grabbed me for a hug and our laughter echoed. Finally it felt as if there was some life in this place. It just needed an excuse to burst free. A little like when I'd opened my eyes to Crownsville after moving from Des Moines. Mrs. Shankles would have been proud.

Twigs snapped on the edge of the clearing. Delane dropped his arm from my shoulder. We spun around, Delane reaching for his sword, just as Sol and the horses stepped out from between the trees.

For a guy who'd just chased demons through the forest, Sol didn't appear breathless. In fact, I wasn't sure how he seemed. The slightest trace of a frown appeared on his face as he looked from me to Delane. He handed Delane the reins to our horse. "I could hear you two from a mile away," he said.

Something had bugged him, but it was impossible to tell what it was. We'd got the horses back, we were in one piece, what more could he want? A second ago Delane and I had been laughing and hugging, now I felt like it had been wrong to celebrate the fact that we were alive. I wanted to ask him what was wrong, but as always with Sol, I doubted he'd tell me if he didn't want to confess. I'd never met a guy so difficult to read.

"You're okay," I muttered, instead. "What were you thinking?"

"That without the horses we'd be lucky to make it another hour. Those things are still out there. You need to stay quiet."

Okay, I really didn't want anything to happen to him. I certainly didn't want my guts to plummet like they had when he'd sprinted after the horses. But . . . come on.

"Does he ever lighten up?" I whispered to Delane.

Delane considered the question for some time. "Not so much. But he's right. We should move on before we run into more imps. They always gather in the valley."

We continued our trek through the never ending woodland, down the never ending slope to the valley floor, the red mist our only company. My hip throbbed. My butt ached. Even Delane's spirits seemed to have sunk.

"The mist," I said, after what felt like hours of silence. "It gives me a headache."

"It does that," said Sol. Whatever mood had gripped him earlier seemed to have left him. He'd slowed a little over the last few miles. Now he rode at our side.

"Where does it come from?"

"It's residue from all the dark magic conjured here during the Great War. It's trapped in the valley. It could take years to fade." He shifted in his saddle. "I wonder if the valley can ever go back to what it was."

"What was it like?" I asked.

"It was once one of the most beautiful places in Brakaland," replied Sol. I caught his sigh. "The mist builds during the day. It should clear a little by morning."

The sunlight had faded by the time we stopped to rest, and I was desperate for the break. I made my announcement as soon as my feet touched the ground: "I've got to go."

"Go where?" asked Delane.

"Girls' business," I replied. "I'll be over there." I pointed off to . . . well, to where there were more trees and mist. I unbuckled my sword, glad to get rid of it—master wielder that I now was. I handed it to Delane. "And if you don't mind, please turn your backs."

Sol smiled, but for some reason, Delane still appeared mystified. Maybe whichever of the thousand races he came from didn't, as a rule, have to pee.

Though I didn't go far from the temporary camp, I couldn't see the guys as I made my way back to the horses.

"Hello?"

I cleared my throat and tried not to think of shadow imps popping from out of thin air.

"Guys?"

Sol and Delane couldn't have gone far or have expected to be away for long, because their packs lay on the ground. Increasingly nervous, I stroked one of the horses, mostly for the comfort of touching a living thing. That was when I heard their voices.

I say voices, but it was whispers, the kind of whisper you make when you're trying really hard to keep your voice from rising. I slipped between the horses to get closer.

"Solandun, we can't take her there. What are we supposed to tell her?"

"We don't tell her anything. We sleep there and then leave in the morning. It's the safest place to camp."

"It wouldn't feel right."

"I understand, Delane, but getting her out of the valley is most important. Orion is only a few hours from the house. We're trusting luck if we stay out in the open tonight."

I crept toward the voices.

"Then let's choose another house," insisted Delane.

"Who knows how far we'll have to go to find one that's standing. We can't risk the villages after dark; there's too many demons lurking around for them to be safe. We know the house can be secured—like last time."

"This isn't like last time. This is piling lies on top of lies."

"It's not a lie," said Sol.

A few more steps and I caught sight of Sol's back.

"It's pointless throwing all this at her," he said. "It won't change anything, Delane. She has to go back."

"But it's not up to us to make those decisions for her."

Good manners dictated that I should have stayed hidden or turned back for the horses and waited for them to return as if nothing had happened. I'd had enough of good manners.

"What decision?" I asked, and stepped out from the trees.

Sol spun around. Delane cringed and then looked to the ground. "I'm going to check the horses," he said. He patted Sol's shoulder as he walked off. It was a typical guy-avoiding-bad-news move. Some things never changed, no matter what world you lived in.

Sol and I stood in silence. He seemed ready to speak a few times only to change his mind and clam up.

"Well?" I asked.

He looked truly uncomfortable. "Mia, I—"

"Yeah, yeah," I replied, my patience with the whole cloak-and-dagger routine wearing thin. "You were talking about something to do with me, some place we have to go."

The red mist snaked about Sol's feet, adding to his air of mystery.

"There's a place we can stay in the valley," he said. In the forest's gloomy light, the golden streaks had faded from his hair. Now it appeared dark against the gray of his shirt. "We can get there before nightfall. That puts us close to Orion for the morning."

Unconvinced by his tale, I shook my head. "So what about

'We don't tell her anything. We just sleep there and then leave in the morning.' Or are you just going to keep your secrets?"

He studied me, hard. "Does it really matter to you?" he finally asked. "Even though it won't change a thing?"

"Sol, it matters," I replied. "I may not know much about Brakaland, but I'm not an idiot. I know something more's going on. It has to do with my parents, doesn't it?"

He didn't reply.

"Come on, Sol," I urged. "I need to know."

"All right," he said, struggling to hold my gaze. He straightened. "It's about your father."

I'd been expecting that, or something like it, but still those words hit like a blow to the side of the head. "You know who he is," I whispered.

"Yes."

"He's not the Suzerain, is he?" I asked, and laughed. The sound was as hollow as my joke.

"No." Sol was serious.

"At least that's a relief." I wandered to a large rock and sat, trying to remain calm. Calm and reasonable had got me information from Sol in the past. He really wasn't a guy for histrionics. "I already guessed that my parents knew this place." I said. "How else could I have come by the necklace? I'm guessing they were Runners."

Sol sat on the ground in front of me, his posture open. As soon as his expression softened, I wondered if maybe we were actually more similar than I'd thought. I didn't know Sol's story, but both of us had built walls around ourselves. I could feel mine crumbling.

"Mia, you have a great life in Crownsville," he said, his voice soft and deep, his eyes taking in every inch of my face. "You don't have to worry about any of this. You have your friends, school, a future where you can be anything you want."

I saw sincerity in those gorgeous eyes. He was trying to protect me? That was the reason for his silence? But as much as I was learning about Sol, there was just as much he still didn't know about me.

"I just want to be whole," I said. "I want the truth."

"All right." He took a deep breath. "Mia, your father is from Brakaland. And so are you. You were born here. At the place where we hope to camp tonight."

# FIFTEEN

'd said that I wanted the truth, but sitting with Sol in that clearing, I wasn't sure I was ready to hear it. Before, Dad was anything I wanted him to be. Imagining him as a total loser usually made me feel better about being abandoned. Now he was close, if only in thought, and he came from a world that a day ago I hadn't even known existed.

"No wonder Delane freaked out," I said.

"He wasn't happy going behind your back like that," said Sol.

"But you were?"

"If it keeps you safe, then yes."

A week ago I would have laughed in Sol's face if he'd told

me this. But too many things had happened for me not to believe his words.

"So I'm a Brakalander like you," I said, simply. "Where do I get my passport?"

"You already used it," said Sol.

"And *Pops*? Is he alive?"

Sol nodded.

"Over here?"

Again.

"Not a Runner?"

"No."

So I'd guessed that part wrong. How much more was there for me to learn?

"Then who is he?" I asked.

"His name is Bromasta Rheinhold," said Sol. "And he's a great man."

I laughed—snorted, really. "Yeah," I said. "Great at dumping his kids." My voice had turned shaky and that wasn't a good sign. It usually signaled a meltdown. "Wow. So my name isn't Mia Stone and I'm actually an illegal alien. It's a lot to take in."

Sol shook his head. "Those things don't define who you are, Mia."

"You sure about that?" I asked, unconvinced.

I couldn't help but think of all the times I'd looked at other families, like the Burketts or the Bakers, and wished for what they had. Even though I'd known it was stupid. Even though I'd sworn to myself that life was what you made it, that everyone had problems, and that everyone wanted at least one thing they couldn't have. That was what I'd had to believe, because of my dad. As much as I'd wanted my family to be like the Burketts, wallowing in misery about the fact that it wasn't, wouldn't change the future or the past.

And Jay? Jay just got on with things. He was tougher than me, always had been. I was just better at putting on a front. I'd had seven more years' practice. Now my dad was real, and I didn't know how I felt about that.

Wherever I'd come from and whatever that meant, there was one thing I did understand: None of this was Sol's fault. Shooting the messenger wouldn't change the message.

"So you really know who he is?" I said.

"Yes."

"Then you must have known who I was too. This whole time." It was a logical argument.

"I knew before I even went to Crownsville," said Sol, holding my gaze, "but I didn't know it was *you*. I knew you were at the school. When you stopped me and asked about the dream bird, that's when I put it together."

"And Jay?"

"I knew you had a brother."

Calm and reason faded. I felt *hot* and, I admit, a little overwhelmed. All this time and Sol had known answers to questions I'd been asking all my life.

"So where is he?" I asked. "This great Bromasta Rheinhold."

"He's fighting in the West," said Sol. "Your father's a legend, Mia, a close friend of the king. He—"

I stopped him with a raised hand. "*King?* You have a king? My father knows a king?"

Sol brushed dust from his leg, again uncomfortable. "There are many kings in this world," he said. "But it's not what you think. The king is an elected official. Our king, my king, holds the West, but it's a constant battle against the Suzerain."

"So where does my father fit in all of this?"

"Your father was a warrior in the great war against Elias," Sol replied. "This was before Elias became the Suzerain. When he was defeated, a law was passed that banned magic in Brakaland. It was called the Purge. It was argued that without magic, what had happened in the war couldn't happen again. It was the biggest mistake we ever made. Many magicians fled to your world, fearful of persecution or arrest, and took with them the tools they used in their skills. Others sought refuge with Elias and joined him in hiding. So when Elias resurfaced, he had all the power and we could no longer beat him.

"From the start, your father didn't agree with the Purge. He left the West in protest, traveled here, and became a Freeman of Welkin's Valley."

So my father was known throughout Brakaland, yet not known by his own children? I wondered what he'd done to earn such legendary status, what was so special about his life here that Jay and I had simply been unable to compete for his attention. Part of me wanted to know more, another part wanted him to remain the shadow that had dumped me in Des Moines. A ghost.

"So this is Welkin's Valley?" I asked, determined, however I felt, to prove to Sol that I could handle this latest revelation.

"It's where we're sitting and where we'll camp tonight," Sol replied. "Welkin's Valley has always been the seat of the Freemen. They're self-governed, swear no allegiance, and don't join fights in the wider world. When Elias returned, this was one of the first places to fall. This had always been a battleground, because it rests between Orion and the Ridge. Your father fought here in a battle against Elias that brought death to more than half the Freemen. When it was over, those who survived headed west to join the fight on the king's frontier."

"And my father's still there?"

"He's still there," confirmed Sol.

"Then why abandon us? Sol, why not take us too?"

"To save you from war, Mia," said Sol, sadly. "He knew Elias. He knew what would follow."

"So he dumped us on the Other Side." I was starting to freak out again now that it was all sinking in. "And what about my mother? Is she alive? Is she from here? Pete told me she was in prison."

Sol raised his hands, trying to calm me. "I think she's alive," he said. "But I'm not sure."

"And Jay's mom?"

"I don't know, Mia."

"But my father must," I said. "He needs to know what's happened to Jay!"

"He may already know."

"Then why isn't he doing something about it?"

A million thoughts tumbled through my mind. My grandmother in Des Moines. Who had she really been? Jay's tattoo. Sol's tattoo. Pete alone in Crownsville, whoever Pete was. And of course, the necklace.

"My father had the Solenetta," I said. "He hid it with us."

"It was safer out of this world than in."

"Not anymore," I replied, finally understanding that I was in Brakaland for a reason, as was Jay. "The Suzerain must have found out. That's why the demons kidnapped those boys. They were after Jay. They thought he had the Solenetta. What will they do to him, Sol?"

"We don't know," he replied.

An unsettling feeling gripped me. "Then we have to hurry. The Suzerain will know he doesn't have it by now. Or any of those boys. Sol, they'll kill them!"

I clenched my hand into a fist and squeezed as hard as I could, needing that jolt of pain to bring me back to what was important: finding Jay and getting out of Brakaland. The great Bromasta Rheinhold, the Solenetta, the Suzerain—this world could keep them all. Jay and I had survived this long without them. I'd be damned if they were going to turn our lives upside down.

Except they had already turned our lives upside down. Because of them, Jay, a ten-year-old boy who played baseball and computer games and goofed around with Stacey Ann Baker, had been snatched. A boy who should have been home, not lost in another world.

"What if they've already killed him?" I said, unable to believe I'd uttered the words.

"Mia, nothing has happened in Orion to make us think that those boys are dead."

I paused, seeing Sol in another light. "Us?" I asked. "Who are you? Why are you involved in this?"

"Mia, we're fighting the Suzerain."

"Like a resistance?"

"In some ways," he replied. "We're known as the Sons of the

West. There are many of us in the towns and cities. We infiltrate Elias's networks, but answer to the king. Everything we do is to stall the Suzerain's plans, to protect the Barrier until he is removed from Brakaland forever."

So Sol was a freedom fighter, an underground warrior. Hope soared. "Then you can get us into where they're holding Jay."

He sighed, looking anywhere but at me. "I don't know if we can."

"You have to! Sol, don't tell me this is hopeless. Don't tell me all of this and then step away. Jay's all I've got!" Suddenly the great Bromasta Rheinhold, the Solenetta, and the Suzerain mattered a whole lot.

I'd thought if only I hadn't broken into Old Man Crowley's, or if I hadn't asked Sol about the dream bird, or if I'd never sat with Andy on the Ridge and seen Sol's tattoo, then none of this would have happened. I could have continued on oblivious, worrying about nothing more than what I'd wear to prom with Andy and who'd watch Jay when I was at work. But I knew those weren't the things that had brought me here. "Here" had come for me and Jay. It had come for the Solenetta.

But what could *I* do? Mia Stone from Crownsville. Mia Rheinhold from Brakaland. I didn't even know who I was anymore! Would I march into Orion and demand the bad guy give me back my brother? As soon as Malone's gang put the

Solenetta in the Suzerain's hand, those kids were toast. What use were they once he had the stones he'd searched two worlds for? I was crying before I even knew I'd started. They were great gulping sobs a million times worse than when Willie and I called in pizza and watched old weepy movies like *Titanic*.

Concern on his face, Sol reached for me and I tumbled into his arms before I could stop myself. He felt like I'd imagined. Hard. Strong. Living proof that you could hold back the charge of fifty sentinels with a look more dangerous than any weapon or spell. If only he could show me how.

Sol wrapped his arms around me. What else could he do after I'd collapsed in his lap and with my head buried in his shoulder? With my face pressed against his warm neck, I tried to banish everything but him from this one moment. Maybe, for just a second, this didn't exist. Sol could go back to being the new guy at school and we could be sitting in the woods by the Ridge. But I couldn't hold the dream. We were in too deep for that.

"We don't have to stay at the house," he said, not letting go, his grip tighter than ever.

Right then? That was the least of my worries.

"No," I said. "If you say it's safe, then that's where we should go."

I pulled away, though I really didn't want to. For some reason, being wrapped in Sol arms felt like the safest place to be. Mopping up tears, I tried a smile. "I'm usually more prepared than this. I carry tissues."

He laughed and pulled me back to him, his hand stroking my hair. *Heaven*. "You don't always have to be tough, Mia."

"I'm not tough," I said. "Ask Delane about the shadow imp. Not my finest moment."

"You'll get the next one." He said it like he believed it. "And we will find Jay. I promise you, Mia."

I realized then how Rip had felt when Sol had grasped his shoulders and told him that we'd make it through the valley. Because, right then, I believed Sol too.

"Am I interrupting?" Delane peered hesitantly from behind one of the trees. I untangled myself from Sol and together we got to our feet.

"He told you," said Delane.

"Yep," I replied, and shot a half smile at Sol. "He did."

"And you're okay?"

In Crownsville, okay was a relative term. Rusty's crapped out again, but that's okay. You get regular Coke when you ordered diet? Okay, too. But this?

"I'm fine," I said, though really I wasn't. "Can't you tell?"

Delane smiled. He held out his hand. The red orb glowed on his palm. Just what we needed. "More demons?" I asked.

Sol draped his arm across my shoulder and led me back to the horses. "Welcome to Brakaland," he said.

When we reached the valley floor, Rip, Crowley, and Bordertown seemed a dream within a dream I could no longer clearly remember. We chased the setting sun, every step taking me farther from Crownsville but closer to understanding my past. Whatever followed us stayed well back. Waiting for dark, no doubt.

The horses' heads hung low. Burdened by two, mine in particular looked ready to drop. If we had anyone to thank for our escape, it was those guys.

A vast and beautiful land surrounded us. Forests grew on the valley slopes. A fast-flowing river coursed to our right. To the west stood a distant row of mountains, their caps golden beneath the rapidly sinking sun. How they could be there, when we were still so close to Crownsville, I could not explain. But there they were. And with snow on the peaks, too.

As beautiful and majestic as the land appeared, it was barren. There were no birds, no squirrels, or rabbits. There wasn't even a gutterscamp. It was just grass, trees, rock, and the ever-present mist.

"There were once thriving towns here," said Sol, as if catching my thoughts. "Narlow. Hamley Hold. All deserted now.

Fortknee's the only valley town where you'll find people these days, but then Fortknee's close to the valley's edge. It's easier to stem the tide of demons there."

"What did the people here do?" I asked, thinking of my father, a warrior withdrawing to this remote spot.

"Many things," said Sol. "Years ago, the Freemen signed a covenant with the king. Anything they made, grew, or found here was theirs. No taxes. No levies. It meant they were on their own. But that's exactly how they wanted it."

I tried to picture the place bustling with life. It was difficult. "How far to the house?"

"Not far," said Sol. He glanced at the golden explosion above the mountains. "We should reach it before dark."

Daylight faded to dusk, which lingered on and on as if to give us one last chance to reach safety. I was nervous, both about what horrors might still pursue us, and to see the place where I'd been born.

Signs that life had once thrived here appeared. Fence posts. Tumbledown cabins. Wagons abandoned on the overgrown, cobbled roadside. And then bones, in the grass and on the road. Some were large, as if from cattle or horses. Some were so twisted or overgrown that I couldn't imagine what creatures they'd come from. And then there were the human bones. Femurs. Skulls. Left here like garbage on the side of the road.

The golden dusk faded to peach, pink, and then lavender. Distant shrieks—not human, not animal—carried from the forest and higher ground.

"That doesn't sound good," I said.

Sol agreed, if the look on his face was anything to go by. He scanned the forested slopes, then shot me a reassuring smile. "We're almost there."

The road veered left, and a narrow track emerged through the undergrowth. Weeds choked the broken-down fences. The trees thickened along the path. The track again turned, opening onto a huge clearing. There was a barn, a paddock, and a pond, all of it shrouded in the mist from the magic conjured long ago.

But it was the house that held my gaze. It was bigger than I'd expected, with two floors and a wraparound porch. Its dark wood was slightly bleached by the elements.

Stunned, I held my breath. I knew it was the place. Truly, I did. Or was my mind just playing tricks? I *wanted* it to be this house—a picture-perfect cabin lodged between the forest and the mountains, home to a Freeman of Welkin's Valley.

This was the house where I'd been born.

# SIXTEEN

"Can I go in?" I asked.

Sol squeezed my hand. A couple of hours ago I would have done anything to have him touch me again. Now I was so numb I could hardly feel him there.

"Go ahead," he said. "Look around while we get the place ready for tonight."

It sounded simple, but like so many things in life, when it came down to it, it was harder than it looked.

Sol watched my first tentative steps. After my meltdown earlier, I was determined to appear strong. I dropped my pack on the porch, then opened the door and stepped inside.

I entered into a kitchen with a range, wood burning, I guessed.

Did they have oil or gas? And a table, like the table where I'd sat with Pete and Jay a thousand times. Pots on a dresser. Dust covered every surface, but other than that, it was untouched by time or nature. There were two other doors: one to the left, one to the right. A narrow staircase stood in the corner.

I inhaled deeply, thinking maybe I'd catch a whiff of something familiar. You know, like animals who can tell their kin by scent. All I smelled was damp, musty wood. But had I really expected anything more? I'd been born here, never lived here. Any notion that I knew this place was plain old crazy.

The floor creaked beneath me as I crossed the kitchen. Through the door to the left was a larger room with a stone hearth and chairs upholstered in fur and hide. It was like a stage set for a show with the lights dimmed and with actors waiting in the wings. Or it was a museum. Bromasta Rheinhold's museum. My dad.

"It'll wear off."

I'd been so enthralled I hadn't noticed Sol enter. He'd rolled up his sleeves, lean muscle visible in his folded arms.

"What did you say?" I asked.

"You said, 'This is too weird,'" Sol replied, his expression soft. "I said, 'It'll wear off.'"

So I was talking to myself without realizing it. Not a good sign.

He smiled warmly, the gesture so open it left me aching for him to hold me again. "For what it's worth," he said. "I think you're handling all of this really well."

"You do?" I asked, surprised.

"Yes," he said. He didn't expand on his comment, but drew a deep breath and turned to the table, almost as if to hide his face. "We're going to move this outside so there's room for the horses. Can you check upstairs? Especially the windows."

"Of course," I replied, grateful for the task. "It'll give me something to do."

The staircase loomed. I grasped the rail and headed up, imagining footsteps overhead. I'd always believed that a building could absorb its history, just as when I had sat in the empty gym at school and could almost hear the shouts and screams of a thousand games played there. Might some memory of my father stalk the upper floors of the house, his spirit embedded in the timber beams?

Off the upstairs hallway, I found a bedroom. A rug lay on the floor, blue with a white flower woven in the center. On a shelf sat a corn doll, about the size of my hand, with long yellow hair and a scarlet dress. It was the same as a doll I'd made at a craft camp years ago in Des Moines. I didn't know where that doll had gone. I'd thought it had gotten lost in the clutter at Grandma's, then tossed out with all the other junk after she'd died. I stared at its painted face, suddenly convinced that this had been my room.

I had been a baby when Grandma had taken me. There was no way I could have remembered this place. And even if the room had once belonged to me, it didn't now. It belonged to this house.

Mind adrift between the two worlds, I stepped up to the window and peered out from between the woolen drapes. The kitchen table stood in the yard. Delane had found buckets for the horses from somewhere and the water inside them glistened. But it was Sol I watched.

He made for the barn, head down, on a mission. Willie had nailed it about Sol. He *was* 100 percent, sugar-coated, eye candy. But I was starting to think he was much more than that. He'd been so warm and kind when I'd sobbed on his shoulder, and then again, downstairs. He was literally a world away from the aloof newcomer he'd been at school. That Sol had been the one to tell me about my dad felt strangely intimate.

I sighed.

"Just check the windows, Mia. Get a grip."

The next room was identical to the first. I rattled the window. It was secure. Feeling more confident, a little more like myself, I flung open the next door. I screamed.

A floor to ceiling, wall to wall mass of gray cobweb crawling with huge, brown spiny legs confronted me. I say legs—I didn't hang around long enough to take in much of anything else. I bolted out, slamming the door behind me. Chills coursed my spine. I slapped my hair, shivered and shook, as I tried to shed the creep factor from my skin.

Footsteps thundered up the stairs and Delane darted into the passage. "We heard a scream, a bang!" he gasped.

I pointed at the closed door. "There," I squeaked. "They're in there."

Delane stalked to my side, his brow low, ready to fight. "What is it?" he whispered, his body tense.

"It's about twenty huffing great big spiders!"

Delane paused, his eyebrows raised. "Mia!"

"What do you mean 'Mia'?" I grabbed his arm. "Delane, there are twenty huffing great big spiders in there!" Clearly Delane misunderstood the seriousness of the situation.

"How big?" he asked.

"What do you mean how *big*?"

"Well," he made a gap between his hands about the size of a dinner plate, "this big? Or, this big?" He widened the gap to the size of a garbage can lid.

"The first!" I squealed. "You get spiders that other size?"

"Some," he replied, seemingly not the least bit disturbed. "Don't you?"

"Not anywhere you'll ever catch me."

Before I could save him from certain doom, Delane opened the door. Legs scurried to all corners, forcing an encore of the *Mia Stone: Elastic Limbs* extravaganza. Several of the foul fiends held their ground. Motionless, they eyeballed me with legs outstretched. At least ten inches across, each spider had a scarlet slash along its hairy, brown back.

"Stripe-back nest," said Delane. "Impressive."

Not a description I'd use. "Are they poisonous?"

"Nah. Just ugly." He closed the door. "They're actually handy to have around. Stripe-backs eat scroachers—nasty little critters that chew their way through anything."

"Can you get rid of them?" I asked. With one eye on the door, my mind contemplated an overnight stay in an already populated house.

"Tricky," said Delane. "I had one in my bedroom when I was young. You could hear it in the walls. Thing is, they're too fast to catch. This one demolished a chair in, like—"

"I meant the stripe-backs!"

"Oh," he laughed. "Sure, you can get rid of them. Just pick them up and throw them out."

Like that was ever going to happen. I tried to free myself from what Willie would call, "A State of Revoltitude." I shook out my limbs and cried, "Blahhhgrhllahaa."

"You're having a good day," commented Delane.

That earned him thump on the arm. "I feel like I'm on a twisted student-exchange program."

I don't think he knew what I meant. He leaned back against the wall and folded his arms. His grin faded. "Mia, just so you know, I always voted 'aye' on telling you about Bromasta."

The stripe-backs momentarily forgotten, I nodded. "I know," I said. "Sol's the secret keeper."

"He has a lot on his mind," said Delane. "But Solandun's no liar, Mia. He's worried about you. This place isn't like where you're from."

Talk about understatement. "No," I said. "We don't go around knocking each other's blocks off, if that's what you mean. Well, not most of the time."

A little twinkle, like Pete's when a good mood struck him, entered Delane's blue eyes. "Do you miss it?"

"Sort of," I said. As soon as I said it, I thought of the cafeteria at Crownsville High, my bedroom at home, and Rusty vacationing over at Reggie West's Motor Repair and Salvage. I sighed. "Delane, I just want to stay alive long enough to find Jay."

"Then you should help with some last-minute preparations." He playfully slapped me on the back, no doubt revenge for my well-placed thump. "Want to try some magic?"

\* \* \*

To me, magic meant wicked old witches and *abracadabra*. But that wasn't how they did things in Brakaland.

I balanced an orb on my palm and gazed at the purple grain inside. Delane and I stood just off the porch. Sol perched on the railing, watching us with one eye and the valley slopes with the other.

"Ready?" asked Delane. He looked as excited as when Jay came home with a new game. "Just squash it."

I wanted to—*I really wanted to*—but it was like holding a pin to a balloon and not knowing when you'd hear the *BANG*.

"I thought magic was banned."

"That was way before," Delane replied, waving the thought away. "Besides, this is basic stuff. We use whatever we can get our hands on these days."

I focused on the orb. "Won't I get cut?"

"Mia, I promise. Just crush it, and then throw it."

Okay. I could do this. "One. Two . . ."

I held my breath, crushed the orb between my palms, and made a tossing motion, but there was nothing to toss. As soon as I'd applied pressure, the orb in my hand vanished and heat entered my palms. A flash of silver, like fairy dust, sparkled in front of my eyes. I checked my hand to find no blood and no orb.

"Told you it was easy," said Delane. He pointed up. A ball of purple light was suspended above us. "Now watch."

Purple rays radiated from the ball of light like spokes on a wagon wheel. They stretched rigidly in every direction, ten feet in length, an amethyst star twinkling in the air.

"I did that," I said, and feeling rather proud of myself, I grinned at Sol. "That's my spell."

Sol laughed and flashed me a glimpse of an orb in his hand. "Watch this."

He jumped from the railing, crushed his orb, and tossed it about twenty feet from mine. As if drawn by magnetism, the rays from Sol's spell joined with the spokes from mine until an intricate lattice hung above our heads, glistening purple in what was left of day's light.

"It's a repeller," said Delane, taking more orbs from his pack. "We'll connect them around the house."

"And the demons can't get through?"

"Not a chance."

That was more like it. "Then let me do another."

"But space them apart," Delane warned. "We don't have that many. So aim well."

The purple lattice grew. Heat radiated from its shimmering threads. Like a pretty version of the stripe-back nest, the entire house was soon cocooned in a web of purple light.

"We can pass through it," said Delane, and demonstrated by slicing a hand through the beams. "But not demons. Repellers do dreadful things to their blood."

"Good," I replied. Anything to exact revenge on a shadow imp. As I rummaged through the pack for more amethyst orbs, my hand chanced on a yellow sphere that was slightly larger in size. "What's this one do?" I asked, making a grab for it.

Sol leapt to my side. "Careful," he said. He grasped my wrist before I could touch the orb. "These make a big bang. Blow us to the stars, and we won't have to worry about demons."

I didn't get chance to apologize. A scream echoed through the valley.

Except for the spell of protection around us, it was almost dark. From what we could see, the trees stood silent and still. All that moved was the crimson mist.

"Just in time," said Sol.

Delane bounded over. He grabbed the bag off the ground. "Who's hungry? We've got Snickers."

Now I really had heard it all. *"Snickers?"*

"Tiamet brings them over," he continued. He entered the house, leading us to the den. "For Rip. He loves them."

The state of Rip's teeth finally made sense. "Pure sugary goodness. You know, we have lots of tasty treats on the Other Side."

"But Snickers have to be the best."

The repellers cast a purple glow into the den. The demons were out there—I was certain of that—but there was no way they could get inside.

Sol lit a fire in the hearth as Delane and I brought blankets and rugs from around the house and prepared for a night on the floor. Sol's fire soon warmed the den.

After eating our nutritious supper, Delane wandered to the window.

"Maybe the demons won't find us here," I said, though we'd created a huge purple beacon.

"No chance of that," replied Delane. He motioned for me to join him.

Blackness hung heavy outside, an ominous curtain shrouding whatever lurked in the void. Through a gap in the lattice, something lurched by the barrier, larger than a shadow imp or visage demon.

"That looked like a tallon demon," said Delane. "Very nasty."

I sensed Sol come up behind me. His chest brushed my back as he too peered outside.

The demons had increased in number, but I saw only Sol's reflection in the murky glass. Every time he breathed I felt his chest move against me. I was no squirt, but I always forgot how tall he was until he was right beside me. Did he have the faintest idea how I felt when I was around him?

I didn't feel that way around Delane. Delane was cute, cute enough to spin heads at Crownsville High. But butterflies didn't migrate through my gut when I saw him as they did when I was with Sol.

I caught Delane looking at me, then Sol. And though the expression was barely perceptible, I was sure he frowned.

Another shriek rang from right outside the house and the look on Delane's face lifted. He leaned in to the window. "Looks like we have more company," he said. "Here they come."

# SEVENTEEN

Picture a crowd on TV. A riot or a protest. Picture surging bodies, snarls, pumping fists. That's how they came—a mass of demons, all different breeds, all drawn by the spell and the scent of what hid behind it. One by one, they launched at the purple web. One by one the web threw them back.

"They're looking for weaknesses," said Sol.

"But we're safe, right?" I asked.

"For as long as the spell holds."

"And how long's that?"

"Long enough."

Only the demons closest to the magic web were visible.

Several were winged, like gargantuan bats, and soared above the rabble, their ghastly faces tinged with purple light. They paid each other no heed. All they wanted was us.

"This can't go on all night," I said. "Surely, they'll—"

A thud came from above. We all stared at the ceiling. Another thud. A wailing screech followed.

Sol dashed to the door. "There must be a gap. They're on the roof!"

Delane snatched up the pack with the remaining spells and hurried after him. It was like the shadow imps in the forest all over again. "You're not going out there," I cried, trailing behind.

"Not me," said Delane. He thrust the pack into Sol's arms.

"But it's crazy out there," I said, trying to force Sol to look at me. He wouldn't. "It's suicide, Sol. I'm serious. Don't do it."

Another thud. And another. My heart just about hit the ceiling.

I grabbed Sol's arm, tugged. Finally, he looked at me. "Sol, there were only a couple of them in the woods earlier. There're a million out there now."

"And they're trying to find a way in." He took my hand and gently removed it from his arm. "Keep the door shut. Don't come out, for any reason."

He left the den, closing the door behind him.

I turned on Delane. "You're just going to let him do this?" I asked. "Delane?"

The banging took on rhythm. Fists pounding on wood, shaking the rafters above us.

"Delane!"

This wasn't right. If it had been Willie, Kieran, or Seth, I would have tied them to the ground before letting this insanity take them. Or we would have stood at each other's side, fighting to the death as one. After everything we'd been through together, I couldn't leave Sol out there alone. Determined to intervene, I snatched my sword from the hearth and headed for the door.

Delane was already a step ahead. He slammed his back against the door. "You're staying here," he said, a touch of Sol's tone in his voice.

I brandished the sword like a baseball bat, ready to swing at anything that threatened Sol's life. "Get out of my way."

"Mia, he'll make it."

"Delane, nothing, not that tattoo, not some spell is going to stop that many demons! Now get out of my way."

"And what do you plan to do?" he asked, his back still bracing the door. "Take them on like the shadow imp?"

As soon as he said it, I pulled back, stung—though, of course, he was right.

"Then show me what to do with this thing," I begged. I pointed the sword, planted my feet, trying to make him see that we could help. "Delane, show me how to use it!"

Delane grabbed my wrists and placed my open hand around the fist that gripped the sword. "You hold it firm," he said, and squeezed. His eyes narrowed. "And if anything comes through that door, you ram that blade through its gut so hard that it comes out the other side."

My breath caught in the back of my throat. It wasn't what I'd wanted to hear. "And what about Sol?"

Delane shook his head. "Mia, there are things out there worse than shadow imps and visage demons. There are creatures with claws like razors that can slit your throat with a touch. Demons that spit poison into your eyes, blinding you before they tear you apart. You, me, we wouldn't last a second out there, but Solandun carries the Lunestral. You don't know its strength." He squeezed my hands once more before releasing his grip. "He'll make it."

A different sound came from above. Delane raised a hand for silence. He placed a finger to his lips. *Thud. Thud.* The sound rumbled through the house. A shriek that could shatter glass followed.

Delane did not move. "He's on the roof," he whispered.

"He'll break his neck!" I cried.

Delane tracked the sounds overhead. "I don't think so."

Energized, he grabbed my arm, urging me to follow him to the window. I dropped the sword with a clang.

Mayhem continued outside. There was no sign of Sol.

One of the winged demons had surely swooped down and taken him, I knew it. I waited for his body, broken, yet beautiful, to plunge to the ground. Sol had taken one risk too many. It would be his last.

How much longer could it go on? I wanted to dive into the nearest chair, to scrunch my eyes closed, and stick my fingers in my ears like the big baby I really was. But I couldn't. I had to know. I had to see.

Then a flash lit up outside like a nuclear blast. A boom, louder than thunder, shook the house. The explosion filled the air with limbs. The horses brayed in the kitchen, their stomps adding to the confusion. We braced for a second wave. It didn't come. Something landed outside the window.

"You wanted to know what the yellow spell did," said Delane. "You just saw it."

I'd been dazzled by the flash, so all I saw were purple streaks and the afterglow of white light burning in the back of my eyes. But I made out a blurred silhouette close to the window. A second later, the door off the porch opened and there was movement in the kitchen.

"It's him," said Delane, gesturing me to stay back as he darted through the door.

Sol's voice carried. "It's holding," I heard him say, between deep breaths. "Mia?"

"She's fine," replied Delane. "Solandun . . ."

Their words faded into whispers and I hurried to join them. I got no more than a couple of steps before Delane reappeared, alone. He closed the door behind him. "He's okay," he said, beaming.

Then why was Sol hiding in the kitchen? I knew I should trust Delane, but I had a feeling in my gut that something was wrong. "He's hurt, isn't he?" I asked, dreading the answer.

"He's checking upstairs," Delane replied, like it was no big deal. "Mia, don't worry."

Only, I was worried. I'd heard Sol on the roof. I'd seen the explosion. "How can I not worry with you two around?"

Delane hurried to the fire and gave it a poke. He looked like a guy trying to be busy.

Sol's steps sounded overhead, but my anxiety didn't lift. I couldn't explain the feeling, but I had to see Sol for myself. "I should check if he needs a hand," I said.

"Mia, he's just securing upstairs. How could he be doing that if he was hurt?"

It was a very good question. How *could* he do that if he'd been sliced open by a razor-sharp claw and was bleeding to death, or had been blinded by a poison-spitting demon. What the hell was the matter with me?

I groaned. "You two drive me nuts," I said. "I can tell when you're up to something. You'd happily tell me about Bromasta, but you won't tell me what's going on here."

Delane put his arm around me. "Nothing is," he said.

Five, then ten minutes passed. Sol did not reappear. The demons had already returned in numbers, the explosion only a temporary deterrent. Now they'd regrouped. They looked pissed.

"They really don't give up, do they?" I said.

"Not when they're hungry."

"But they're all so different. How many kinds are there?"

Fights had broken out among the demons. There were creatures of green, blue, red. Pale ones, as nasty as the shadow imps, of which I was certain I caught a couple in the crowd. And the winged ones, scaled harpies, with claws like the ones Delane had described.

"There are thousands of types," said Delane. "Demons interbreed and get nastier with each incarnation. When Elias opened the Warnon Mines, he took many of the demons there and bred them himself, creating his own monsters."

"Like the visage demons?"

A gangly demon hurled the body of a smaller, rotund creature at the barrier. I heard the thud when it fell to the ground.

"Visage demons are different," said Delane. "Some were once men, some were demons of other breeds until Elias got his hands on them."

*"Men?"*

"From all of the five families. It's a long story. Not all demons are like this," he added, gesturing outside. "And not all demons came from the Warnon Mines. There have always been demons in our world, but they were separate, rarefied."

With an ear trained for a sound of Sol, I listened to Delane's tale. "Rarefied?" I asked.

"It means they're like me."

"You're a *demon*?"

"No," he laughed. "I'm Samu—one of the five original families—but rarefied, pure. I have no other blood but Samu. There aren't many of us left."

I'd been curious about Sol's and Delane's roots ever since Old Man Crowley had told me about the families in Border-town. I wasn't sure if it was polite to ask them about their blood-lines, but Delane had brought it up himself, and I was itching to know more.

"You have no blood from the other families?"

"Not a drop," Delane replied. "It makes it difficult to find a girl. My family is determined that we keep the line pure."

"You can't see whoever you want?"

"Not if you want to get your hands on the family silver."

I'd never considered that. Crowley had just said that Braka-land was a melting pot of families and breeds. I couldn't imagine what it meant for Delane. He was the nicest guy ever. He could take his pick of girls. I was pretty sure Willie would take him in a heartbeat. But an arranged marriage? He deserved to be with someone he loved, regardless of what his parents planned to do with their money.

"So what's special about the Samu?" I asked, wondering why it was so important that Delane's family remain pure.

"We're tough." He took my hand and placed it against his chest. "Can you feel that?"

I wasn't sure what I was expected to find. "Just your heart."

"Now here."

He moved my hand to his right side, just above his hip. And there it was. Another beat, as strong as the first.

"You have two!"

"To cleanly kill a Samu requires two accurate shots," said Delane. "Our hearts rejuvenate. If one is hurt, the second still beats while the other heals. Only time and age slows a Samu heart. And we live a long time."

"Longer than humans?"

"Much. Our bones are tougher, too. Not a single Samu bone has ever broken since the five families appeared in our world."

This was pretty cool. I was becoming friends with a guy who had two hearts and indestructible bones. "Impressive. And what about Sol?"

Delane paused. "Solandun's not rarefied," he said. "But that's different."

"How so?"

He watched the demons continue their rampage. "That's up to him to explain."

But when Sol returned, I was more concerned about checking that he was okay than asking about families and bloodlines. His hair was wild. His shirt was disheveled. Sweat glistened on his brow.

"You're pale," I said, hurrying to his side. "You okay?"

He lingered in the doorway, massaging his back at the waist, twisting as if something had pulled. "I'm fine. You?" he asked, checking me all over as if *I'd* been the one fighting demons.

"All in one piece," I replied, confused. "Thanks to Delane."

"She wanted to go out and fight," added Delane. "I told her it was a bad idea."

"Very bad," said Sol. He looked from me to Delane, and the shadow I'd caught on his face after the imp attack returned. "The spell's holding," he muttered.

"Thanks to you," I replied. I nudged his arm, trying to jolt him out of the mood with a joke. "But you have to stop with the crazy action stuff, Sol. You don't have to be the big hero to impress me."

"I wish you'd told me that before," he said, with a half smile that interrupted my heartbeat more than any shadow imp or visage demon ever could.

I smiled back. "So what now?"

"We rest," said Delane.

He said it as if it was the easiest thing in the world, despite the circus going on outside. Delane hunkered down in the corner close to the window. I pitched a spot by the fire. I'd barely gotten comfy, when Sol laid his rug beside me. It was only when he sat that I noticed a small red stain on the back of his shirt.

"Sol, you're bleeding."

He laid his sword beside his makeshift bed and shook out his blanket. "It's nothing," he said.

"You haven't even looked."

He glanced at Delane, who was watching us from the corner, then he turned to face me. "It's really nothing," Sol said, when he caught me still watching him.

I studied him closely as he sat. For the first time, he looked almost weary. His eyes appeared to have darkened; liquid black ringed the iris.

I drew up my knees, trying to hold on to the fire's remaining warmth. As I moved, Sol reached a hand toward my face. Convinced he was about to randomly kiss me, my heart stopped.

"You have cobweb in your hair," he said.

"Oh," I said, half disappointed, and then, "OH!" when I remembered the stripe-backs.

"It's just a little. Hold still." He gently brushed the strands of web from my hair and then quickly pulled away, almost apologetic. "I think I got it. You really should rest now."

But I lay awake long after the fire had faded to embers. Screams raged outside. The horses stirred in the kitchen. I couldn't sleep, no more than on the night that Jay had disappeared. Through everything that had happened during the day, thoughts of Jay had never left me. I could almost hear his voice, like one of those strange echoes I'd heard in the Wastes. I'd thought no further than finding him and getting him home—whatever that entailed. But now I knew that Jay was a Brakalander, too. A castoff like me. An exile. And I was the one who was going to have to tell him.

Or maybe I wouldn't tell him. I'd take him home and we'd continue as normal. We'd pretend that Brakaland and the great Bromasta Rheinhold didn't exist. We'd simply be Mia and Jay Stone, who lived on the outskirts of town with their crazy uncle.

I stared at the ceiling beams. Maybe Jay's room had been the one with the stripe-backs. I imagined him bounding downstairs in the morning, ready for a day of sword fights, demon slaughter, and lessons in magic. He'd probably love it.

"Can't sleep?" asked Sol.

I turned onto my side to find him watching me. "I don't

know why," I said, quietly, careful not to wake Delane, whose deep breathing echoed across the room. "I feel like I've worked three shifts and run a marathon all in one day."

"A marathon?"

"Twenty-six point two miles."

Sol heaved himself onto his elbows. "We've come farther than that today," he said.

"On horseback."

"That's true."

However far we'd come, I was certain I'd never forget the things I'd seen in Brakaland. The image of that rabbit in the Wastes would forever be imprinted in my memory. I thought of Crownsville's new subdivisions on the west side of town. All the land that way, which had been shared between Crownsville and Brakaland, would become the Wastes.

I didn't know how to fix the problem, I didn't even have a clue where to start, but there was one thing I was sure of: What was happening to Brakaland was wrong.

"Sol, if we're squeezing you out, then isn't the Suzerain right? Wouldn't it be better if you fought back?"

He looked surprised by my question, or maybe he was just shocked that someone from the Other Side even cared. "There are some who believe so," he said. "But imagine the Barrier coming down in Crownsville. What would happen?"

It was a good question. "The army would be out faster than you can say 'domestic terrorist.'"

"So the sides are already drawn. What happens next?"

"I don't know. First we'd faint," I joked, "then I guess we'd talk."

Sol shook his head. "Elias won't talk. He'll strike. What do you do?"

Don't ask me why, but I bristled. "We hit him right back!"

"And?"

I sighed. "And Elias will hit again." It all seemed like such a hopeless mess. "Sol, America gets blamed for everything that goes wrong on this planet, but you can't blame us for this. We wouldn't want war any more than you would."

"But war would come," said Sol. "With the Solenetta in Elias's hand, the Equinox will spread, starting a chain reaction that can't be stopped. Picture demons streaming onto the streets of towns and cities all across your world."

I tried to picture it. Visage demons in Crownsville? In Omaha, Chicago, at the White House. "You're saying we'd wipe each other out."

He shrugged. "One day it would end," he said. "After we'd destroyed enough of one another that there would be no point in fighting anymore. Now picture the world. The Barrier's gone. What's left of two different worlds would be thrust together."

"It'd be chaos."'

"Ripe ground for someone to take over."

Finally it made sense. "Elias."

"Mia, Elias doesn't want to attack your world for the good of Brakaland," said Sol. "Nothing he's ever done has been for the good of Brakaland."

"But you can't sit here and wait to be squeezed into oblivion."

"There is a plan," he said, keenly. "The Treaty of Roi. It's a proposal to form boundaries between your space and ours. We can't reclaim what's gone, but we could halt what's in progress."

A treaty, like in the books I'd read for Rifkin's debate, "The clash of civilizations has no basis in reality." How was I ever going to complete my assignment knowing all of this? Treaties. Agreements. They never worked. "Sol, no one even knows you're here. Who'd believe you?"

"It would mean letting the Other Side see us," Sol replied. "A host of emissaries would enter your world." It didn't look as if the prospect pleased him. "But it will take time. Until then, the priority is to keep the Barrier intact and stop Elias's war, or there'll be nothing left worth saving on either side of the Barrier."

I flopped back, listening to the demons outside, trying to get straight all I was involved in. And then I thought of Jay and none of it seemed important. "Sol, we've still got a chance to catch the gang, right?"

"We should. I'd never planned going much farther than we

did tonight. The Orion road is faster terrain, but it swerves north before it veers toward Orion, and the gang won't travel through the night on the Orion road. Not with the Solenetta."

"Demons?" I asked.

"Thieves," replied Sol. He looked to the window where black shadows danced beyond the purple light. "Mia . . ."

I waited for him to continue. "What is it?"

Though I'd thought Sol had been checking the demons, I noticed that he was actually looking at Delane.

"What's wrong?" I asked.

He sighed and then straightened. "It's nothing," he said, as he turned back to me. "You should sleep. We'll leave early in the morning. I'll keep watch if it helps."

I lay beneath my blanket for the longest time, trying to tune out the screams. Somewhere upstairs the stripe-backs crept through their web, and the corn doll lay on her shelf. But neither creepy beasts nor memories of a childhood I'd never known could distract me from Sol. He remained on his back, his eyes to the ceiling, alert. *I'll keep watch if it helps,* he'd said. And it did. His unblinking gaze was the last thing I saw before I finally fell asleep.

# EIGHTEEN

Whether it was because of sharing a house with the horses or sharing a room with two guys, a musty odor hung over the place when I awoke. I grabbed my blanket and crept to the window. In the dawn's first light, the demons, and all trace that they'd been there, had gone. Only the purple lattice remained, though it had faded to lavender. Even the red mist had cleared.

Sol and Delane slept, so, taking care not to wake them, I tiptoed to the door, crept past the horses, and slipped outside. The crisp morning sparkled with dew. Pale sunbeams struck the mountains and glistened on the pond beside the paddock.

From across the valley, a faint pounding, like a distant drum-beat, could be heard. That was the only sound.

Glad to be in the fresh air, I sat on the porch's bottom step, my blanket beneath me. A feather lay on the grass beside my feet, deep, yet bright blue, and almost a foot long. I picked it up, entranced by the green iridescence that shimmered where sunlight caught the tips of its soft vanes. It was a beautiful thing, vibrant and full of color. But then I thought about the bestiary outside last night and it immediately lost its appeal. I let it fall to the ground. There was really only one thing on my mind. Today we'd reach Orion and that meant finding Jay.

Yesterday, Orion had just been a word, a vague *somewhere* in a world I didn't know. Today it felt tangible and real. Reaching Orion was about the Solenetta for the others, and if there was anything I could do to help stop that war, then I'd gladly lend a hand. But whatever magic lay in the Solenetta's stones, it was still just a necklace and, I suppose, I didn't truly believe that a piece of jewelry could cause so much trouble. Jay was flesh and blood. My little Spud.

"You're awake early."

I turned to find Sol on the porch, his hair tousled from sleep. The color had returned to his skin and he looked strong and refreshed. After how pale he'd been last night, it was a relief.

"There were drums," I said, pointing toward the horizon. "Or something like that."

"I heard them too." He sat at my side, his long legs bent, his arms resting on his knees.

"Demons?" I asked.

"Maybe. But we don't have to reenter the forest. We should be fine."

We sat in silence, but this was different from the awkward pauses when he'd driven me to Mickey's. I felt no pressure to speak. It was like a regular morning—as if we were the first up after a night camping at Jacob's Lake.

"You were right about the mist," I said eventually. "It's cleared."

"It'll build again during the day," said Sol. "It's always the same in the valley."

Almost as much as his stoicism, I was growing to hate the sadness in Sol's voice whenever we talked of his home. I chased those fleeting moments when he opened up with a smile or laugh, and I'd see the humor and mischief inside. It seemed hard for him to let go and relax.

I knew Sol could get along fine without any help from me, but still, as I watched him on the step, I battled the urge to put an arm around him and say, in my own stupid way, that I got that life sucked here, that nowhere was perfect, and that one day

I hoped it would get better. Thinking that way had gotten me through the dark times in Crownsville.

Instead, I asked, "How far is it to Orion?"

"We should reach it by noon," he replied. And there it was. That little flicker of fun in his eyes. "*If* Delane ever wakes up."

I smiled. "It's quite the bromance with you two."

He frowned. *"Bromance?"*

"You know, buddy love. Guys together through thick and thin."

"We grew up together," said Sol. "He's more brother than friend."

"Like me and Willie." I laughed as I imagined her striding across the valley floor toward us. "She'd bust a gut if she could see me in this dress."

"The dress suits you," said Sol. "You look good in red."

I took a double take at him, but he wasn't making fun. What was it about me and guys who liked red? It was the only thing Sol had in common with Andy.

"You'll see Willie again, Mia," he said.

"I know."

Sol was the only one here who knew where I came from, who knew about Crownsville High, and about my life on the Other Side. All I knew about his world were sentinels and visage demons.

"I don't get how there can be mountains here," I said, wanting to know more about his world. "That people on the Other Side can't see them."

"Maybe the Other Side does see it," he replied. "Like in the evenings, when the sun sinks beneath the clouds, and for just a moment, you catch something out there—a mountain, a river, a city in the sky."

I watched him, unable to look away from his striking profile. He twisted toward me, almost stealing my breath with his smile. "I once heard that we're the ghosts you sometimes see on the Other Side."

He leaned in to me as he spoke, his shoulder nudging mine as if to draw me into his words. I stared at him. I mean, I was *staring* at him, my eyes vacant and glazed. I hesitated.

There's a line between enjoying some eye candy and wanting to gorge on a whole bag. I'd not knowingly stepped over it, but no matter how many times I imagined a touch or a kiss, Sol and I could never be more than a dream. Anything else would bring a long descent into a world of hurt.

I snapped out of my daze, reminding myself that I actually had to speak. "So Duddon Malone is the poltergeist in your closet? Gives new meaning to the term 'closet monster.'"

Sol threw back his head and laughed. "It certainly doesn't sound like something you'd want to run into. It would scare me half to death."

*"You?"* I gasped, in mock horror. "I don't believe that anything scares you."

His gaze penetrated mine and his smile faded. "Some things scare me."

I took a deep breath, his sudden intensity catching me off guard. "But still," I continued, hastily. "In the Wastes we saw Onaly, but Onaly can't see you. The Sleeper Hill Giant appears in both places, the mountains only here. How?"

"There are places that appear on both sides," said Sol, back to his normal, businesslike self, "some only here, some only in your world. But don't confuse that with what you saw in the Wastes. There's nothing natural about the Wastes." He shrugged. "I'm no expert. I never paid much attention in school. Barrier lore is tediously boring. I doubt if there are many left who truly understand it."

"I think I get it. The Barrier isn't a wall or a fence."

"That's right," said Sol. He seemed impressed that I understood. "The Barrier isn't a solid boundary you can touch. It doesn't begin or end. It exists everywhere. It's all around us. The gateway at the Ridge is one of many weaknesses."

"Then this world is really another dimension."

"But connected to your world," said Sol. "All the worlds are connected. As I said, I'm no expert. Once Elias resurfaced, school didn't seem so important. I just wanted to get out and fight."

Though Sol had been at Crownsville High, I couldn't picture him in class, on either side of the Barrier. "So you have school here," I said.

"We have school," he replied. "It's different."

"No algebra or Spanish?"

"We learn languages from the Other Side. And then there's history and culture. Weaponry. And some magic, though not as much since the Purge."

This was wild. Sol a student in Brakaland. It was a whole new side of him. "I feel like I know you," I said, wanting him to continue, "but I don't. What about your parents?"

"My mother died when I was eight. My father's in the West. I have a younger sister, two younger brothers."

"You must miss them. Doesn't your father mind you being out here?"

"He knows it's important that we keep close to the Ridge. What happens there is crucial to understanding the Suzerain's plans."

"But it's so dangerous. You're pretty much in the lion's mouth."

"Things are different here," said Sol. "The path to adulthood starts earlier, at eleven for boys. That's the age when you travel, you train to fight, you learn to survive, so that you can earn yourself the right to be called a man."

Jay was almost eleven, just a kid. If he'd stayed in Brakaland, he'd soon begin his journey into adulthood. And me? My senior year started in the fall, and then college, my ticket out of

Crownsville. But what if my father had kept me here? What on earth would my life have been like?

"What about women and girls?" I asked. "Do they fight?"

"They fight," said Sol. "If that's their path."

I'd never seen him so relaxed. Any more laid back and he'd give Andy a run for his money. Wrapping my skirt around my legs, I shifted to face him. "So have you earned the right to be called a man?"

"Not yet."

"Is that why you joined the Sons of the West?"

It was the wrong question. A stern look entered his eyes. "I joined the Sons of the West because this is part of our home," he said, his chin raised. "It belongs to the people; it can't be given up to the Suzerain."

Hastily backtracking, I tried to lighten the mood. "Puts my problems in context. What college to go to. What to wear to prom."

"The dance?" asked Sol.

"I have a hot date," I replied, hoping he'd catch the flippancy in my tone. It didn't feel like a balanced exchange of information. Sol talks about fighting for his country, and all I could come up with was prom. I wasn't even sure why I'd mentioned it. Maybe just to remind myself that my life in Crownsville was real. "Andy," I said. "He's a really nice guy."

Sol's gaze again fixed on me. "And lucky, too," he said, quietly.

There's that moment when a guy says something random, like Andy offering to take Jay to the cages, that drives you to spend hours analyzing every word—*Did he say it like this, or did he say it like that? Did he mean this, or did he mean that?* Then somehow you break the code and you think maybe, *maybe*, that guy you'd been dreaming about might actually like you, too. That was how I felt right then.

"I want to show you something," said Sol. He got to his feet and offered me his hand.

Still dissecting his previous comment, I took his hand, and together we wandered to the edge of the paddock where the river flowed beyond the pond.

"The river's called the Ritter," he said, pointing to the babbling water. "It comes from the mountains, feeds the valley, or used to. All of this, from the Ridge to the western ocean, is Brakaland, the greatest of this world's kingdoms. To the north, Hillsvale. In the east, Roul. To the south, Valaray. Then over the ocean lies Balia, the island where the Barrier was created and where the Solenetta was made. The Balians are keepers of magic and legend who nurture the energy from which they say all magic flows. The people there won't join this fight. They fought in the Great War against Elias and it didn't go well for them. So they remain isolated, knowing that if the Suzerain opens the Barrier and Brakaland falls, the other kingdoms will topple one by one and they could be all that remains of this world."

I stared into the distance, imagining kingdoms and countries, worlds continuing on forever. "And beyond Balia?" I uttered.

"Beyond Balia are places few of us have ever seen," said Sol. "There are more kingdoms out there, but what they suffer, I do not know."

"And then there are worlds within worlds," I said. "Like the demons breaking through the Warnon Mines?"

"There are no limits."

"It's like learning history all over again," I said, almost mesmerized by his words. "It could take a lifetime to know everything about this place."

"Several. Ten days' walk from here lies the Falls of Verderay where the water flows true green into a lake of the same color, and when it rains, the droplets break on the lake's surface like emeralds that have fallen from the sky."

Sol's energy rose as he spoke, his love for this world clear in every word. A tiny part of me swooned as his rich voice carried me along for the ride. I imagined us together, swimming in green water with emerald rain falling all around us.

"To the north is Byron's Garden," he continued. "Byron's a Flora Demon who's been here since the beginning of the world. He never leaves his garden, and no other demon can set foot there. It's supposed to be amazing. You see creatures and plants that can be found nowhere else." He paused, his gaze fixed on the horizon. Sadness returned to his face. "Word from your world is that a power plant is planned where Byron's Garden grows. The Barrier can't absorb something like that. It'll give up on the garden to save what it can around it. It'll be gone."

The magical tale he'd spun vanished like smoke in the breeze. All of it—Byron's Garden, the Falls of Verderay—gone.

"Then the Treaty of Roi has to work," I said.

"Yes."

"And if it doesn't?"

He paused, then playfully elbowed my side as he lowered his lips to my ear. "Then we'll have to wipe you off the face of the planet," he whispered.

"Funny," I said, as he pulled away grinning. "So we're back to square one. What do you believe?"

"I believe that the treaty will work," he said, once again serious. "We must do everything in our power to make it work. It's time for the lines between the worlds to be drawn once and for all, and for the Barrier to be sealed forever. Mia, it's better if the worlds remain strangers to each other. We're too different to mix."

After everything I'd seen, I kind of agreed. "It's like a poem we read in school," I said. "Oh, East is East, and West is West, and never the twain shall meet." I was surprised that I'd said it—me reciting poetry to Sol. But I knew what I was trying to say. Sol was from here, I was from Crownsville, and there was nothing could be done about it. "Kipling, or someone," I added, and shrugged off my intensity with a smile. "I can never remember."

"Maybe he knew this world too," said Sol.

"Maybe he did."

I took a final look around, then noticed Delane on the porch. I didn't know how long he'd been there; but he watched us with that same strange look he'd had last night. Standing so close to Sol, I wondered if Delane had seen us hand in hand, and wished I didn't feel like I'd been caught doing something I shouldn't.

"Delane's up," I announced, and Sol turned to see.

"At last," he said, and without a second's hesitation, he was striding for the house.

I lingered a second longer, watching as he headed for Delane, wondering if the time we'd just spent together meant as much to Sol as it had to me. I doubted it.

"Mia, come on," he called back, energized to be leaving. "It's time to move."

From the back of our horse, I took a final look at the house. The damage the demons had wrought to the roof was clear from a distance. A huge hole spanned several of the boards. We were lucky to be alive.

In our hurry to get to Orion, we were kind of leaving a mess. My blanket remained where I'd left it on the step, the kitchen table still sat on the grass outside. My gaze scanned the upper floor, then paused at the cobweb-filled window. I couldn't help but think that behind it, spider eyes stared back.

Not yet mounted, Delane strung our packs to our horse's side. "What, in the name of the stars, do you have in here?"

"In what?" I asked.

"In this pack!"

Oh, that. I'd made a quick sweep of the ground floor before we'd left the house. There was plenty of stuff we could use: a couple of blankets, some rags from the kitchen (for bathroom breaks), a switchblade I'd found in a cupboard . . .

"We got caught off guard a couple of times yesterday," I replied, casually. "It's just in case."

Delane muttered something I didn't catch, maybe about defense mechanisms and garbage. After securing the bulging pack, he jumped aboard.

Not long after leaving the house, we entered the town of Narlow. Delane told me it had long been a trading post between Orion and the valley.

"We can't stop," said Sol. "Not if we're to cut off Malone's gang."

The horses' steps echoed off the cobbled streets. As in Bordertown, there were scars from battle. But unlike my first view of Brakaland, there was something light and wholesome about Narlow. Flowers grew in the overgrown yards, pretty drapes hung at windows. More a village than a town, it was easy to imagine the place filled with workers and families. I pictured kids, excited to be off the farms, running like crazy through the streets, just like the kids did on Saturday mornings in Crownsville.

"That's the Gathering Hall," said Delane. He pointed to a stone building to our right. Wide steps led to heavy double doors, which had fallen from their hinges. "It's where the villagers made their last stand against the demons and where most of those who died were killed."

I gazed into the blackness beyond those doors and wondered if their bodies were still inside. Who would retrieve them? They didn't have the UN or the Red Cross or anyone who swept into war zones to clean up other folks' messes. I guessed the bodies stayed where they lay until only bones remained, like the bones we'd seen on entering the valley.

"The survivors finally evacuated," said Delane. "They headed into the forest to Maslian's Caves where they waited three weeks to be rescued."

*Three weeks!* Had my father not abandoned me, how easily I could have been with them. "There must be something that can be done to bring this place back."

"There is," replied Sol. "Cast out the Suzerain and send him to hell with the demons."

It was a touch ambitious for my watch. Rescuing Jay and the Solenetta would have to suffice.

A couple of hours later, a tall stone obelisk, like something from Rome or Ancient Egypt, appeared on the side of the road.

"That's it," said Delane. "We've made it out of the valley."

The trees and brush soon cleared. Wider roads joined ours. And then people appeared. A woman, like Willie's double from Bordertown with spines on her arms, sat on a boulder at the edge of the road and watched as we passed. It was both strange and reassuring to see other people again. It was easy in the valley to feel like the only three alive.

"We're close to Orion," said Sol, pointing to a gang of Runners recognizable by their jeans and jackets. Some had the look just right. Others? Not so much. Like the guy in sweat pants and a suit jacket. I wasn't sure he'd ever seen a copy of *Vogue*. But the Runners had one thing in common: They all looked human. I guess the Brakaland folk knew enough about the Other Side to know that green scales were definitely last season.

Sol stopped on the peak of a rise in the road. We drew up alongside and looked down into a gap between the hills. And there it was, like the magical city Sol had spoken of earlier. Orion.

# NINETEEN

don't know what I'd expected, but this wasn't it. Orion was a city surrounded by a great white wall. From the high peak on which we stood, thousands of rooftops were visible with smoke rising from chimneys. The infamous Gates of Orion were beneath us, barred, wrought iron barricades, the height of the wall. Guards blocked the entrance. But the guards weren't sentinels and that, I supposed, was a good thing.

At the far edge of the city stood a spectacular structure as white as the city walls, and as wide as the whole of Orion. It was built on several terraces, its upper levels higher than the rooftops of the houses below. Eight or nine towers soared above the terraces. No windows adorned the towers but, from a distance, I could clearly make out the steps that spiraled the towers' outer walls from base to tip. I wasn't sure what purpose the stairs served. Security? If nothing else, they offered anyone fool enough to climb them a view right across the Brakaland Plains.

It was Orion's palace, I guessed. I guessed something else, too. "That's where they've got Jay."

"It's the Velanhall," said Sol, catching my comment. "It once housed the Alderman Council of the Plains. The Suzerain has taken it over. He has no right to be there."

And neither did we. Yet somehow we had to find a way in.

"So what do we do?" I asked. "The gates look heavily guarded."

"I'll go see if there's any trace of Malone's men," replied Sol. "Wait here. This shouldn't take long."

I dismounted, glad to give both our horse and my butt a well-earned break. Sol disappeared from view and there was nothing else to do but watch the Velanhall's ominous towers. Jay was so close, yet he might as well have been on the opposite end of the earth.

Delane had dismounted. He adjusted the packs on our horse. "You're wasting your time, you know," he said.

Certain I'd heard him right, but having no clue what he meant, I shrugged. "Sorry, what?"

"Solandun," he said. He continued to fiddle with the packs as if to avoid my gaze. "The two of you together wouldn't work out."

I didn't need a mirror to know I looked stunned. I immediately turned my back to him. Call it ego preservation. "I don't know what you're talking about," I muttered.

"I'm pretty sure you do."

He came to my side, close—too close when all I wanted was to hide my face and pretend this conversation wasn't happening.

"You're really nice, Mia," he said. "I'd hate to see you disappointed."

There's a playbook Willie and I had devised for moments such as this. It contained one tactic: deny everything.

I feigned a laugh. "Delane, you're way off base. Sol? Come on. *Seriously?*"

"I've seen you," said Delane.

"Seen me what?" I asked. "I need him to help me get my brother back. That is all." I folded my arms, which felt too defensive, so I forced them back to my side.

Delane looked down toward the gates. I didn't dare follow his gaze in case I caught sight of Sol and further betrayed my feelings. *Betrayed my feelings?* What was I even thinking about? It wasn't as if there was anything between us. What Sol had said about Andy being lucky? He was just being nice. But I'd latched on to it like a fool. Where there could be no hope, I'd let hope grow.

"Mia . . ."

"*What?*" I said, attempting another laugh. "Seriously, Delane. You've—"

"Made a mistake?" he asked, clearly uncomfortable. "Then you won't mind if I tell you something."

"Tell me what?" I asked, not sure I wanted to hear what he had to say.

"I've known Solandun all my life," said Delane. "I know what his life in the West is like."

"And what is it like?"

"It's different," he replied. "There have been lots of girls in his past—girls who've come and gone. He's not looking to get tied down to anyone, especially someone from the Other Side. Mia, Solandun only thinks about defeating the Suzerain, securing the treaty, and having the Barrier sealed forever."

And there it was again. The Barrier. Me on one side. Sol on the other.

"Mia, Solandun crossed the Barrier to protect the Ridge and to stop them from taking the boys. There was no other reason."

Whether he knew it or not, he may as well have punched me in the gut. It would have hurt less. "Yeah," I said, and this time I did fold my arms. "But he didn't do a very good job of it, did he?"

Sol returned to find me on one side of the road and Delane on the other. We'd been that way for—I don't know—twenty minutes? As each minute had passed, I'd sunk deeper and deeper into a black mood I couldn't shake off.

"How'd it go?" I asked Sol as casually as I could, aware of how Delane might misinterpret every word or gesture.

"Better than we could have hoped," Sol replied. "Malone's men are already here. A gang from Fortknee saw them pass about an hour ago."

"And how's that better than we hoped?" asked Delane.

"Because the Suzerain isn't here," said Sol. "And he won't return until tomorrow."

"Then we've got time."

Sol nodded. "Malone's gang will have to wait to hand over the Solenetta." He took a deep breath. "But there is a problem."

"Only one?" I asked. This being Brakaland, I highly doubted it would be a small one.

"For now," said Sol. "I've been talking with some Runners at the gate. They say Malone's messenger told the guards that a group of three escaped the Bordertown sentinels and could be heading this way. The guards and the gang are looking out for us."

That *was* a big problem. "Isn't there another way in?" I asked.

"There are other gates, but they're equally risky. That's why I wanted to arrive here first. It's the reason we cut through the valley. It will all be for nothing if we're arrested at the gates."

I stared at the towers and my resolve stirred. Mooning over

Delane's warnings wouldn't get Jay or the Solenetta back. Soon this would all be over, and what would it matter how I felt about Sol when I was back on the Other Side? What had Delane said? Girls come and go. Brothers were forever. That's when I came up with my plan.

"Then we should split up," I said. "They're looking for a party of three. We'll go in one by one."

"And how do you intend to get past those guards?" asked Delane.

A small group in jeans and jackets and sweatpants passed us on the road. "Orion's a trading post, right? It's full of Runners."

"Go on," said Delane.

"Then we play to my strengths. It's a Runner's job to know the Other Side. And who here knows the Other Side better than me?"

"It's risky," said Delane, once I'd filled them in on the details of my plan.

"It's perfect," I replied. "It'll work."

For once, Sol was on my side. "Wait for us outside Morningstar Stables. It's opposite the gates; you can't miss it. Huge yellow sign."

"Morningstar Stables," I said, with a nod.

"Don't talk to anyone but the guards. We don't want to push our luck. Take this, too," he added. He handed me a squishy Snickers from his pocket. "It might work on the guard if he gets testy. And take care." He placed his hands on my shoulders and squeezed. *"Please."*

I didn't want Sol to let go. But I had a point to make to Delane: Mia Stone was in Brakaland to rescue her brother, not to mope over some guy.

"Okay," I said, and reached for my pack. "Now turn around. I need to change."

I admit, my plan was genius. That it also meant dumping the dress was like the double chocolate frosting. But I was nervous. Very nervous. This was the first time I'd be alone in Brakaland, and success hinged on my performance. Stumble, and the audience wouldn't pelt rotten fruit, they'd clap me in irons. I ran through everything Sol and Delane had told me. Be calm. Stay relaxed. Act like you belong here.

I walked the road to the gate, just little old me among the gangs of seasoned Runners. I knew Sol and Delane watched but I resisted the urge to check back. They were alone and it was a perfect opportunity for Delane to tell Sol that he suspected I had feelings for him. It didn't ease my nerves.

The closer I got to the gates, the less I thought my plan a work of genius. There were no sentinels, but the guards, though smartly dressed in uniforms of gray, appeared little friendlier than their brutish Bordertown counterparts. I'd already seen them turn two people back.

"Next."

Two guys approached the gates. I could hear little of their conversation beyond the noise that rang from Orion. It was busy in there, much busier than Bordertown. Though the streets were partially visible beyond the gates, I couldn't yet see the stables. But, boy, had I taken Crowley's advice to heart. I trusted Sol without question. The stables would be there. I prayed that I could find them.

"Next."

That meant me. I approached the guard, a lanky character of about Pete's age.

"Name."

"Poppy Fellows," I said. It had been Sol's idea. I wondered if Poppy might have been one of the girls who'd "come and gone."

"Where you headed?"

"Rickter's," I replied, like it was the most natural thing in the world. "Got something for him to see."

The guard's eyes narrowed. "Are you a Runner? You talk funny."

Okay. We'd prepped for this one. "I spend a lot of time on the Other Side," I said, trying not to sound as if I read from a script.

He was suspicious, I knew it. Time for Plan B. I took my cell phone from my jacket pocket and flashed it at the guard. His manner immediately switched. "I haven't seen one of those for a while."

"It's a good one too," I said, doing my best QVC demonstration. "Normally I wouldn't come this way, but I heard Rickter's been getting these to work. Worth twenty times more, then."

He eyed my crappy old phone as if it were a Rolex watch. *Moron.* I mean, it wasn't even a smartphone!

"Are you from Bordertown?"

"Fortknee." Another of Sol's lies. "Bordertown's flooded with Runners. I'd rather sell my stuff without Duddon Malone fleecing the profits."

The guard snorted. "We've had more of his lot already today."

"Well, they won't get their hands on this." I snapped the handset shut.

The guard stepped back. Orion beckoned. "Let me know if they get that thing to work. I've never seen one that actually does."

I didn't hang around long enough for the guy to have second thoughts about Poppy the Runner and her busted cell phone; the priority was to get out of his sight and reach the stables. Only, it looked as if that might be easier said than done.

I'd emerged onto a fan-shaped concourse, about half the area of a football field, constructed of sand-colored flagstones, which radiated out from the gates. On either side loomed Orion's curved white walls, though the curve didn't seem as pronounced from the inside. A line of shops and stores had been built in the wall's shadow, crooked little places with roofs of different heights. At first glance, I saw a pottery shop, a dress store, and what had to be a butcher, judging by the carcass hanging in the window.

Traders, with multicolored awnings above their carts and stalls, filled the concourse. Their cries rang as they hustled their wares. Someone, somewhere, was grilling, the scent a mixture of bacon and beef. Having eaten only Snickers since I'd left Crownsville, my stomach growled.

I headed toward a cluster of buildings with narrow streets between them. Each street I passed was different. One, barely ten feet wide, ran long and straight with rows of three-story town houses on either side, each painted a different color—lemon, lilac, sky blue, peach. The next street was covered by a sandstone roof, and beyond the arched entryway, the dim tunnel inside was lit by flickering lanterns. A green and white mosaic paved another street.

There was no sign of the stables, so I cut back toward the center of the market, dodging traders and their customers, recognizing some as races I'd seen in Bordertown.

I pushed on, only the tops of the gates visible behind me, when a couple passed on horseback. I followed them to a wide arch between two white buildings. A straw-strewn courtyard lay beyond. A yellow sign hung from the archway: Morningstar Stables. Bingo.

Alongside the stables ran a wide road. At one end of the road were the gates, at the other, the Velanhall. I stopped. Even from a distance of about twenty blocks, its towers loomed over Orion. I wished Jay knew I was coming for him.

"One hurdle at a time, Mia."

I stifled a scream. Sol had crept up behind me, his horse at his side. I studied his face, praying Delane hadn't told him that the girl from Crownsville might be harboring a secret crush. To my relief, Sol didn't look like he knew.

"I can't stop thinking about him up there," I said. "I feel like I should be doing something."

"You are," said Sol. "More than most ever would." He turned back to his horse and withdrew my sword from his pack. "You forgot this."

I took it, used to the weight, though it still felt clunky in my hands. "It's probably time I gave up pretending I can use this," I said, and handed back the sword. "We're not destined to be together."

Our hands touched and I realized how prophetic my statement was. I held on for maybe a second too long before releasing the sword to Sol's steady hand.

*Not destined to be together?*

Willie loved symbolic moments.

This one sucked.

\* \* \*

We headed deep into Orion, on the east side of town. I kept an eye on Delane, who'd yet to speak a word to me since we'd regrouped. I didn't want bad blood between us. I'd never been one to hold a grudge. It wasn't his fault that he'd noticed the feelings I thought I'd hidden. He'd been doing me a favor, really, warning me off Sol. A favor my rational self completely understood, even if my stupid hormones didn't want to hear it.

But our earlier conversation didn't seem to be on his mind as we wandered Orion's back streets. Delane straightened his shirt about five times. When he ducked to catch his reflection in a window, I couldn't help but ask, "Are you checking your hair?" He couldn't have thought I wouldn't notice.

"What? No."

Sol glanced back and smiled. Really, I couldn't let this pass. "You are," I teased. "You're fussing with your *hair*."

*"No."* He stopped, and then shrugged. "But how do I look?"

"Like a guy who spent a night on the road," I replied, confused. "Don't think you can change that now."

"Doesn't hurt to try."

But whatever it was Delane preened for, he'd run out of time. Sol stopped at a door in the middle of a terrace of town houses. He unstrapped his pack and rummaged inside.

"What is this place?" I asked. The house was constructed

279

from dark gray stone and stood three stories tall. Tiny windows, embellished with stained-glass inlays of plants and flowers, peppered the front.

"It's home to a member of the Sons of the West," said Sol. "We use it whenever we're in Orion."

He took from his pack a white oval disc, which he placed into a recess beside the door, then covered with both his hands. *Click*. As easily as that, we were inside. I followed Sol and Delane, happy for them to provide a buffer for whatever shock might come next.

Inside, the house was nothing like Rip's. In fact, it was like nothing I'd seen in Brakaland. We entered a hallway where elaborately framed mirrors hung over swathes of purple gossamer fabric. A floral scent carried through the air, rose or lavender, heady and sweet. To the left was a staircase illuminated by candles, which sat on ledges.

I hung back with Delane, but Sol strode to a closed door at the end of the hall, and without knocking, entered a second room. A light, breathy squeal followed.

"Guess she's home," said Delane, with a grin wider than the Cheshire Cat's. "Get ready to meet Vermillion Blue."

Intrigued, I followed to the next room. Stronger floral scents floated through the doorway. There were more breathy squeals. I stepped inside.

And then my jaw just about hit the ground.

# TWENTY

Vermillion Blue didn't look much like a *Son* of the West to me.

She was supermodel tall and blessed with the kind of curves usually reserved for the calendars that hung at Reggie West's Motor Repair and Salvage. And she was blue. Well, a silvery gray, which caught the light and was as flawless as an airbrusher's dream. Scarlet hair, lustrous and thick, tumbled to her waist. It shone like nothing I'd ever seen. If Vermillion Blue ever set foot in the States, she'd get one hell of a lucrative contract with Pantene.

She was dressed from head to toe in white, all six foot whatever of her. Her dress was sheer, yet somehow managed to cover what it was supposed to. I'd never seen such perfect features. Full lips. Straight nose. And her eyes? As gorgeous as her skin and framed with scarlet lashes.

It sounds like I'm making a big deal about this. Maybe I am. But here's the thing: Vermillion Blue was wrapped around Sol like cotton candy on a stick, and Sol didn't seem too sorry to be in that predicament. Her long arms squeezed his shoulders like a boa constrictor dancing with its prey, her amble chest crushing his. And she was kissing him. On the mouth! As if the whole world wasn't standing at the door and watching.

Suddenly, I felt very plain. Very plain and very boring.

"I thought he only cared about defeating the Suzerain," I muttered.

Delane caught my comment. He leaned in to my ear. "Vermillion's an exception to most rules."

Apparently so.

Vermillion released Sol from her clutches and then, much to his delight, it was Delane's turn.

I tracked Sol's path as he moved to the side of the room. He didn't appear any worse for the encounter, nor did he appear shocked that Vermillion was squeezing the life out of Delane, too. What a welcome. I guess they really did do things differently over here.

Then it was my turn.

I wasn't going to hug her. Seriously, I was not going to have my face mashed against that chest. She approached like a figure skater, all gliding and elegant, looking down on me from up there on Blue Mountain. I put out my hand.

"Mia Stone," I said.

That threw her. She hesitated, looked back at Delane, and then tentatively offered me her hand. "Vermillion," she said, her voice clear and light.

"Good to meet you," I replied hastily, and shook.

It was only when she'd stepped away that I noticed the room; Vermillion had a knack for eclipsing most things around her. It was a kitchen, much like the kitchen at my father's house, with a table and benches, a range, and a row of low wooden cabinets, though the walls were painted pale blue and every surface held a vase containing some kind of flower. There were mirrors everywhere. I guess Vermillion didn't like to lose sight of herself even when cooking. Who could blame her?

"You have to tell me everything," she said, watching me as if I might change my mind and decide to join the love fest. Once it was clear that I wouldn't yield, she turned her attention back to the guys. "I didn't expect to see you so soon. Solandun, the last I heard you were on the Other Side."

"I was," said Sol, still safely out of her reach. "It's a long story. We came through the valley from Bordertown."

Vermillion again glanced at me. "The valley? But why?"

"It's the Solenetta," said Sol.

Vermillion spun back to Sol, and the draft from her hair wafted across my face.

"It's here," he said. "It's back."

For all her "faults," Vermillion was a good listener. As we sat around the table and talked, she never once interrupted Sol's tale.

"I never expected this," she said, once Sol had finished. "If the Solenetta lands in the Suzerain's hands then war could quickly follow."

"That's why we have to get it back."

"And we will," she said. "We must. But I'm shocked. No word of these events reached me."

"There was no time," said Sol. "We barely escaped from Rip's before the sentinels were on us. But the guardsmen will know by now—Malone's men will have seen to that. Can you help us?"

"Help you?" she asked, tossing her hair in a cascade of scarlet tresses. "I would crawl naked across the Wastes to ruin that monster's plans."

Sol smiled. "We'd settle for knowing which safe house Malone's men are using."

"That shouldn't be difficult," she replied. She rose like a pre-Raphaelite vision bursting into life. "Now take some rest. Get cleaned up. I'll have news for you within the hour."

\* \* \*

*Get cleaned up.*

I had to concede Vermillion that point. Stringy didn't come close to describing my hair. I hadn't been near a toothbrush in two days. Vermillion was all fresh and larger than life. Me? I looked like a gutterscamp. I was pretty sure I stank like one too.

I was given a room on the top floor, homelier than the one at Rip's, but clear of the chaos and clutter of my own room in Crownsville. The bed was waist high, with a pillow top that screamed to be slept on, and a comforter in crisp, bright lemon.

An hour ago, I would have welcomed a nice, comfy bed, but I was still kind of sulking about seeing Sol in Vermillion's arms. Why had I thought the Sons of the West would be a bunch of guys like Rip and Old Man Crowley? No wonder Delane had warned me. He'd known who waited to welcome Sol back to Orion.

I flung open the closet where Delane had promised I'd find clean clothes. An entire wardrobe hung inside, everything from the gray uniforms I'd seen on the gate guards to flowing gowns of lavender and green—Vermillion's, no doubt. I decided to stick with my jeans and closed the door. No point trying to compete with Vermillion Blue.

The sound of running water brought me to the window. A

tiny walled yard lay below with a gate that opened onto the alley behind the house. Steam rose from a wooden cubicle tucked in the corner. From the shoulders up, there was Sol.

I'd seen Sol without a shirt before, but catching another sight of him, I knew the image of Sol by the river that lived in my memory was simply a shadow of Sol in reality. His tanned skin was tight across his triceps and shoulders, so I could see their every movement in perfect definition. Water cascaded from pipes on the wall. Hopelessly yearning, I thought of the Falls of Verderay and Sol and me swimming in the green water. Only hours had passed since I'd listened to Sol's tale on the grass outside my father's home with my hand locked in his. It felt like a million years.

*Don't do this, Mia.*

I wasn't used to handling this stuff without Willie! It's a best friend's responsibility to keep this kind of daydreaming in check. Without her, my senseless crush had spiraled out of control.

"I've brought towels." Delane waited at the bedroom doorway with arms full of linen.

*Great.* There was no way he hadn't seen me peeping at Sol.

"So the shower's outside?" I mumbled, pointing to the window, trying not to seem like some sort of pervert. "Rustic."

"Don't let Solandun stay out there too long," Delane replied, as he entered the room. "He's an infamous hot water thief."

"I'd settle for a bucket of water right now. Any temperature. I stink."

Delane laughed. "I'm pretty sure that's me."

He lingered like a little old woman with something to say. After being confronted with Vermillion Blue, I really didn't think I could face another lecture.

"You look tired," he said.

"Just nervous. Worried about Jay. Part of me wants to go up there, bang on the door, and tell them to hand him over. Not a great plan."

"We'll think of something." He took the linen to the bed, cringing slightly. "Mia, I want to apologize for what I said earlier."

"You don't have to." I really didn't want to dwell on Sol. I had a feeling it wasn't healthy. "Delane, it was nothing. Silly, really."

"It's not my business what you do with Solandun."

"We're not doing *anything*," I said, and thinking of the way Vermillion Blue had kissed him, I meant it. "It was just the valley. We were all freaked out. And then there's Jay and the Solenetta and . . ."

Nobody had ever looked at me the way that Delane looked at me then. He looked *sorry* for me.

I spun around, wanting to hide my face. Only, now I could see outside. Sol had left the shower. He stood in the yard, towel wrapped low around his hips, the Lunestral visible in all its glory. The water from his hair and shoulders dripped down his back, the sunlight casting life into the dream bird.

He was perfect to me.

Defeated by my feelings, I reluctantly faced Delane. "It's me who should apologize," I said. "You're right. I haven't been able to stop thinking about him since I first saw him."

Delane didn't reply.

"And it's not because it could never be," I blurted, not sure where the words were coming from. "He's different from other guys. He's so committed to everything he does. He never thinks about his own safety to help someone else. He risked his life for us in the valley. *Twice.*"

I started to pace, the words pouring out of me.

"And he didn't want to tell me about my dad," I continued, "but he did it anyway, because he knew I needed to hear the truth. And the way he loves Brakaland. Delane, you should have heard him talking this morning about the places here. At home, guys just moan about how everything sucks and everything's lame, but they never *do* anything about it! Sol's family is in the West, yet Sol's *here*, trying to change this world for the better. He even came to Crownsville to fight. *Alone.* I can't even imagine what that must have been like for him. But he did it, because it was the right thing to do."

I stopped. Delane's eyes were wide like a guy who'd just had a bomb dropped on his head. I must have sounded crazy to him. Just another girl who'd fallen under Sol's spell.

"I guess you've heard it all before," I stated, embarrassed.

Delane's shocked expression faded gradually. He leaned against the bed and let out a deep breath. "Actually," he said. "No."

*No?*

"But all the girls you mentioned . . ." I trailed off.

He began to smile. "Mia, those aren't the parts of Solandun girls usually focus on."

I snickered. "He is hot," I said, sheepishly. "Did I mention that?"

Delane faked a look of deep thought. "I'm sure you meant to." He stretched back on the bed, propping himself up on his elbows. "Are you going to tell him how you feel?"

"No way!" I exclaimed, as I sat on the comforter. "I'll get over him. Got no choice, right? I mean, even if we didn't live in different worlds, he's still got Vermillion draped all over him."

Delane pulled back his head. "You think Solandun's with *Vermillion?*"

"Well, aren't they? It was hard to miss that greeting, Delane."

He laughed, hard. "That's too funny. Mia, Vermillion's rarefied Simbia. Notoriously emotional. Notoriously *loving.* Get my point?"

I think I did. We had a name for that type in Crownsville, too.

"So they're not together?"

"Never. Ever," he said.

The news made me feel slightly better.

"You're not going to tell him about any of this, right?" I asked. "Sol, I mean."

"I won't say a word," Delane replied. "And I'm still sorry for what I said earlier."

"We're buddies, Delane," I said, and flopped onto my back beside him. "If you can't tell it to me straight, then no one can."

Sol had left some hot water, and after washing the valley out of my hair, I felt ready for anything. I relinquished the shower to Delane, then retired to my room to dress and towel dry my hair as best I could. There really was something to be said for confessing. I felt lighter—freer. What had passed between me and Delane would remain a secret. It was time to get my head out of the clouds over Sol, and focus on Jay.

I hadn't heard Vermillion return, but as I left my room I caught her and Sol's voices coming from the kitchen. I went downstairs.

". . . word of what happened has reached the West," said Vermillion, as I approached. "They've known for some time. If news of this latest development reaches them, they might decide it's time to destroy the Solenetta."

"Which is why we have to get it out of Brakaland before they find out," said Sol.

"You're not tempted to destroy it yourself?"

"No," Sol replied. "Never."

That surprised me. The second I got back to Crownsville, I planned to hurl the thing into the river. Well, perhaps not. But there was no way I was keeping it, regardless of whether or not Willie thought it was the perfect accessory for prom.

I entered the kitchen to find them at the table. Sol had changed clothes, swapping one gray shirt for another. His hair was damp from the shower.

"The boys are being held in the Velanhall," said Vermillion. "It's no secret."

"Jay?" I asked.

Vermillion looked up on hearing my voice. She gestured for me to join them. "Solandun has been telling me your story."

"Has anyone seen the boys?" I asked.

"Periodically. They've been taking them to the Nonsky Fault."

I slid onto the bench beside Sol. "Where's that?"

"It's a Barrier weakness," Sol replied, "less than a mile from here."

"They're planning something up there," said Vermillion. "There's a camp of sentinels. They've been taking the boys."

"You think they have solens?" asked Sol.

"What use would they be without someone to use them?"

I didn't understand. "Can't anyone use them?"

"Not without a spell to create the reaction," Vermillion replied.

"And there's no spell powerful enough to harness an entire solen's power," I added. "Other than the Solenetta." I smiled at Sol. "See? I pay attention."

"Whatever they're doing isn't working," continued Vermillion. "They bring the boys back to the Velanhall a couple of days later and then no one returns to the fault for weeks. Another caravan left the city yesterday, heading for the encampment."

"With the boys?"

"We don't know. The wagons were covered and the spies we sent haven't yet seen any children. But whatever they're doing, they're making ready for another attempt, probably to open the Barrier. And now the Suzerain returns. Coincidence?"

"Unlikely," said Sol.

"I heard a rumor that a new boy arrived recently and that he is Balian." Vermillion glanced pointedly at me. "I am guessing that is your brother. I sensed Balia when you arrived here."

"My father's from Brakaland," I said. "I don't know about Balia."

"Then maybe they know something we don't. Maybe they really do have solens and they think this boy is their shot at an Equinox. But without the Solenetta it could never be a true and lasting reaction."

"But what does any of that mean?"

"It means they're going to be hugely disappointed," said Sol. Then, to Vermillion, "So Malone's using the safe house on Maslian's Square?"

"Yes. I saw three of his men there; I don't know how many more there are. Tomorrow there will be a parade in honor of the Suzerain's return. You know the type of men Malone hires. They enjoy a drink or two. There will be parties for the parade all over town. I'm sure they'd happily join the festivities given the right persuasion. That would give you a chance to slip in. Until then, you'd need an army to penetrate their defenses. It's a window, Solandun. A narrow window, I grant you, and not foolproof. Some of Malone's men will undoubtedly remain to guard their prize. But for sure, as soon as the Suzerain is settled and granting audiences at the Velanhall, they'll be up there to make their trade."

"Then maybe we have a plan," said Sol. "I'm going to go up there and sniff around." He turned to me. "Want to come?"

And get him out of Vermillion's hair? It was an easy decision. "This isn't another one of your crazy missions, is it?" I asked.

Sol's eyes widened in mock outrage. "Just a stroll!" he said. "I promise. No trouble."

# TWENTY-ONE

knew it was Malone's place as soon as I saw the eye painted above the door. It gave me the same creepy feeling as the tattoo on Malone's hand. "Do you see it?" I asked.

"I see it," said Sol. "We need to be careful."

He lowered his head as we passed the hideout, a wide gray building, one of many that edged Maslian's Square. There was no sign of activity on our first pass. The ground floor windows were shuttered and the eye was the only sign of life. "Can it see us?" I whispered.

"Best not to find out."

"Then we can't go in through the front tomorrow."

"Probably not a good idea anyway," said Sol. "It's busy around here."

Maslian's Square was smaller than the concourse inside Orion's gates, but it was no less populated. Hundreds of windows overlooked the square. No doubt they'd be filled with spectators—witnesses—during the Suzerain's parade. Preparations were already underway. Sentinels patrolled, pushing back stall holders and erecting barriers along a route, which cut through the square and continued on to the Velanhall. It was heavily guarded chaos in the making.

"Let's check out back," said Sol.

The rear was little better. Malone's hideout backed onto a long, stuffy alley that reeked of garbage. The rear windows were shuttered, too, so there was no peeking inside. There was one door, which Sol discreetly checked to find it locked, but no eye.

"There's one of those things by the door like at Vermillion's," I said, picturing the oval disc Sol had used to enter the safe house.

"It's a bond key." He checked the length of the alley. All clear.

"Any chance your key would fit? They look about the same size."

"It's not that kind of a key," he said. "It's a spell. They were popular before the Purge."

I took another look at the shallow recess as we again passed the door. "Any chance we could find a key to fit?"

"Not many people can make bond keys these days," Sol replied as we headed back to the street. "Besides, there's no way to replicate the spell in the lock. Bond keys use blood rites."

"Blood rites?" I blurted. "Like *real* blood?"

It was a relief to be back onto the square where the air was fresh. Shame we had to be talking about blood.

"Blood was often used in spells," said Sol, as if it was the most normal thing in the world. "It was a way to link an object of value to an individual."

He led us to a bench on the opposite side of the square, safely out of sight of Malone's eye. Once seated, he took Vermillion's key from his pocket. "There's blood encased inside," he said.

I'd thought about touching it, then I changed my mind. "Your blood?"

"That's right. The lock at Vermillion's knows it's the blood of a friend. If it senses the same blood in the hand that uses the key, the lock will release."

Whatever Delane had said about Vermillion and Sol not being together, I'd seen how Vermillion had greeted him. And Sol had a bond key. To her house.

"So how come you have one?" I asked.

"You can connect a lock to many keys," he replied. "As long as it recognizes the blood, it'll open."

It wasn't quite what I'd asked, but Sol could be tricky when he wanted to be.

"It's still gross," I said, looking away.

"It's secure. Some of the strongest spells ever conjured used blood rites. You have to know what you're doing with them, though; they can get messy."

I slumped forward. "You're a fun date, Sol."

He laughed. "Sorry. I can't compete with your prom."

"Instead of fruit punch and chaperones, you have sentinels and visage demons. That's hard to top."

"I doubt you'd want either of those at the dance."

I wouldn't have minded seeing Sol in a tux, though, but that wasn't ever going to happen. The only thing we had to look forward to was storming Malone's hideout and then somehow getting Jay out of the Velanhall. No orchid corsage required for that.

"Just so you know," I said, after taking another look at the eye. "I don't have a good feeling about this plan."

Sol turned toward me, surprising me with a penetrating stare. "And why's that?"

"There could be dozens of them in there." I was determined to keep my mind on the business at hand, which was difficult when Sol looked at me that way. "I'm useless in a fight. You can spot Vermillion a mile away. That leaves you and Delane."

"I hope there won't be a fight," said Sol. "Get in, get the Solenetta, get out."

"Which we can't do if the place is packed with Runners."

"I doubt there will be more than a few men in there. It's not Malone's style. There's no safety in numbers in Orion. Here you lie low, keep your head down, otherwise you're attracting thieves. And this place is full of thieves."

"Like us?"

"We're not stealing, Mia. We're taking back what's yours."

"And if we don't get it?"

He paused. "We'll get it back."

But then what? We still had to get Jay. And what about the other boys? We'd have to make it to the Ridge and across to Crownsville without the whole of Bordertown noticing. As soon as the Solenetta disappeared, Malone would know it was us. If the Ridge had been guarded before, it'd be impenetrable by the time we reached Bordertown.

I saw the Solenetta in my hand, picturing myself using it to reopen the Barrier. And then Crownsville. How could I explain where we'd been? What would I do with the Solenetta? Whatever Sol had said to Vermillion, there wasn't a chance I was keeping that thing. More and more, I thought the safest plan was to use grains to cross the Barrier and leave the Solenetta here where it belonged. Using it on the Ridge was skywriting that it had returned to Crownsville. The Suzerain's demons would come for it and the race would begin again.

Thinking of the Solenetta, my mind flashed back to something Vermillion had said. "Sol, what did Vermillion mean about me and Jay being Balian? If my father's a Freeman, then she must have meant my mom, Jay's mom too. But why would she say that? Unless she knows something I don't."

His gaze roved the square, but he wasn't patrolling as he'd been before; he was avoiding me. "Vermillion's rarefied Simbia," he said.

"I know. Delane told me."

"Simbians can smell a family from a mile away. They can sense how a person's roots have evolved from the original five families. She sensed Balian in you."

"You told me Balia was where the Solenetta was made."

"It was," said Sol. "A long time ago."

"But she said Jay was Balian too."

He had that look again, as if he was sizing me up. Right away, I guessed that he knew something more.

"Sol, it's where he went, isn't it?" I said. "My dad. After he dumped me. He went to Balia."

Sol slowly shook his head. "Mia—"

"Sol, you can tell me. You won't hurt my feelings. He dumped me. End of story. I've had plenty of time to come to terms with that fact."

"I'm sure it wasn't like that."

"And I'm sure it was." I nudged his arm, wanting him to

know that he didn't have to tiptoe around me. "Look, Sol. As great a guy as you say he is, my dad bailed. You have your father, even if he is in the West."

Sol leaned forward, his hands covering his mouth as he thought. Though the street bustled around us, the space between us fell silent.

"Mia," he started.

I smiled, warily. "Bad news always follows whenever you say my name like that."

"It's not bad," he insisted, but he wouldn't look me in the eyes. All I could see was his strong profile. "It's something I should have mentioned. I . . ."

He stopped, frowned, and gestured across the square.

The door to Malone's had opened and a short, stocky man—definitely a Runner, judging by his sweatshirt and jeans—exited the house. Sol sprang to his feet. "Now's our chance."

Conversation forgotten, I asked, "We're gonna follow?"

"If we find out where he's headed, we might learn something useful," he replied. A mischievous twinkle entered his eyes. "And besides, I can't bring you to Orion and not show you a good time."

"This *is* a good time," I announced, as we ducked into yet another doorway. "Is this what you do with all the girls?"

We'd stalked Malone's guy down Orion's main street. No one less than a full-blown mind reader could have guessed we were trailing him. The afternoon light had faded and the evening traders had taken over the town. We kept back, using the crowds for cover, all the time inching closer to Malone's man.

"He's heading for that side street," said Sol.

We were jogging by the time we turned off the road, entering into a dim alley of ramshackle stalls and storefronts, bursting with shoppers. Within seconds, I'd lost sight of our quarry.

"Now what?" I kept close to Sol, worried we'd get separated in the throng.

Sol, head and shoulders above most of the crowd, gave the alley a quick scan. "He's entered that store."

Tucked behind Sol's arm, I dodged the elbows of passersby and trusted he could navigate us through. Nearby, a pencil-thin man on a podium danced to the beat of a drum. His limbs rolled like dough as he posed in time to the music, creating a series of contorted shapes, which were perhaps even creepier than the eye above Malone's door.

"Here," said Sol, and he forged a path to a store opposite Elastic Man's stage. He pretended to watch the performance. "Can you see him?"

I peered around and there, at a counter inside the store, I caught sight of Malone's man. "Yep," I said.

"Then I need you to do something." He rifled through his pocket and then dropped a few coins into my hand. "Go inside and browse. Listen in. If we're lucky, he'll let something slip."

I clutched the coins as I took another look inside. I'd said I wanted to help, but . . . "Can't you do it?"

"I shouldn't go in there," he said.

"You mean they know you?"

"Maybe."

*Maybe? What kind of an answer was that?* I shot him a scowl. "All right," I said, skeptically. "But stay where I can see you. I'll never find my way back if we get separated."

"I'll be right there," he said. He pointed to a stall to the right of the contortionist's podium. "Good luck."

I went in before I could chicken out. A bell tinkled above the door, announcing my arrival. So much for stealth. Inside, it was gloomy and cramped and smelled of a stomach-churning mix of dust, wood, and syrup. Ceiling-high shelves with jars and bottles of every color caught the light from the orbs in a rusted chandelier.

Head down, I wandered to a rack close to Malone's man and feigned interest in a bottle of *Sour Soc*, whatever that was. I listened.

"Two crates," said Malone's man. "And you'd better throw in some bottles of Duddon's poison."

"You're expecting Malone?" asked the proprietor, a five-foot, ninety-pound weasel-like man with thin, greasy hair. "Can't remember the last time I saw Duddon in Orion."

"He's on his way," said the man. "He'll be here for the parade."

"Then you'll need more than two crates. How many is he bringing with him?"

"Just a few. Two crates will be fine."

I stole a peek in time to catch Malone's man counting on his fingers. He got to seven before he stopped. "Better make that three crates," he said. "To be delivered at two."

"And someone will be there to collect? The parade starts at two and I don't want my man turning up to an empty house again."

"There'll be a couple of us there all day," retorted Malone's man. "Don't be late."

I kept my head down as he left the store, analyzing the *Sour Soc* like it was the most interesting thing on the planet. Inside, I cheered. We'd discovered that Malone was coming to town.

"Is that all you want?"

Startled, I realized the storekeeper had turned his attention to me.

"Erm."

I flashed a smile, dumped the coins on the counter and prayed there'd be enough. The storekeeper scowled but, to my relief, took a couple of the coins before pushing the rest across the glass.

"Thanks," I said, turning tail as fast as I could.

"Hey!"

I spun back, panicked, certain he somehow saw my guilt.

"You forgot your bottle."

Silly me. I grabbed the *Sour Soc* from his hand and then barreled through the door onto the alley.

"You said seven," said Sol for the fifth time.

"I said he *counted* to seven. And that there would be at least two people in there all day."

We'd left the alley and were wandering Orion's streets. Excitement for tomorrow's parade was palpable, especially among the kids, a group of whom (including one with a green beard) darted past with wooden whistles and streamers, parents nowhere in sight.

"And the delivery's at two," said Sol.

"Yeah. Are you thinking what I'm thinking?"

"If you're thinking we could intercept that delivery, then yes."

"That's what I'm thinking," I said. "Oh, and I got you a bottle of *Sour Soc.*"

I handed it over.

"Haven't seen this stuff in years," he said as he flipped the bottle cap and took a sniff. He pulled away. "That's nasty."

"That isn't what you're supposed to say when someone offers you a gift."

"You want it?" he asked, offering it to me.

I took a sniff before conceding his point. "It smells like feet."

"Not yours, I hope."

I thought of my old sneakers festering on Rusty's backseat. "Course not."

Sol held on to the bottle, and as we passed an old woman shaking a basket for change, he handed it to her. "For you," he said.

The woman looked as if her birthday and Christmas had come all at once. The power of *Sour Soc*. It never failed to please.

"So Malone's coming to town," said Sol, when we moved on. "I knew the little worm couldn't resist."

He was in full stride mode. It was kind of hard to keep up. "I'm guessing you two have a history."

"He's a clawcurling snake."

"You don't have any claws." I hesitated. "Do you?"

"Only on the full moon." He must have caught the look on my face. "Joke."

"You never can tell in these parts."

Though I'd yet to fully catch my bearings, I was pretty sure we were headed away from Vermillion's, not that I minded keeping Sol to myself. He pointed out landmarks as we walked.

The boarded-up building that had once housed the Magician's Guild. Maslian Rock, a giant statue of the Freeman who'd discovered the caves where the people of Welkin's Valley had hidden after the siege in Narlow. And the Evening Song Fountain with its breathtaking cascade of multicolored waters. But it wasn't until we reached the Velanhall that we stopped.

The palace was larger than anything I'd ever seen. The row of cream-colored mansions adorned with flags and banners that faced the palace were far grander than the homes on Orion's back streets. This was obviously where Orion's powerful resided.

We crossed to the Velanhall's steps, great marble monstrosities that led to the terraces above. I looked up, up, up to the towers, which rose like beacons against the deepening sunset. I shivered.

"They don't hold people in those towers, Mia," said Sol.

"Are you a mind reader?"

"Lucky guess."

I traced the steps that spiraled the nearest tower's outer wall and figured there had to be at least five hundred. A huge star was engraved in the stone near the top.

"It's the Morningstar," said Sol, catching the direction of my gaze. "It symbolizes hope. As the sun rises, it strikes the tower and the star shines for a few moments. It marks a fresh start, another chance on a new day."

I stared at the Morningstar and wondered if Jay could see it too. "I wish he knew I was here," I said. "That he's not forgotten."

"Kids are tough, Mia. If Jay's anything like you, he'll be fine."

"Jay's more resilient than I am."

"I find that hard to believe," Sol replied, softly.

I turned my back on the Velanhall and sank onto the bottom step. "Ever since Jay came to Crownsville, I think he's been dreaming of this place. He remembers his mother, you know. He said they took her."

"Not having parents must have been hard for both of you," said Sol.

"It was harder for Jay," I replied. "He'd play games with swords and magic. I just thought it was something that boys did. But I wonder if he remembered all along that he was from here."

"Mia, he couldn't have known much."

"I'm not sure," I said. "I think this place has always been inside him."

I watched sentinels patrolling, remembering the horrific chase through the woods surrounding Bordertown.

"Sol, about the plan," I said.

He sat at my side, his legs close to mine, his presence once again a comfort. "What about it?"

I felt the Velanhall looming behind me, its huge towers symbols of its impenetrable power, with Jay captive somewhere inside.

"I think we should get Jay first," I said.

Sol tilted his head as he listened—he *was* listening, I could see it all over his face. "Mia, getting into this place won't be easy."

"Exactly," I said. "Once we have the Solenetta, you're going to want to get it out of Orion. No one's gonna stay to help Jay." I put my hand on his knee. "Sol, please don't get the Solenetta back and then bail on me."

My words clearly shocked him, and I felt bad for thinking he might do that after everything we'd be through.

"Why would you even say that?" he asked.

I took a deep breath. "It's like the Solenetta is all anybody cares about! I can't leave without him. I won't."

Sol took my hands before I could pull away, his grip strong. "Mia," he said, his expression serious, his eyes filled with assurance. "I promised. And I'll promise again. We'll get Jay out."

"You swear. Like on a blood rite?"

"I'd swear on anything," he said, squeezing my hands. I could almost feel the power of his promise passing from his hands into mine. "I'd cut out one of Delane's hearts and swear on that if it would make you trust me."

I couldn't help but smile. "He wouldn't be too happy about that."

"He can get by with one. Mia, you can't ever believe that I'd leave your brother in the hands of that animal."

"No," I said, and I meant it. "But I could believe that you'd try and get me and the Solenetta out, then worry about Jay later."

From the sudden change in his look, it was clear I was closer to the mark. "It's dangerous for you here, Mia."

"And more so for Jay. He's all alone, Sol. He doesn't have you looking out for him."

"Mia, believe me," he said. "He does."

He released my hands. The switch had flicked. All the control, all the restrain was back. He was wound so tight I could almost feel him pulsating beside me.

"Mia, there's something I have to tell you."

I braced myself. With this kind of buildup, the news was sure to be huge. Or bad. Or both. There were no ribbons and rainbows when Sol was struck with this mood.

"About Jay?" My voice was shaky.

"About me."

He looked uncertain. He was *nervous*. My heart raced.

"I should have told you before," he said. "I meant to. I wanted to, but . . ."

He frowned, struggling for the right words.

"What is it?" I asked. "Sol?"

Still he fought against whatever it was he had to say. I reached for his arm, desperate to urge him on. "Sol?"

Nothing.

"Solandun."

He turned. The light from the sunset caught in his eyes. "That's the first time you've called me that," he said, his voice barely a whisper.

"I guess," I replied. "I never really thought about it."

"It's just a name, right?"

"Of course."

"It doesn't mean anything," he said, almost to himself.

I scowled. "Okay, now you're freaking me out."

I looked away, hoping a little personal space might help him open up. It didn't. Hating the silence, I was ready to speak, but stopped as my gaze caught a figure sprinting across the square.

"Is that Delane?" I asked. "It's Delane."

Sol saw him too, for he got to his feet and protectively reached for my hand, the moment forgotten. "This doesn't look good."

Delane skidded to a stop in front of us. "I've been looking all over for you," he said, panting. "Vermillion said you were at the hideout."

"We took a detour," said Sol. "What's happened?"

Delane glanced at Sol, then licked his lips and looked at me, clearly uneasy. "It's Bromasta," he said. "He's here."

# TWENTY-TWO

'd once sworn that when I finally saw my father, I'd slap his stupid face. But I couldn't. He didn't have a stupid face. He had a handsome face, worn, but handsome. He was dark in the hair and eyes and, at the moment, in need of a shower and a shave.

He sat in Vermillion's kitchen in a long black coat, much like Old Man Crowley's. Flakes of dry, crusty mud covered the sleeves. When he got to his feet, his presence loomed, tall and broad.

I'd always wondered how we might meet, but I'd never dreamed it would be in Brakaland. And my father had never looked like this in those dreams, more like the guy who'd sold me the bottle of *Sour Soc*. The scenes I'd imagined usually involved me burning with rage, demanding the apology that, deep down, I believed Jay and I were owed, and then showing him the door as he had done to us. That was how it was supposed to be. I never once imagined that it would feel this surreal.

The house was empty, except for us and Sol, who hung back in the doorway, arms folded. He nodded when I looked back to him, reminding me that I probably needed to speak.

"We came through the valley," I said, hesitantly. "I saw the house."

It wasn't much of a start. What was I supposed to do? Throw myself into his arms and squeal, *I love you, Dad!*

"I'm relieved it still stands," my father replied.

"You haven't been back?"

"I doubt I could ever go back," he said.

He pointed to the bench on the opposite side of the table. I sat, back straight, chin up, feeling a little like when I'd interviewed for my job at Mickey's. *Here's a resume of my life, Dad. Sorry you're not in it, but you were busy with other things.* But I didn't want to talk about me.

"You know your son is here," I said. "That Elias, or whatever his name is, took him and six other boys."

My father's gaze never once left my face. "It's why I came," he replied. "I received a message not long after it happened and

I immediately set out. I have been traveling night and day."

What did he want? A Boy Scout badge?

"A message from whom?" I asked.

"From your uncle, Petraeus."

*Petraeus?* "You mean *Pete?* But Pete's in Crownsville."

He took from his pocket a palm-sized stone, sapphire in color and highly polished. He placed it on the table between us. I snatched it up. "I've seen this before! On the living room shelf."

"It's a parler stone," said Bromasta, still watching me intently. "A communication device. This is one of a pair. Your uncle holds the other."

"So you've been checking up on us."

"More regularly than you know."

I ran my finger across the surface and caught my face reflected back. My frown was so deep it reminded me of Oscar the Grouch. I pictured Pete alone at the house. I saw the blue stone on the bookshelf. Crownsville had never seemed so close. "We should call him."

Bromasta took the stone from my hand and laid it back on the table. "There's nothing Petraeus can do to help."

"But he might care to know that I'm still alive!" I caught the accusation in my tone as soon as I'd said the words. I paused. This wasn't about Pete and polished stones. "What are you doing here?"

"I came for you and Jaylan."

"His name's *Jay*. And you've had years to do that. Why now?"

"Because everything your mother and I'd planned for you has unraveled."

My heart kicked as soon as he said "mother." This was going to be harder than I thought. He was holding back, almost as much as I was. You could see it in the tension around his mouth, the deep ridges on his forehead, and the white knuckles of his clasped hands.

"Where is she?" I asked.

"She is gone."

"Gone? Or dead?"

He failed to reply. It didn't take a genius to put it together. "It's because of what she did, isn't it?" I said. "She stole the necklace."

It was only when Bromasta looked to the doorway that I remembered that Sol was there. "How much does she know?" he asked him.

"Not much," replied Sol. He turned away, clearly wanting no part in the conversation. "I'll be outside if you need me, Mia." He closed the door behind him.

"Why did you leave us?" I asked, as soon as we were alone. "I can look after myself, but *Jay*? He's just a kid."

"We had no choice," said Bromasta. He shifted in his seat and the scent of horse and sweat rose from his coat.

"I'm supposed to believe that?"

"Giving you up was the hardest thing I've ever done, but I wouldn't have done it differently. If I'd had my way, you would never have come back here."

At least he was honest.

"Too late now," I said. "Why did they kill her?"

It was clear we were cut from the same cloth; he kept his emotions almost as tightly reined as me. But that one question finally made a crack in his businesslike facade.

"Because of who she was," he said.

"And who was that?"

Pain entered his eyes—deep, heartfelt pain, more physical than emotional, and right away I knew that he'd loved her.

"Your mother was the rightful keeper of the Solenetta."

It took a couple of seconds for that to sink in. I'd spent so many years profiling a woman I'd never known, a thief, or worse, languishing in jail, serving time as she deserved. My father's declaration turned the entire theory on its head. All these years, I'd thought my mother was the worst kind of scum and she'd done nothing wrong? The Solenetta had been rightfully hers?

"Your mother's name was Ilalia," he continued. "She was Balian. Born of the bloodline descended from the creators of the Barrier. They, and only they, have the power to manipulate the solens and create a true and lasting Equinox." He'd regained his calm manner. It suited me fine. I could handle calm and collected.

"Then how come other people can use grains?" I asked.

He nodded slowly. Was that a trace of a smile?

"You're sharp, Mia. Tell me what you know."

"Not much," I replied. "A solen grain is in an orb, the orb contains a spell, the spell allows the grain to open the Barrier. But there's no spell strong enough to harness the power of a complete solen. Right?"

"That's right."

"But you said someone with Balian blood doesn't need the spell. That they can open the Barrier using only a solen. So even if Elias finds a solen, it's worthless without one of that bloodline to use it?"

"Without a spell, which he cannot conjure, there would be no reaction. There's no doubt Elias has solens, Mia, yet he's been unable to open the Barrier."

"And that's why he's taken Jay," I said. The explanation felt right as soon as I said it. It wasn't simply about the Solenetta. Elias had been drawn to Jay because of where he'd come from.

"I just assumed Elias was looking for the Solenetta and that he'd thought Jay had it," I stated, my argument gaining strength. "But he was looking for someone Balian—someone who could use a solen. He must have given up on the Solenetta. He's just trying to open the Barrier any way he can.

"But it doesn't make sense. Of all the Balian people, why Jay? Why those other boys? I don't get it!"

"It will be hard to understand unless you know it all."

"Then tell me," I urged.

His hands formed a pyramid beneath his chin, the skin around his eyes crinkling as he watched me. "From the beginning of the Barrier," he said, "the Balians knew of the connection between the solens and the Equinox. Having created the Barrier, they devoted themselves to remaining its master. They experimented, tested its powers, its limits. They found that individual solens created a brief, temporary Equinox. It was the idea of a Balian Elder to link solens, to harness their power in a single entity that alone could effect a true and lasting Equinox."

"So they made the Solenetta?"

"And in doing so, created an object of such power that it could transform the future of our world and its Barrier. They did not fear what could be brought about through individual solens; it was a reaction they'd long ago mastered."

"And the Solenetta?"

"An entirely different entity, one of such strength that anyone who wielded it could induce the Equinox at any Barrier weakness, however small. Using the Solenetta required no training, no skill. It is a key that opens the Barrier.

"Such power would need all of Balia's protection. So they made a decision. In each generation there would be one—and only one—bound to the Solenetta by magic. Only one could use it."

"And at one point that was my mother?" I asked, stunned.

"It was," said Bromasta. "And Elias, through his many travels, his many guises, learned this. Your mother left Balia during the Great War. It is a long story I have no care to tell you and one the Balians would rather forget. Still, Elias hunted her to the valley."

"He destroyed the valley to find her?"

"Partly. The valley wasn't safe anymore, for anyone, especially Rheinholds. We took you when you were just a baby and gave you and the Solenetta to Petraeus. He hid you on the Other Side with a woman we knew from this world."

"Grandma," I said, nodding.

"She was no blood relative, Mia. She was a magician who'd fled following the Purge. She had the skills to protect you. She kept you safe. Petraeus kept the Solenetta himself—away from you, where you and it were safer still."

"But you said only one in each generation could use it. That was Mom." Chilled, I paused. "Hold on. I used the Solenetta on the Ridge."

"That is right, Mia," said Bromasta. "The Solenetta was passed to you. You are its rightful owner."

Clearly he'd made a mistake. Why would it pass to me? I'd never even been to Balia! It belonged with someone who knew what they were doing, who understood solens and the Equinox and magic, not a high school student from Nebraska! Bound by magic? What did that even mean?

But I saw myself on the Ridge, the Solenetta in my hand, the Barrier opening before me. And the night the demon had taken Jay, the Barrier had been closing by the time I'd gotten there. That is, until I'd stepped onto the Ridge with the Solenetta around my neck and the great wall of light had expanded. The Equinox.

"You passed it from Mom to me," I said, disbelieving though I understood. "Before you sent me to the Other Side."

Bromasta nodded. "Using a spell Ilalia conjured. We had no choice. Elias would never have given up looking for her. It had to pass on. With you and the Solenetta safely on the Other Side, we eluded Elias for many years. When Jaylan was born—"

I straightened. "We have the *same* mother?"

"Yes."

The blonde in the photograph with the sad but beautiful eyes. *She was my mother too.* "What happened to her? How did she die?"

"Eventually Elias's men found us," Bromasta replied. "They took her. Though the Solenetta was safely beyond his reach, Elias found other solens and tried to force Ilalia to use them to forge another opening, however insignificant it might be. Your mother resisted. She was strong, Mia, but strength only lasts so long."

Horror-struck, I listened to his tale. No wonder Sol had kept quiet about the necklace. If I had been in his place, I wouldn't have wanted to be the one to tell its story either.

"Increasingly desperate, Elias searched for those of your mother's bloodline, determined to find any person who could connect with the solens in his possession. Balia itself was closed to him. Following the Great War, they'd barred their doors, creating an impenetrable web of spells and enchantments. All Elias could do was to look for others in Brakaland who shared Ilalia's blood. That was when I removed Jaylan from this world."

"And that's why they've taken him." My voice strained. Everything that had happened since Alex had disappeared, since Jay had seen his mom in the cornfield, flashed before my eyes. "They found out you had a son on the Other Side, they just didn't know who. Elias's demons weren't snatching random kids. They were looking for *Jay*. They're going to make him open the Barrier."

"They'll fail," said Bromasta. "Without the Solenetta, Elias cannot create a lasting Equinox, no matter how hard he deludes himself that he can. He's looked for the Solenetta. He hasn't found it. All he has is a pitiful belief that the son of Ilalia Rheinhold might bring down the Barrier with individual solens."

"But he might know something you don't! He has Jay. He has solens."

"You're not listening, Mia. An individual solen is dumb without a mind tuned to its power. Jay does not have that power."

"How can you know that? You haven't seen him for seven years!"

Pain again entered Bromasta's eyes. "When I took Jaylan to the Barrier, I placed a solen in his young hand," he said. "Nothing. Away from this world, he's never learned the skills necessary to manipulate the stones. He cannot help Elias. Only the Solenetta, in the hand of the one bound to it, can create the lasting Equinox."

"Then Elias is on a false trail."

"There is only one who can use the Solenetta, Mia. Only one that it hears. You."

I put my head in my hands and tried to digest what I'd heard. For the first time since stumbling into Brakaland, the story did actually make sense. All of it. Only, it was impossible. "This is bad."

"Not as bad as you think," Bromasta replied. "Elias doesn't

know you exist. He knows only that Ilalia bore a son. He doesn't realize that she passed the Solenetta to her daughter long before Jaylan was born."

"He knows someone opened the Barrier," I said. "You should hear the talk in Bordertown!"

"But he doesn't know it was you. That is our greatest strength. And now we have to get you out before you're found."

"And if I am found?" I asked. "I'm not my mother! I can't stop the Barrier from opening. I've already used the Solenetta and I didn't even know what it was then! We'll have to destroy it. I'll use grains to get me and Jay back."

"It can't be destroyed, Mia."

"Of course it can," I exclaimed. "How else did they get grains? They ground up solens. Let's grind it up."

"It can't be done. The Solenetta cannot be destroyed."

I felt like a time bomb waiting to go off. My mother, Jay, Pete, me—all of us were wrapped up in a tale of which I wanted no part. And then there was this man, Bromasta Rheinhold, my father.

Stunned, speechless, I sat as Bromasta wearily removed his coat and placed it on the table. Beneath his coat, he wore a deep green shirt, the sleeves rolled up to his elbows. I frowned.

"The tattoo," I said, pointing to his arm. "You have the tattoo."

Bromasta glanced at his forearm where the Lunestral lay strong and true.

"I was the king's man for many years, Mia," he said. "Before the madness of the Purge forced me out of that court of lies. But I am the king's man in my heart. Many who support his reign bear his mark."

*The mark of a king.*

"That's what it means?" I asked, my mind racing. "It's connected to the king? Then why did you tattoo Jay?"

Bromasta shrugged, clearly surprised by my interest in something he obviously considered of little note. "The Lunestral's protection is always granted to the sons of those who stand at the king's side," he said. "I am now a Freeman, Mia, but King Solander is my friend. A good friend. An old friend. The Rheinhold family stands by him, no matter what disagreements we may have had in the past."

For the first time in my life, I wished I had that tattoo. I'd swap it for the Solenetta any day of the week. I'd seen how invulnerable Sol had been to the demons and the shadow imps.

My heart kicked, then raced. My mouth dried. I stared at Bromasta, but I saw only the dream bird's wings in red and gold, green and blue stretched from shoulder to shoulder, from neck to hip on Sol's back.

"Sol," I said. "He has the tattoo."

"Solandun? But of course. He is descended from the Lunestral. Its power is in his blood."

"The king," I said, my voice falling into a hush. "You said his name was *Solander*?"

"Solander the Second of the House of Beseye."

Everything slipped into place. Sol's father was in the West. Malone's wariness around him. Why Sol had worried he'd be recognized at the store.

"It can't be," I whispered, though already I knew it was true.

Solander.

Solandun.

Sol.

I looked at my father. "He's the king's son."

I sat on the steps in the alley outside Vermillion's walled yard, my emotions lurching between shock, embarrassment, and rage. Solenetta? Fate of the world? A long-lost father turns up on the doorstep? Small fry. I'd fallen hook, line, and sinker for a guy descended from the dream bird. I'd fallen for the king's son.

Okay, I knew it could never have been. I knew I belonged in Crownsville and Sol belonged here. But it had been nice to pretend.

There was no pretending anymore. The time we'd just spent together walking Orion's streets. When we'd stood side by side in the valley and he'd told me about the Falls of Verderay. I'd gotten it all wrong. It was as Delane had said. Sol thinks about one thing and one thing only—defeating Elias and closing the Barrier forever. And I was the means to do it.

A chirrup came from across the alley, and from behind a crate, a gutterscamp scurried into the open, drawn by the scraps of food left here during the day. It offered me a cursory glance before darting back behind its crate where I knew it watched me.

"Hey, buddy," I said, strangely glad for the company and wishing my life was as straightforward as a gutterscamp's.

Its eyes peered out. I pulled the Snickers from my pocket, the one Sol had given me to bribe the gate guard. "I know you want this," I said. I took off the wrapper and held it out. "Come and get it."

The gutterscamp took a couple of dancing leaps, but stayed well back. It watched me, head to one side, its long neck stretched. I tossed him the candy bar. The little guy snatched it up.

"You really shouldn't feed them."

It was Sol. I hadn't heard him open the gate to Vermillion's yard behind me. The gutterscamp took one look, and then bounded into the shadows. Stomach churning, I turned away. "It looked like it hadn't eaten for days."

"It'll follow you everywhere now."

He stepped through the gateway, then sat at my side without invitation. I pulled away.

"What's wrong?" he asked.

There was no avoiding this, no matter how much I wanted to. What was I going to do? Hide from him until the moment I stepped back through the Barrier?

"He told me everything," I said.

Sol leaned forward, trying to catch my eye. I stared at his hands, unable to trust myself to look at any other part of him. From this moment on, he was strictly off-limits, rescuing Jay our only connection. The illusion of him was fading like ripples on the surface of a pool.

"I was in Crownsville to watch you, Mia," he said. "Why else do you think I'd go to that awful school?"

"I don't know," I replied, empty inside. "You tell me."

Before I thought to stop myself, I looked at him. His expression had reached an even deeper level of intensity: his brow straight, his eyes narrowed, the muscles in his jaw tightly clenched. It felt like a billion years since the first time I'd seen him from the Ridge.

"You see now how important it is that you leave," he said.

"And how important it is that you stay."

He frowned.

"He told me *everything*, Sol," I said. "So what do I do? Bow like Gus?" I hesitated. "*Gus*. He knew about this, didn't he?"

Sol's manner switched the second it became clear that I knew who he really was. His shoulders sagged. He covered his face with his hands, drawing a deep breath through his fingers. When he reappeared, he looked resigned.

"Gus is from this world," he said, clearly deciding to ignore the most pertinent part of the massive secret I'd unearthed. I wasn't about to let him off so easy.

"And how many others knew the heir to the throne of Brakaland was hanging out in Crownsville?"

He stiffened at the sting in my tone. I was glad.

"It isn't like that, Mia," he said, his voice low, with a faint hint of warning.

"I think it's exactly like that," I snapped. "The dream bird—symbol of the king. That's a pretty big set of wings you carry around with you."

"I tried to tell you," said Sol. "I wanted to. Outside the Velanhall, I was trying to find a way. Will you let me explain?"

"You don't have to explain," I replied. "You said it yourself a thousand times: Nothing's changed. I want my brother back and I want out of this place. I want school. I want Willie. I want to forget that any of this ever happened."

He flinched. Or did he cringe? How simple my life must have seemed to him. He was the king's son, a fighter in a great and endless battle. He was as rooted in this world as the trees and rocks I'd seen in Welkin's Valley. And he was surrounded by women, like Vermillion Blue with her supermodel curves and major-wow skin, who knew exactly who he was, and what it would mean for them if they could land him.

And me? Well, I was just Mia Stone from Crownsville, Nebraska. Silly old Mia who'd thought she'd met a guy who overshadowed the great Andy Monaghan. When, all this time, I'd just been a pawn in his war.

I couldn't explain that I was heartbroken, mortified, because that meant confessing how I felt about *him*, and that just couldn't happen. Not now. But what I felt more than anything was crushing disappointment. I had been growing to trust Sol so deeply, and all that time he'd concealed the essence of who he was.

I brushed my hair from my face and pulled myself together. What else could I do? I'd felt sorry for myself for long enough. "So what time do we hit Malone's tomorrow?"

Sol held my gaze, drawing back any trace of emotion until it was almost as if we'd never talked at all. "I think it's best if you don't come."

"I'm sure that's true," I remarked. "Doesn't mean that's what's going to happen."

"Mia, after all your father—"

"Please don't call him that."

"After all *Bromasta* told you. Our greatest weapon is that the Suzerain doesn't know you exist."

"I'm not a weapon. And I'm coming."

"I'll not have you risk yourself like that."

*Risk myself?* This was a joke. As if he cared. As if *any* of them cared.

I got to my feet, anything to get away from him. "Sol, all any of you care about is that stupid necklace."

"Mia . . ."

I groaned. "Here we go again! Mia, what? You think I can't fight? You think I can't battle day in and day out and still have the strength to turn and smile sweetly to the world? Well, I can. I've spent my entire life doing it, thanks to that *man* in there."

"He's your father, Mia," said Sol. "And he's a great man."

"Then lucky for you he's on your side. We'll get your necklace and then you can do what you want with it. All I care about is Jay."

I barged past him for the gate before he could say another word, fleeing from the weight of shock and disappointment that grew heavier and heavier on my shoulders. Too many thoughts raced through my brain. I could not escape them.

Determined to avoid any more confrontations, I charged through the house and locked myself in my room. And then I did the only thing I could think to do, the only thing that could take me away from this nightmare.

I slept.

# TWENTY-THREE

woke to raised voices. Daylight streamed through the window. I bolted upright, convinced I was back in my bed in Crownsville. But then I realized that the voices weren't Pete or Jay's and that the faint perfume I smelled wasn't mine or Willie's. Fully dressed, I threw back the comforter and headed for the door. My stomach growled as if I hadn't eaten for weeks. But none of that mattered. I crept downstairs.

"Bromasta, she can do it."

It was Sol, his voice a hurried whisper. Bromasta's quickly followed.

"I did not send my daughter away only to have her return to this! She can't control the Solenetta's power. It would be her hands that opened the Barrier. Her hands that started the war."

Hating that I'd gotten pretty good at all this sneaky stuff, I perched on the bottom step and strained to hear what was happening in the kitchen.

"She won't leave without Jaylan."

"She will do as she is told. She's my daughter, Solandun."

"You don't even know her! She's strong. She's held that family together. I've seen it."

Silence. I gripped the banister, preparing for a quick escape should the kitchen door open. Whatever they were talking about, Sol was clearly on my side, which surprised me after our conversation last night.

"Is there something going on between you and my daughter?"

A second pause. I held my breath for Sol's reply, knowing the answer, yet wanting to hear it from him nonetheless.

"There's nothing between us."

"I deserve to know."

"There's *nothing.*"

My stomach fell.

"Because I'll not have her mixed up in the politics played out there in the West. Her mother and I left court for a reason. I don't want that kind of life for her."

"Bromasta, this is about Mia and the Solenetta. She has every right to fight with us. Who but she can say that the fate of the Solenetta is also literally a fight for her life?"

Another pause. This one was weightier, strained. My skin prickled from the adrenaline that flooded my veins. A fight for my life? Whatever that meant, it didn't sound good.

"You didn't tell her," said Sol.

I scootched to the edge of the step, closing the gap between myself and the kitchen, if only by inches, so as not to miss a single word.

"She is my *child*, Solandun."

"Whose blood is in the Solenetta."

"As it was once my wife's blood. Yes, I know we are bound to that . . . *thing*."

"Then she doesn't know what will happen if the Solenetta's destroyed?"

"You think I'd let my child live under a death sentence?" he spat.

*Death sentence?* Bromasta hadn't mentioned anything about blood or death sentences yesterday. He'd said the Solenetta had been passed to me, like it was no big deal, like it was the most natural thing in the world. What kind of game were they playing?

"There are many who still talk about doing it," said Sol. "If they know of this trouble, it'll give them all the ammunition they need to argue that it should be destroyed."

"Why do you think I got Mia and the Solenetta out of this world? Why do you think I sit here now, my own child a stranger to me?"

"Linnett has my father's ear—"

"Linnett is a spineless wretch. He has more faces than a visage demon."

"Yet his supporters grow in number. They'll come for it, Bromasta. And this time not even I will be able to persuade my father not to destroy it. Is that what you want?"

"How dare you! I gave up my children to prevent that."

"But that's exactly what will happen if we don't get the Solenetta back and it and Mia out of Brakaland. She has a right to help us do this, Bromasta. She has a right to fight for her own life."

The kitchen door opened before I could bolt, not that I could have run if I'd wanted to. My heart had emptied and the blood that it once contained had pooled in my feet.

It was Sol. As soon as he saw me, he froze. I shook my head, unable to do anything else. The walls closed in; the reflections in Vermillion's mirrors repeating the scene over and again. Behind Sol, I caught Bromasta's figure pacing the kitchen. Whatever this new revelation meant, I knew I couldn't face the man who'd cursed me with this inheritance.

I spun around to the front door and was out on the street in seconds. With no clue where to go, I sprinted toward the alley at the back of the house. All I wanted was to be alone because being alone was the only way I would ever be safe again.

A distant drumbeat, like I'd heard in the valley, drifted through the streets as ominous as any demon's scream or sentinel's call. I stopped. It was the parade, or some preparation for it. The Suzerain was back and the Solenetta might soon be in his hands.

"This can't be," I cried. "It isn't real!"

"Mia."

Sol stood at the head of the alley. It was Sol as I wanted him to be, his face overflowing with concern. Still, I put out a hand to keep him away, needing my space if only just to breathe.

"The veins in the stone," I choked out.

He didn't flinch. "Your blood."

*"How?"*

"A blood rite. They made the change when you were a baby. When they knew the Suzerain would come for Ilalia."

The tale got worse and worse. With each new revelation, I felt my grip on reality slip a little further away. A week ago none of this had been in my life. Now my very existence was threatened by a complex war I barely understood.

"Why would they do something like that?" I asked, my voice on the edge of hysteria. "Sol, Bromasta said it was just a spell. He didn't mention any blood rite."

Sol took a step closer. He stopped when I waved him back. "They had no choice, Mia," he replied. He raised his hands, a promise that he'd keep his distance. "The Solenetta had to pass on from Ilalia."

"But Bromasta said she could control it, that she could resist its power."

"Only with solens. Not with the Solenetta. It was too great a risk to keep the Solenetta bound to her. They passed it to you and thought you'd be safe on the Other Side."

"So if it's destroyed, I die too?" My voice rose yet another notch. "Did I get that right? Who wants to destroy it, Sol?"

"There's a faction that has my father's ear," he replied, and this time he stepped forward. I didn't stop him. "They've argued for it to be destroyed ever since the Purge. It's those who believe that magic is too dangerous and unpredictable to be kept in this world."

"Why do they get to decide? They didn't make the Solenetta. It isn't theirs."

"That won't stop them," he said. "Your father, me, many others—we've kept the Solenetta's location a secret. But there are many who would see it found and destroyed. You're nothing to them, Mia. Dispensable. A worthy sacrifice."

I knew it must have been hard for Sol to tell me about the blood rite. He hadn't wanted to tell me about Bromasta and the house I'd been born in and that information wasn't even in the same league. But I could tell that he was determined to see this story through.

"They'd see me dead?" I said, unable to believe it could be true. "Even though they know Bromasta?"

"Especially," said Sol. "He has enemies at court.'

"Enemies that would see his children killed?"

"Enemies that care more about preventing Elias's war on your world than saving one life."

And I was that life. I was infuriated. Everything bad that had happened in my life had all been because of that necklace. I'd had never known my parents because of it. Despite all of that, I'd fought to get where I was at school and at home. Seventeen years of hard work. They weren't taking that away from me.

"Then we really have to get that thing back to Crownsville! I mean that. We have to get to Malone's. Sol, you can hear the drums. The parade's starting."

"We still have time," he replied.

As if my bones had suddenly melted, I slumped against the wall, overwhelmed by everything I now knew. "On one hand, the Solenetta's preserved and I start a war. On the other, the Solenetta's destroyed and I'm toast."

"Mia, no," said Sol, his tone laced with regret. He came

toward me, stopping right in front of me until all I could see was him. "Neither of those things will happen."

"You can't know that."

"I won't let them happen."

"How can you stop it? Can't we take it to Balia? They can do what my mother did. They can pass it on. They can keep it there."

"The Balians won't intervene," Sol replied. He drew closer. "I told you that things didn't go well for them during the Great War. Your mother thought they should help too. That they could use the power of the Solenetta against Elias, that they could use it for good. She was Balia's brightest star. Of high blood, keeper of the Solenetta. Adored.

"But then she met your father. She fell in love. She never returned to Balia, and the Balians never forgave your father for taking her away. They turned their back on us and the Solenetta, knowing that its presence in Brakaland would keep the threat of war alive forever. It was their punishment for stealing their daughter."

"Then I'm done for," I said. "There really is no hope."

"Don't say that." Sol took my hands, gripping them tight against his chest. "You said it yourself last night: Nothing's changed. We get the Solenetta. We get Jay. And then we get you both back across the Barrier. You're strong, Mia. You know how things are now. You know what to look out for. You know there are people in Crownsville who can protect you."

"Is Crownsville even safe anymore?"

"Safer than here."

But Crownsville would never be the same. Gone were the days of volleyball and debate. How could I even think about such things when I knew I was the key to starting a war between two worlds? It would never end. Some night Elias would send a visage demon and what could I do to stop it? I wasn't my mother. I'd never even met her. How was I to learn all she'd known about solens and the magic of Balia?

"How can life change so quickly?" I whispered to Sol.

Our hands remained entwined, tight between our chests. Inches more and we'd be as close as you could get without doing things you really shouldn't do in an alley behind somebody's house. This was the place I'd prayed to be, right? But being close to Sol felt more complicated than ever. He was still the king's son. And I was now the girl with my head on an executioner's block.

But staring death in the face had done something to me. I didn't care about consequences anymore. What could be worse than what I knew? I had to tell Sol how I felt about him before it was too late.

"Sol—"

Before I could start, Sol's lips drew closer to mine. Hands

holding the side of my face, he guided me into his kiss. Everything forgotten, I reached for him, too. His fingers grazed the back of my neck, the pressure of his touch increasing as he held me to his lips—not that I had any intention of pulling away. His other hand slid down my back and then gripped me tightly at the waist, drawing me in until our bodies touched at every point.

With my head tipped back, I swayed in his arms, but Sol wasn't about to let me fall. Never once missing the beat of his kisses, his arms encased me and he effortlessly drew me closer, almost lifting me off my feet. Heat rose between us.

Craving the touch of his skin, I reached for the hem of his shirt and felt the firm muscles in his back. He responded immediately to my touch, his gentle kisses taking on a harder edge until it was impossible to know who wanted this more.

And then he stopped.

Our faces remained together, almost cheek to cheek, the tip of Sol's nose grazing my skin, his breath warm against my ear. "Mia, I'm sorry," he whispered, his voice soothing and deep.

*Sorry?*

"I shouldn't have done that."

He'd kissed me. *Sol* had kissed *me*. Was it possible he felt for me what I felt for him? I had to know.

"Just tell me why," I gasped between breaths. "I didn't think you . . . When did you . . . ?"

"Always," he said. "It was Delane who stopped me."

There was no space between us, no room to breathe. He had to feel how fast my heart was beating. I stepped back, but didn't get far, as the wall behind me blocked my retreat.

"He told you?" I asked, shocked that Delane would break his promise to me and tell Sol how I felt.

Sol looked down at my face, his body towering over mine. "Told me what?" he asked.

Then Delane hadn't told him. "Nothing," I stammered. "It's just . . . I don't believe this is happening."

He analyzed every inch of my face, his expression so earnest, so open and honest. How was I ever going to keep my hands off him?

"I wanted to tell you, Mia," he said, "but there didn't seem any point. None of this was about me. It was about you. As if you needed me harassing you on top of everything else."

"*Harassing me?*"

"I think you're beautiful, Mia," he said. "Smart. Tough. The way you've handled everything that's happened—it's unbelievable to me. How I felt? That was my problem. I couldn't let it get in the way. Your safety came first. Always. I thought about telling you, but then I saw how close you'd grown to Delane and I . . ."

"*Delane?*"

"The two of you were always laughing, finding fun, even

during the worst of what had happened. I could see how close you'd grown."

"It was that or go crazy," I replied, frantically. "Sol, it didn't mean anything."

"It meant something to me." He took my arm, squeezing my wrist as if willing me to understand. "Mia, Delane is like my brother. Whatever he wanted, if I could give it to him, I would. But not you."

This was a dream. The times Sol had watched us with that strange look in his eye . . . "You were jealous of Delane?"

"I'm not proud of it," he said. "And if there is anything between you, please say, and you won't hear another word of this from me."

"Delane's my friend, Sol," I replied. "That's all."

Sol's eyes twinkled, his lips moving as if to smile. I couldn't let him smile, not if we were to avoid doing things you *really* shouldn't do in an alley behind somebody's house. I slid from between Sol and the wall, certain that if I didn't move I'd be unable to stop myself from dragging him to the ground there and then, to hell with the world and its problems. That couldn't happen. There was too much I had to say.

I put a few feet of distance between us before I spoke, "Then I'd better tell you too. Delane knew I was crazy about you. He saw through me from the start. He warned me off."

Sol frowned. "What did he say?"

"That all you care about is the war and that there isn't room in your life for anything else. I have to know, Sol. Is that what I am? Just another pawn in your war?"

"Mia, no," he said, aghast. "Why would you even ask that?"

"Because this is complicated," I replied. "Sol, just think about your life. You have all of Brakaland to worry about. You're the king's son, remember?"

He came at me, his long legs covering the small gap between us in an instant. "I remember," he said, his voice low. "And for just a second, why don't you think about what that means."

Right away, I saw the change in his expression. It was the look he'd flashed the sentinels in the Wastes. Shoulders back, head up, a warning of danger in his eyes. That was how he looked at me then. He looked like a king's son.

"Every second watched," he said. "Every decision crucial. So few people I can truly trust. The daughters of men I can't stand thrown in my path night and day all to further ambitions at court. A click of my fingers and whatever I want is there— money, friends, *girls*."

I flinched. "Is there a point to this?"

"Yes," he replied, and he took my hand. "*You* are the point. I never told you who I was because I cared about you, Mia. I didn't want that between us. People change around me when they know who I am. You're one of the few people whom I can truly trust."

The intensity in Sol's expression dissolved. He wandered to the step at Vermillion's gate and then sat.

"I'm sorry," he said. "Mia, you just say the strangest things sometimes. If this was about the war, Jay would have gone to the Suzerain and that's where he'd stay. Jay can't manipulate the Barrier. It would help our cause more to let Elias keep the boys and waste his time wondering why he can't forget his Equinox. If this was about the war, I could have taken the Solenetta on the Ridge and you would never have seen me again."

"You would have done that?" I asked.

"I didn't because of you, Mia. The night Jay disappeared, I went back to the Ridge with the Solenetta and the grain I'd saved for my return. If the police hadn't been searching the rise, I might have crossed over, and never come back. Instead, I returned to Tiamet's, and used the map to search for other weaknesses where I could sneak through.

"But I couldn't do it. I couldn't stop thinking about your face on the Ridge when Jay'd disappeared and how you'd looked at me when I'd lied about what had happened. Your brother was gone and you'd never know where he was and you'd never get him back. Your life would have changed forever. You had friends, but you were an island among them, different. Jay being gone would have isolated you even more. I know how that feels."

I hung back, arms folded, stunned that he'd felt this way and never said a word. "Do you mean your life in the West?" I asked.

"You don't want to hear about that."

"I do." Wanting to be close to him, I joined him on the step. "You must have given up so much in leaving your home. I can't believe the people at court let you do it."

"It was my choice," said Sol. "Besides, I answer to no one but my father."

"So what's it like out there?"

"It's a city of politics," he replied, his voice thick with disgust. "Politics and pandering. I was born into it, but I've never wanted it. Everyone's too busy forcing their own agenda, scrambling for a place close to my father. I have only to ask and there would be a place for me on my father's council. No one refuses the king's son."

"Instead you're sitting on a step with me," I said.

He smiled. "Which is exactly where I want to be."

"But you're in the middle of a battleground here, Sol. It's dangerous, especially if you're recognized."

"Everything is dangerous these days," he replied. He leaned back on his hands, his legs outstretched. "I volunteered for the Sons of the West as soon as I was old enough to be of help. My father supports that decision. It was the right thing to do. Talk only takes you so far; if we're to defeat Elias, we need to be where we can see him."

"And if your father . . . you know."

"You mean, what happens if he dies?"

I shrugged.

"A king here isn't the same as a king in your world, Mia," he said. "He is an elected official. My father was elected because he comes from the line of the Lunestral and that is needed in a time of demons."

"So if something happened to him you'd be elected too?"

"It's too soon to say."

I thought about what he'd told me at Bromasta's house about one's path to adulthood in Brakaland. "But that's why you're here, isn't it? You're proving yourself worthy."

"No," he said. "I am here to help stop Elias's war on your world."

The drums continued their thrum and the occasional cheer rose from the streets. Here we were, sitting side by side, talking of blood rites and kings of faraway places moments after sharing our first kiss. Brakaland and its problems weren't about to wait for us.

"This is a mess. What are we going to do?"

"I don't know," said Sol.

I welcomed his hug. The space between his shoulder and his

neck—it was like it was made for me, it fit just right. I squeezed back as hard as I could. The Suzerain himself couldn't have made me let go. Being with Sol felt like home.

We broke from the embrace, but Sol's arm remained around my shoulders.

"You know Bromasta's going to kill you if he finds out about us," I said. "He didn't seem happy about the prospect of you and me."

Sol grinned, his face alive and alert. "Bromasta, I can handle. I'll have him thrown in jail."

"Do that anyway," I declared. "I still haven't forgiven him for dumping us."

"But one day you will," said Sol. "You have the capacity to forgive, Mia. I see it in you."

I didn't want to admit it, but he was probably right. What would I, or anyone else, have done in Bromasta's place? Could I have left my kids in Brakaland when I knew what their futures would be? That would have been as cruel a choice as the one Bromasta had been forced to make in hiding me and the Solenetta. Don't get me wrong; he was a stranger to me. As hard as I tried, I couldn't find any trace of daughterly love simmering inside me. But I did now feel bound to him. Our family had been destroyed in order to keep the Solenetta safe. I couldn't let that sacrifice be for nothing.

"We should get ready for Malone's," I said, though inside I felt reluctant to leave. Sol and I should have been together to talk and to touch. There was no time.

He gently held my face. "Mia, after all you've heard, do you really think you should come?"

I held Sol's gaze, drawing on his strength, determined he see my strength, too. "More than ever," I replied. "It's my blood. I want it back."

He kissed my forehead, his hand stroking my hair. "Then we better break the news to Bromasta."

We found Bromasta at the kitchen table studying architectural plans. As soon as we entered, he looked up.

"It's the Velanhall," he said, gesturing to the papers. "I don't know what changes Elias has made to the place. The Velanhall was never used for prisoners. But he must have Jaylan somewhere secure."

My father appeared fresher than the night before, but the wrinkles around his eyes were deep. The parler stone lay on the table, but I didn't ask about Pete. Bromasta had been right about that. Pete couldn't help me now. It was time to play my cards.

"I understand why you didn't tell me about the blood rite," I said. "All that matters is that I know. It's better that I know."

Bromasta pushed the drawings aside. "A million lifetimes wouldn't be long enough to make amends for what we did to you."

I glanced at Sol before joining Bromasta at the table. "My life's actually been pretty good," I said. "I'm not saying that I never thought about you or hated you for leaving. I certainly didn't think you were in another world."

He took from his pocket a notebook bound in battered leather and held together with a silver cord. He opened it to a wallet-size photograph, which had been tucked between the pages. "It's the only one I have," he said, and handed me the picture.

It was my second-grade portrait, the one with the blue turtleneck and missing front teeth. "Where'd you get it?"

"I have my sources," he replied. "I always knew how beautiful you'd grow up to be, and I was right. How could you not, when your mother was the most beautiful woman in the world?"

I handed back the picture, suddenly self-conscious of Sol seeing my toothless grin.

"Parting with you and Jaylan was the hardest thing I've ever done."

"You did what you had to do," I said. "Now it's my turn. The Solenetta is a part of me. I have a responsibility to keep it safe."

He watched me intently and a look of pain entered his eyes like when he'd spoken of my mother. "Why did we ever give you up?"

"Because you had to," I said. I offered him my hand. "A truce?"

It was like looking in a mirror when he smiled. "Of course," he replied, and shook back.

His touch broke something inside me. This was my *father*.

"Okay," I said. After a moment, my hand fell back to the table. "Now how the hell are we going to get this thing back?"

# TWENTY-FOUR

Sol drew a map of the streets around Malone's safe house, and we huddled around it on the kitchen table.

"Cloaks on as soon as you're in position," he said, again pointing to our marks in the alley behind the hideout. "Mia, you're in charge of supplies. Stay close to me or Delane. Under no circumstance does anyone pass by the eye out front."

"And me?" asked Bromasta.

Since calling our truce, Bromasta had barely moved from my side, but he seemed resigned to the fact that I was going to Malone's, and for that I was grateful.

"You really shouldn't come," said Sol. "You're a dead man if you're spotted out there."

"One could say the same for you," Bromasta replied.

"But my face isn't plastered across every reward board in town."

This was interesting news.

"Is that *true*?" I gasped.

Bromasta made a sound in the back of his throat that might have been a "yes." So my father was a wanted outlaw. It was actually pretty cool.

"What did you do?"

Bromasta shuffled, uncomfortable in the spotlight. "I put the Solenetta far from the Suzerain's reach."

"And wiped out one of his demon armies on the Theadery Plains," said Delane. "The Suzerain doesn't forgive and forget."

So Sol had been right. My father was a legend. And by the sound of it, a hell-raising legend at that. "You really did that?" I asked, impressed.

Bromasta raised an eyebrow and scowled at Delane. "It was a long time ago."

"But not forgotten," said Sol. "We can't risk your being spotted with us. We go in as opportunistic thieves—nothing more."

There was one problem we hadn't yet discussed. "So how do we intercept the delivery guy without anyone noticing? It's a pretty big part of the plan."

"We lure him somewhere quiet," said Delane.

"And how do we do that?"

Delane grinned. "That'll be with Vermillion Blue."

Vermillion entered on cue. I kept my gaze firmly off Bromasta's face. Having seen the "Vermillion Effect" in action, I thought I'd vomit if I caught the same dreamy look in my dad's eyes.

"No offense, Vermillion," I said, as she sandwiched herself between Sol and Delane, "but everyone in town must know who you are. You're not exactly hard to spot."

"Then we will make it hard." She snuggled against Delane. "Delane, you choose. I know you have favorites."

"Twenty-eight," crooned Delane. "Do twenty-eight."

I tried not to laugh. Vermillion was growing on me, especially since I knew that she and Sol weren't together. I don't think I'd ever met such a self-confident person. I would have loved to have seen her in action with Kieran and Seth; she'd turn them both into quivering wrecks.

Though Delane looked like he'd be happy to have Vermillion stay at his side forever, she swept to the corner of the room where she drew back a curtain revealing an alcove of shelves, crammed with bottles and jars. "Twenty-eight," she said, scanning the rows. "Here she is."

She returned with a small green jar. "Beseye," she said, and, after unscrewing the lid, removed a strand of long, dark hair. "A touch of Balian, though weak." She inhaled. "And Fauna Demon somewhere along the line. Unusual mix."

Beyond mystified, I stared, as mesmerized as Delane. "I love twenty-eight," he said, almost drooling on the table.

Stunned and slightly repulsed, I watched as Vermillion placed the tip of the hair on her tongue and then closed her mouth.

The change started gradually: a couple of twitches beneath Vermillion's skin. Her lips, firm and plump, pursed to a heart. Her ice-blue eyes darkened to brown. Vermillion's scarlet hair blackened and then *receded* into her scalp until it lay at shoulder length. Her silvery skin transformed to tan. And as all of this happened, the metamorphosis gained pace elsewhere. She was shrinking, for one.

There was no violence or jerkiness to the transformation. Everything slipped and slid, like melted chocolate poured into a mold. And where it settled, it set, until finally Vermillion was gone, and a petite dark-haired girl, who couldn't have been much older than me, stood in her place, her body dwarfed by Vermillion's long white gown. The girl—*Vermillion?*—smiled and the entire face came alive with a stunning, exotic beauty. She looked Hawaiian to me—big brown eyes, golden tan, glossy waves of ebony hair. Gorgeous.

I scanned the others' faces, but they weren't shocked like

I was. Delane in particular. The only way I could describe his expression? Half-baked.

I looked back at the girl. "You've got to be kidding," I blurted. "Did that really just happen?"

"I'm rarefied Simbia, Mia," said the girl, her voice deeper than Vermillion's. She batted huge black lashes at Delane. "A shape-shifter. And this is number twenty-eight. Delane's favorite. Do you think our man will like her?" She raised her arms and twirled. Vermillion's gown almost slipped down to where it shouldn't. "Now excuse me," she whispered, and she pulled the strand of hair from her mouth.

"You are still Vermillion, right?" I asked. I couldn't help it.

"Of course," she replied, as she returned the hair to the jar. "But I need a template to change. I found twenty-eight in Jova City many years ago. So *beautiful*.

"'Vermillion,' she said to me. 'One day I will be old and ugly. Use this hair. Keep my beauty alive.'

"Now she is a part of my collection." She pointed to the jar-filled closet. "And now I must change this dress. The girl is so short. How did she see anything from down here?" Clutching the dress to her body, she breezed to the door, but not before she shot Delane another provocative wiggle.

"We're gonna use Vermillion to get into the Velanhall, right?" I said, as soon as she'd gone. The costumes in the upstairs closet finally made sense. "She could transform into a guard."

"She'll be part of the plan," said Delane.

"But this is perfect. She even has guard uniforms in the upstairs closet. It's simple."

"It's not as straightforward as you think," Bromasta replied. "Not even a guard can wander at will into the Velanhall."

Okay, so my father was a glass half-empty kind of action hero. I'd yet to hear a better suggestion.

"Let's just worry about Malone for now," said Sol. "We're going to need the decimators. Where's the bag?"

"It's upstairs," replied Delane.

I jumped to my feet. "I'll get it," I said, glad to prove I could be useful. "I am supposed to be in charge of supplies."

Inside the guys' bedroom, the bag of spells lay on a chair beneath the window. I checked what was left—a handful of repellers, plenty of the exploding decimators Sol had used on the demons, and a couple of larger greenish-yellow orbs that I didn't recognize.

The distant drumbeats penetrated the room's silence and my nervousness returned. It was getting close to the time when the celebrations would begin in earnest and the parade would start its slow journey through Orion's streets. And the Suzerain? Was he already here? Might I even see the man who'd brought so much darkness into my life?

I stared at the decimators as I envisioned the parade marching by. Just one man had caused so much trouble. I imagined him waving to the crowds, me among them. I'd shuffle closer to the road, reach into my pocket and . . .

"Did you find it?"

I snatched up the bag and spun to find Sol at the door. "They're right here. I was just coming down."

He closed the door and then sat on the bed. "Mia, are you sure you want to do this?" he asked.

"I'm sure," I replied. "I'm nervous, though."

The drums rolled and I clutched the bag of spells more tightly. This was it. Any minute we'd leave the house, and, with a little luck, the Solenetta would be back in my hands. Would Sol stick to his word? Or would he force me back to the Barrier as fast as he could? That was all for the future. First, we had to get the necklace back.

"Do you really think this is going to work?" I asked. "Malone must know who you are. Why doesn't he say something?"

"He knows only that I work for the king," said Sol. "He doesn't know I'm his son."

"Then why doesn't he turn you in?"

"Because if he does, he knows what will happen to him when we topple Elias. You don't earn loyalty from a rat like Malone. You trade it."

Happy to spend these last few minutes alone with Sol, I came to his side, trying not to think what it would be like to fall back onto that bed with his arms around me. Now really wasn't the time.

"He's going to know it was us," I said, carefully placing the bag at my feet, conscious of the decimators inside.

"But we're not going to give him proof."

"Does that even matter?"

"Depends on what Malone does once he finds the Solenetta missing. He may say nothing and slope back to Bordertown to lick his wounds. Coming clean to the Suzerain creates problems for him, too: why he didn't pass it to the Bordertown sentinels; why he hung on to it here. I'm sure he could talk his way out of it, but any deal with the Suzerain is risky. If he does confess, things could turn bad here. It could be dangerous for you."

"Don't worry about me." Changing the subject, I said, "Besides, we've got Vermillion on our side. I can't believe no one told me about her. Did you see my face?"

Sol laughed. "You said Delane told you."

"He skipped that part."

"I'm not surprised," said Sol. "Delane's been wildly in love with Vermillion since we were kids. She came to court when we were eight or nine. That was it for Delane; he's never been the same since. He's incapable of rational thought when she's around."

"Then you've known her a long time."

"She knows my father from years back."

"How old is she?"

"Older than you think."

I recalled Vermillion's tale of the girl from Jova City. How long ago had that been? Was the girl now old, her fears realized? Or maybe she was dead, her wish immortalized in Vermillion's skin. I wasn't sure if it was romantic or creepy.

"Vermillion doesn't swipe hair off pillows, does she?" I asked, thinking of my bed next door.

"You don't want to end up in one of her jars?"

"No, thanks. She's gorgeous, but I feel like she's dangerous, too. Like a cute dog that might bite."

"You have good instincts," said Sol. "You should never underestimate Vermillion. She's one of less than a hundred rarefied Simbia left."

"Why so few?"

"They've always been rare," he replied. "And then Elias hunted them to virtual extinction."

The Suzerain. Was there no misery in Brakaland that he hadn't caused?

"I don't understand why he'd do that," I said. "I'd want the Simbia on my side."

Sol slowly nodded. "He used their blood to create the visage demons."

Sickened, I pictured Vermillion in all her glory, tried to imagine towns, cities filled with other beautiful Simbia. And then I thought of the visage demon beneath my window in Bordertown—cold, cunning, devoid of all the life that made Vermillion what she was.

"That's awful," I said, though the words didn't come close to describing how I felt.

"He's found other ways to do it now, using what he learned from working with Simbian blood," said Sol. "But he's made very dangerous enemies of those who've survived. Vermillion amongst them. She joined the Sons of the West, determined to make him pay. I have no doubt she'll achieve that. Shape-shifters are formidable opponents."

It was all so wrong, as wrong as Narlow's deserted streets and the sentinels who struck fear in Bordertown. How far would that monster go to get what he wanted? Did he care about anything, or anyone?

"Sol, if you had the chance," I said, "if you got close enough, would you kill him?"

Sol had a curious look in his eye. "I don't know," he said.

"But you must have thought about it."

"Many times."

"He can't be allowed to get away with this. He's destroying your world."

"What do you think this is all about?" he asked, raking his hand through this hair.

"I don't know," I replied. "Boys playing games?"

"If only it were." He twisted toward me and placed his hand on my leg, forming a small intimate space between us. "He's dangerous, Mia. He sees a world without the Barrier—a collision of cultures that could never endure. We know so little about what he plans to do next. We only know that we can't let him get started." He took my hand and his fingers entwined with mine. "Just stay close to me out there, okay?"

I smiled. "Like glue."

"I'm serious. You shouldn't even be coming."

"But you know there's no way to stop me, so you're stuck."

"This isn't a joke," he said, but he was smiling too.

Yearning simmered inside me. It was both addictive and terrifying that I could feel this way about one person. He leaned in for a kiss, a light brush of his lips against mine. It wasn't enough. Nestling in, I rested my hand on the bed, my other reaching for his face, his hair. *Stop, world*, I chanted. *Just stop.*

Sol kissed me once more, his gaze lingering on my eyes as he pulled away. He didn't want to stop either. I could see it in his face. With a half smile, he groaned. "We have to go," he said. "You definitely won't change your mind and wait here?"

I shook my head.

I watched him head for the door, torn between following him or calling him back. I suddenly had a shiny new plan. We could rescue Jay and then stay here, hidden, forever. No one would know. I could be with Sol. Elias could have the Solenetta. Without me it was useless to him anyway. Until he discovered how to break the spell that bound it to me, or cracked its secret in some other way. . . .

With Sol's back toward me, I glanced at the bag on the floor and images of the parade returned to my mind. I hated this Finneus Elias, and that wasn't a word I used very often. I *hated* him. But maybe there was something I could do about that.

As Sol left the room, I reached for a decimator and dropped it into my pocket.

# TWENTY-FIVE

A massive boom resonated through Orion's streets and an explosion of multicolored stars cascaded across the sky.

"I guess that's it," I said. "It's started."

"Then let's hope the celebration brings out most of Malone's men," Vermillion replied.

We waited at the head of a dark passage, which cut between the stores on the side street where Sol and I had followed Malone's man. It was quieter here than the day before; most of Orion's population lined its main thoroughfares. Rubber Man and his audience had gone. I peered down the street to where Delane casually waited on the other side of the store. We'd be in place for some time. I prayed we hadn't missed our man.

"Still nothing," I said, and shuffled back. "I don't think I've ever been this nervous."

"Think of the result. It is worth a little fear."

Vermillion remained in the shadows, almost invisible in a long black cloak. A deep hood shrouded the face of the Jova City girl. "Sol told me what happened to the Simbia," I said, and looked beyond her to where, far back in the gloom, Sol waited too. "I'm sorry."

"It is long past," the Jova City girl's voice replied. "But it will be avenged when that monster and his demonic hordes are wiped off the face of this land."

"I don't know how you can to be so close to him and not try *something*."

"I have patience," she said. "Great patience."

I adjusted the bag on my back, heavy with cloaks and spells, ropes and bindings, and thought of the decimator in my pocket. Would the chance come to use it? For Vermillion and the Simbia, for the valley, for Jay, for me.

A familiar chirrup came from close by. Round eyes watched us from a gap where the bricks had crumbled from a wall.

"Just a gutterscamp," said Vermillion, with a loud exhalation.

The eyes blinked twice and then disappeared through the gap.

"It scared me to death," I gasped.

Heart pounding, I caught a breath before again peering around the corner toward the store. A man headed our way with crates piled high on his cart. Delane was hot on his heels. This was it!

"He's coming," I said. I offered Vermillion a final smile. "Good luck."

With everything in place, I sauntered onto the street and to the window of a storefront across from the passageway. From out of the corner of my eye, I tracked the man and his cart. Thirty feet. Twenty . . . Hand dangling loosely at my side, I made ready to shoot Vermillion her signal.

Ten . . .

Five . . .

Now!

I pointed to the ground.

A heartbeat passed and then Vermillion burst out of the alley and into the delivery guy's path.

I'm not proud to say that I learned a couple of things from Vermillion that day. From the moment she threw back her cloak, the delivery guy was doomed. She exploded brighter than the fireworks that sparkled overhead, a rich aroma of flowers and spice sweetening the air around her. Never once missing a beat, she kept to her story—ironically about a necklace, a gift from her dying mother, which had fallen into a drain.

"Help me," she urged, her chest pressed against the man's arm, her eyes wider than a gutterscamp's. *"Please."*

"But my cart!" spluttered the man, though his eyes seemed more interested in what was bursting out of the front of Vermillion's dress. "It'll get nicked. Find someone else."

He was not yet convinced, which meant it was time for "Concerned Onlooker" to take a shot at the Oscar.

"I couldn't help but overhear," I said, springing to the man's side and prying his fingers from the cart. "You can't just leave her. I'll guard this. Show us where you dropped it, lady. We're right behind you."

"You're so kind," purred Vermillion, and seizing the helpless guy's hand, she led him into the shadow-filled passage.

Once the guy was safely off the street, I parked his cart about thirty feet down the narrow passageway. Ahead, Vermillion simpered in the man's arms. She led him toward a deeply recessed doorway, close to where Sol lingered, hidden in shadow. Soon Delane appeared off the street, heading after the pair. With Sol waiting ahead and Delane following behind, the man would not escape.

I spoke no word to Delane as he passed, but handed him the rope he needed to bind the man and the strip of old blanket that would serve as a gag. By the time the man was found or freed, we'd be long gone.

My role complete, I left the cart in the passage, and returned to the street to keep watch. Distant music played. Fireworks exploded overhead. Barring a disaster, everything was in place.

Though I knew I shouldn't, I glanced behind me, hoping Sol and Delane were going easy on the guy, but I could see little in the shadows. It was probably for the best. Sol beating up on Malone was one thing; the weasel deserved it. But the delivery guy? He was just in the wrong place at the wrong time.

It didn't take long for Sol and Delane to complete the job and emerge onto the street, leaving Vermillion to transform into the delivery man.

"He won't get out of that for a while," said Delane, when he and Sol joined me.

"Tell me you didn't hurt him."

"Of course not!" he exclaimed. "The poor man was just trying to make his delivery."

"Yeah," I said. "Right into our hands."

A couple of minutes later, wheels rattled on cobbles behind us. Vermillion had picked up the cart from where I'd left it. The Jova City girl was gone.

"That's just freaky," I said, when I saw Vermillion's latest incarnation clothed in the delivery guy's brown pants, yellow shirt, and boots. "You didn't leave him naked!"

"Don't worry," said Delane, and winked. "Vermillion left him her dress."

"Here's our spot," said Sol. We ducked into a doorway in the alley behind Malone's hideout. "Cloak on."

We'd sprinted across town, leaving Delane to track Vermillion as she navigated the crowds with the cart. All we had to do was wait.

"It's crazy out there," I whispered, as I put on a cloak from the pack and raised the hood.

"Should make it easier to get away."

"We've got to get in first."

Sol periodically checked the alley as I rummaged through the bag for Vermillion's spells. It was all planned. She'd gain entry as the delivery guy, then stun Malone's men with a decimator. Following her signal, we'd enter, find the Solenetta, then get our butts back to the safe house as fast as we could. Simple.

"Don't forget the counter spell," said Sol, as he adjusted his cloak. "Never release a decimator in a confined space without the protection of the counter spell or you'll knock yourself out in the blast."

"Got it," I said, and held up one of the large greenish-yellow orbs.

The minutes crawled by until, finally, the rattle of wheels

approached and then the cart and Vermillion appeared. Gaze forward, she offered out her hand as she passed. Now she was safely off the street, I placed the two spells on her palm before ducking back into the shadows.

Delane arrived moments later. "The parade's at Tanner's Row. I'd say that gives us fifteen minutes before it passes this way and the crowds start to thin."

"Is that long enough?" I asked, offering him a cloak from the bag.

"It'll have to be."

"And Vermillion?" asked Sol.

Delane peered out, paused, then drew back into the doorway. "Just gone in."

This was it. Though Sol and Delane appeared calm, panic rose in my guts. I pressed myself against Sol's side, searching for the reassurance his physical presence usually provided. For once, it didn't work. Too many things could go wrong: Vermillion wouldn't get past Malone's men; she'd forget to use the counter spell and knock herself senseless with the decimator; or we'd get in and the Solenetta wouldn't be there.

"Get off! *Get off*, why don't you?"

I snapped out of my worrying to find Delane tugging at his leg. A gutterscamp had appeared at his feet. It pawed the hem of his cloak.

"Get off," he said, yanking again. "It was in the other alley too. It must have followed us across town."

"It followed us from Vermillion's," said Sol. "Mia was feeding it last night."

Delane stopped, mouth agape. *"What?"*

Suddenly conscious that this was my fault, I pretended nothing was wrong. "That was him?" I asked. Its cute round eyes peered up.

"Mia, you never feed a gutterscamp," said Delane, and again yanked his cloak away.

"Well, I know that now," I replied. "Go on, boy. Beat it."

The gutterscamp gave a final tug, and then sprang off down the alley.

"I only gave him a Snickers," I muttered.

Delane brushed down his cloak. "You know they carry screes. Get those in your hair and you'll—"

I never found out. A muffled bang traveled the alley. A long, trilling whistle followed. Vermillion's signal.

Sol peered out. "It's her," he said, and the gutterscamp was forgotten. "We're in."

Three men lay passed out on the kitchen floor with the delivery of bottle-filled crates scattered around them. Vermillion, in her delivery man's guise, ushered us past.

"Malone?" asked Sol.

"Not here," Vermillion replied in the man's voice. "Hurry. I'll bind them. You find the Solenetta. Mia, the bag."

I handed it to her, then followed Sol deeper into the house.

Inside it was cool and quiet, the only noise the sound of distant singing. A narrow hallway bisected the building with doors on either side. Paintings, of what appeared to be Orion's streets, hung on the walls. About halfway down the passage, a narrow staircase led to the second floor. I tried to listen for footsteps overhead, but the singing from the parade grew louder, like a choir walked the streets, their voices airy and light, their words lost in the melody.

"You go up," said Sol. "Call to me if you find anything."

Jittery, I climbed the narrow stairs to a square landing. Three doors edged the space. Body braced for what might follow, I opened the closest one.

Malone's Bordertown collection had been impressive. What greeted me here was a nightmare. There was not an inch of space to squeeze anything more into the room. Pictures, clothes, teddy bears, saucepans filled it floor to ceiling. There was even an old tin bathtub buried beneath the clutter. If Willie was right and collecting trash really was a defense mechanism against misery, then Malone had some serious issues. Fifteen minutes until the parade passed by? It would take me fifteen hours just to get through the door.

*Mia* . . .

Suddenly frozen, I turned my ear to the air. "Hello?"

Silence followed, but I'd definitely heard my name. Poised to run, I listened for the others downstairs. Nothing.

*Mia* . . .

Again. Definitely a voice. In fact, it was a whole host of voices whispering at once. And that song I thought I'd heard outside had grown louder.

I turned slowly, fixing my gaze on the opposite door, convinced that was where the voices came from. The song rose again.

*Mia-hasee-ah-mia-si* . . .

"Who is that?"

Heart thumping, I crept to the door and gently pushed it open. Beyond lay a large room, decorated with heavily carved furniture and richly woven rugs. Daylight flooded through a wide window. Sweet perfume lingered. The singing voices swirled, beautiful, lighter than anything I'd ever before heard. Certain again that they must have come from outside, I hurried to the window where crowds mingled below, jockeying for position in readiness for the Suzerain. Sentinels and guards kept them back. There was no choir.

. . . *hasee-mia* . . .

"Who's there?"

*And what were they saying?* I made for the door, but got no more than a few steps before I stopped. The hair on my arms bristled. The skin on my neck tightened. I felt *watched*. There was no other way to describe it.

I looked back to the window, expecting to see a face peering through. But no face appeared. *What was I thinking?* I was on the second floor!

Then maybe it was the four poster bed and the beady eyes of the animals that had been carved into it that had me on edge. Their teeth and claws looked as if they could spring to life and pounce.

Spooked, my gaze swept to the side of the bed. A wooden jewel box lay on top of an end table, its image reflected in the mirror behind.

*Mia . . . mia . . . mia . . .*

I dashed across the room and snatched the box from the table. The voices I'd been hearing soared as something shifted inside it. Heat rose from the wood. This was it. The Solenetta. It had to be.

Hands trembling, I opened the lid. As soon as I saw those golden stones, relief flooded through me. The stones were unharmed, the veins intact. Even the chain's broken clasp had been repaired. Elated, I threw back my hood and reached inside. Images burst in my mind when I touched the Solenetta. Crystal blue waters. Mountains and streams. Birds flying above forested peaks. Fountains. Palaces. It was almost as if I stood inside the scene. It *was* my name they'd called. It was the voice of Balia. . . .

"You called out!" Sol stood at the door, his eyes wide with concern.

The images vanished. The song ceased.

"Sol, I found it!" I gasped. "It called to me."

Sol hurried to my side, the concern on his face morphing into relief. *"How?"*

"I don't know. But I saw a place. I think it was Balia. I *heard* them." I laughed. "Sol, I got it back!"

Sol tentatively touched the stones as if he expected something wild and miraculous to occur. The solens did not respond.

"Mia, we have it," he said. "Now let's get out of here."

I was never going to lose it again. Ever! I securely fastened the necklace around my neck, then tucked the stones safely beneath my clothes.

Sol glanced out of the window, waiting for me as I secured the necklace. "It's crawling out there," he said. "We should go."

I put the box back on the table, then went to raise my hood. I stopped. My heart raced at the reflection in the mirror behind the box. I backed away, tentatively touching Sol's arm. I pointed up.

Malone's eye watched from the ceiling. I don't know how I'd

missed it—it was at least twenty inches across. I knew what I'd felt watching me. I glanced at the jewel box—there was no lock or bond key. With those voices singing and my name whispering on the air, I'd never stopped to wonder why Malone would leave his treasure so unprotected. Now I knew. He'd been spying on us the whole time.

"We're in trouble," said Sol. His gaze on the eye, he gestured to the window.

A gang of at least ten sentinels closed in on the house, pushing bystanders out of the way as they approached.

"What do we do?" I cried.

"We run."

He didn't need to say it twice. We tore downstairs.

"They know we're here!" Sol yelled. "Everyone out."

Vermillion guarded the men, who were blindfolded and bound in the kitchen. *"How?"*

"There's an eye upstairs," I replied, as Delane rushed into the kitchen. "He knows we're here. There are sentinels heading this way. They're right outside!"

"But did you find *it*?" said Delane.

Sol was already at the door. He stripped off his cloak. "We got it," he said. "Cloaks off. We split up. Get back to Vermillion's—any way but by a direct route."

"I don't know the way," I said.

Sol opened the door. He cautiously checked the alley. "You're coming with me," he said as he hurried Vermillion and Delane through the door. "If we get split up, follow the towers to the Velanhall. I'll find you there."

I grabbed his hand, the magic and mystery of the Solenetta long gone. Malone knew it was us; even if I hadn't lowered my hood, he would have seen my reflection in the mirror. Border-town would definitely be closed to us now. Would we even make it back to Vermillion's?

"Vermillion and Delane are gone," said Sol, after again check-ing the alley. "You ready?"

I nodded.

"Then let's see how fast you can run."

We didn't get far. No sooner had we entered the alley than grunts and growls came from close by.

"They're coming," I said.

We sprinted left, toward a narrow passage close to Malone's that cut back to Maslian's Square. Sol stopped. He pressed his back to the wall and peered around the corner. He quickly pulled back. "No good," he whispered. "They've blocked it."

I ducked low and peeked. A sentinel gang waited at the head of the passage. Their aim was unclear. Keep others out? Or keep us in? I checked in the direction of the house, expecting more sentinels to stream into the alley from behind.

"We can't go back," I said. "We'll never make it past the house."

"Then we'll have to run for it."

"Toward the *sentinels*?"

"If we wait much longer, they'll cut off the other end of the alley too."

"But they'll see us go past," I whispered.

"Keep your eyes forward, your head up, and whatever you do, don't fall."

I took a couple of breaths and tried to gauge the distance to the street. I used to get pretty good times in track. The end of the alley couldn't have been much more than a hundred meters.

"This is nuts," I said.

"You can do it, Mia."

I again checked behind. The sentinels had not emerged from Malone's.

"Remember," said Sol. "Head to the Velanhall."

I hesitated, no longer liking the tone in Sol's voice. "Sol—"

He squeezed my hand. "You've got the Solenetta," he said. "Don't look back." Before I could stop him, he tore toward the gang of waiting sentinels.

It was an utterly psychotic act. And all just to give me a few precious seconds to get away. I couldn't waste them.

Head up, eyes forward, I sprinted as hard as I could. A hundred meters had never seemed so far. All I could picture was Sol among the sentinels that guarded the passage. He *was* crazy. He couldn't fight that many. And outrun them? He didn't stand a chance.

A deep voice called from behind—*"Get her!"*—and I stumbled as I glanced back. Sentinels poured out of Malone's. Their gargantuan feet pummeled the cobbles as they picked up speed. But thirty . . . twenty . . . ten meters and I'd make it to the street, thanks to Sol.

The sounds and scents of the crowd drew me—cheering, clapping, and a sweet aroma like melted toffee or fudge. The Solenetta bounced around my neck, pounding against my skin like an external heartbeat. It was a part of me. I couldn't let them take it back.

Five . . . four . . . three . . .

A final push and I burst free of the alley.

To the right, the street was almost empty. But to the left, a large group had gathered on the corner of Maslian's Square. I headed for them with one mission in mind: lose the sentinels in the masses. Another group merged with the one on the corner. And then another. And another.

A cry went up from behind, *"That way!"* But it was too late. I was already deep in the crowd.

The drums beat ever louder. Bodies surged to catch sight of the Suzerain's approach. Elbows out, I forced a path in the direction of Malone's hideout, searching for Sol. There was a commotion as the sentinels pushed through the crowd.

Head down, crushed on all sides, I pressed on. But it was no good. For every forward step I took, the crowd forced me three steps to the side. Bodysurfing the mosh pit had never been my thing. Claustrophobia hit. Fireworks exploded overhead and massive cheers erupted. With a final surge, I was pushed forward and out into the front of the crowd.

A wide path arched across the square to the street that led toward the Velanhall. Lines of guards held back the masses. On the far left, the Suzerain's cavalcade appeared.

It started with a row of sentinels and then a troop of guards who marched in step with flags and pennants outstretched. Dancers came next. Musicians. Acrobats and jugglers. The Rubber Man from yesterday posed on a moving platform.

The people went crazy around me. Why did they cheer the man whose plans would see Brakaland enter a war with no end? How did the Suzerain dare to face the people when he was responsible for so much death? Cheer as they may, no one knew that I stood with the one thing the Suzerain most wanted around my neck—something I would never let him have.

I scanned the faces in the crowd, searching for someone,

*anyone*, opposed to this madness. Instead I caught movement on the opposite side of the square. A group of guards had broken free of their duties and pursued a figure that dashed along the edge of the crowd. Sentinels followed.

"Sol," I whispered. I ducked between the guards to see better. It was no good. Every time I moved, one stepped to the side and blocked my view. I jumped, feigning interest in the parade, cheering and clapping with those around me.

One guard broke from the line to push back a man who'd stepped onto the route. The pursuit across the square became clear. A young man darted in and out of the crowds. But it wasn't Sol.

It was Delane.

The parade forgotten, I pushed into the guards, battling to get out into the street.

"Keep back!" bellowed a guard.

The chase continued. Delane swerved in and out, heading to the right and somehow keeping out of reach of the guards he passed. The sentinels gained speed. Another pack approached from the right. Clearly, Delane hadn't spotted them. He was sprinting right for them!

The flag bearers at the head of the parade were less than fifty feet away. The crowd went crazy and pushed again. Delane ran toward the sentinels.

Gripped with panic, I reached into my pocket. My fingers closed on the decimator I'd saved for the Suzerain. I had no choice; I couldn't let them take him. Eyes closed, I said a prayer. And then I crushed the decimator between my palms and hurled the spell into the crowd across the square.

# TWENTY-SIX

Energy surged from the epicenter of the blast, knocking me, and everyone around me, off our feet. The drums stopped. The music ceased. Chaos erupted.

Terrified I'd be crushed, I scrambled up as the crowd began to flee. The guards, many of whom were also down, battled to hold back the herd. Delane was nowhere to be seen.

A man beside me got unsteadily to his feet. He pointed a shaky finger at me. "She did it!"

Time to go. I spun around. Three guards approached from the rear.

"It was her!" cried the man, outraged. "I saw her throw it. She tried to kill the Suzerain!"

Guards closed in to my left. Sentinels to my right. Soon they'd formed a wide ring around me. Onlookers drew close until a deep wall of bodies surrounded me. There was nowhere left to run.

One of the guards broke free of the ring. "Is this her?" he shouted, heading my way. "Is it her?"

An annoyingly familiar voice again rang: "That's her! I saw it! She was after the Suzerain!"

Frozen, I didn't dare speak. I glanced at the sentinels on my right, praying they weren't the ones who'd chased us from Malone's. I was in big trouble if they recognized me.

The crowd fell silent as another guard entered the fray. He was taller with a scarlet uniform, which stood out against the other guards' gray. "Is this the one who released the decimator?" he demanded, forcing his way to the front.

"This is the one," said the first guard, again pointing at me.

"Then take her!" the leading guard barked. "Make way for the Suzerain!"

The ring of guards closed in. A hand grabbed my arm. As quick as that, I was under arrest.

As they herded me away, the enormity of what I'd done hit me. In one stupid moment, I'd blown our entire plan. As if they would ever have caught Delane with all those people! Malone would be looking for me too—the eye had seen me. It wouldn't take long for the guards to put it together. And here I was, alone, arrested, and with the Solenetta around my neck.

The guards marched me from Maslian's Square to a covered, sentinel-drawn wagon. There was no sign of Sol.

"In," said the guard to my right. He flung me forward. Another guard waited by the cart.

I took another look for Sol, but, other than a few onlookers, there was no one on this part of the street. I climbed up, slipped between the tarp flaps at the rear of the wagon, and then perched on one of the two benches inside.

The tarp blocked much of the sunlight, and the air inside was close and hot and smelled vaguely of mildew and sweat. Veering between stunned disbelief and outright panic, I grasped the Solenetta beneath my shirt and prayed for it to call to me again, to offer me some kind of help.

How was I going to get out of this? I prayed that Sol or Delane or *someone* had seen what had happened. They could save me. Or Bromasta—he'd defeated a demon army on the Theadery Plains! Busting me out of a wagon couldn't be so hard. But what if they didn't know? Sol would be waiting for me on the Velanhall's steps. Delane, if he had any sense, would be sprinting to Vermillion's as fast as he could. I'd be clapped in irons before they'd even realized I was missing. Word would spread of what had happened at Malone's. And then the Suzerain would come for me.

Rocking through the cobbled streets, we slowly made our way through Orion. From time to time, the flaps in the tarp caught in the breeze and I'd catch sight of a sentinel guarding the step at the rear of the wagon. I crossed "make a run for it" off my dwindling list of options.

The wagon stopped abruptly and a guard appeared at the rear. "Out."

Tall white buildings surrounded a courtyard filled with wagons and horses, guards and sentinels. A white tower rose into the clouds above. It was the Velanhall.

Seizing my arm, a guard led me to a wooden desk manned by more guards. "We've got another," he said, and hurled me toward them.

"Crime?"

"Releasing a decimator in a public place and within reach of the Suzerain!"

It didn't sound good when he said it like that.

The guard at the desk watched me from beneath thick bushy eyebrows. "Speak!"

But what to say? I'd never been in trouble with the cops or even at school. My attitude to authority was pretty straightforward: Do what's expected of you, keep your head down, and people pretty much leave you alone. Now I had to think—fast. And that was difficult mid-meltdown.

"It was an accident," I stuttered.

Bushy eyebrows shot into the guard's hairline. "An accident?"

"Yeah." I glanced at the guard at my side. "It was in my pocket and . . ."

"And?" asked the man.

"And I thought it was going to get crushed." I watched closely for a hint that they were buying my story. It was difficult to tell. Best to keep talking. "We were packed really tight. So I took it out to keep it safe, but this guy behind me pushed and . . ."

The guard at the desk leaned forward. One of the eyebrows sunk. "Where are you from?"

I forced myself to hold his gaze. "Fortknee."

It couldn't have been more than a couple of seconds that we stared eye to eye. It felt like hours. If brains were made of clock-work, then this guy's cogs and pulleys were definitely whirring. His finger drummed the desk. His mouth twitched at the corner.

"Fortknee," he said. And then, with a dismissive shake of the head, he backed down! "I haven't time for this. Seventeen arrests already today. She'll have to wait. Take her to the pit."

Without a word, the guards at my side forced me through a door at the rear of the courtyard and into the Velanhall.

My first thought when we stepped inside was that I'd passed through yet another Barrier. This was one of Sol's worlds within a world, a vast concourse of polished marble with columns that

rose to a high, vaulted ceiling. The room stretched on forever—
it had to run the width of the entire Velanhall, at least the length
of a city block. In the center lay a crystal-blue pool, larger than
the pool at Crownsville High. Water blossomed from fountains hidden beneath the surface. Two or three hundred people
walked here, all of different races. Their voices and footsteps
echoed.

I didn't get long to take in the space before one of the guards
shoved my shoulder and marched me to the left, away from the
pool, and toward a narrow wooden door.

"Stop!"

One of the guards grabbed my jacket. Confused, I turned,
just as the guard to my right sank to his knee. One by one, everyone in the concourse did the same. Silence fell. Only a small
group of about twenty remained on their feet. They headed
toward us, flanked by sentinels and guards. Then the sentinels
parted. There stood a tall, thin man dressed in a three-piece suit
of pale gray.

As soon as the man stepped forward, those who'd walked
with him also bowed. The Solenetta grew heavy around my
neck. I resisted the urge to grab it.

It had to be. I knew it.

Finneus Elias.

The Suzerain.

I don't know where he'd got that suit, but it was definitely from somewhere expensive and it was definitely from somewhere on the Other Side. He appeared neither young nor old and had cropped dark hair. You might have guessed he was a lawyer or a stockbroker. He certainly looked out of place here. He moved with the confidence of a man who didn't care that everyone watched him. In fact, he looked as if he enjoyed it. The heels of his polished black shoes clipped the marble floor.

"So this is the young lady who disrupted my parade," he said, his voice smooth and deep. I noticed his eyes—one purple, one gray. These were the eyes of the man who'd killed my mother. "So now I am rushed back here when my people wished to see me on the streets. What is your name?"

I knew what I wanted to yell—"I'm the sister of the boy you snatched!"

Instead, I said, "Poppy Pillows," then kicking myself, added, "*Fellows*. My name is Poppy Fellows." My voice echoed off the marble walls.

He looked as though he was trying to remember the name. "You don't seem certain."

"It's Poppy Fellows."

The fountains trickled in the background. The guards breathed deep at my side. Tension was ripe in the air.

"You speak as an American, Poppy Fellows."

Sweat broke out on my palms. Talking to the guard had been tough, but this was unreal. I couldn't take my eyes off him.

"I'm a Runner," I said, determined, yet failing, to keep my voice calm. "I spend a lot of time on the Other Side."

"As do I," he replied, seemingly oblivious to everyone around us. "Poppy, you are a young and pretty Runner. What is your trade?"

He had to ask. Reluctantly, I pulled my phone from my jacket pocket, again conscious of the Solenetta heavy beneath my shirt. "I've got this." I held out the phone. "It doesn't work."

Elias's gaze never once left my face as he took the phone, flipped it open, and ran his finger across the buttons. The keypad and display lit up. "And now it does," he said.

He began to pace and I felt all of us—me included—waiting on his next word. My runaway heart pounded in my ears.

"You remind me of someone," he said, and stopped in front of me. "Like the dark shade of a little light I have found." His mismatched eyes narrowed. Long fingers reached for a lock of my hair. "I have ways of making people speak the truth, Poppy," he warned.

He stood as close to me as Sol had been in the alley that morning, but now he turned, his arms wide to the crowd, bringing our audience back into the exchange.

Scarcely able to believe I was still standing, I struggled to hold my ground. "I'm telling you the truth," I stated.

"That you accidently released a decimator in Maslian's Square?" He spun back to me. "That's what they told me. It is difficult to release a decimator by accident," he added, his tone suddenly chirpy and light. "You have to squeeze them, you see, Poppy." He clasped his hands tightly together. "You have to *mean* it."

Though his lips were curled into a smile, there was no friendliness in his eyes.

"Poppy, you're going to the pit," he said, and leaned in as if we shared a secret. "While you're there, I want you to think hard about this tale of yours. Not least an explanation for this."

He handed me my phone, the screen still brightly lit. Willie and I grinned back, red-faced, elated in our Crownsville High volleyball uniforms, the court and net visible in the background. I looked back at the Suzerain.

"Think hard, Poppy," he whispered. "I look forward to your revised tale." He stepped away. "Take her down!"

I moved, following a shove from the guards. Gradually the concourse returned to life. I felt eyes upon me, not least the Suzerain's. He knew. He'd seen the wallpaper on my phone's display. Why would a Runner be playing high school volleyball?

I took one look back before we left the room. Far across the concourse, a new group of guards entered the Velanhall.

Between them hurried a small, fat figure. My already quivering heart picked up its beat. However bad my situation was, it could soon get worse.

It was Malone.

The guards escorted me through a dingy tunnel deep beneath the Velanhall. Torches cast flickering amber light on the stone walls. The scent of earth and moisture rose. I constantly checked over my shoulder, certain I'd catch the Suzerain striding down the tunnel with a furious Malone on his heels.

"Face forward," snapped one of the guards, offering me another shove.

My hands balled into fists. I swore I was going to punch him if he touched me again.

The passage ended at a square antechamber. Two sentinels stood guard at a wall of thick black bars. Light from the chamber's torches barely penetrated the gloom beyond, but in what dim light there was, I could see the jagged walls of a rock cavern. There was an icy draft. Though I was glad I wore my jacket, I still shuddered.

One of the sentinels unlocked the bars and a guard ushered me inside. "Get comfortable, Poppy Fellows," he said. "And don't forget the Suzerain's advice. I'd have a long think about what you were really trying to do with that decimator."

I stepped through without comment, determined not to flinch when the bars slammed behind me. I failed.

A vast cavern rose into blackness, a kind of empty nothingness, the true scale of which I could only imagine. Moisture dripped from above and collected in pools at my feet. The ground sloped gently down.

I took a final look behind me. The guards had gone, but one of the sentinels watched from the bars.

"Sleep tight," it growled.

I walked slowly through the corridor of blackness. Far ahead, it was impossible to tell how far, a light flickered, but reaching it meant navigating the blind patch around me. I shuffled to the cavern wall and pressed a hand against the damp rock. With tiny steps, I forged my way through the darkness.

Colder drafts brushed past my skin. I imagined visage demons and shadow imps waiting in the blackness. Winged harpies, like the ones at my father's house, surely hovered above. One wrong step and they'd swoop down, opening my throat with their razor-sharp claws—

A hand grabbed my arm. I screamed from the pit of my gut.

"Mia!"

Gripped with terror, I lashed out at the arm around me. Then my brain latched on to the voice. Uncertainty and then relief hit.

"Sol?"

His voice rang again. "It's me. Stay still." His hand touched my shoulder. "Hold on to me. There's another torch ahead."

I clutched Sol's hand as he led me through the darkness and into the light. A torch, almost burned out, hung from the wall. As soon as Sol's face appeared in the pale glow, I launched myself into his arms. "Thank God," I gasped, and clung on to his shoulders, my face buried in his neck. His scent washed over me. I held it deep in my lungs, a magical elixir offering me strength. It was him. It was really him. I reluctantly pulled away. "What happened to you?"

"I got arrested for attacking the sentinels," he replied, reaching for my hands. "Mia, why are you here?"

I told him what had happened.

"A *decimator*?" he said, once I'd finished.

"I *know*," I replied. "They'd almost captured Delane; I couldn't think what else to do."

I couldn't tell if he was secretly impressed or if he simply despaired that I'd caused so much trouble. I didn't care. He was here with me. That was all that mattered.

"Thank God you're here," I said. "The Suzerain just questioned me himself! I told him it was an accident, but I know he didn't buy it." I handed him the phone. "He just touched it and it came on. Look at the photograph. Does that look like a Runner to you?"

Our backs to the distant guardroom, Sol stared at picture.

"This is bad," he said.

"I'm pretty sure they think I was aiming for him."

"Very bad."

"And don't forget—" I yanked down my collar and flashed him the Solenetta.

His shoulders sagged as soon as he saw it. "We've got to get you out of here," he said.

"What about you? You're in big trouble if he recognizes you."

"He won't."

"Don't be so sure. There's something about him, Sol. When he was talking to me, it was like he knew *everything*. Or that I was ready to tell him everything. What if they search you? What if they see the Lunestral? I'd say the king's son is a pretty big prize. And it gets worse." I again checked for the guards. "Malone's here. And he looked pissed. If the guards hadn't dragged me down here, he would have seen me."

Sol shook his head. "Even if Malone tells the Suzerain what happened, there's no reason for them to link it to you."

"What, not link it to the girl they think tried to assassinate the Suzerain? And what about you? Arrested for attacking sentinels on Malone's doorstep! Even if they don't link *us*, they're going to tear this city apart looking for the Solenetta."

"Which will keep them distracted."

"For how long?" I asked. "Sol, Elias told me to 'think over my story.' He said something about dark shades and a little light he'd found. I think he meant Jay."

Sol paused, thinking over my words. "There's no way he can know you and Jay are connected," he said.

"I would have agreed before," I replied. "Not now. He's gonna come back for me, Sol, and I don't think Poppy the Runner is going to hold up for long. With some idiot at the gate, maybe. But this guy? I've got a bad feeling, Sol. When Elias speaks to Malone he's going to know it was me. We know what he's capable of. We know what he did to my mother."

I gestured to the phone. "I'm not kidding; he just touched it, Sol, and it came back on! How does a person do that? This guy's not using magic orbs—the magic is coming from him!"

"Have you tried to use it?" asked Sol, and handed back my phone.

I pressed the call button and then held it to my ear. "No signal. And anyway. Who would I call? Willie? She's bailed me out of a few tough spots, but this is a little too much to ask." I flipped it shut and then wedged the phone back into my pocket.

"I don't think it's as bad as you say," said Sol. "Not yet. The best case is that they let us stew for a while and then release us."

"And if they don't?"

He didn't reply.

I glanced around, but other than darkness, rock, and the spot of light at the guard station, there wasn't much to see. "There's got to be a way out of here."

"I've looked," said Sol. "This place is huge."

"There has to be a way. We'll split up. We'll keep looking."

"All right." He reached for the torch on the wall. "Take this. And be careful."

"You'll need one too."

Sol peered into the darkness, the gold in his eyes catching the torch's flame. "I'll be fine," he said.

"What, so you can see in the dark?"

"Better than most."

As soon as we set off, I realized that Sol's description had been an understatement. The place was huge multiplied by ten. The deeper into the pit we walked, the more chambers and passages opened on either side.

"I'm going on ahead," said Sol. "You check these caverns. Head back when you're done. I'll find you from the light."

Torch hot in my hand, I headed across the cave to a narrow passage forged through the rock. Water dripped until soon my hair and shoulders grew damp and the torch smoked from the moisture. Like a mythological labyrinth, the passage twisted and turned. Long dead torches occasionally appeared, but most were so damp they wouldn't light when I offered them a flame. Openings appeared here and there. All led nowhere.

I don't know how far I'd gone when the passage veered into a larger chamber. I held the torch high and checked for an opening or shaft. Nothing. But it was drafty—the breeze had to be coming from somewhere. I pushed on, checking the shallow pools for a sign of flowing water.

I stopped.

At first, I thought it was a gutterscamp curled up against the rock. But as I pointed the torch, I knew right away that it was something else. Wide, frightened eyes peered out from beneath a brown mop of hair. Tears had cleaned paths through the grime on his cheeks. I saw the Ridge. I saw Crownsville. I saw the window booth at Mickey's piled high with fried chicken.

"Alex?" I gasped. *"Alex Dash?"*

# TWENTY-SEVEN

Seeing Alex, it was as if the time I'd spent in Brakaland had suddenly vanished. Alex meant Crownsville, where life made some kind of sense and I
wasn't the confused and uncertain shadow of myself that I'd
become since arriving in Brakaland. The past days had been so
crazy I'd never considered how amazing it would feel to see
someone from home. Two worlds collided. Alex was someone *I*
knew—and he was someone who knew Jay.

I wedged the torch into a gap in the rock and then crouched
in front of him. "Alex, it's me," I said, hand on my chest. "It's Mia.
Mia Stone. From Mickey's."

He was filthy, his eyes wide and white amid the grime.

"What are you doing here?" he asked.

"I'm stuck here too."

He blinked a couple of times as if to clear his eyes. "Is my mom here?"

I reached for his hand. "No," I said, and gave it a squeeze. "But you're gonna see her real soon. I promise."

His sneakers slipped on the rocks as he struggled to rise. His jeans were damp, his T-shirt torn. It was hard not to imagine what he'd been through.

"My brother, Jay," I said, my voice echoing down the nearby passage. "Jay Stone, from your class. Is he here?"

"He was," said Alex. He still looked at me as if he couldn't quite believe what he saw. "Those big muscle guys? He kicked one of them. Then they took him and the others."

*Jay was alive!* I tried not to smile, picturing Spud giving a sentinel a firm boot to the shin. That was Jay, all right.

"When did they take them?" I asked, shuffling closer.

Alex shrugged.

"Do you know *where* they took them?"

"I think to the hill," said Alex.

I gestured that I didn't understand.

"It's where they took me," he said. "There was a camp and lots of the big guards. They made me hold a stone."

A solen. It had to be.

"Was it like this?" I asked, and showed him the Solenetta.

Alex's eyes brightened. "That's it! But only one. And not as big. They made us hold it, and then they brought us back here."

And they'd taken Jay there too. They were about to be disappointed again.

I took another look at Alex's disheveled appearance. "Alex, how did you get here?"

"I don't know," he said. "I was chasing Buster and then I saw . . ." His eyes glazed.

"Saw what?"

"Grandpa Dash. But Grandpa Dash is dead. Or maybe—am I dead too?"

"No," I said, pulling him in for a hug. This wasn't the time for a lesson on visage demons. "And neither am I. You've been kidnapped, Alex. But we're gonna get you home. The other boys too." I reached for the torch and took his hand. Alex pulled back.

"You have to take Benny," he said.

Confused, I shook my head.

"Benny," he said. "They didn't come for him this time." He turned for the back of the cave.

I held up the torch and followed.

"Benny doesn't come out much," said Alex, as he led me into a narrow passage. "He hides back here. But they find you. You can't hide forever in this place."

We stopped at a gap in the rock. I pointed the torch inside.

In a closet-sized hollow, a little boy was curled on a nest of leaves, the slimy stuff that collects in storm drains after a rain. He was tiny, younger than Alex and Jay, barefoot, and dressed in a T-shirt and shorts. Bony knees and elbows jutted from his pale, wasted limbs. He watched us with a half-open, lethargic eye. He reeked of dried vomit.

Stunned, I passed Alex the torch. I squeezed inside and knelt at the boy's feet. "Are you Benny?" I asked.

"Ben Griffin," the boy whispered.

I recognized the name from the news. He'd been one of the first boys to be taken. He'd been here for almost six months! Deep, bubbling rage surged inside me.

"Can you get up?" I asked, struggling to keep the anger out of my voice.

"Don't want to," Ben whispered. He snuggled deeper into his nest.

"Benny doesn't talk much," said Alex. "I don't think he can walk very well either."

I shuffled back, hating to leave Ben for even a second, but knowing I had no choice. The splintered remains of a torch rested in a sconce on the wall close by. I snatched it down, hands shaking as I ripped the shreds of damp tinder from the cord that bound it. A clump of dry twigs appeared beneath.

"Alex, I need you to wait here with Ben," I said, and poked the kindling into the flaming torch in Alex's hand. "Can you do that?"

He nodded.

"Keep the torch up and I'll be able to find you. Don't move."

"Where are you going?" he asked. A tear glistened in his eye.

"Be brave," I replied. I leaned in for a reassuring hug. "I'm gonna go get help."

Adrenaline saw me through the return journey to the main cavern. Two images flashed—one of Ben Griffin wasting away in filth, one of me on the Velanhall's concourse with the Suzerain in my reach. Why had I wasted that decimator in the crowd? I should have rammed the thing down his evil throat. But then again, if I'd never released the spell at Maslian's Square, I wouldn't be here. I would never have found Sol and Ben and Alex. I would never have learned that Jay was alive.

I found Sol prowling the area where we'd split. "I've found two of the boys," I said. "It's not good."

We raced back to find Alex still waiting at Ben's den. When Alex saw that I wasn't alone, a smile blossomed on his face.

"This is Sol," I said, ushering Sol forward. "He's going to help you too. And he's really tough, so don't think he can't get us out of here."

Sol shot me a warning look. I shrugged. I knew it was a big promise. But these were kids, right?

I pointed to the gap where Ben hid. Bent at the waist, Sol shuffled through. As soon as he was clear of the rock, I passed the torch in to offer him some light, then poked my head inside. As the cramped space lit, Sol dropped to his knees, Ben's body tiny beside him.

"Do you think it's safe to move him?" I asked.

Sol wasn't about to wait and find out. He got his arms beneath Ben's emaciated frame, and then, as if he were air, lifted him from the nest.

"We'll go back to the main tunnel," I said, backing up to let Sol through.

"And then we're leaving?" asked Alex.

Sol emerged carrying Ben. Seeing them together like that, my voice caught in my throat. "We're leaving soon, Alex. Let's just get Ben out of here first."

Once back in the main cavern, the boys settled in a dry alcove close to where Sol and I had first talked. Alex took charge of Ben, his chirpy whispers carrying on the air. Satisfied they were safe, I led Sol out of their hearing.

"Did you find a way out?" I asked.

Sol shook his head. He simmered; his jaw tense, his back straight. I told him everything that Alex had said about Jay.

"It must be the Nonsky Fault," I said. "Vermillion was right. He's trying for the Equinox."

Sol had not spoken a word. He blinked as if waking from a deep sleep. "I'm going to kill him," he said.

The tone in his voice scared me. This was a side of Sol I'd never seen. I'd seen him angry at what had happened to the valley, at the demons, at Malone. But never had he been this measured, this dangerous.

"If I have to call out the whole of the West," Sol said, his tone even. "If I have to burn every brick of this place down, I will kill Elias."

I reached for Sol's hand. "But you'd never do that. You'd never hurt the people here. The Suzerain knows it. He's always got that over you."

Sol looked down at me and a little of his anger faded.

"Sol, that kid's not going to make it if we don't get him out of here."

Alex still entertained Ben, pulling faces, prancing around, trying to keep what was left of the poor kid's spirit alive. I caught Sol watching them. Fire burned in his eyes. Tears fell from mine.

"It's me that monster wants," I whispered. "It's my fault."

Sol pulled me to his chest, his arms wrapped tightly around me. "It's everyone's fault," he said.

Hours must have passed, but in the monotonous gloom it was impossible to keep track of time. I'd wrapped my jacket around

Ben and hugged him close trying to keep him warm. Alex was slumped at my side, his head resting against my shoulder. We waited for Sol to return from another search of the pit.

Every few minutes I looked back at the distant guardhouse. In every moment, I expected a commotion and for the Suzerain to appear. So far there'd been no sign of activity. But how long would that last?

"Have they even fed you down here?" I asked Alex.

"Bread and stuff."

"Do they bring it in?" I asked, wondering if we could rush the guards when they entered the pit with food.

"They leave it on a tray on the other side of the bars," said Alex. "And then they throw stuff at you when you reach for it."

"That's not very nice."

"They're dipshits," he said.

"Alex!"

"They are. I'm glad Jay kicked one."

I rocked Ben in my arms and again looked to the bars. "Me too," I said.

Sol's flickering torch eventually reappeared. I'd stopped asking—*Anything?*—about six hunts ago. Everything I needed to know was written on Sol's face.

"I had no idea this place was so big," he said, as he crouched beside us.

"It's huge," said Alex. "Simon tried to walk around it once."

"Simon?" asked Sol.

"Wilkins," I replied. "One of the other boys."

Still hunkering down, Sol tapped Alex on the arm. "And did he reach the end?" he asked. "This Simon Wilkins."

Alex shook his head.

Sol smiled. "Then maybe he should have walked backwards."

Alex had latched on to Sol ever since we'd hooked up. It had taken all my powers of persuasion to keep him beside me whenever Sol ventured deeper into the cavern. Now they grinned like brothers.

Alex looked from me to Sol. He scrunched up his face. "Backwards?" he said.

"It's just something I heard," replied Sol. "If you walk backwards for long enough, you'll eventually find your way back to the front."

Alex frowned. "Huh?"

"You should try it," said Sol, again smiling. "It'll pass the time. Keep you warm."

Up for the challenge, Alex sprang to his feet. He began to walk backward into the cave.

"But don't trip on the rocks," said Sol. "It doesn't work if you trip on the rocks."

*"Really?"*

Sol shrugged. "That's what I heard."

Alex continued with arms outstretched. Soon he'd left our haven of light.

"Alex, you do realize he's making this up." I nudged Sol in the ribs, though inside I was grateful that he was keeping Alex amused.

Alex's voice echoed back. "I wanna see. I wanna—"

A gargled scream reverberated. A dull thump followed. Sol leapt up. A second passed and Alex reappeared. He pointed into the gloom.

"Something's out there," he cried. "It touched my leg."

Sol dashed in front of Alex, guarding him from whatever was out there. "Did you see it?" he asked.

"Only felt it," Alex replied. He peeked out from behind Sol's arm, his head barely reaching the height of Sol's chest.

The commotion stirred Ben. He raised his head as Sol inched closer to the darkness, all of us on high alert. Something was out there.

Away to our left, a low figure scuttled across the rock. A cry echoed—"*wheep, wheep*."

"What is it?" whispered Alex to Sol.

Sol peered deeper into the gloom. Not a muscle in his body moved. He sniffed the air. "Mia," he said. "I think it's a friend."

I gently released Ben before joining Alex and Sol where the

dark met the light. I squinted into the blackness. Whatever was out there moved around—you could hear loose rocks shifting beneath its feet, followed by a whistle and then a chirrup.

"It can't be," I breathed. "Sol, it's my gutterscamp. It's the same one."

"I think so," said Sol. He took Alex's arm and together they retreated so as not to scare it away.

Alone, I crouched and reached a hand into the blackness. "Hey, bud," I said. "It's me, Mia. Remember me?"

The gutterscamp leapt closer. Light flared in its eyes.

"How'd you get in here?" I whispered, desperate not to alarm him. "Come on, buddy. I won't hurt you."

I glanced over my shoulder to Sol. "There must be a way in," I said.

Alex still peered out from behind Sol's arm. "What is it?"

"It's a friend of mine," I replied. I couldn't hold in my smile. "I told you we'd get out."

"It knows the way out?"

Out of reach, the gutterscamp swayed side to side.

"He got in here somehow."

Beyond elated, I got back to my feet. "We have to follow him," I said. "He can lead us out."

Sol was already helping up Ben. Alex headed for the gutterscamp.

"Not too close," I whispered, and I reached for his hand. "Give him some space or you'll scare him off."

The gutterscamp remained close to the wall, sniffing at the puddles on the ground.

"What's it doing?" whispered Alex.

"I have no idea," I replied.

With Ben in his arms, Sol came to our side. "Gutterscamps can sense movement through the ground," he said. "It's probably just checking for danger."

As if the creature had heard Sol's words, its neck shot straight up and its gaze pierced the blackness from which it had emerged. It leapt off into the darkness.

"Now," said Sol. "Quickly."

I snatched up the torch and hurried after them. We stayed as far back as we dared, desperate not to scare the scamp away, but fearful that it would vanish into the black void. Hope rose with every step. We were going to get out—I knew it. There was no way we could have come through the Wastes, the valley, Malone's, only to be snared like rats in a trap, waiting powerlessly for the moment when the Suzerain realized who I was.

The gutterscamp froze.

"Stop," whispered Sol.

Huddled around the torch, we watched as the creature

reared onto its hind legs, its tail outstretched for balance. A clatter of rocks came from deeper in the cave.

"Did you hear that?" I uttered, breathless. "Something's out there."

The gutterscamp darted for the wall. It clung to the rock, its gaze fixed in the direction of the sound.

"Back," said Sol. He took the torch from my hand and placed Ben into my arms. "Mia, take the boys."

For a bag of bones, Ben felt pretty heavy. Desperate not to drop him, I shepherded Alex back to the wall. Alone in the center of the passage, Sol stood in a circle of light, his chin raised as he again sniffed the air.

I pulled Ben closer to me, expecting that at any moment some fell creature would lope into the light and take Sol down with a single swipe.

Sol lowered the torch, his head tilting as he peered into the darkness. Without warning, he dashed forward. Panicked, I began to follow before realizing that I was holding Ben. I'd barely put him down, when a smiling face appeared in Sol's light. Certain my mind was playing tricks, I froze. Delane stepped from the gloom with Vermillion, back to her normal self, close behind.

As soon as he saw us, Delane's grin widened. "We thought we'd never find you," he said, as he and Sol hugged. "What is this place?"

"Elias's guesthouse," replied Sol.

I don't know who was more shocked to see them, me or Sol. From the look on his face, I was willing to give Sol the edge.

"Surprised?" asked Delane.

"Relieved," said Sol. "And yes, surprised."

I still couldn't believe it was them. But if it was some kind of cruel trick, then there was no way Sol should see them too. You couldn't share a hallucination.

"I don't believe it!" I squealed. I dashed into the huddle, grabbing hold of Vermillion as she joined the celebration. I even forgave Sol when he gave her a big welcome hug.

"How?" I gasped.

"The little critter showed up at the house," said Delane, gesturing to the gutterscamp. "It was going mad. I knew it had to be the same one. I'd seen what had happened at the square. I knew they'd taken you." He shook his head. "Mia . . ."

"I know," I said. "I'm crazy. Should never have done it. What was I thinking?"

"I was going to say thanks," he said. He pulled me in for a hug.

"It was for the shadow imp," I replied, hugging back. "But I still owe you for the stripe-backs."

The gutterscamp lingered in the background, more interested in a bug crawling on the rocks than the fact that it had just saved our lives.

"Never feed a gutterscamp, eh?" I said, as I stepped away from Delane.

"An act of kindness repaid," Vermillion replied.

I inched toward the creature, expecting him to scamper away as he always did. To my surprise, he stretched out his hand. My fingers grazed soft smooth skin.

"Screes, Mia," warned Delane.

"It's worth it."

We touched for a couple of seconds before the gutterscamp pulled away. I wished there was a way to say thanks.

"Let's get out of here," I said instead. I turned for the boys. "This is Ben. And this is—"

Alex stood behind Sol, a familiar expression on his face. Eyes as round as silver dollars, jaw pretty much on the ground, he stared at Vermillion.

I rolled my eyes. "Not you too," I said, and gave him a nudge. *"Alex!"*

Alex continued to gape; he was lost in Vermillion's world.

"Delane, you'd better take him," I said. "Maybe he'll snap out of it once we're moving."

Vermillion had already intercepted me. "He can come with me," she said, putting her arm around Alex. Her fingers went to his hair. "A little boy like this would make a—"

"I don't think so," I said, horrified by the thought of Alex ending up in one of Vermillion's jars. "He can stay with me."

Delane led on with the gutterscamp slightly ahead, and Sol at his side carrying Ben.

"He led us through the sewers beneath Blood Alley," said Delane. "A wall's collapsed down there and there's a tunnel full of gutterscamp nests that leads to a shaft. The Suzerain can't know or he would have sealed it." He stopped and then pointed up. "It's pretty tight, especially if one of us has to carry the boy."

About twelve feet up there was a black opening in the cavern wall. The gutterscamp bounded up and through.

"We have to climb," said Delane. "Vermillion, you first."

Vermillion took Alex's hand. She led him to the wall.

"You next, Mia."

"Ben first," I replied, and ushered Sol forward. "He's been here longer."

Sol had barely taken a step with Ben when a loud clang resonated through the pit. We all froze.

"That was the gates," said Sol. "They're coming. Move. Go."

A shout boomed. I just about shed my skin.

"Poppy Fellows!"

My stomach turned. "That's me," I cried.

"Poppy Fellows! Make yourself known!"

# TWENTY-EIGHT

Put out the torch," said Sol. He thrust Ben into Delane's arms. "They'll see."

We were far from the guardhouse, but already two tiny clusters of orange light were visible some way back in the cavern.

Panicked, I bashed the torch against the rocks, convinced that at any moment we'd be spotted. It refused to die.

"It's not working!" I said, searching for a pool of water in which to drown the flames. "Delane, go. Get them out."

"POPPY FELLOWS!"

Clinging to the wall, almost in reach of the shaft, Vermillion and Alex clambered upward. "Go!" I begged, wrestling the torch. "Sol, they'll see us."

Seconds sped by. The window for escape was rapidly closing.

"There's no time," said Sol. "Mia, you have to go."

"I'm not leaving you here," I replied. "Sol, it's me they want; if they don't find me they'll know something's going on."

Delane still held Ben in his arms. "Solandun, we won't all get through in time," he said. "Any second they'll see us."

"Why haven't you gone yet?" I asked, forcing him toward the shaft. "There's time to get the kids out. Delane, you have to help Ben, but you have to go now. If they catch any one of us crawling through that gap, they're going to follow. We can't let them find out how you got in here."

He did not climb.

*"Please,"* I urged. "Save the kids. Get them to Bromasta—tell him they've taken Jay and the boys to the Nonsky Fault."

Finally Delane nodded. "All right," he said. He gestured to his side where a dagger hung from his belt. "Solandun, take it. Use it."

With Ben clutched to his chest, Delane scrambled up toward the shaft. I moved away from the cavern wall, offering the sentinels a target far from where the others escaped.

Sol hung back, close to the wall, the dagger firmly in his grip.

"I'll be right behind you," he whispered. "Take care."

He vanished into the darkness before I could reply.

Torch quivering in my hand, I walked toward the sentinels.

"Drop the flame!" commanded one as soon as I was in reach.

I dropped the torch.

"Hands up."

I raised my hands.

"Now follow. The Suzerain awaits."

Though I allowed my face to show no emotion, inside I screamed. The Suzerain had spoken to Malone. He knew. But the others would be safe and that was all that mattered. With Sol somewhere behind me, I gave myself over to fate. In minutes, we'd be free or we'd be dead.

We passed the spot of our makeshift camp, passed the opening to the passage where I'd found Alex. There was still no sign of Sol. Cold sweat covered my skin. My breaths, already shallow and rapid, grew faster with each step. I struggled to focus, concentrating only on the sentinels, the bobbing torches in their hands, and the fast approaching light of the guard room. The bars appeared. Two guards waited beyond.

"Bring her through," said one. "She's to be taken to the council room."

My gaze fixed on the guard as he moved to the lock. The rattle of steel against stone followed. If Sol meant to strike, it had to be now; there was only so long I could delay before stepping through that gate. Careful not to betray that Sol was behind me, I looked to the ground, dragging my heels, counting the seconds until the chance to escape would be gone.

*Come on, Sol!*

Sol flew from the shadows.

The first sentinel fell from a dagger through its throat. The second had barely turned when it suffered the same fate. Carnage exploding, the guard at the gate yelled as he scrambled for the bars. Too late. I'd snatched the second sentinel's torch before it touched the ground. Vaulting its body, I thrust the flames at the guard's hand. With a scream, the guard pulled back. It was all the gap Sol needed to burst through the gates.

He moved as fast as a sentinel, almost flying, his movements both powerful and effortless. One thrust of the dagger and the guard at the gate went down. A leap and the second joined him on the ground. Blood flowed.

I leapt over the fallen gate guard, joining Sol in the antechamber, ready to fight. The gate guard moaned, grabbing the bars as he struggled to rise. Face pale, his front soaked with blood, he toppled back, dragging the gate closed as he fell. He collapsed to the ground and did not move.

I dropped the torch and darted for the now locked gate. It was our only way back to the shaft. "Sol, it's a bond key!"

Sol was checking the second guard for signs of life. "Do you see the key?" he asked.

Frantically scanning the ground, I found it in the out-stretched hand of the fallen guard. "It's here!"

Together, we dragged the guard's body back to the lock. Sol placed the key into the recess. He covered it with the guard's hand. The lock did not release.

"It's still locked," I said, tugging the gate. "Why isn't it working?"

The guard's hand fell from Sol's grip. It landed with a thud on the floor. "He's dead," said Sol. "The key needs living blood."

I glanced into the pit where the secret shaft waited for our escape. And then I thought of the Velanhall, vast and bustling, above us. "We'll never make it," I whispered.

The fear I felt was not visible on Sol's face. He surveyed the room, at the fallen guards and the blood trickling on stone. "We have to try," he said.

With no choice but to press on, we sprinted up the passage toward the Velanhall, our steps echoing behind us. Freaked by the Suzerain, I'd paid little attention on the journey down, but I marked the endless corridors and passages that opened around us. "It's impossible. We'll never get out."

"We've made it this far," said Sol. He stopped at a junction to another passage. He peered around. "It goes up."

Glued to Sol's side, I reached for his arm. "Guards?"

"It's clear."

At every junction, Sol stopped and checked the way. The stone labyrinth stretched on and on. It was eerily quiet.

"This is all wrong," I said, after six or seven turns. "They must know by now. The place should be crawling with guards."

Slightly ahead, Sol slowed. "I was thinking the same thing."

We paused in the passage, Sol looking one way, me the other. Still we remained alone. "What if it's a trap?" I whispered.

His back against the wall, Sol fingered the dagger at his side. "Then we're heading straight for it."

We sprinted on, the route growing steeper the farther we ran. Finally, we turned a corner and a set of stone steps rose before us. A wooden door stood at the top. Though I'd wanted nothing more than to get out of this place, that door set my mind on edge. Passages were one thing; you could see ahead and behind. Imagining what surprises lay behind that door made me very uneasy.

Sol started the climb. Grabbing what breath I could, I followed. At the top, Sol placed his ear to the wood.

"Anything?"

"Nothing."

"Maybe it's locked." I anticipated us bursting into the Velanhall's concourse and half hoped it would be true.

Sol tried the handle. "It's open."

His hand fell as he turned to me. Sweat glistened on his brow, but he wasn't sucking air like me. He leaned in and without a word planted a light kiss on my damp forehead.

"What is this, good-bye?" I asked, hoping a joke might mask my terror.

"It was for luck," he replied. "Ready?"

I nodded, shook my head, and then nodded again.

Sol pushed open the door.

It appeared to be an empty guard room, about ten feet wide and twenty long. Eight chairs surrounded a table in the center. Sheets of dappled sunlight, which entered through the narrow open windows that lined the walls, brightened the room. Another passage continued on at its end.

Relieved to have found nothing worse and hungry for fresh air, I dashed to the nearest window and pushed my face into the breeze. The sun hung in the west. Orion's white stone gleamed beneath us; we'd come higher than I'd thought. Distant sounds rose from the city.

"We must be in the base of a tower," said Sol, at the window beside mine. He pushed up, trying to force his body through the gap.

"Are you nuts?" I exclaimed. He looked as if he were trying to jump.

"Too narrow," he said, as he dropped back down.

"Too high," I replied.

"At least we'd be outside."

"But that's not much good if we're halfway to the moon."

He looked like he was about to smile. Instead he frowned, then sniffed.

"What is it?" If there was one thing I'd learned in Brakaland, it was to always trust Sol's nose.

His gaze went to the open door through which we'd entered. "Demons," he said.

Any thought of escaping through the window fled as we dashed to the door. A visage demon, with several more behind it, was climbing the stairs.

"Brace it," yelled Sol.

I slammed the door as Sol grabbed a chair and wedged it beneath the handle. As soon as it was secure, I grabbed another chair and then another and another, stacking them haphazardly against the wood.

"What do we do?" I spluttered.

"We have no choice," said Sol. "We keep running."

We'd gone no more than a few steps before the first bang came at the door.

"Don't stop!" yelled Sol.

The passage at the head of the room led to another set of

stairs. A second room, identical to the first, appeared at the top. On and through. Up another set of stairs. A crash sounded from below. Screeches echoed.

"They've broken through!" I hollered. "Sol!"

We sprinted into the next passage. A spiral stone staircase, dimly lit, waited at the end. There was no other way onward.

Sol ushered me up. "Go!"

I ascended as fast as I could, my hands gripping the walls as I counted the steps beneath my feet. Twenty. Thirty. All the training sessions I'd skipped in the gym returned to haunt me. My lungs screamed.

"Keep going!"

Forty. Fifty. Sixty. There had to be a way out—somewhere! Or a way back down! I suddenly felt as I had in the Wastes when I realized that the sentinels had herded us there on purpose. This must've been the same. There *was* no way to escape, and the visage demons knew it.

My head down, arms pumping, I was watching my feet so I wouldn't trip, when I crashed squarely into a door above. Off balance, I fell back onto Sol. He grabbed my waist before I could topple down the stairs. With his free hand, he yanked open the door. Fresh air and daylight flooded into the tower.

The flight of stairs we'd climbed continued on through the door, only now the steps coiled around the outer wall of one of the Velanhall's towers. All I could see was gleaming white stone.

"We can't go that way!" I gasped.

Screams carried up from below.

His hands tight on my shoulders, Sol forced me to look into his eyes. "Mia, you have to trust me," he said, rapidly. "Tell me you trust me. Say it."

Air rushed into the tower like water gushing from a broken dam. It whipped our faces and hair. Sol never released his hold, his eyes penetrating my soul, his fingers crushing my bones. The look in his eyes. Was it Sol admitting defeat? I remembered sitting with Sol on the grass outside my father's home, and the night in Border-town when I'd first seen the visage demon and had cried at Sol's side. But mostly I recalled the first time we'd spoken at Crowns-ville High with radios blaring from the parking lot and students streaming by. The moment when Sol had truly entered my world.

I glanced down the steps. The demons were drawing closer. I gazed back at Sol, who was watching me keenly, his hands tight on my shoulders.

"I do," I said. "I really do."

"Then follow me."

He pushed me through the doorway and out into the blus-tery air. The wide, white steps spiraled the Velanhall's tower all the way to the clouds. It wasn't the best idea, I know, but I looked down. Orion lay far beneath us. At least two hundred feet of air separated us from the Velanhall's roofs. It was what I'd feared. The only way down was back.

"This isn't a good idea!" I gasped, my vow of trust already forgotten. Dizzy, I grabbed at the tower's white stone. Sol brushed past me, continuing to climb.

"Just run!"

"Run where?"

Screeches carried up the spiral staircase.

"Up! Mia, you have to move!"

I ran, but to what I didn't know. Death? That and the clouds were all that waited for us on top of the tower. All I'd wanted was for the others to get away and for Jay to be safely home in Crownsville. I would have given anything for that. But regardless of the dangers we'd so far survived, I'd never thought that saving Jay might cost me my life. Everything I'd wanted, everything I'd worked for—college, Willie, the chance to just get out of Crownsville and be *something*—flashed before my eyes and, just as quickly, faded. Those things were gone.

The wind kicked and swirled against the tower. We continued up and up. At least I'd get my view of the Brakaland Plains before I died. At least I'd have one last chance to look across the land and think of Crownsville and everyone I loved waiting safely on the Other Side.

My legs heard my heart. Though heavy beyond belief, they carried me up. The cold air cooled my sweat and brought goose-flesh to my arms. I thought of Ben Griffin wrapped in my jacket and prayed that he and Alex were safe with Vermillion and Delane. This final flight toward death was worth it, as long as I knew that at least two of the kids had made it out. I imagined them at home, their parents spoiling them rotten, celebrating their return with hamburgers and ice cream.

Tears fell as I pictured home and all the stupid things I'd never do again. Never again taste my favorite combo at Harper's Ice Cream Parlor? Black raspberry, chocolate chip, French vanilla . . . This wasn't how it was supposed to be! But we were cut off from escape—nothing in front but a dwindling number of steps, nothing behind but demons. Would I really let them take me? Or could I take that leap and put both myself and the Solenetta forever out of the Suzerain's hands?

I ran out of steps to wonder.

After passing me on the stairs, Sol had already reached the top of the tower. Miraculously, he didn't seem breathless. He gazed over Orion, head high, shoulders straight—the King of Brakaland's son.

Speechless, panting, I collapsed onto the third step from the top. I peered over the edge of the tower. Black cloaks swirled below us as the demons mounted the coiling staircase. They streamed in line, twenty, thirty, forty visage demons. Not even Sol and the Lunestral could save us from this crowd. "They're coming," I said, my throat dry.

The first demon appeared about ten steps down. It stopped. I don't know how a creature with no face could portray such hatred, but I felt its disgust with every ounce of my being. Others formed a pack behind it until a black wall of bodies sucked the light from the bright white stone.

Though I saw little point in delaying the inevitable, I shuffled up to the next step and took another glance into the void of open air. But when I thought of spreading my arms, of taking that final leap . . . I couldn't rise. I wanted me and Sol to live. The only way that could happen was to give myself up.

I looked down at the demons. A familiar face, repeated over and over, gazed back at me. The visage demons had seen into my heart. Only this time, they hadn't found Jay. They'd found *Sol*. All the wasted moments between us swirled through my mind. The real Sol waited just a few steps away and here I'd wasted our last few seconds thinking of ice cream and surrender.

The demons screamed, the collective sound of their call piercing my ears. I raised my hands to block out their cries, then froze.

A swath of gray fabric fluttered in the breeze, landing at my feet. I glanced at the fabric, perhaps a flag liberated from the parade by the wind. But then the color looked too familiar. And was that a sleeve hanging loose across the step?

Confused, I twisted to face Sol.

Then my eyes widened and my heart leapt.

I couldn't believe what I saw.

# TWENTY-NINE

Sol's wings reflected every ounce of light. In green, gold, red, and blue, each spanned more than six feet. Shaped as eagles' wings, they formed a rigid line from his shoulders, like two great arms held out to his side with a curtain of feathers across them. This was the Lunestral's power in all its glory.

Sol stood tall and strong, his bare chest out, his wide shoulders back. His eyes had blackened and bore into the demons' with the Lunestral's steely gaze. Thick red veins—I could see scarlet blood pumping through them—had risen to the surface of his skin. The Lunestral made real in man.

Delane's words tumbled back to me. *Solandun's not rarefied. But that's different.*

Sol was descended from the dream bird. Its power slumbered in his blood. A power unleashed on the visage demons paralyzed by his gaze.

He held out his hand. I didn't take it. The wind carried my whisper. *"How?"*

I didn't expect him to reply, I mean, it wasn't even really a question, just a barely evolved thought that had escaped my lips. I got to my feet and inched closer with tiny, uncertain steps. Sol held still and bore my gawking with good grace, as if he knew it was better just to let me see. No words could truly explain what had occurred.

I ducked beneath the tip of one of the wings. Soft vanes brushed against my hair as I passed. The wings sprang from Sol's upper back in the exact place where the tattooed wings met the Lunestral's body. The inked image of the dream bird lay between them, but now its wings were real. His shoulder blades had shifted, rotated, and the muscles around them firmly braced the wings. Two deep gashes had opened along the length of his back. Each was at least a foot in length. Blood trickled from one.

Sol glanced over his shoulder and the wing beside me separated the air as it made a gentle beat. His eyes were so, so black—not a trace of white remained. But they were still Sol's eyes. It was still him.

I skirted back to the front of the tower and looked down on the visage demons. Not one had moved since Sol's metamorphosis. It was as if someone had simply pulled a plug. Their menacing aura had gone.

"We really should go," said Sol.

"You mean, fly?"

"Unless you'd rather go back the way we came."

I turned away from the demons and scanned Sol's wings from tip to tip. Huge. Powerful.

"You said you trusted me, Mia."

I looked out over the city. We were so, so high . . .

"I do," I said. It was the time to prove it.

Unsure of the recommended form for flying with one's crush turned dream bird, I put my arms around his neck. "Like this?"

"You'd hang like a dead weight. I need to lift you."

I clung tight as he swept me up. His wings commenced a slow beat, casting a deep thrum as they sliced the air. I tapped him twice on the back of the neck.

"What's that for?" he said.

"It's for luck."

I couldn't help but smile. This was so surreal, so *amazing*. Minutes ago I was preparing to say good-bye to Sol and the world. Now we had risen like a Phoenix from the ashes. Or in this case, a Lunestral. My heart beat in anticipation of taking to the sky.

"Okay," I said, and held tighter. "Like on a one, two, three?"

"Like on a right now."

Sol moved with such speed, I barely felt us go. One great leap and we were off and out.

The wind stole my breath. My stomach flipped. Face buried against Sol's shoulder, I screwed my eyes shut. The whoosh of his beating wings was the only sound I heard over the rushing wind.

"The masks," said Sol. "They're moving."

I wanted to look, but that would involve opening my eyes and I was kind of pretending that we were still on top of the tower, or on a really windy street.

"Mia, it's okay to open your eyes."

Easy for Sol to say; he'd done this before. But was I really going to spend this amazing experience with my head buried in his shoulder? I tightened my grip and peeked open an eye.

Orion lay far beneath us, its main thoroughfares cutting like runways toward the outer gates. The black veins of darkened alleys threaded through the city's heart. Beyond the walls spread the Brakaland Plains, the road to Bordertown a pale ribbon in a patchwork of brown and green. Forests grew in the distance, the mountain I'd seen from the valley lay hazy beyond. I could see how far that mountain actually stood from Welkin's Valley; it had seemed much closer from the ground.

Though it remained difficult to breathe against the rushing currents, from over Sol's shoulder I could see that we'd already sunk below the tops of the towers. The visage demons spiraled back down the steps of the Morningstar tower, their black cloaks stark against the white stone. Soon the Suzerain would know we'd escaped.

"Can you find Vermillion's?" I asked. It was only then that I noticed Sol's labored breathing. Knowing it couldn't be a good sign, I held on tighter. "What's wrong?"

"My wings are meant for one," he replied.

"Then we need to get down!"

"I'm looking."

Though we descended smoothly, the rapidly approaching rooftops made my stomach flip. A little like in the Wastes, the sounds of the city popped into life. Clear among them, a tolling bell.

"Does that mean the same thing it did in Bordertown?" I asked.

"They've called out the guard."

"Then they must know already. Sol, the demons saw your wings. Elias will know who you are!"

The beat of Sol's wings slowed and again we dipped lower, the ground clear beneath us. We were close to the wall, east of the gate I'd first entered, but far from Orion's main streets. Sol straightened. His legs pushed down, and we dropped onto a shadowy, deserted courtyard between a tight cluster of buildings. As soon as we landed, Sol gently put me down. Then he dropped to his knees and lowered his head, his breaths deep.

I knelt before him and cautiously touched his shoulder. "Is it always this bad?"

"It's flying with two," he replied between breaths. "Give me a second and I'll be fine."

"Take as long as you need. I'd be dead if not for you. Or in front of the Suzerain. Or . . ."

He looked up. Some of the blackness had already faded from his eyes. His wings lowered. They softly swept the ground. Looking at him this way, my heart skipped a beat. I didn't care that the bell tolled or that windows overlooked us on all sides. I saw only Sol. I finally saw him complete. He was beautiful.

"Why didn't you tell me?" I asked, dropping my hand from his shoulder.

"I thought it best to stay quiet after the way you handled the whole 'king's son' thing."

"That little thing?"

"Yes," he said. "That."

His breaths now normal, the black still fading from his eyes, he shook his head. "I'm Beseye, Mia," he said.

"But not rarefied."

"Few are. The Beseye were the first to abandon the pure lines and mingle with other beings."

I glanced at his wings. "But . . . a *bird*?"

Hands on his thighs, he took a couple more deep breaths. "The Lunestral was a bird in form only. It was a spirit, a force of nature. The Beseye were communicators and their strong senses allowed them to link with those spirits, the spirits of animals, beasts."

"And the Lunestral's spirit entered all of them?"

"Some," he said. "Other Beseye linked with different spirits—spirits from the sea, the forests, the mountains. This all happened thousands of years ago. A spirit bond sometimes skips generations only to reappear years later. But my family's line has always run strong with the Lunestral's blood."

"Which is why you have those gorgeous wings."

It should have been weird to be kneeling with a guy whose very being was linked to another creature, whose *wings* carpeted the ground behind him. But it wasn't. Bird. Man. Whatever. It didn't matter to me—this was how he was *supposed* to be. The Sol from before had been perfect. Now he was more than perfect, more than the mythological creature from the book he'd loaned to me, more than simply the king's son.

I kissed him before he could say anything more. I tried to put everything I wanted to say into that kiss. I didn't have any words left that could explain what he meant to me. He was my dark light.

His hands grazed my face, my hair, my neck. Needing us to be closer, I crawled onto his lap, holding him so tight I wasn't sure I could ever let go. His skin bare beneath my hands, I felt his muscles beneath his wings, the feathers caressing my fingers as I stroked his smooth, tight skin.

Sol responded to my touch with increasing fervor. Raising himself up on his knees, he held my body in an unbreakable hold. His lips moved to my ear and then my throat. This felt so right. My hands entangled in his hair, I knew we had to stop, but stopping was hard when Sol's every touch led to the promise of more and more and more.

"THEY LANDED OVER HERE!"

Then we stopped. It was a man's voice that had called.

My face hot, my breathing shallow, I pulled away slightly. "Where did that come from?" I whispered into Sol's ear.

Sol didn't move. His lips lingering beneath my jaw, the side of his face pressed to mine, I felt his breath on my skin as he spoke. "The next street, I think," he said.

We scrambled to our feet, checking all around for a sign of the guards. But it wasn't guards who watched us.

Though I'd not noticed her when we'd landed, across the courtyard sat a woman on a stool washing clothes in a large tin tub. She was older, maybe in her fifties, and was a little rotund with one of those matronly chests that burst out all over and refused to be constrained by anything made by man. Still scrubbing, she looked up to the sky, then looked at Sol. She harrumphed.

"It's a long time since we've seen the Lunestral in Orion," she said.

Realizing that the woman knew what the wings meant, I glanced at Sol.

"It's been here," he said, his eyes narrowing. "Only hidden."

"THIS WAY!"

"That sounded closer," I gasped. I grabbed Sol's arm, knowing we had to move, confused why he stood here humoring some old lady and her laundry.

The woman leaned forward on her stool. "There's no love for the Lunestral in Orion these days," she said. "Best put those wings away, lad."

She was so right. Sol was a dead man if they caught him; he'd fully revealed himself as one of the king's line.

"SOMEWHERE DOWN THESE STREETS!"

The woman got to her feet. She wiped the suds from the front of her dress. "Get in here." She jerked a thumb toward the house behind her. "You can hide until they've gone."

With great relief, we slipped into the tiny house, leaving the woman to her laundry and the guards who suddenly swarmed onto the courtyard. We entered into a small, square room. A window, draped with yellowing net curtains, looked out over the street. Safely out of sight, I peered into the courtyard. The guards walked toward the woman, who remained at her tub. She was pointing them toward the neighboring streets.

"She's sending them away," I whispered. Relieved, I left my post at the window. "That was too close."

Sol's head was bowed. His wings slowly retreated.

"Does it hurt?" I asked.

He nodded. With his head low, he was the image of a fallen angel with the world on his shoulders. I wished there was some way I could lessen his pain.

"And when they come out?"

"Not as much," he replied.

I crept behind to watch the wings retreat. His muscles twitched and clenched as they clawed them back into his body. About two feet of each remained. As the feathers retracted, they flattened, folding in and over themselves as if a powerful vacuum sucked the air from their vanes. It was clear from this close that pockets on either side of his spine held the wings—his entire physiology different—and that it was the muscles in his back that kept the openings shut. As the gashes slowly closed, I remembered his bloodied shirt on the night of the demon attack in the valley.

"This is why you didn't come into the den," I said, as I wandered back to face him. "At Bromasta's. After you released the decimator that night."

"Delane didn't think you were ready to see."

"He was probably right," I replied. "And here I was, worried you'd fall off the roof and break your neck."

He smiled. "I'm good on roofs."

His transformation complete, we crept back to the window. The woman still talked with the guards and was giving them hell, if her gestures were anything to go by.

"Mia, neither of us wanted to keep things from you," said Sol. "But you understand why it was better that we did."

"I understand," I said. "I just wanted to know you—the *real* you. I still do."

"I was born with this blood," said Sol. "It's part of who I am."

"Then you've always been this way?"

"Not always," he said. "The change doesn't manifest until seven or eight, when the wings begin to develop inside. You're isolated as soon as the process starts, mainly to counter the other changes that happen then too. Your senses sharpen and it's disorienting, dangerous for a while. Beseye who share the Lunestral's line gather when the change is complete. If the wings are strong and true, then the Lunestral's mark is later applied to the skin."

"The tattoo."

"Yes," he said. "The Lunestral is the mark of my family, and now is also the symbol of the king. But it's only those with the Lunestral's blood, those with the wings, who wear the tattoo on their back."

"Your parents must have been proud when it happened to you," I said.

"It was expected."

Out in the courtyard, the guards finally left. The woman headed for the house.

"Here she comes," said Sol.

The door banged and the woman entered. "Tyrants," she muttered. "Suzerain? There's the joke! He's in every part of our lives. Boil a cabbage and he knows about it." She brushed past me and then snatched a blue shirt from a chair in the corner. "It's my son's," she said, tossing it to Sol. "It should fit."

Sol caught the shirt. "I won't forget this kindness," he said.

"Not forgetting those of us in Orion is thanks enough."

"You're not forgotten," said Sol.

Another harrumph from the woman and it was back to business. "Which way you headed?"

"The Sheffer District," said Sol, as he pulled on the shirt.

"Then you're in luck. I sent them off toward Bembam Road. But I wouldn't hang around too long. They saw you come down. They're not going to give up their search any time soon."

Fully dressed, Sol held out his hand. "Thank you."

The woman glanced at Sol's hand before wiping her own down the front of her dress. "Here's a promise," she said, and proudly tipped back her head. "I'll shake your hand on the day the Suzerain is dead."

Vermillion threw open the front door the second we knocked. "The bells," she said, ushering us into the safe house. "The guards! We didn't know if they were for you. I am too old for this! I am too old!"

"I'm glad you made it back safely," said Sol.

"Yes," said Vermillion. "Through water and filth and—"

Delane darted out of the kitchen. He snatched me up into his arms. "You are certainly not boring to have around!"

"The kids?" I asked, as soon as my feet touched the ground.

"They're fine. Go see."

Alex greeted me with a hug. I'm sure Ben would have too if I could have pried him away from the huge plate of food before him. Color had already returned to his cheeks.

"We have to get Jay," I said, as soon everyone had gathered in the kitchen.

Sol looked to Alex and Ben, and then quickly glanced around the room. "Where's Bromasta?"

I paused. I'd been so relieved to be back in one piece, I hadn't noticed he wasn't there. I caught a look pass between Vermillion and Delane.

"He's gone," said Delane.

"Gone?" I blurted. "You mean he couldn't even stick around long enough to—"

Delane shook his head. "To the Nonsky Fault."

Stunned, I pulled back. *"Alone?"*

"He left as soon as I told him about Jay," said Delane. "We couldn't stop him. And now the gates are bolted and they're not letting anyone in or out. I don't know what he plans to do, but he rode out just in time."

What he planned was obvious: a suicide mission. Vermillion had told us the camp was heavily guarded and Bromasta had gone there alone! With Alex and Ben missing from the pit, the Suzerain would know someone had rescued the kids. Every guard under his command would be heading to the fault to secure the other boys. I knew Bromasta had beaten Elias's demon army, but I was betting he hadn't done it single-handed. He'd be killed; it was as simple as that. And just when he'd come back into my life.

"We have to go after him," said Sol.

I agreed.

"But we'll never get past the gates," said Delane.

"Then we'll use the Down Pass," Sol replied.

Vermillion headed to the jar-lined shelves. "I have a bond key for the pass."

Delane was still not convinced. "But we'd need horses to reach the fault. We can't take horses through the Down Pass."

"Leave the horses to me," said Vermillion. She returned with the bond key in one hand and a squat black jar in the other. She slammed the jar on the table. "Number six."

I wasn't sure who lived in jar number six, but having seen Vermillion's transformations I trusted she knew what she was doing.

"Do we have more decimators?" I asked, feeding off the energy that sparked in the room. Even Ben had caught the bug. He jiggled at Alex's side, a hunk of bread clutched in his hand. This was it. We were going for Jay.

"Mia, there's a box of decimators beneath the shelves," said Vermillion, pointing toward the jar-filled alcove. "Delane, you'll find a torch for the pass in the closet beneath the stairs. You'll need weapons too. Fetch the swords."

I hurried to the shelves to find a small wooden chest containing decimators. Vermillion handed me a leather pack, which I immediately began to fill with the spells.

My heart pounded, but this time it wasn't from fear. It was excitement, exhilaration. I couldn't wait to see Jay! But even more so, I was proud. Bromasta Rheinhold—my *father*—had raced off to save his only son, even though he must have known he'd stand no chance against a camp filled with sentinels.

Delane burst back into the room, having retrieved the swords from the upstairs bedroom. There was a torch wedged beneath his arm. "What about the boys?" he asked.

I glanced over to Ben and Alex, who hovered by Sol's side. A sinking feeling entered my gut. One of us would have to stay behind to watch them, and it was pretty obvious who that someone would have to be. We needed Vermillion to use the bond key for the pass and to find us horses. Sol and Delane were the muscle. That left me.

Sol took his sword from Delane and then looked back to where I lingered at the shelves. "We'll take the boys with us," he said.

"You've got to be kidding," I exclaimed. "It's too dangerous."

Sol's brow lowered. The lines on his forehead deepened as he frowned. I noticed that the room had fallen silent.

"We have the Solenetta," he said. "We'll find Jay and the other boys, then use it to open the Barrier weakness at the fault and get you all back to the Other Side."

I could feel Delane watching me. Vermillion, too. Sol was

serious. Of course he was serious. Why would we wait even a second longer in Brakaland when the chance for me and the boys to escape was staring us in the face? I'd known this moment was coming—it was all I'd wanted when I'd stepped through that wall of light what seemed like a million years ago. But *now*?

"What about Bordertown?" I asked, my voice caught somewhere in the back of my throat. I couldn't look at anyone but Sol.

"Mia, we won't make it back to Bordertown," he said. "Especially not with the boys. This is your chance to go home."

Vermillion and Delane hurried the boys out of the room. Sol and I stared at each other, at an impasse. He was right. Bordertown? We'd never make it. The time to escape Brakaland was now and the key to opening the Barrier hung around my neck. But somewhere inside me, my heart clung to the time I might have with Sol on the journey back to the Ridge. During those days we could have talked, explained to each other how we felt, and then said a long and fitting good-bye before the Barrier closed behind me. In my mind, it was all planned. But not like this.

Delane poked his head back into the room, breaking the tension. "We have to go," he urged, "before Elias sends more guards."

Sol hastily left the room, leaving me with Delane.

"This is it!" he said.

"That's right," I replied. I reached for my jacket, which Ben had left on the back of his chair. "I'm going home."

# THIRTY

We scurried through Orion to a deserted bazaar close to the city wall, a street of pale stone lined with empty stalls and strewn with crates. A cloaked Vermillion led us to a stall about halfway down.

"The Down Pass was built for smugglers," she said, checking to make sure we hadn't been followed. "Usually for bringing things in." She ducked behind the stall. "Pass me the key, Mia."

I took the key from the pack and then followed Vermillion. She tossed aside a moldy old rug and knelt by a trapdoor. There was a space for a bond key beside it.

"Delane, light the torch," she said.

The lock clicked as soon as Vermillion inserted the key. She threw back the door to reveal steeply descending stone steps. Delane had been right: We would never have gotten horses down there.

"This is it," Vermillion said, pocketing the key. "I'll meet you at the other end." After ruffling Alex's hair, she disappeared down the street.

Delane led with the lit torch. I followed with Alex and Ben. Sol, at the rear, closed the trapdoor behind us. We proceeded to file through a long, deep passage. Graffiti covered the walls, most in a language I couldn't read. There were symbols and motifs, crests and insignias, and some sketches that described only too clearly what the artist really thought of the Suzerain.

I tried to think only of saving Bromasta and Jay, but nothing could drive Sol from my thoughts. Everything between us had only just begun. Now it would end too soon.

I guess we walked for about fifteen minutes, mostly in silence. I responded to the few things Delane said with one-word answers. I didn't trust myself to say anything more. Ben and Alex seemed to be holding their own, but occasionally I looked back at Sol, barely visible in the shadows at the rear of the pack.

We stopped at another set of steps leading to a second trap-door. As soon as Delane unlatched the lock, we emerged into what remained of the day. We stood on the outskirts of a wood.

Orion was far behind us. Birds sang. It sounded like a funeral dirge to me.

Free of the city, I waited with the boys as Sol and Delane whispered off to the side. It was as if we'd come full circle, back to the days of "Don't tell Mia." It no longer mattered. We were on our way to rescuing Jay and that was all I needed to know.

We'd been there for a while when the sound of hooves approached from the west. Worried we'd been followed, I grabbed the boys and pulled them deeper under the cover of the trees. Once they were safely hidden, I crept back to the edge of the wood.

A mounted sentinel, a horse tethered on either side, cantered toward Sol and Delane. Surprisingly, neither raised their swords. It was only when the sentinel reached them and scarlet hair erupted from its bald head that I realized why: This was Vermillion's number six. The sentinel's shoulders narrowed, and Vermillion appeared, her long limbs bare beneath the sentinel's tunic. She dismounted.

I rounded up the boys. "Okay," I said. "Time to go."

They rushed out to greet Vermillion. Alone, I lingered among the trees, not wanting to leave but knowing that every second we wasted could be Jay or Bromasta's last. When I'd stood before the Suzerain, even when I'd learned what those veins in the Solenetta truly were, I'd never felt as condemned as I did now. I was torn between two worlds: Jay in one, Sol in the other. Crownsville. Brakaland. I hated them both in that moment. I wanted only one world, one that was just for me and Sol. Guilt hit—*hard*. Jay was in danger. And I wanted those things I'd told Sol I wanted. I wanted Jay back. Willie. Even Pete. But I wanted Sol, too—the one thing I couldn't have.

A twig snapped behind me. Sol had followed me into the wood. He waited some distance away, his face devoid of expression, but I knew him too well now not to recognize the subtle hints of emotion. His arms too tense at his side. His gaze focused—too focused. The tiny twitch of the muscles in his jaw. Sol was hurting, just as I was.

This was it. Our final moments alone. The chance for me to tell him how I really felt. The birds sang. The breeze rustled the leaves in the canopy above. And I couldn't think of a single word to say.

"Are you ready to ride?" he asked.

"You should probably ride with Ben," I muttered.

"Probably," said Sol. He didn't move. Didn't flinch. "But I want to ride with you."

Delane had once warned me about Sol and horses. We'd soon outstripped the others. I clung to him tightly as the ground steadily rose toward a hilltop camp marked with tents. Beyond the camp rose a second hill. It was taller than the first, with a white stone arch as high as a two-story house on its peak. The Nonsky Fault. Peachy tints from the start of sunset struck the arch's stones.

On the hill closest to us, sentinels swarmed the encampment. Among them, a lone figure fought.

"Sol, faster!"

Sol must have noticed the battle too, for I'd barely gotten out the words when he spurred on the horse. We galloped up the hillside, Sol low over the horse's neck, his sword already drawn.

I could now see Bromasta clearly. At least twenty sentinels surrounded him. I counted seven or eight already down. Another fell as Bromasta drew his blade across its gut. The harder the sentinels fought against him, the faster Bromasta's sword flew. I'd never seen anything like it. He was unstoppable. My dad.

Sol slowed the horse. "Wait here for the others," he said. "Hide the boys."

I dropped down as soon as we stopped, opened my mouth to wish him luck, but Sol had already gone.

It couldn't have been more than a minute before the others arrived, but standing alone it felt like eternity. "Delane, get up there!" I yelled. "Hurry!"

Delane passed Ben and the bag of spells into my arms as Vermillion and Alex dismounted their horse.

"We can skirt the camp," said Vermillion. She slapped Delane's horse on the flank. "Go!"

Dust from the dry earth swirled as he tore away. Abandoning her horse, Vermillion pointed left. "Up the hill. This way. Quickly."

Keeping low, we headed for a tent on the camp's perimeter, little more than a utilitarian tarp anchored to a wooden frame. Vermillion ducked inside. "It's clear," she said, holding open the flap. "Boys, hurry. Mia, you too."

Screams and snarls rose to my left. The clash of steel echoed, but I couldn't see the fight beyond the city of tents between me and the battleground.

"Look after the kids," I said to Vermillion. Armed with the pack, I secured the strap across my shoulders, which bolstered my courage. "I'm going to find Jay."

If it had been Sol or Delane, they would have stopped me. Not Vermillion. In her long battle against the Suzerain, she knew that sometimes a girl just had to take action.

"Then be careful," she said. Her scarlet lashes grazed her cheeks as she looked down. She smirked. "Solandun will kill me if anything happens to you."

I paused. Vermillion *knew* about me and Sol? Was that what she meant with that smirk? I couldn't imagine Sol spilling his guts to her. It really wasn't his style. And we'd been pretty careful to keep quiet about what was happening between us, especially with Bromasta around. "You know about me and Sol?" I asked.

Vermillion gasped in mock outrage. "I'm Simbia, Mia!" she said. She winked. "I smelled it on his skin in the moment you entered my house."

The flaps fell shut. Vermillion disappeared.

I smiled. So I had two priorities: not to get caught or killed. As much as I wanted to check the battle's progress, doing so would probably put me on a fast track to one or both. Stooped, I darted tent to tent, not daring to shout Jay's name and attract the sentinels' attention. Every tent I checked was empty. But the kids had to be somewhere—Alex had been sure of that.

I tore across a gap between a tent and a larger canvas pavilion, and caught sight of the battle. I couldn't see Bromasta, but Sol fought a cluster of sentinels on the fringe, taking down two in the few seconds I watched. Delane, deeper in the melee, felled another.

I scanned the larger pavilion. That's when I saw the hut. It stood on the periphery of the camp, a wooden shack, its one window barred. It had to be the place. Anticipation rose. Everything else forgotten, I sprinted over and peered through the window.

Six tiny stalls lined the interior—three on each side—each with a bolted door and a small barred window. There were no guards inside. I checked the door. There was neither a lock nor a spot for a bond key.

Disappointed, knowing there was little chance the sentinels would leave the boys so unguarded, I opened the door.

"Jay?" I whispered, not expecting a response.

Silence.

"Jay?"

Nothing.

I'd been so sure this was the place; it was the only sturdy building I'd seen in the entire camp. Where else could the boys be?

"Mia?"

A pair of small, disembodied hands appeared at the bars to my right. Another pair appeared on the left.

"Who's there?" called a voice.

"Get us out!" cried another.

Stunned, I dashed door to door, looking down through the bars to see faces I recognized from the TV and newspapers. Simon Wilkins from Crownsville. Darryl Someone from Markham Creek. It was really them! Like a crazed activist set loose in an animal lab, I slid the bolts as I went. I guess the Suzerain saw no need for bond keys in a camp this heavily guarded. He was mistaken.

"JAY?"

I slid the last bolt. Jay launched out of his cell and into my arms. Overwhelmed with relief, I crushed him harder than a magician grinding solens for grains.

"What are you doing here, Mia?"

"I came for you!" I cried.

His voice muffled against my shoulder, he could barely squeeze out a word. "All this way?"

"All this way." I pushed him back, checking him for injuries or marks. He seemed fine. Time rewound and I was back in Crownsville, tearing through the cornfield with the multicolored light dancing in the night sky. "Jay, why did you run from the house? Didn't you hear me yell?"

He shrugged—a total, one hundred percent, that's my Jay, shrug. "I don't know," he said. "I saw—" His expression turned distant, and I imagined his mother—*our mother*—beckoning to him between the rows of corn.

"I know what you saw," I said.

The boys had gathered around us, faces painted with joy. Some of them had been here for almost as long as Ben. I couldn't imagine how it must feel for them to be free.

"Is this everyone?" I asked, not wanting to let go of Jay's hand.

"There's Alex and Ben," said Jay. "But they didn't bring them with us. Ben's sick. I think he's—"

"He's here," I said. "Alex too."

Jay pulled back. "You got them out of the pit?" He looked to the others, always a leader. "This is Mia," he said, all puffed up. "My sister." Then to me, with a touch of awe: "The pit? Really? *You?*"

"I had help," I replied, charmed. "And we're gonna need more of it before we get out of here."

Simon shuffled closer, a little dazed. "Where are we going?"

I offered him a friendly nudge. "We're going home."

Skirting the battle alone had been tricky. Navigating it with five newly liberated boys was beyond challenging.

"You've got to keep down," I hissed, for the tenth time.

"Who's fighting?" whispered Darryl.

"Some friends," I replied. "And they won't thank us if we're spotted."

We crouched behind the large tented pavilion close to the hut. It was a little too close to the battle for comfort, but the only place large enough to offer cover for six. But we couldn't stay there forever. Somehow I had to get the boys safely back to Vermillion. And there was the fight, too. I couldn't stand not knowing what was happening to Sol, Bromasta, and Delane.

"Can't we fight?" asked Darryl.

"You're not going anywhere near that mess."

"I wanna get 'em."

"Well, forget about it, because it's not going to happen!" I crawled to the end of the pavilion and peered out.

The three guys raged amid a great mass of sweaty, grunting beasts. Blood soaked Delane's torn sleeve. Sol ducked as a sentinel swung a fist aimed for his head.

My heart stopped. Another beast approached him from behind. Sol stepped back, right into its path. Bromasta's warning cry rang across the camp. Sol turned. He effortlessly swung his blade at the sentinel's leg. It collapsed.

I drew breath, but it was just a temporary reprieve. The guys couldn't keep this up forever.

"How does it look?"

Jay had crept up behind me. He crouched at my side.

"Like they're totally outnumbered," I said.

"We have to do something."

What that was, I had no clue. I put my head in my hands to think and noticed my pack at my hip. I looked at the boys, eagerly awaiting our next move. The answer became perfectly clear.


"There's to be no funny business," I said to the boys as they huddled around me. "You do what I told you to do and you do it only when I say."

"Got it," said Jay, with a nod.

"Got it," repeated the others.

"Okay." I took a deep breath. "Everyone ready?"

Five heads nodded.

"Then here goes."

Heart pounding, I stepped out from behind the pavilion. "HEY! MORONS!"

The sentinels turned like a pack of rabid beasts. Sol's eyes widened as he spotted me. I gestured for him to move. When it was clear he didn't understand, I opened my hand and flashed the decimator in my palm. As the sentinels moved en masse toward me, I caught sight of Sol grabbing Delane's arm. The two retreated, slashing the sentinels in their path. I could only trust they'd take Bromasta with them.

Heart still racing and not in the slightest bit convinced that we could pull this off, I crushed the orb between my palms and launched it into the oncoming pack. The first line went down in the blast.

"NOW!" I screamed.

The boys scurried from hiding. One by one they pitched their spells into the chaos. The more they pitched, the faster I handed them spells from the bag. Jay pitched a killer, right into the path of five furious-looking sentinels. They toppled like pins to the ground. The blasts were deafening. The flashes were blinding. But the boys and I kept on until the last decimator had been thrown and silence fell over the camp.

Now Sol stalked the fallen, his sword ready, his figure hazy amid the clearing dust. Most of the sentinels were out cold. Some groaned and struggled to their feet. It was time for the guys to finish the job.

"Okay," I said, turning to the boys. "Everyone back. You are *not* watching this part."

A collective groan rose from the group, but there was no way I was letting a bunch of kids watch the full-blown slaughter I knew was to come. To my relief, a distraction soon appeared. Vermillion, half-clad in the sentinel's tunic, hurried toward us with Alex and Ben at her side. I went to cover Jay's eyes.

"We saw it," she said. "They had no idea what was coming!"

I couldn't help but smile. "Weren't they great?"

"And brave," said Vermillion. Her gaze turned dreamy. She viewed the boys like they were a rack of designer clothes laid out just for her . . . and her jars.

Guessing any one of the boys would happily donate a whole head of hair to Vermillion's collection, I pulled Jay closer. He shrugged me off. It wasn't Vermillion who'd caught his interest. He peered across the battlefield, eyes squinting through the swirling dust and smoke, to where Bromasta checked for surviving sentinels.

*"Dad?"*

I'd been grinning since our victory. Now my smile faded. I didn't know how Jay could have possibly remembered Bromasta, but, clearly, he did. Free of my grip, he tore between the bodies of the fallen, vaulting their outstretched limbs. I didn't stop him.

"DAD!"

I watched, stunned, as Bromasta finally heard his call. He lowered his sword. A smile appeared. The weary years he carried on his face were wiped away.

"Jaylan!"

Unaware of anything around them, Bromasta scooped up Jay as if he were air. Their greeting couldn't have been any more different from my and Bromasta's frosty first meeting in Vermillion's kitchen.

I took a couple of hesitant steps, wondering if I should join their reunion. Something held me back. This was Jay's moment and I didn't feel a part of it.

With the last of the surviving sentinels dispatched, Sol approached me.

"It's good that Jay remembers," he said. He looked from Bromasta to me. "Isn't it?"

"I guess," I replied. I didn't know. The adrenaline that had carried me through the battle drained to my feet and then seeped into the ground. Only emptiness remained.

"We should move, Mia," said Sol. "Before more sentinels arrive."

Sol rallied the troops. One by one, they headed off toward the arch on the second hill. At the front of the pack, Bromasta carried Jay on his shoulders, his sword in Jay's hand. Only I lagged behind. My reunion with Jay in the hut suddenly felt flat. Jay should have been on *my* shoulders. He should have been laughing and joking with *me*. I was the one who'd spent six years taking caring of him! I was the one who'd gone through hell to get him back. I wanted to tell him all the things that I didn't say enough in Crownsville—that he was the bravest, coolest kid I'd ever met. But I didn't think anything could tear him away from Bromasta's attention. Especially not a sister jealous of her own father.

It was ridiculous. I knew Sol would laugh when I confessed all this later. He'd tell me I was crazy. He'd say I was—

I stopped.

There was no later.

I looked to the arch, now an ominous beacon. These were my last minutes in Brakaland. My last minutes with Sol.

He walked way ahead with Delane.

"Oh, God," I whispered, and picked up my pace. "Sol! SOL!"

I only got a few feet before a voice called out. A shiver traveled down my spine.

"Not so fast, Mia Rheinhold."

# THIRTY-ONE

M
y name is Mia Stone," I said, and I turned to face the Suzerain.

I had no idea how long he'd been there or where he'd come from. Thin air? I didn't know. He stood about twenty feet away, still in his three-piece suit, oblivious to the carnage around him and the sulfurous odor that lingered from the decimators. I stared him down. What else could I do? There really wasn't any place left to run.

"That was impressive," he said, as he strode gracefully toward me. "But I can't allow you to steal my treasures so easily. Come with me now and we can avoid more bloodshed. I am a man of peace, Mia."

Peace? Sol had once called him a man of persuasion. His words didn't persuade me.

"Tell that to my mother," I said.

He knew who I meant. He'd called me Rheinhold. It didn't faze him.

I wasn't sure if the others had noticed my absence. In a way, it was better if they hadn't. Elias would shed their blood. Mine was too precious for him to waste.

"I know of your escapades in Bordertown," he stated. "I know what you stole from Master Malone. I want the Solenetta, Mia."

And yet, I remained unmoved. I wanted Sol. Didn't mean I was going to get him. "I won't create your Equinox."

"I truly doubt there's anything you can do to stop it."

I defiantly kept my silence.

"Your choice, Mia," Elias said. "Please don't test me."

I held my ground. No was the only answer he was going to get.

Elias slowly nodded. "Then rise," he commanded, surveying the sentinels at his feet for the first time. "Rise with flame and fury."

Smoke rose from the sentinels' bodies and sparks ignited the air. One by one, the fallen got to their feet. Flames burst from their skin. The heat was intense. The stench of burning flesh, atrocious. Flanked by his flaming army, Elias again faced me.

Smoke coiled about his body—pale smoke, the color of his suit, as if it emanated from the fabric. Then fire burst around him, the air aflame. The grass at his feet ignited. It shriveled to black.

"Come with me, Mia," said Elias.

The sentinels moved as one. Beneath the flames their features melted. Flesh became bone. I choked on the scent of billowing smoke.

So this was to be my death. I wouldn't give myself up to him, not even to save my own life. Everything the Suzerain had done to me and my family, whether he knew it or not, had created the person who stood before him. A resilient person who would face his fire and not give in.

"Mia," said Elias, his warning clear in his tone.

I stared Elias in the eyes. "I'd rather burn."

The sentinels advanced. Little more than ten feet separated me from their flames. A few steps more and I would get my wish. Ready to meet my fate, I closed my eyes, said good-bye to the world, and took a step forward.

At least that was the plan. I'd barely lifted my foot when I was hauled back from the army of fire. Disoriented, and sprawled on the ground, I scrambled to my knees. Bromasta faced the sentinels, sword in his hand.

"Never, Elias!" he yelled over the roaring flames. "Turn your gaze from my daughter or I will take out your eyes."

The Suzerain did not reply. He opened his arms and the line of sentinels parted. From Elias's limbs, a fiery torrent flew at Bromasta. Through the smoke, I saw Bromasta go down.

A cry came from behind me and Sol, Delane, and Vermillion, her hair streaming like a river of blood, sprinted toward the battle, their figures blurry through the shimmering heat haze.

I could reach Bromasta first, if I could just get through the fire unscathed. Elias couldn't take him—not like this. To protect us, he'd given up his chance to see his children grow. I couldn't let him give up his life, too. I launched myself into the flames.

"DAD!"

Flames roared around us. They'd caught the sleeve of Bromasta's shirt and had seared the hair on the side of his head. I bowled into his body, wrestling him back from the fire.

"Mia, no!" my father gasped.

I turned my back to the Suzerain, shielding Bromasta's body, waiting for the moment of agony as my skin burst to flame. It didn't come. Instead a deep cold spread from my neck and into my limbs. Sharper than biting ice, it coursed through me with the force of rushing white water. Not daring to let go of Bromasta, I felt the Solenetta's power growing with each second. Voices sang from somewhere inside it. It was the song I'd heard at Malone's, only this time I understood the words. It was the voice of Balia, the part of me inherited from my mother's blood. It sang of the solens—the sunstones—birthed in the southern deserts. It wanted the heat. It drank the heat. It would not be conquered by flame.

Its words strengthened and guided me. Answering its call, I tore the Solenetta from my neck and held it out to the fire. Winds of flame coursed into the stones. The song of the Balians soared.

I wish I could say that I knew what I was doing, that deep down some understanding existed between me and the Solenetta. I couldn't. I held on for dear life, bolstered by the knowledge that Bromasta had broken free of the flames. My father was safe.

The Suzerain's furious roar shook the camp. Still the Solenetta absorbed the heat of his attack.

Bromasta's voice rang out, "Finish it, Mia!"

I looked at Elias through the fire. I saw the sentinels frozen before him. My grip on the Solenetta loosened. My muscles relaxed. I envisioned the Suzerain consumed by his own fire.

The Solenetta heard me. A ball of vibrating light formed around my hand and the stones spat back the power that they had absorbed. A tornado of flames tore at Elias. His screams shook the hilltop. The sentinels exploded in a wave of ash. The wall of fire flared and then it, and the Suzerain, disappeared.

Stunned, I stared at the rings of charred grass where the

army had just stood. Elias was gone. He was really gone. For good? I didn't know. Dead? I had no clue. But he'd disappeared.

I fell back, the Solenetta dormant in my outstretched hand. Jay appeared beside me, his eyes wide with awe.

Unable to believe it was over, I waited for Elias to reappear. Slowly, I relaxed. It was over. The Solenetta was again just the Solenetta. No burns, no marks touched its surface. Its veins—*my veins*—glistened as always.

"I never knew it could do that!" said Delane.

"Me neither," I replied.

Sol and Vermillion helped Bromasta to his feet.

"You're hurt," I said, rushing toward him. "He would have killed you."

Smoke wafted from Bromasta's arm, the skin on one side of his face painfully scorched. "But for you," he replied. He held out his hand to shake, just as I'd done to call our truce in Vermillion's kitchen.

I stared at Bromasta's outstretched hand, picturing Jay triumphantly riding our father's shoulders after the battle. I remembered the goofy portrait of me that he carried in his worn notebook. I'd always thought of fathers in terms of what they did, ticking off the points for every good deed—holidays, birthdays, cheering from the bleachers at soccer and baseball. But Bromasta had never been there for me or Jay through any of that time. Instead he'd given us a chance to live, had thanklessly devoted himself to keeping us safe, while he'd stayed here alone to fight for Brakaland. I saw his sacrifices as if they lay in his outstretched hand.

"You want to shake?" I said. I laughed. "Are you kidding me?"

I threw myself into my father's arms.

We stayed that way for the longest time. In three days I'd gone from hating a man I'd never known to embracing my own flesh and blood. He was real and he was my dad—I couldn't ask for anything more than that.

"We should move," said Delane. "Those fireworks are sure to bring out more guards."

Then this was it. I pulled away from Bromasta. "You all have to get out of here," I said. "Quickly."

"Let's see you safely back first," Bromasta replied.

Vermillion headed off to where she'd ushered the boys to safety at the base of the second hill. I looked for Sol. He'd hung back since Elias had vanished, and hadn't spoken a word. Now he'd taken charge of Jay, leading him toward Vermillion and the other boys, Delane jogging to catch up with them. Time ticked away.

"I can't stay," I said, as I walked with Bromasta. I wasn't sure who I was trying to persuade.

"Nor should you," he replied. "You have a life elsewhere."

"I mean, what would I even do here?" I added, unable to take my eyes off Sol. "I can't fight. All that with Elias was just a fluke."

Bromasta stopped me with a touch on the arm. "Mia, you have the hardest job of all of us," he said. "You have to guard the Solenetta. You have to take care of Jaylan."

"And you?"

"Back west there's much to be done," he replied. "Elias is gone, but I doubt if it's for good. We must press this advantage. And quickly."

Sol would probably go there too; they'd waited so long for an opportunity like this.

"You have the parler stone," said Bromasta. "Petraeus will show you how to use it."

"I'll use it," I promised.

"I'm proud of you, Mia, whether that means anything to you or not."

"It means a lot. I'll try not to blow it."

"You won't," said Bromasta. "Of that I am quite certain." He smiled, a proper smile, as wide as the one he'd offered to Jay. "Now go and be with your friends. We can't linger for long. Delane was right—more guards are certain to arrive."

Jay had turned back for Bromasta. I passed him as I hurried to catch up to the others. That was one good-bye I didn't want to see. "Quick as you can," I said. "We've got to move."

By the time I'd reached the base of the second hill, Sol was already marching the kids up to the arch. I half hoped, half wondered if he was trying to avoid saying good-bye as much as I was. Paranoid that I'd start the Equinox before we spoke, I tucked the Solenetta, which was still in my hand, safely into my jacket pocket. Vermillion and Delane waited for me at the bottom of the hill.

"Ready?" asked Delane, when I reached them.

"I think so. Take care of yourself."

Delane grinned. "Never. Don't forget about us."

"As if that's humanly possible. Let's hug it out before I cry." I pulled him in, my Brakaland buddy, the guy Sol had thought had meant more to me than just an amazing friend. Looking back, it was insane.

Our hug complete, I hung back for Jay, who brought up the rear with Bromasta. They walked hand in hand, Jay chattering away about something I couldn't hear. Jay's face was upturned, the look in his eyes almost starstruck. I hated to break their moment.

"Ready?" I said, offering my hand to Jay.

He didn't take it. He shuffled closer to Bromasta, his gaze cast to the ground.

"Jay, I know it's hard," I said, hating to see him this way. "But we have to go."

Jay looked up, frowning, his hand tight in Bromasta's grip. "I want to stay."

Nothing that had happened could have prepared me for those words. Of course Jay would come home with me; I'd come here to rescue him, the thought of him safely back in Crownsville was the only thing that had kept me sane.

"Jay, you can't," I protested. "You've got school."

Jay's mouth set and I knew it meant trouble.

"Jay," I warned. I looked to Bromasta for help.

"Mia is right," said Bromasta, softly. "It's too dangerous here. You have to go with your sister."

"But I don't *want* to go back," said Jay. He held tight to Bromasta's arm. "Dad, I want to stay with you."

As soon as Jay said those words, the look on Bromasta's face changed. He'd been soft with Jay yet, at the same time, serious and firm. Now he looked as he had when we'd spoken of my mother in Vermillion's kitchen. I caught tears welling in his eyes and panicked that all the emotion of being apart from his son was about to be released.

"Jay," I said. "Let me talk to Bromasta alone, okay?"

"I'm not leaving!"

"Jay," I said. *"Please."*

Jay shuffled reluctantly toward the other boys at the arch.

"This can't happen," I said to Bromasta, as soon as Jay was

out of earshot. "You have to make him understand."

"I'm not certain he can understand."

"Just think about it. What on earth would you even do with him?"

Bromasta sighed. He looked to Jay with a distant expression on his face. "I'd take him north," he said, as if he wasn't even sure himself. "Solander's soldiers protect the land there. It's well-guarded. Safe."

"But then what?"

Bromasta's eyes softened. It was as if he saw it, he and Jay together, a reality he'd never considered possible, now in his reach. "From there we'd head west," he said, and nodded. "If we veer south at the mountains, we'd be far from Elias's battle-grounds. From there we can reach Solander's court."

"But you said you didn't want us at the court!"

"These days there are few places as safe as Solander's court," he replied. "I have friends there. Few, but loyal."

I looked at Jay, who waited as if the whole world lay on his ten-year-old shoulders. I thought of his life in Crownsville—his baseball, his computer games, Stacey Ann Baker. He had all that, yet something always had been missing. All the kid wanted was to be with his father. Only in our family could that be like asking for the moon.

I paused, trying to conjure Bromasta's vision of Jay growing up in the same way that Sol and Delane had in a king's court. Was that what I wanted for him?

But when I thought of Sol and Delane, I realized that was exactly how I wanted Jay to be—brave, selfless, smart. I was certain that if Bromasta thought he could get Jay safely west, then safely west they'd go. And who better to protect Jay than the legendary Bromasta Rheinhold? Besides, was Crownsville really any safer? If Elias was alive, he knew about me. How long before he searched for us again?

My reservations collapsed beneath the weight of one simple realization: I couldn't make Jay leave the two things he'd been searching for his whole life—Bromasta and Brakaland.

"I can't believe I'm agreeing to this," I whispered.

"If you have any doubts, Mia, then he will leave with you."

"I don't doubt you. I just . . ." I sighed and looked into my father's eyes. "I don't doubt you," I repeated.

"Then I will break the news to Jaylan."

Bromasta headed for Jay. I lingered for a second, trying to get my head around how quickly life had once again changed, trying to imagine a future in Crownsville without Jay. Bromasta had survived all these years without him. Somehow, I had to do the same.

I turned for the hill and then stopped.

Sol waited about six feet away. I didn't know how long

he'd been there, but as soon as I saw him, my heart raced. "You heard?"

"I heard."

"Did I do the right thing?"

"He belongs with his father, Mia," he said, approaching me. "This is a chance for that to finally happen."

"I know," I said, and meant it. "But would you trust Bromasta? With Jay, I mean."

Sol responded with a subtle nod, his gaze never once leaving my face. He reached for my hand, our fingers linking, hands palm to palm.

"Then I guess that just leaves you and me." I squeezed his hand as tightly as I could and battled the tears I knew were about to fall. "Sol, I . . . ."

His fingers came to my chin and he gently raised my face to his. "Mia, I'm coming with you."

I knew I'd heard him wrong. There was just no way. He was going to head west, like Bromasta, to press the advantage following Elias's defeat.

"To Crownsville," he said.

"You're serious?" I whispered, still gripping his hand. "Please don't tell me this is a joke."

He smiled. "I don't believe we've seen the end of Elias, Mia. His magic is powerful. Until I see his body, I won't be convinced he's gone. You need someone to look out for you, more than just Petraeus. At least until things calm down."

Sol was coming with me to Crownsville! I wasn't going to lose him. Not yet.

"We have to move, though," he said. "Did you hear the horns?"

I hadn't heard anything but Sol telling me he was coming back to Crownsville.

"They're coming," I said, regaining my senses. "Bromasta and Jay! They have to get out of here."

We ran to the others where I scooped up Jay for the hug of a lifetime. "No swords," I said, crushing him against me. "And no more kicking sentinels. I'm serious."

"I'll be good," said Jay.

"And I'll make certain of it," added Bromasta. After seeing him take on the sentinels, I believed him. "Now go, Mia. You'll hear from us. Often."

Though I knew I'd done the right thing, letting go of Jay was hard. A horn blew.

"Contact Petraeus as soon as you're safely away," said Sol to Bromasta.

"The moment we're clear of Orion," Bromasta replied, his arm around Jay.

Sol and I walked to the arch. Smiling at the boys, I took the Solenetta from my pocket. "It's time to go home."

Colored mist swirled under the arch. The Equinox was beginning.

The others watched from the bottom of the hill. Orion, aflame from the light of the setting sun, stood far beyond. A brigade of mounted guardsmen tore across the land, dust churning in their wake.

"Barrier's open, Mia," said Sol. He stepped through the veil of brightening multicolored light that filled the archway, the boys at his side. They vanished.

My gaze settled on Bromasta and Jay. "Good-bye," I whispered.

The Equinox strengthening, I slipped into the shimmering lights, and emerged in a field in the middle of nowhere.

The same sun lowered in the west. Brakaland was gone.

"I want my mom," said Ben. "Where's my mom?"

I wished I knew. I stared at the spot where Bromasta and Jay had last stood. There was no hill in sight. In fact, there was nothing but acres of browning pasture and a dilapidated barn in a neighboring field. Nevertheless, I pictured Bromasta and Jay, Vermillion and Delane, and the sentinels charging from Orion. Did they gallop west toward this very space in a world within a world?

"Mia, the Solenetta," said Sol. "The Barrier won't close while it's in your hand."

I spun around, aware of the lights, which spread rapidly into the sky. I pushed the Solenetta into my pocket. The Equinox retreated, the colors fading before they finally disappeared as if absorbed by the early evening air.

The kids waited in a huddle, looking to us for the next move. Slowly it sank in that we were back. And in the middle of a field. In the middle of nowhere. With six kids who were depending on us to get them home. Six kids who had suddenly reappeared.

"We didn't think this through," I said. "Sol, what the hell am I going to tell the cops?"

"I'm thinking," said Sol. His gaze rested on the barn in the neighboring field. "Tell them you were looking for Jay on the Ridge and that you were kidnapped too. That you found yourself here." He pointed to the barn. "In there."

"That's my story." I rolled my eyes.

"It'll work," he said.

I stared at the barn. It was half falling down, hardly the lair of the infamous Crownsville Kidnapper.

"Don't mention me," said Sol. "It'll only confuse things."

"And if the kids talk?"

"Who'd believe them?" he replied. "Especially if you stick to your story. Get them away from here. Make it look like you've escaped. Get a few miles and then call the police."

"And what about you?" I asked. Sol was in his Brakaland gear, as out of place here as I felt.

"You can do it, Mia." He kissed my forehead. *For luck.* "I'll be waiting for you in Crownsville."

There was nothing left but to put the plan into operation. I rallied the troops before leading them off across the field and toward what I hoped was civilization, all the time getting the boys straight on the story, warning them that no one would believe that they had been in Brakaland. After about a mile trek, we found a road. We followed it for a mile or so farther before we stopped. A sign stood on the grassy shoulder.

CROWNSVILLE: 60 MILES

Was that how far we'd come? Through Bordertown, the Wastes, the valley, Orion.

Sixty miles.

I took out my phone and placed a call. The cops picked us up twenty minutes later.

# THIRTY-TWO

An hour passed. Then two. Then three. Still the cops did not release me. They entered in and out of the hospital's private waiting room where I sat, a never-ending stream of nameless, frantic faces. Only Sheriff Burkett refused to leave my side. He'd arrived about an hour after we'd been picked up, astonished, almost bewildered by the news he'd picked up on the wire. Pete hadn't reported me missing. Now word of my disappearance had exploded.

"We're trying to track down Pete, Mia," said the sheriff. "Just hang tight."

Oh, I was hanging tight.

Night had long since fallen outside and an image of the

room with its nondescript paintings, soft lamps, and overstuffed armchairs was reflected in the wide window. Two worlds. One solid and real, one existing in some kind of dreamy haze.

"Try not to worry," the sheriff added. "As soon as we catch the kidnapper, we'll find out where he's holding Jay. We'll get Jay back."

I didn't reply. There was no need. I'd spun my lies. All I had to do was wait.

And then the wait ended. The door opened and another cop entered. Sheriff Burkett sprang to his feet.

"News?" he asked.

The cop perched on the seat beside me, his look despondent. "We found it burned," he said. "The barn's gone. I'm sorry. The kidnapper got away."

I closed my eyes and tried not to smile. *Sol.* It had to have been him. He'd burned the barn to cover our tracks. Our story was safe.

"Mia, is there anything else you can tell us?" the cop asked. "Anything you might have forgotten?"

It went like this: I'd been searching the Ridge for Jay on Friday night when I'd been grabbed and hurled into the trunk of a car by a man I couldn't see in the darkness. He'd taken me to a barn in the middle of nowhere, where I'd found the six kidnapped boys. Jay had not been among them.

The man had left us tied up in the barn, returning with food and water two or three times over the next two days. On the final day—today—I'd managed to break free of my bonds and get myself and the boys to safety. It was a simple story. A stupid story. And it was working.

"There's nothing else," I said. "How are the boys?"

"They're with the doctors," the cop replied. "Their parents have all arrived. I don't need to tell you that you're a hero in their eyes, Mia. In all of our eyes."

I glanced at Sheriff Burkett who was nodding in prideful agreement. If only they knew the truth.

Struck with guilt, I stared into my lap. "What happens now?"

"We comb the barn for evidence," replied the cop. "We keep looking for the kidnapper. We keep looking for your brother."

With the Solenetta safely stuffed in my pocket, I pictured Jay as I'd last seen him at the Nonsky Fault. Where was he now? A world away from the lie that would forever be a part of my life. I couldn't wait to get home and use the parler stone, to tell him of the trouble he'd caused—he'd love it. The cops would search; they'd never find him. And then one day they'd give up the hunt and this would all be forgotten. For them. Never for me.

I looked to Sheriff Burkett. "When can I go home?" I asked.

"Not until Pete gets here. He has some explaining to do, Mia. I want to know why he didn't report you missing."

"You know Pete," I said, rushing to Pete's defense. The last thing we needed was Child Protective Services breathing down our necks. "He's always in and out of the house. We barely see each other some days. He might not have even noticed I was gone." I wasn't convinced my explanation was helping Pete's cause. "Honestly, he would have called you if he'd known I was missing."

"Perhaps," said the sheriff skeptically, then changed the subject, "You're sure you won't see a doctor?"

"I'm sure."

Four hours passed. Five hours.

*Come on, Pete.*

Sheriff Burkett's phone rang and he left the room to answer it. It was the first time I'd been alone. Restless, but so tired I could sleep for a week, I wandered to the window and looked out over the parking lot. A large pack of reporters were gathered by the hospital's brightly lit entrance. How the hell was I going to avoid them in the coming days?

The door to the room opened, and I turned. Sheriff Burkett entered with simmering anger in his eyes, his face red. He looked disgustedly away from the man who followed him into the room, a man with unwashed brown hair, a three-day beard, and sparkling blue eyes. Balian eyes.

Pete's gaze locked with mine.

I'd done it. I'd made it. I was home.

\* \* \*

We didn't speak until we entered the kitchen at home and the door was safely locked behind us.

"All this time," I said to him as we sat at the table. "You never spoke a word."

It was the same old kitchen, the same old Pete. Only not anymore. There was energy in his eyes, a visible lifting of the weight of the secret he'd carried for so many years.

"It hasn't been easy," he said. "But it was necessary."

He took from his pocket the parler stone—an exact replica of Bromasta's.

"I spoke to your father. He and Jay are safe. They should reach Solander's encampment early tomorrow morning."

"Vermillion and Delane?"

"They're with them."

I was glad, though a touch worried about Vermillion being unsupervised around Jay's hair.

"And us?" I asked. "What happens now?"

"I teach you," said Pete. "You listen. You learn."

Pete had emptied his pocket, so I emptied mine. I placed the Solenetta on the table.

"Hide it," said Pete, barely giving it a glance. "Don't tell anyone where—not even me."

"I'll bury it so deep it'll never be found," I said.

"And when the cops question you again, stick to your story.

Don't veer, no matter what the boys say. You offer one face to the world—a sister hoping for her brother to be found."

I hesitated, not used to seeing Pete so in control. "You know everything that happened," I said. "Don't you?"

"From the moment the first boy disappeared," Pete replied.

He *was* different. I could see it in his every movement. It was clear on his face. He'd known about Sol, about Gus, about countless Brakaland exiles here in Crownsville. He was part of a bigger world, one I'd never noticed though it was all around me. But now I knew. There would be no more secrets between us.

"Can you do it, Mia?" he asked. "Can you live a lie?"

I was about to reply when lights shone from the driveway and a car pulled up outside the house. Wondering who it could be since it was the middle of the night, and hoping to hell it wasn't the press or the police, I darted to the window, Pete a step ahead. But it wasn't reporters. It wasn't even the cops.

I tore out of the kitchen and onto the porch. Willie was dashing toward the house, her eyes wide, her face pale in the moonlight. "Mia, I don't believe it!" she gasped. "I just spoke to Dad. I knew something was wrong when you didn't return my texts. I just thought you were freaking about Jay."

A second later we were collapsed on the porch step, wrapped in each other's arms. I knew right then that everything would be okay. I'd knuckle in, play my part. I didn't have to lie—not to the people I cared about most, not to Willie, not really. Because that was the thing with me and Willie: Sometimes there was just no need for words.

I found him on the Ridge the next day, back in jeans and a T-shirt. It was the Sol I knew from before madness had entered my life.

"I went to Crowley's house," I said.

"I've not long been back."

Sitting beside him on the grass, I looked out over an invisible world. "I feel like I should wave to Rip. Let him know we made it."

"He will have heard," said Sol. "It'll be the talk of Bordertown."

The plains stretched before us, empty and endless, Onaly and the Sleeper Hill Giant the only sights.

"I still can't believe you burned down the barn. It's all over the news."

"It was falling down anyway," said Sol. He grinned.

But other loose ends remained. I'd spent most of the morning with Willie. She'd warned me that her dad wanted to talk to me and that the cops were already in town.

"I'm not sure that Sheriff Burkett's buying it," I said, "especially about Jay. It won't be long before one of the kids says something about Brakaland."

"And the Solenetta?" asked Sol.

"Top secret location. Pete made me hide it."

"That's good."

"And if they come back for it?"

The golden flecks in Sol's eyes twinkled in the sunlight. "We'll be ready."

He drew me into a kiss that chased any thoughts of danger from my mind. I savored every sensation—the touch of his fingers as they grazed my cheek, his hand on my neck beneath my hair. Why care about tomorrow, or the next day, or the day after that, when I had Sol now?

Our kiss ended and we lay on the grass and watched the clouds gather in thick clusters. They drifted to the east and I couldn't help but wonder if those same clouds had passed over Orion or over my father's house in the valley. Did it matter which world those clouds belonged to? Or had Sol been right when he'd said that all worlds were connected?

You see, no matter how quickly life changes, some things always stay the same. Take the lights, for instance.

There have been strange lights in Crownsville for as long as I've lived here. Lights on the Ridge; lights on the river; lights that seep from the ground and then float to the sky in clouds of colored mist.

There have always been strange lights in Crownsville.

Now I know why.

# ACKNOWLEDGMENTS

To Nathaniel Jacks, my amazing agent, who always said "when" not "if", and who helped me turn something raw into something real. Huge thanks to you, Nat, and to everyone at Inkwell.

To the entire Simon Pulse team for making me feel so welcome and for all your hard work on this book. Immense gratitude to Angela Goddard for designing the most amazing cover. Wow. Special thanks go to the gorgeous Anica Rissi for taking a chance on this story, and Annette Pollert, my wonderful editor, who is just so awesome she blows me away. Annette, I'm so lucky to work with you. Thanks for loving Mia and Sol as much as I do.

I offer a bootay shake to everyone in Purgatory, and raise a spezna to the Next Circle of Hell. You guys are the real deal.

Huge hugs to Cueball and JoJo for madness, mayhem, and

days at the Branch. I'm throwing an outdoor disco on your behalf. You know the moves.

To the formidable Walsh clan: Sunny, Susan, Doug, Bridget, Maggie, Emma, Mark, Paige, Mac, Lily, Donovan, Charlie, Matt, and Cherie. Home doesn't feel so far away when I have family like you.

To all my family across the Pond—especially Mandy, Fintan, David, and Tanya. Mandy, thanks for reading over all these years and for never suggesting that I was crazy to keep going. To David and Tanya, who were there on the road trip that started this story no one could ask for a better brother and sister-in-law. And to Mum and Dad, who never doubted I could do this. I hope you're watching from somewhere up there.

Finally, to Mike for reading this story and then telling me that it was the one. Like Willie, I believe in fated love. This one's for you. Always.